Average Joe

Playing Dirty
book one

KRISSY DANIELS

ISBN: 979-8-9866316-0-8

Published by Kiss Me Dizzy Books

Edited by Corinne DeMaagd
www.cmdediting.com

Cover Design by Okay Creations
www.okaycreations.com

Cover Photo by Michelle Lancaster
www.michellelancaster.com

AVERAGE JOE

KRISSY DANIELS

For all the moms
whose babies have
flown the coop.
I'm sending hugs.

PROLOGUE

Marley

"You shot me!"

"I'm sorry!" Frantic and pleading, I repeated, "I'm sorry. I'm sorry" as I climbed over the fallen man, peeled off my Guns 'N Roses T-shirt, and balled the fabric over his oozing wound. "Don't die. Please don't die," I begged. Despite my best efforts, sticky fluid saturated my shirt and his.

I pressed harder, hoping to slow the blood loss, only to draw an agonizing scream from the man beneath me. With violent grunts, he bucked his hips, attempting to throw me off his thighs.

"Stop squirming. I have to stop the bleeding." I squeezed my knees together, desperate to hold him steady.

"Get off!"

"Hold still." I leaned to the right, stretching, walking my fingers across the floor toward the fallen phone, so, so close to calling for help.

"You goddamn motherfucking cuckoo-ass crazy bird." He curled his bottom lip between his teeth with a groan. "You shot me."

"I swear, it was an accident." My fingertips grazed his cell, shoving the lifeline farther from reach.

I needed therapy. My temper was out of control. Why had I touched that gun? I hated violence and blood—oh, God, the blood. I hadn't meant to hurt him. Yet, there I sat, all one hundred and twenty-three pounds of me, fighting with two hundred and something pounds of pissed-off, wounded man-beast. He would not die on my watch or because of my recklessness. Engaging my thigh muscles, I surged forward, stretched, ignoring the sharp twinge in my ribs, and curled my fingers around the thin metal.

"Got it!" I held the phone high in the air, but it was a short-lived celebration. The bugger slipped right out of my gore-slicked hand and landed with a thud on Joe's head.

He yelled words not fit for any ears.

"I'm sorry. I'm so sorry!"

"Get"—his large hands cinched my waist—"off." His face contorted as he lifted me with supernatural strength. "You maniac!"

My butt hit the hardwood floor with a spine-cracking *thunk*.

Joe rolled to his side, sucked in two breaths, then pushed to his feet. Fists clenched, face red with rage, he stalked toward me.

I was dead, and I was too young to die. I crab-walked backward to no avail, my elbows hitting the wall before my shoulders and head caught up.

"I'm sorry. I'm sorry. I'm sorry," were the only words I could manage.

Joe stood over me, his chest rising and falling in rapid, violent bursts, the dark stain spreading halfway down his leg, soiling his jeans.

"We need to call an ambulance. Let me call for help before you kill me."

His red eyes narrowed. "Kill you?" he snarled. "Yeah, that sounds good. Maybe that's what I'll do." He tilted his head in a thoughtful gesture, his gaze aimed at my feet for a long moment before bouncing back up to strike me with a death glare. "I'll make it slow, too."

He'd always been larger than life, but now, towering

over me, contemplating the many ways he could end my life, he seemed bigger, omnipotent even.

This was not how I'd imagined my last moments on earth, dying at the hands of my terrifying neighbor, the ex-con, the man who'd made my life miserable for the past months.

The man who'd stolen my heart.

CHAPTER

One

*M*ARLEY

"Come on!" I shouted to the metal beast. "Start. Please. One more time. I know you've got it in ya."

My rusty, tired, yard-sale lawnmower stood like a cow in a field. Unmoving. Unmowing. Unmotivated. I dropped one foot on the bumper, grabbed the plastic handle, and pulled with all the fight I had left in me, yanking the string with a hard jerk.

Nothing. Not even a halfhearted sputter.

Defeated, I bent forward, hands to knees, head down, catching my breath, glaring at the lush green blades beneath my feet.

My neighbor and dear friend, Alice, had been in the hospital for two weeks due to a tumble in her rose garden, where she'd hit her head on a concrete bench, the same garden seat where we'd spent many hours discussing love, life, and all that was right and wrong with the world. While she was laid up, I focused my spare time on keeping her property pristine because I wanted her to have zero worries when she came home. Her yard was her pride, and that rose garden, her joy.

I dropped my ass to the dewy ground in her front yard, squinted up at her pale yellow, two-story Craftsman, and couldn't help but smile. I'd managed to keep her hanging baskets alive, the front flowerbeds free of weeds, and the driveway clear of moss. My arms were full of scratches from the countless hours spent in her rose garden around back.

The lawn, however, was a whole different battle, seeing as the grass seemed to grow two inches per day, and my well-used machine could no longer hack the thick greenery.

I looked across the street to Mr. Slavic's half-acre paradise and considered borrowing his Toro when a different machine altogether drew my attention to Alice's driveway: a large, rumbling, black-and-chrome motorcycle.

The bike rolled to a stop in front of Alice's garage, its growl rattling the windows. The man straddling the Harley wore dusty jeans, thick-soled boots, and a mountain of muscle. A tapestry of ink peeked out from under his black T-shirt on both arms.

First impression? Pretty boy, he was not. Trouble in a pretty package, he most definitely was.

Mystery rider planted one boot on the ground, then hoisted his log-sized thigh over the bike, offering me a front-seat view of a high, tight ass. The type of ass that conjured wicked images.

The man turned, removed his helmet, and wiped his brow with the back of his forearm. His gaze brushed over me like I was nothing more than a dandelion sprouted in a patch of greenery before he strode with purpose up onto Alice's porch, impressively skipping two of the steps. He shoved a key into the doorknob, walked in, and disappeared with a hard slam of the door.

I sat, my butt damp, processing the past sixty seconds. I looked down to find that entirely too much of my cleavage was showing. Not that the man had taken the time to notice. Seriously, any decent human would have at least acknowledged my presence, maybe offered assistance or asked what I was doing in the yard that he must know wasn't mine. Which reminded me—who was he, anyway? Why did he have a key to Alice's house? I was her favorite neighbor, and I didn't even have a spare.

I hopped to my feet revved and ready to storm Alice's front porch, bang on the door, and demand answers, but the guy came back outside, shirtless, and stalked toward me, his glower daunting. Sweet mother of mercy, he was mammoth —stacks upon stacks of earned muscle that had to have taken years of disciplined training. Colorful tats covered his well-conditioned chest, but I couldn't make heads or tails of the art through my blurry vision.

I swallowed the fear and cranked my chin upward to meet his glare.

"How much is she paying you?" he grunted, shoving a hand into his pocket and pulling out a wad of cash.

"Who?"

"Alice." He looked over his shoulder and nodded at the house. "How much does she pay you to take care of the yard?" His gaze raked the length of me, his expression apathetic at best.

Good Lord, his eyes—sleepy and swollen like he'd smoked weed for a week straight, but huge and framed with thick lashes, and so damn beautiful I almost sighed.

"The yard? Oh. No." I waved away the misunderstanding. "I don't work for Alice." I pointed a thumb over my shoulder. "I live next door. I was helping out while Alice..." I tucked my hands into the pockets of my cutoffs. "Wait. Who are you?"

"Listen." He scrubbed his forehead with the back of his hand. "I'm sure she would've appreciated the kindness, but I'm here now. I'll take care of the yard work." With his glum declaration and not so subtle blow off, he turned on his heel and marched back toward the house.

I followed, legs moving double-time to keep up with his long strides. "Wait."

He ignored me.

I sprinted to reach the top of the steps before he could ascend, then turned to meet him eye to eye. "You didn't answer me. Who are you?"

I was no longer dumbstruck by his scary beauty. I was pissed. And I wasn't wholly convinced he even knew Alice. He looked every bit the criminal with the tats, the muscles, and his fuck-the-world attitude.

I hit him with the same glare I gave my employees when they tried to bullshit me, the same angry warning I shot my customers when they got out of line, my *don't mess with Mama Bear* scary face. Only, my glare didn't faze him. He shot daggers right back with his puffy, red-rimmed, glorious blue eyes.

"Why do you have a key to her house? Explain, or I'm calling the cops."

The man dropped his head. His shoulders sagged, and he released a long breath. "Marley, is it? I've had a long fucking day." He moved around me and reached for the door.

"Wait." I shoved myself between the massive man and the sturdy oak frame at my back.

"Christ, woman. Get out of my way."

"How do you know my name?"

He slammed a palm into the jamb above my head and braced his body.

I slapped my hands to his chest in defense, a move I immediately regretted. A grumble vibrated his pecs beneath my fingers, a slew of profanities flew my way, the world spun, and I found myself pinned against the porch railing.

"Go home." With a grunt, he released my arms and headed back inside.

Alice was my neighbor. My dearest friend. I wasn't

about to let some stranger into her private space. She wasn't home to fight, so I would fight for her.

I followed that tight, beautiful ass right into the kitchen.

"You have a death wish or something?" he asked, voice raspy.

"You need to leave," I ordered, pointing at the door.

"Why would that be, little one?"

Little one? Oh no, he did not. I shoved a pointed finger between those marble-hard pecs. "I don't know who the heck you are, but this is Alice's home, and I'll be damned if I let you come in here and—"

Scary guy stumbled, slamming his back against the wall before sliding down, down, down and landing with a thud.

Elbows to knees, he hid behind his hands, and the hulking man sobbed.

Despite my irritation, my heart broke for the guy.

Men didn't cry. Men were emotionless globs of lies and selfish motivations. What was I supposed to do? Walk away? Leave him on the floor to drown in his ocean of misery?

I scanned the room. A fresh bouquet sat on the kitchen table—daisies, Alice's favorite. A worn leather jacket hung on the back of a kitchen chair, and two suitcases waited at the bottom of the stairs.

I hurried to the hall closet where the tissue supply resided, snagged a box, jammed a finger through the perforated hole, then crouched at the man's side.

When I tapped him on the shoulder with my offering, he raised his head, red eyes finding mine. So weary. So damn broken. Through jagged breaths, he managed to say, "She passed today. I didn't make it home in time."

"Who passed?" I croaked, fearing the answer.

"Alice," he muttered, barely keeping his shit together.

No, not my Alice. Deep anguish pulsed through me, the

pain bone deep. Like a drunk snake, I crumpled, coiling to the ground in a messy heap. "Today?"

"This morning," he mumbled, ripping tissues from the box.

"But the doctors said..." The doctors had warned me she might not survive her stroke. I'd visited her only two days ago. "I mean, I thought she was doing better." I had tried to convince myself that she'd be home in no time, that maybe the little twitch in her fingers the last time I'd held her hand meant she was going to wake up.

"Goddamn!" He slammed a fist into the linoleum. "I was one day too late."

With increasing pressure, I sunk my teeth into my bottom lip. I would not cry in front of this stranger. I would break down later, where I could fall apart, cuss, scream, and mourn yet another loss in the privacy of my home.

"Who will make arrangements? I have to..." I pushed to my feet, heading for the drawer where she kept her address book. Then I remembered, Alice had no family. Well, except for her brothers-in-law, whom she had said were never worth mentioning, and a nephew she'd helped raise, who had done time upstate for God knows what before going off the grid. Alice suspected he'd joined his father's "satanic biker gang." Her eyes would tear whenever she'd brought him up, and a bottle of gin would appear out of thin air.

"I have to call the funeral home. The church. Yeah." I nodded like a bobblehead. "The church. Maybe they'll help. I've never had to do this before. I don't know what to do."

"I got it," came a gruff reply.

"What?" I asked, thumbing through her list of contacts as if I would find answers in her embellished handwriting. I needed a task, a distraction from the paralyzing grief.

"I got it covered." He cleared his throat. "She's my responsibility."

"Who are you again?" I asked, the room going blurry.

"Joe." His voice was wet and garbled, his pain palpable.

"Joe who?" I slammed the address book on the counter. "That tells me nothing."

"I'm her nephew," he said, head hung low while he fisted his hair.

I'd spent hours upon hours with Alice, drinking tea or gin, talking, gardening. One thing I knew sure as shit was that she claimed no family except for—oh crap, her no-good nephew.

"No." My body tensed. "Alice's only nephew broke her heart and went to prison for a crime so awful she couldn't speak about it. That's what she told me."

"She exaggerated. He got out. I mean, I got out," he said to the floor. "And it was... I was..." His voice broke. After a painful silence, he whispered, "Too fucking late."

"You're trying to tell me that you're Little Joe?" I locked my emotions down tight and rifled through the drawer until my fingers met the sharp metal corner of the frame that I knew resided in the back. I pulled out the photo. "You're this scrawny, buck-toothed kid?"

"In the flesh," he grumbled. "Got my teeth fixed. How about that?"

"Where's your scar?"

He dangled his arms over his knees, tilting his head up to shoot me a glare. "What scar?"

"She told me the story about the cat in the tree. Where's the scar?"

"Fuck. Seriously?" He slammed his palms on the floor, shoulders bunching tight.

"I'm not leaving this house until I know who you are. Show me, or I'm calling the cops."

My mention of the police had the opposite effect I'd expected. The beast smiled. "You're crazy. You know that?"

"You're stalling." I backed into the counter and slid my hand into the drawer, feeling for the box cutter I'd used three weeks ago to help Alice open her latest Amazon order. Stupid move, entering the house alone with a stranger.

I stared into the face of danger and watched, trembling, while he curled his legs underneath himself and slowly rose to stand. The man had murder on his mind, judging by the way his muscles flexed and twitched, and the way those blue eyes, once anguished but now dark with fury, held my gaze and rendered me immobile.

I hadn't noticed the size of his hands, the long fingers, the map of veins under the skin, until he raised those beasts to his belt. Slow and steady, he undid the heavy metal clasp.

Jeans next. Pop, pop, pop went the buttons.

Shit. Shit. Shit.

"Crazy fuckin' woman," he murmured, turning, giving me his back.

The violent knocking in my chest grew painful as he lowered his jeans and boxers to his knees, revealing the ninth wonder of the world. Aside from the scar stretching from hipbone to butt crack on his right cheek, his butt was perfection. Purrr-fection. The longer I stared, the more I realized that the disfigurement only added to his appeal. And Lord have mercy, those thighs were thick and athletic, the perfect size for pinning a willing participant against a wall.

Shit.

He was Little Joe.

Joe the ex-con.

I couldn't have been more mortified. That was until he turned, arms held wide, pants to his knees, enormous cock swinging in the breeze. "Satisfied?"

My breath hitched. Holy freaking monster dongs, the man was hung.

Not appropriate, considering the news of the day. Had he no shame?

The rays of a thousand suns hit my cheeks. The blade slipped from my trembling, sweaty palm, hitting the floor with a terrible clang, jerking my attention from the Holy Grail of cocks.

"I, um. I gotta go." I turned, tears flowing, and made a mad dash for the door.

CHAPTER
Two

MARLEY

The last guest, an elderly man who had introduced himself to me earlier as Larry, seconds before commenting on my "plump, fresh titties," commanded Joe's attention for over an hour. Adorned in a gray suit, slick loafers, gold rings on his fingers, and a heavy gold cross around his neck, the man reeked of old-school debauchery—a mob boss from a bygone era.

I'd met a handful of Alice's friends over the years. I'd dined with them, sipped tea in the rose garden, listened to endless stories about long-lost loves, grandchildren, and hip surgeries.

The gentleman—and I use that term loosely—was someone I'd never before met, never heard of, and did not want in Alice's home. For that reason alone, I had stayed well past my welcome.

I ignored Joe's sideways glances, the subtle hints that my time was up, and made myself useful by collecting dishes and garbage left behind on the hardwood furniture Alice had kept in pristine condition.

Trash in the bin outside, dishwasher loaded, floor mopped, and countertops sparkling, everything looked as it should.

Except things weren't as they should've been. My friend wasn't sitting in her favorite chair or making me tea while offering passive-aggressive dating advice. Alice was gone. Dead and buried. I never told her how much I loved her or that our friendship had kept me grounded while my world fell apart around me. I didn't get to say goodbye. Alice was gone. Like Dylan. Like Warren. All the most important people left me.

In the quiet of the empty kitchen, my heart broke. I shattered, crumpling into a heap of sobs and weary bones on the lemon-scented linoleum.

With a grunt, Joe lifted me off the floor and settled me onto a kitchen chair.

Warm, spicy breath hit my face. The tissues were soft but rough under the press of his strong fingers while he wiped my tears. Never had a man touched my face with such clumsy tenderness, and the intimate gesture ignited a deeper ache in my chest.

A bottle of gin landed on the lace tablecloth in front of me.

"You broke into her Hendrick's?" I searched the room, expecting Alice to shuffle around the corner and scold us.

Joe settled in the seat across from me. "Way I see it, she'd want us to finish this bottle in her honor."

He pushed a glass filled with ice and clear liquid my way.

I studied the small scratch in the tumbler. "Alice never filled my glass this full."

Joe laughed. "She always gave me too much."

I swiped a knuckle under my eyes before lifting the crystal. "To Alice."

Glasses clinked. I opened my mouth, relaxed my throat, and let the liquor soothe me from tongue to gut, numbing every sensitive spot along the way.

Joe hadn't cried at all since the funeral started. I envied

his strength. He'd removed his suit jacket and tie, and the silver-blue dress shirt made the blue of his irises sparkle.

"Who is Larry?" I nodded to the corner where the man had last sat. "I've never met him before today."

Joe refilled my glass, then topped off his own, his expression giving nothing away. "Nobody." He looked down at the table, his eyes narrowing, jaw clenched. "Thanks for cleaning up." Crossing one black-socked foot over his knee, he leaned back and looked as if he planned on staying awhile. He tapped a rhythm on his glass, staring right through me, and the silence, the weight of his glare, heightened my sorrow.

Instead of offering words of comfort or begging for a hug, which I desperately craved, I finished my drink in one long draw. "I'm sure you want me out of your hair."

He looked over my shoulder and blinked, then sighing, brought his gaze back to me. "Have another drink."

One more wouldn't hurt. The hooch was good. Besides, I couldn't bear the thought of saying my final goodbye to Alice. Not sober, anyway. I nudged my glass closer to Joe, and he poured me another shot.

"She was my best friend," I said, raising the gin in salute.

Joe nodded, his eyes welling with emotion. "She was my favorite human."

I sipped slowly, savoring the flavor, welcoming the numbing buzz. "I feel like when I leave, that's it. She's gone for real. I won't see her, smell her, feel her arms around me."

When he smiled, his whole face got involved—forehead wrinkles, eye crinkles, dimples. "She gave the best hugs, didn't she?"

"The absolute best." I curled my arms around myself, remembering Alice's last embrace. "And she always knew when I needed one. I never had to ask. She just knew."

Joe shifted in his seat, coughing. "Thanks for being here."

His eyes sizzled, raking the length of me, lingering on my mouth for an uncomfortable spell.

I licked my lips, a knee-jerk reaction and a bad, bad, terribly bad move because Joe moaned a low, hungry moan.

He shifted again, tossed back his drink, and refilled both of our glasses. "Last call. Then you should probably go."

The big man with killer muscles and a *don't fuck with me* aura slumped in his chair. Jaw set hard, he rasped, "Or you could stay."

Those words, that thick voice, rumbled through me like a thunderstorm. "Why?"

"Why?" He huffed. "Because you're beautiful. And I want to bury my grief in those gorgeous curves."

I downed my glass in one swallow. "You're drunk."

"So are you. And you're still sitting there. And you're licking those lips, staring at me like I'm about to be your next meal."

Stupid liquor. I gave him my standard response. "I can't get involved with a criminal."

His face reddened, muscles bunched. "I'm not asking for your heart. Just need to get lost in a soft body for a while."

I respected his honesty.

Call it bad judgment, loneliness, grief, whatever, but I craved a physical connection. To be touched, noticed... needed, maybe.

I wanted to bury my pain, too.

And damn, there went my tongue again, sweeping between my lips.

One second, Joe was seated across the table; the next, he towered over me, hands in my hair, tongue tangled with mine and, God bless the man, he kissed like an awkward teen, big and sloppy and desperate. He didn't take long to find his rhythm, though, and when he relaxed? Sweet coffee with cream, that man savored my mouth like making out was his only care in the world. One hand wandered down my back, then lower still, and without breaking contact, he scooped me off the chair and dropped me on top of the table. His hips split my thighs wide, forcing the hem of my dress to my hips.

The man was strong, and he seemed to vibrate with need, every inch of his hardened body taut to the point of snapping.

Aching to hurry the pace and starving for a distraction from the sadness, I raised my fingers to his tie and made quick work of undoing the knot and discarding the damn thing.

He yanked at the *V* of my wrap dress, exposing my lace bra, and cupped my breast, rubbing his strong thumb in a slow circle over my hardening peak.

His buttons proved troublesome. Frenzied, I ripped the shirt open down the middle, desperate to get to the brutal heat hiding beneath the fabric.

Joe stepped back, shrugging out of his sleeves, and ditched the barrier somewhere over his shoulder. His gaze bounced from my boobs to my mouth, his cheeks flushed, lips parted and wet.

His chest rose and fell. "I haven't been with a woman in ages."

"Been a while for me, too." I snatched the bottle of gin, took a swig, then offered him another drink.

"Got a lot of pent-up energy." He lifted the bottle to his lips, paused, and said, "Soft and sweet won't be an option."

I leaned back on my arms and raised an eyebrow, ignoring the fuzzy tingles clouding my vision. "That a challenge?"

"Shit." Two deep dimples appeared before he took a long draw from the bottle. "You're perfect."

He came at me, rushed and clumsy. One thousand pounds of virile male, unbridled, unleashed, and un-freaking-believable.

. " . " . " . " . " . " . " . "

"Rise and shine, sleeping beauty."

Despite the rich timbre of his voice, every syllable hammered spikes into my skull.

The sheets rubbed my skin like sandpaper. I moved to kick them off, my blood going cold when my feet hit something hard and hairy.

Shit. Shit. Shit.

The bed bounced. Warm flesh poked my backside, and a heavy arm lopped around my waist, fingers splaying over my stomach.

I held my breath, praying the beast would go back to sleep.

His chest rose and fell. A gentle tug, and our bodies were flush, melded together, back to chest, ass to groin.

Heat rushed through me. Dear Lord, the man was huge. And not just the part of his anatomy nestled against my butt crack.

I silently cursed the gin sloshing through my veins, my stomach roiling.

Warm lips grazed my shoulder.

Visions of empty bottles, broken tables, and acres upon acres of bare, colorful skin flashed behind my lids.

I squeezed my legs together, the memories of all we'd accomplished over the past drunken hours causing heat to swell between my thighs. Damn, I was tender. Damn, the man was well endowed. Damn, I was in trouble.

Mourning sex was incredible. Waking the following morning, however, sucked hairy balls.

Not only did I suffer an inconvenient hangover, but I carried an unbearable burden of guilt for desecrating Alice's home. I would never be able to look at a La-Z-Boy recliner without blushing.

His kisses wandered lower, as did his fingers, meandering over every erotic point of contact on my body.

I refrained from arching into his ministrations, stifled my moans, and remained still when all I wanted to do was press closer, feel anything other than abandoned by those I loved, and connect with someone, anyone, even a total stranger.

A criminal.

Oh no. No, no, no.

No more bad boys.

What had I been thinking? Had the past thirty years taught me nothing? A few drinks, a hot body, and I'd broken my vow, repeating the cycle that had brought me battered heart after battered heart.

A string of profanities left my lips. I kicked free of the bedding and shrugged free of his hold.

Joe grabbed for me, but I rolled away. I misjudged the size of the bed, and off the edge I fell, hitting the floor with a yelp as pain shot up my spine.

"Ow," I cried, scrambling to my feet, rubbing my backside.

"Jesus, woman, you okay?"

God. His voice was like a well-aged Barolo: rich, robust, and firm, making my mouth water. I surveyed my surroundings and groaned. Heaven help me, we'd fallen asleep in Alice's guest bedroom, on a twin-sized bed, no less.

Time to make my escape.

"I'm fine. I, um..." I searched his room for my clothes, then remembered we'd disrobed downstairs, in the kitchen of all places. "I need to get ready for work." I snagged a pillow off the bed to cover myself.

"Little late for modesty, don't ya think?" Joe huffed. In one smooth motion, he threw off the blankets and, oh, sweet hell, the way his skin stretched over all those bumps and ridges... A girl could go blind if she stared too long.

He hit me with a panty-melting grin. "I'll make you breakfast."

"No!" I shouted, tossing the pillow his way and heading for the door. "For the love of God, go back to sleep." I jogged down the stairs, holding my breasts steady.

"Marley? Marley!" Joe's footsteps sounded above me, then a drawer opened and closed.

I shrugged my dress over my head, snatched my bra, panties, and shoes off the floor, then made a mad dash for the door.

A loud whistle stopped me with one foot over the threshold, two heartbeats from escape.

"What the fuck?" Joe wore nothing but a pair of boxers and stood clutching the banister and scratching the stubble on his jaw.

"I don't have time for breakfast," I threw over my shoulder. "Late for work," I lied, then slammed the door behind me.

Sure, my swift exit was a shitty move, considering the events of the past twenty-four hours. We'd buried Alice, his aunt and my dearest friend. We'd mourned together, soothed each other. Nobody deserved the brush-off I'd just given Joe, but my organs were still bloody and bruised from the last man who'd stormed out my door. I'd sworn off men like Joe. Men like... like every other man in my life.

No good. Low-life. Self-serving.
Criminals.
I attracted them like flies.

CHAPTER
Three

"Fucking fly." I groaned, swatting away the nuisance. I set my coffee on the small dresser and parted the thin bedroom curtains, scenting them for the thousandth time. The lingering stench of cigar flooded me with childhood memories—happier times.

A door slam drew my attention out the dust-spotted window to the yard next door. My new neighbor dashed to her car through the darkness, her long auburn hair bouncing against the hood of her baggy sweatshirt.

Sweet Jesus, that woman.

A grin cracked my face as I recalled the perfection hid beneath her loose clothing: smooth skin made for rough fingers, her body soft where it mattered but tight in all the right places, long, sweet legs, and an ass I wanted to gnaw like bubblegum. Marley had attitude for days—a fighter if ever I'd met one. What was she fighting? I hadn't a clue. I doubted she knew either, but damn, that fiery spirit would be fun to unravel.

I hoped to God there wasn't a man in the picture, because I wanted more.

True, I should've inquired about a significant other before we'd desecrated Alice's house, but in the frenzy of sharing our mutual grief, we'd drowned our sorrows in each other's grunts and moans, and there'd been no room for talking.

I watched from behind my shield of darkness while she settled into her Crosstrek. She ran the engine for a good five minutes while she scrolled through her phone, then rolled out of her long driveway and headed east.

I closed my eyes and allowed one more playback of the previous night when she'd rode me on the stairs, her heavy tits bouncing in my face, my spirit igniting for the first time in years, my body on fire, my libido unquenchable.

When I turned to face the empty room again, grief squeezed my chest. I itched for simple things—a sweet "good morning," a hug, or the scent of pancakes and home-made maple syrup. Alice had been everything good about my youth—wisdom, grace, and the perfect dash of rebellion—and as I turned and studied her room, I couldn't find a lick of regret for what I'd done. She'd given me everything a young man needed, and in return, I'd given her freedom.

Her faded pink robe hung on a giant white hook nailed to the closet door. Purple crocheted flowers trimmed the collar, some of them hanging by frayed strings. Her slippers sat on the floor, toes touching the wall, waiting for feet that would never again fill their vacant space. Her hairbrush lay on the small vanity perched between the bedroom windows, silver hairs tangled in the stiff black teeth. Her bed stayed as she'd left it, one half made, the other with the sheets and blankets thrown back, her pillow still bearing the indent where her head should be lying. At some point, I'd have to change the bedding.

My gut knotted. Another day.

The doorbell chimed, and my dark thoughts dissipated, freeing me from the ghosts. I jogged down the stairs, tore open the front door, and was assaulted by two of the craziest fuckers I'd ever known.

"Ready to catch some fish?" Frank asked, his heavy arm slung over my shoulder as he raked his nails over the top of my head. He'd damn near doubled in size since the last time we'd wrestled.

Then again, so had I.

"Can't wait." I'd missed our early morning excursions and had never been more grateful to see those two knuckleheads.

"Morning." Connor held up a massive thermos, then led the way to the kitchen. "We'll fill this baby, then be on our way." He busied himself with the coffee pot. He was overdue for a haircut, his blond hair hanging in his eyes and messy like he'd just rolled out of bed and hadn't taken a look in the mirror.

"My gear?" I asked.

"In the truck." Frank perched his ass in a kitchen chair, dark eyes aimed my way. His dark brown hair had been recently trimmed, cut close to his scalp—no nonsense, like Frank. "You find anything yet?"

"No." I scratched a nagging itch behind my ear. "But Larry didn't come to the funeral to give his condolences. He was fishing for something." He'd tried more than once to case the house, and Con, Frank, and I had taken turns steering him back into the living room.

Frank, who'd graduated college with me and gone on to become a cop without me, crossed his arms, nodding. "You get anything outta him?"

"No. But I will."

My uncle Larry. Dirty to the bone. He'd had eight years to hound Alice. "Why did he wait for my return to come sniffing around?" I asked the room.

"Don't know, buddy. You talk to any of the neighbors? Maybe Alice confided in one of them?"

"Working on it," I grumbled. Most of the attendees at Alice's service had been neighbors, and though every one of them had come offering casseroles and condolences, I hadn't been in the right headspace to interrogate.

Anger and regret still dominated my gray matter.

"Goddamn that woman!" I slammed a fist on the table, then pushed to my feet, agitated, and stepped into the other room. At times, I hated Alice for being so damn sweet, for making me love her so much, for staying with Uncle Bill, her piece of shit husband. But she was worth the sacrifice, I reminded myself, breathing deep. Alice was worth all the wasted years. After four controlled inhales and exhales, I returned to face my friends again.

Frank stood and tucked his chair back under the table like I hadn't had a fucking meltdown. "That neighbor of yours..." He nodded in the direction of Marley's house. "You hit her up? Maybe she knows something."

"Doubt it." Marley was off-limits, but if I voiced my demand, they'd want to know why. I didn't understand why myself. So I told them, "I'll poke around when the time's right."

I snorted, unable to contain my grin. I'd poked around all right. Poked for hours. I was jonesing for more poking.

Frank's right brow arched. "What's funny? Something going on with your neighbor?"

Before I could rustle up a lie, Con turned, tightening the thermos lid. "Ready?"

"Hell yes." Ready to get my life back on track. Eager to fall into a routine that didn't include guns, drugs, or dodging bullets. I was primed to get back to normal, whatever normal entailed, starting with my two best friends. "Let's catch some fish."

Mom of the Century? Donna Ruiz. The second she'd heard I was headed home, she'd hit up Amazon, Costco, and several men's clothing stores. On my second day back in Seattle, the deliveries had arrived. She'd thought of everything down to my favorite cinnamon-flavored floss.

That wasn't what made her phenomenal, though. What I'd found hard to comprehend, what had eaten at me every day while I was away, was that my mother never once believed I'd committed the crimes for which I'd served time. The lies I'd told. God, the lies. Yet she knew the truth, hard as I had denied her the facts. She knew and had accepted what transpired. She'd never judged, never chastised. Never once questioned or complained when I made her promise never to visit. She'd trusted me completely. For that, I owed her everything.

"Your hair is growing fast," she said, eyes watering as she stared at me through the screen.

"Yeah." I scrubbed a hand over my scalp. "I'll get it cut this week."

Her once blonde hair was now a gorgeous silver-white, and she wore it long. Her skin was still youthful, and her smile still made me feel like a goofy kid.

I missed my mom.

"Catch a big one this morning?"

"Nah." I chuckled. "Wasn't about the fish, though," I confessed. "Guys and I spent most of our time catching up."

"You've got the best friends, Joseph."

I nodded in agreement. "I appreciate the deposit you made in my bank account."

Though I didn't need her gift, I knew better than to offer to give one cent back. But fuck, I hated being in that position, a grown man accepting money from his mother. Lower than low, in my opinion.

"What will you do for work? Do you need me to call Sean and see if he has any openings?"

My mother's cousin, Sean, ran a successful logistics company based in Seattle.

"No. I'm good. Promise. Got everything lined up." Mom had no clue what I'd done to earn a living the past six years. The truth would kill her. Better to let her believe I'd served my full sentence, rather than only two years.

And since I'd lived rent-free, my savings was hefty.

"What a blessing that Alice left you the house, honey. Real estate is outrageous in Seattle. Are you going to keep the property or sell?"

I choked down the ball of emotion in my throat. "Think I'll stay for a while."

I'd inherited the house, along with everything Alice had owned. But I'd trade the two-story craftsman in a heartbeat for one more day with the woman who'd made the best of dire circumstances and managed to keep a mischievous adolescent in check while his mom worked two jobs to keep a roof over his head. Though Alice was my aunt by marriage, she'd treated Mom and me as her own flesh and blood.

Before my arrest eight years ago, my career goal had been respectable and obtainable. After? Options were limited. I could follow in my father's footsteps and continue the family legacy, but that was the easy way out. I'd fought too damn hard not to fall into that cycle.

Connor's sister, Bridget, had offered me a job at Misled. Though I knew the ins and outs of running a club thanks to my six years under Dad's employ, pride kept me from accepting.

Option number three? Frank's old man was about to retire from a career in waste management. He'd put in a good word for me at the local facility. The job was a done deal. Not the high octane, do good, save the world fantasy I'd had as a kid, but real life was an uphill battle, and a man had to learn to roll with the punches.

So, most likely, a sanitation worker I would be.

"I'm so sorry I couldn't make it to the States for the funeral," Mom said, sniffing. "I loved that woman dearly."

"She loved you, too." I sighed, taking in the room. The kitchen was small and cozy, but without Alice, the space seemed vast and empty. "The house doesn't feel right, ya know?"

"Oh, Joseph, this has to be hard for you. She was one of the good ones."

"She was."

Mom leaned closer to the screen, crossing her arms on the table. "So I'd like to make a trip home at the end of the summer. Does that sound good?"

I forced a smile and prayed she couldn't read my deception through the screen. "That'd be great. I miss you so much." Last thing I wanted was a visit from my mother. Not until I had my shit together. Not until I could make her proud. "I'd kill for your mac and cheese right now."

Mom laughed, wiping tears from her cheeks. It fucking broke me to see her hurting, knowing she couldn't hug her only child. But she was safe, alive, and cherished by a good man.

Precisely what she deserved after dear old dad had trampled her heart and left her to raise his son.

"I'll talk to you in a couple of days, Mom."

"Promise?"

"Of course."

"Love you, Joseph." She waved, her eyes welling, face scrunching, then leaned into the camera as she severed our connection.

I stared at the black screen with laser focus, giving that inanimate object all my negative energy, drawing deep breaths until the rage subsided. Once again, I was utterly alone in the home that seemed a castle of silence, every corridor, every room, more cold, vacant, and lifeless than the last.

I lugged the sledgehammer upstairs, pulled the safety goggles over my head, and shoved my fingers back into the gloves I'd removed when Mom had called.

The spare room seemed the best place to start.

I raised the heavy tool.

With all the fury I harbored, I swung and struck, cracking the drywall, and damn, what a great feeling. Swing. Smash. Breathe. Start again. For hours, I beat the shit out of that wall, purging, until I slumped on the floor, spent, sweaty, and too damn tired to care about the shit in my head.

CHAPTER
Four

Joe

Dear Joseph,

I hope my letter finds you well. I understand we were not meant to communicate, but I find myself in a pickle, my dear boy, and while I'm still clear-minded enough, I must, with great urgency, get this message to you, my greatest joy, my pride, the son I never had.

Our years together were precious, weren't they? I was tasked to care for you in your mother's absence, but it was you, Joseph, who took care of me, without complaint, without fail. You loved me. You protected me. You did a terrible, grievous thing for that love, and though my mind is unreliable these days, my memories jumbled, at this moment, pen in hand, I must confess that I remember, at least for now, every detail of that horrid night.

You traded your life for mine. Threw away a promising future for that of a stubborn old woman. I shake now with grief, with disbelief, with gratitude. Tears of anger and shame stain this very page. I'm sorry, from the deepest wells of my soul, to have put you in such an impossible position.

I pray your father's hooks have not burrowed so deep that you cannot shake free, because you see, dear boy, you must come home. William invades my dreams and sometimes appears when I'm awake. My husband haunts me, calling me back to his side, and my time on this earth will soon come to an end.

I'm not afraid for me, Joe, but for my roses.

Who will tend to them? I trust no one but my favorite nephew with their care. Please, and hear my words, remember to dig deep. In their soul, deep down in their very roots, treasure lies. If I could turn William's sins into paradise, imagine the reclamation you'll achieve with a purging of blood, sweat, and tears. Hard work is vital for grounding a lost soul.

Come home so I can wrap my arms around you again. Let me see that beautiful smile once more before I redeem my ticket to the Pearly Gates. Come home and live. Claim your life back.

All my love,

Alice

P.S. I have a new neighbor and friend, Marley Masters. She's feisty and intelligent and watches out for me, much like the boy who saved my life. You have my permission to marry this one, Joseph Kaine.

Alice's last communication.

My hands trembled, making reading difficult, but I skimmed the words regardless, the left tilt of her letters, the curly flair to her t's and i's, and the exaggerated swoop of her y's. Alice did everything with flair.

Every time I'd refolded the pink flowery paper, I'd sworn it would be my last read-through. That letter was the reason I'd come home. Those words were likely the ramblings of an aged and well-used brain, but the Alice I knew had a purpose for everything, and my gut told me there was a hidden meaning.

Vision blurry, I stretched, rolled out of bed, and tucked the letter under my socks in the drawer before dressing to head outside. Step by measured step, I made my way to the center of the small, thorny maze, gravel crunching under the heavy soles of my boots.

Alice's apology garden. Our private joke. Her safe rebellion.

Bill had always been unfaithful—his moral fiber weaker than wet tissue—and cocky enough to believe a new rose bush, accompanied by a few days of ass-kissing, would appease his wife and erase his sins. My aunt, faithful to a fault, had turned his apologies into a beautiful sanctuary.

As a punk kid, I hadn't understood the magnitude of my uncle's wrongdoings. Had I paid attention, pulled my head outta my ass, Alice would...

Fuck. I shook the thought from my head. The past was the past. No changing that shit.

I'd avoided the garden since coming home, reluctant to relive unpleasant memories. With every step closer, my legs grew heavier.

The center of the garden was circular, the ground covered with white rocks and pebbles. A small bistro-style table sat off to the left, one of the chairs knocked over. A cement bench sat to the right, close to the shed, and the shattered remains of a porcelain teacup littered the pebbles beneath.

God. Alice. What were the odds she'd fallen in the same place my uncle had? Was the garden cursed?

Horrid visions of Alice unconscious and helpless, bloody and beaten, dropped me to my knees. My guts twisted, an unholy fire ripping through me. Head in my hands, I breathed through the wave of nausea and tucked the memory away.

Three deep breaths brought the world back into focus. The scent of earth and leaves and spring blossoms calmed my racing pulse. Before rising, something caught my eye. Behind a leg of the bench lay a half-smoked cigar. Laughter bubbled through the heartache. Alice and her stogies. Though I'd never picked up the habit, my rebel aunt had been the first to introduce me to the forbidden novelties of tobacco. I hated the shit, but there wasn't much I wouldn't have suffered for that woman. Chest lighter, I retrieved the soggy stick and headed for the trash.

For the rest of the morning and into the afternoon, I tended to the apology garden, sweating, bleeding, purging, digging deep—like she'd asked—into my soul in search of peace.

More often than not, my thoughts drifted to my neighbor. Feisty was how Alice had described Marley, and feisty had been my first impression.

You have my permission to marry this one.

None of the girls I'd dated had passed Alice's approval. Marley was unique; I'd sensed that, too. Marriage was the furthest thing from my mind, but damn, I needed to know what made that woman tick.

Why? Who fucking knew. The important thing was, I looked forward to the challenge for the first time in too many years.

⁕⁕⁕⁕⁕⁕⁕⁕⁕

The yellow shag rug slipped under my feet as I stepped out of the shower. Flailing, I grabbed the towel rack for support, but the rusty old chrome tore from the wall, chunks of paint and plaster falling at my feet, taking me along for the ride.

Thank God I'd closed the toilet lid, because my bare ass landed on the cold porcelain with a spine-cracking thud.

The doorbell rang again.

I scooped my towel off the floor, secured the cotton

around my waist, and jogged down the stairs. Expecting no one, grateful for anyone, I ripped open the door. Blinding beauty greeted me. Cool air caressed my skin, and the muscle underneath tightened. My cock thickened beneath the damp fabric of the towel.

"Hi, Joe." Marley stood on the porch, her hands in the pockets of a long, baggy T-shirt, or maybe it was a too-short dress. Either way, her legs were on display mid-thigh to ankles. Good God, what a gorgeous sight. White canvas shoes covered her feet. The woman looked young, vibrant, and too damn innocent to have done the things we did in Alice's home only a few days ago.

Her sun-kissed cheeks darkened as she took in my naked chest, my wet torso, the white towel that hung loose on my waist. Her gaze lingered on my bare feet before she shook her head.

Deadly adorable, that one.

"My eyes are up here," I teased, pointing to my face.

"Uh. Sorry." She scratched the base of her neck. "I... um..." Again, her focus shifted to my bare chest, and I couldn't help but laugh and, yeah, I flexed just to mess with her.

"I came by to..."

Arms crossed, I leaned against the doorjamb, the towel loosening, falling lower on my hips, seconds from dropping to the floor. I made no move to adjust, curious how she'd react, egging her on because I couldn't help myself.

Her face darkened from a pink blush to beet red, and just as the cotton gave way, she snapped her hands to my waist, just above my growing erection, and clutched the terry cloth.

"What's the matter with you?" Mumbling cuss words, she twisted and tucked, not gently, then settled the fabric back around my waist. "This is a respectable neighbor-hood," she scolded, like a mother to an errant child.

I stared down at her soft, shiny head of hair and bit back a groan. Voice thick with need, I asked, "You got a man?"

Her gaze snapped to mine. "What?"

"You got a man?" My arms stayed crossed. I wouldn't mess with another guy's woman, but damn, every muscle strained, aching to touch that feminine firecracker.

She stepped back, brows pinched, those full lips slightly parted. If she said yes, I'd have to jump off a bridge.

Marley adjusted the pile of hair on her head, tightening whatever held the soft waves together. "Little late for that question, don't you think?"

True. We'd already fucked, but I'd been drowning in grief and gin. A mistake I wouldn't make twice. I was revved and ready if the lady wanted another go, but we'd both be clearheaded.

I stood tall, studying those exotic eyes, and I couldn't read if she was terrified or turned on. Too far gone to care, I demanded, "Yes or no?"

Taking another step back, she shook her head and whis-pered, "No."

Where the hell was she going? I hooked her waist, spun, and pinned her against the rough shingles. "Good goddamn answer, neighbor," I mumbled before claiming those sassy lips.

Marley's was the only mouth I'd tasted in too many months, and shit, I was out of practice and overexcited, so when she gripped the hair at the back of my head and pulled me away, our breaths labored, I feared I'd gone too hard.

Until she grumbled, "Oh, fuck it," and crushed me with a kiss so greedy and full of pent-up frustration my knees buckled.

The beauty tasted like coffee, smelled like expensive perfume. Too long deprived of life's simple pleasures, I gorged on her kisses and moans, her tight body and soft breasts. God, how I'd missed the simple skin to skin.

Cupping her ass, I lifted her higher. She hooked her legs around my waist, her fingers tangled in my hair, her tongue... Sweet Jesus, the things she did with her tongue. I was seconds from making a fool of myself and exploding all over her stomach.

Ending the lip-lock, I begged, "Come inside."

Panting, she stared at me long and hard, her hooded gaze bouncing between my eyes. She dropped her legs, taking my towel with her, the cotton pooling at my feet, my bare ass exposed to the neighborhood, my rock-hard cock bobbing, throbbing, between us.

She looked down and bit her lip, stifling her laugh, but those wrinkles at the corners of her eyes gave away her plea-sure over my predicament.

"Listen." She slapped a palm on my chest, then jerked her hand away like the contact had singed her skin. "We got drunk and hooked up. But that won't happen again."

Liar. And not a good one. The woman was turned on. I slapped my hands on the house above her head and leaned close, waiting, watching. Her breath hitched, her gaze dark-ened, her lips parted while she studied my chest. Finally, she found the courage to meet my eyes.

I couldn't help my smirk. "If you say so."

Swear to fuck, that grimace was priceless. I got the feeling Marley wasn't challenged often. What a travesty. She had a gorgeous scowl.

Again, she pushed at my chest, and this time I backed off, standing straight but staying close.

Not intimidated, the little firebomb twisted and slipped inside, heading for the kitchen. "I came by to get my spare key back. Alice had one in case of an emergency."

Towel forgotten, I followed. "I haven't found any spares lying around."

"It's in a teacup, second shelf above the toaster. Back left corner." She looked over her shoulder, her glare dropping to my rigid cock, then bouncing back to my face. "Can you put some clothes on?"

"Nah. I like the way you look at me," I taunted, then pushed past her and pulled open the cupboard door where Alice's treasured teacups lived. I reached into the cup in the back left corner and snagged the metal ring. "Do you have a spare to return?" I asked, releasing the key into her outstretched palm.

"No." Her brows furrowed, eyes glazed as if lost in a memory. "Alice never gave me one."

I gestured toward her hand. "You sure you don't want me to hang on to that, you know, in case of an emergency?"

She tossed the key in the air and caught it, then crossed her arms. "No offense, but I don't know you. Why would I give you access to my home?"

Christ, how I wanted to kiss that wrinkle between her eyes. "I don't need a key to get into your home," I teased, winking. "Just FYI."

"Not winning brownie points here," she huffed and headed toward the door.

I leaned against the counter, the hollow in my chest expanding. "Tell me something."

Marley paused but didn't turn around. "What?"

"Why'd you run out the other morning?"

Her left shoulder raised, then dropped. "I woke up in a strange bed, next to a man I just met. That's not me. I can't afford to be so careless."

I couldn't resist. "So our hookup was a one-time thing?"

Marley didn't answer, just walked away. I watched her leave, silently begging her to stay, have coffee, have a good fuck, hell, just sit together in silence. She slammed the door behind her, but then, as I was about to head upstairs, the door cracked open, her arm poked through, and she dropped my towel on the floor.

CHAPTER
Five

I dropped the dirty towel in the sink, cracked open the window, and handed the customer his soy latte with an extra sweet smile. The blue hybrid rolled away, quiet and unassuming. Prius guy was my first customer every morning, never flirted or initiated a conversation, always ordered a grande soy milk latte. He said "please" and "thank you" and never stared at my chest. My favorite type of customer.

Ridiculous, I know, considering I owned three "bikini barista" stands. Pink Sweets was my baby—a chance I'd taken years ago that had paid off better than I'd ever imagined.

Lilly's army green Charger pulled into the lot, the ever-present *boom, boom, boom* vibrating the shop windows.

Moments later she bounced in the door, wearing combat boots, a leather bustier, and a tartan-plaid cheeky skirt. "Wassup, girlie?"

"Same ol' same ol'," I replied, readjusting my bikini top.

Lilly stood an inch taller than me. Blonde hair dyed black, heavy eyeliner, lips that put Angelina Jolie to shame, and a body so tight she looked like a CG rendering. The girl never stood still, ate like a horse, and brought in more tips than all of my employees put together.

The other girls suspected she offered more to the customers than sexy coffee, but they were wrong. Lilly just knew how to work a person. Any age, shape, sex, or size. Any proclivities.

She hung her handbag in the small closet and turned to face me. "You look like shit. Rough night?"

Rough week. "Yeah, didn't sleep much."

Her face softened. "How ya holding up?"

I bit my lip to hide the quiver. "Gonna miss that old coot."

"She loved the shit outta you," she whispered, pulling me into her arms, soothing me with a vanilla-scented embrace.

"God, I loved her, too. I still can't believe she's gone." I broke the hug and turned to wipe down the nozzles on my espresso machine.

Lilly shrieked behind me. "Boss, what happened to you?"

Uh-oh. The evidence of my latest poor decision had mostly faded, but blemishes were hard to hide when you were nearly naked. "Nothing. Why?"

"Don't you nothing me. I see those bruises. Was it that Jackson asshole?" She grabbed her handbag and rifled through. "Where's my phone? I'm calling Marco. He'll set that fucker straight."

Bless Lilly's heart; she always had my back. Marco, her boyfriend, a retired military badass, acted the overzealous big brother, threatening to take anyone down who wronged Lilly or any of her friends. I loved the guy to death.

"It wasn't Jackson." I plucked the cell from her fingers. "Ended things with him weeks ago—the day I discovered he was a dealer." Our tiff had turned violent, but I smiled, remembering the black eye I'd given him in exchange for my fat lip. Hadn't seen him since. Probably wasn't used to girls who fought back. The only good thing I learned from my father was how to throw a punch, and that skill had come in handy more times than I cared to count.

"Oh." She leaned closer, studying my face, probably for signs of deception, then turned to the mirror, Chanel lipstick tube in hand, seemingly appeased. "So? Spill it."

"Nothing to spill. I had too much to drink the other night. Woke with bruises." Not a lie. All the dirty bits that happened between drinking and waking were fresh in my mind, but those memories would stay locked up tight. "I'm really embarrassed, so if you could stop probing, that would be awesome."

"Liar. You never drink alone, and none of your friends would've let you get sloshed enough to hurt yourself." She turned around, perfect brow arched high, and capped her lipstick. "So, either you're street fighting on the side, or you spent the evening being slammed into all manners of surfaces." She grabbed my shoulders and turned me around. "Judging by the placement of those scratches, I'd say a couple walls and a hard floor—not wood, though, maybe tile. Oh, shit. You were pinned into a corner. Yep. That's where those came from." She brushed a finger over my shoulder blade, then palmed my left butt cheek. "And the fucker held your ass. Look at the size of those handprints. How big was he? Six-two, six-three?"

The time had come to retire my skimpy duds and concede to running the show from behind the scenes. Leave the flaunting and flirting to the younger girls with supple skin that didn't take weeks to heal.

"Shut up." I shrugged away and pretended to search for something in the cupboard.

"Was he hung?"

Cheeks unbearably hot, I whined, "Stop."

"How are you walking around today?" she continued taunting.

"Enough!" I half yelled, half laughed. "Get to work." I pointed at the window. "You have a customer."

Lilly stopped teasing during the morning rush but started again at the first lull in cars. "You got fucked raw, didn't you?"

"Inappropriate." I reached for my sweats and tugged them over my hips. "I'm your boss."

The roar of a loud motor vibrated the windows. I glanced at the security camera, praying my rising pulse was for naught, but curse my luck, my neighbor and his beefy ride pulled up to the window.

Shit. Shit. Shit! I dropped to a squat. Why? Who knew? But there I was, and there I'd stay.

"Holy, hot tamale," Lilly spewed under her breath. "Look at this guy."

Oh, I'd looked. Touched. Swapped spit just yesterday. "Looks like trouble if you ask me."

Lilly didn't hear me, already leaned too far out the window. If I gave her a nudge, she'd fall right onto his bike. I busied myself in the corner, down low, where there were sure to be dust bunnies that needed sweeping. Sweet lord, why were my knees so sore? Oh yeah, sex on the stairs. *Note to self: No more riding monster cocks without a cushion for your knees.*

"Morning, sunshine," Lilly purred. "What can I get for you?"

"Americano. Black. Two sugars." Joe's rough timber, even from a distance, vibrated my skin, licking every sore spot with white-hot regret.

Lilly worked the man, throwing her best lines his way before turning away to engage the coffee grinder. I duck walked to the closet, then stood hidden behind the door. I had a clear view of the security screen in the corner of the shop.

To Joe's credit, he was a gentleman. No witty come-backs. No sexual innuendoes. He spoke few words to my master seductress other than telling her to keep the change. He hadn't even ogled her 34DDs.

She watched him ride away, then turned to me, lips pursed, blowing a low whistle. "Did you see the size of those hands?"

Seen them, felt them. Wore their marks on my skin. I laughed, shaking my head no.

"You're white as a ghost." She pressed the back of her fingers to my forehead. "What's wrong with you?"

Wasn't that the million-dollar question? Tell ya what was wrong. I'd let that man penetrate my thick skin, and we'd only just met. Fucking old habits. The air grew dense, the walls closed in, and the space became too small for my stifling emotions. "I need to make my rounds. You good until Carmen shows up?"

"I'll be fine." She connected her cell to the speaker and pulled up her work playlist. "We're hitting Georgetown for drinks tonight. Wanna join us?"

"Oh. Um." I absolutely was not in the mood for drinks or hanging out with Marco and his buddies. In my line of work, being ogled and propositioned was par for the course. Hanging in a bar full of drunk, horny men while trying to relax? No, thank you. "Maybe."

I rubbed the ache in my chest. Lilly knew I would decline, but that never discouraged her from extending the invitation. I hated being away from the house. One day, Dylan would come home. I needed to be there when he returned.

I grabbed my keys and handbag and slipped out, checking the periphery for ex-cons on growly bikes. "Lock up behind me," I hollered.

"Morning, neighbor." The rough greeting came from Alice's side of the shrub hedge that separated her front yard from mine.

My insides betrayed me in disgusting, pitiful ways, heart racing, skin tingling. I stepped off my porch, tripped over a pebble, stumbled, then righted myself, thankful the sun had yet to rise. Jeez, I needed to cool my jets.

I offered a watered-down greeting. "Hey."

Joe jogged around my front lawn, then down my driveway, a pair of loose-fitting lounge pants hanging off his waist and a rumpled T-shirt clinging to his chest. Even in his domestic disguise, the man looked threatening, larger than life, and so dangerously delicious.

For the love of God, what was wrong with me? Was my proclivity toward criminal elements a hereditary issue? Mental illness did run in the family. Maybe a visit to the shrink was in order.

Joe stalked closer, his gaze raking the length of me, wearing a satisfied grin like he'd already had me for breakfast. Beautiful, cocky bastard.

We reached my car at the same time.

Spine rod straight, I asked, "What are you doing up so early?"

"Couldn't sleep." The man-beast invaded my personal space, leaving me nowhere to go but backward until my butt, then shoulders, smashed against my car.

Joe towered over me. He seemed to enjoy making me stretch my neck to make eye contact. His size, proximity, and the way he smelled was the opposite of offensive. What offended me, what I could not accept, was the way my body buzzed and hummed in his presence and that my wits ping-ponged out of control.

"Where you off to?" he asked, voice deep and rumbly like he'd just rolled out of bed and hadn't warmed up his vocal cords.

"Work," came my weak reply.

"Yeah?" His hands landed on the top of my car, his feet caged mine, our hips coming too damn close together. "Never did ask what my gorgeous neighbor does for a living."

Oh, Lord. The man was aroused and unashamed of his blatant desire, his erection thickening between us.

What an erotic sight. I was in the danger zone, ridiculously attracted to a man who would inevitably disappoint. I craved his touch, itched for his attention. But, Joe was a criminal, and too young, I'd learned that men who skirted the law never stayed in one place for long, not even to guard the hearts they were supposed to love.

"Coffee." Forcing my gaze upward, I mumbled, "I own a chain of coffee stands."

"That's perfect," he drawled. "I just so happen to have a thing for coffee."

Yes. Coffee served by scantily clad women. I was privy to that fact but refrained from telling him so. The less I said, the better. Conversation with Joe led to sexy time with Joe because that's how I rolled apparently. I focused on the breadcrumbs caught in his stubble so as not to fall victim to the allure of those thick, butter-soft lips.

"Have a drink with me after work," he commanded.

A lesser woman would've crumpled under that heady gaze.

"No." I shook my head, throwing more vigor into the act than necessary. "I can't."

Joe stiffened, one hand coming to my hip, fingers curling, gripping tight—for support or control, I couldn't tell. And what did his intention matter anyway when Joe was water and I, Marley, was oil squeezed from the dirty souls of all the men before him?

"Why? Got a date?"

On an average day, would a man touch me uninvited, I'd have harsh words, and if chastisement failed to deliver my point, I'd target his baby-makers. I hadn't invited Joe's touch, but his voice soothed, his fingers steadied, and his heated gaze made me swell with need. Sweet mocha latte, he was too close, too handsy, too everything. Instead of kneeing his balls, I whispered, "Just working late, that's all."

The man smirked. "I stay up late, so we're good."

"I don't," came my swift reply. I needed to leave. Flee from the criminal I wanted to ravish in the dirtiest ways.

"Beauty sleep, huh?"

"Yeah." I shimmied free of his grip. "Got a business to run. Need my shut-eye."

Joe leaned in. Closer. Closer still, and he licked those sinful lips and stared at my mouth. Heaven help me, if that man kissed me again, I would die, struck down by the gods of sound judgment. He didn't kiss me. Instead, Joe pulled my car door open, and with a sensual rasp, whispered, "See ya 'round, gorgeous," then waited until I settled in my seat before shutting me in.

Hands trembling, I pushed the start button and fired up the engine. "Have a good day," I said, though he couldn't hear me through the glass barrier. I offered a pathetic wave before reversing out of the driveway.

Joe stepped back, settled in a wide stance, arms crossed over his chest, and waited like a father sending his daughter off to school.

Free from his hypnotic gaze, I drew a deep breath and

then released the air nice and slow, hoping to clear the lustful thoughts from my mind. He'd made a bold move, approaching me like we were long-time lovers. Did he think because we'd fucked in a drunken stupor that I would fall onto his dick every time he dialed up the charm?

Men were idiots.

Case in point: halfway to work, my phone buzzed.

I clicked the Bluetooth button on my stereo. "Hello?"

"Hey, gorgeous," came the voice that never failed to wound me.

Bile rose, my skin prickling. "Don't call me that."

Warren responded with a chuckle that made my gut ache, then said, "I'm gonna be in your neighborhood next week. Wanna see you."

Translation: I need a loan.

Tampering my emotions, I responded, "No. Absolutely not."

Silence. Heavy breathing. "Please, baby. I miss you."

His sickly sweet supplications used to work. Until they didn't. "I don't have time for a visit. Unlike you, I work for a living."

"Just give me an hour. We need to talk."

The more I engaged, the greater his persistence, a lesson I'd learned long ago. I ended the call without a response, sucked in a deep breath, and exhaled the negative energy.

Fucking ex-cons.

Bad news. Every last one of them.

. · . · . · . · . · .

"You have got to be kidding me," I groaned, exhausted and done with men and their bullshit.

I slammed the car into park, cut the engine, and dropped my head to the steering wheel. Two deep breaths steadied my pulse. I bumped open my door and braced for an uncomfortable conversation.

Joe sat on the top step of my porch, beer in hand, six-pack at his side, and damn if he didn't look like he belonged, a man unwinding after a hard day's work. The sight angered me for many reasons, none of which I had the energy to contemplate. Seriously, did he think he could charm his way into my pants with Pale Ale and that strong jaw, and—oh, jeez—those muscles?

Gah. Who was I kidding? He could. And that was my problem in a nutshell. I, Marley Masters, was a sucker for any guy who seemed eager to slay my dragons or rock my world. Trouble with that sort was, they always had an agenda, and no matter how handsome, sweet, or convincing, they always left dragging my heart and guts behind them.

No more. I was done being a doormat.

Let him down gently, the angel on my shoulder whispered. *Kick him to the curb with the sharp end of your stilettos*, the devil croaked. Not until I reached the bottom step did I register the look on Joe's face, forlorn and a little lost, so instead of asking him to leave, I settled for, "Hey."

"Hey." He nodded before pulling a long draw between his lips.

Curse my bleeding heart, the man looked defeated. "How long you been here?"

He studied me, eyes weary before saying, "Half hour, give or take."

"Why?"

His chest rose and fell, his gaze darting to Alice's home, then back to me. "Lonely in that damn house."

His confession stung, salt to my unhealed wounds. I conjured a swift defense. "My porch isn't lonely?"

"Nah. Got the squirrels to keep me company." Joe leaned forward, elbows to knees, blue eyes coming to life, taking in every inch of my body.

Never had a man's attention heated my skin the way Joe's did. Seriously. Ten more seconds, and my clothes would be ash.

Desperate to shut down my libido, I constructed the first layer of bricks and asked, "Well, at least it'll only be a few more days, right?"

"What?" He blinked, finding my eyes.

"That you'll be in Alice's house."

Shoulders sagging, his bottle hit the cement with a loud clunk. "A few more days?"

"The funeral is over. I just assumed—"

"That'd I'd go home?" He leaned back on his elbows and straightened his legs, crossing them at the ankles. Sweet mother of mercy, he was long lines and honed edges and too beautiful to be any sort of good for me.

"Well, yes," I said, forcing my gaze above his waistline.

"Gorgeous, that *is* my home." Joe laughed, the sound warming my soul. His words, however, tightened the ever-present knot in my gut.

A beautiful bad-boy ex-con living next door, twenty-four-seven for the foreseeable future? Heaven help me.

"So, you're staying?" I snapped, my voice raising an octave, my heart lurching, my purse dropping off my shoulder.

Joe's brows pinched. He looked at the ground, then back to me, shaking his head. "Jesus. You're an ego killer."

Gah, I was a bitch. It wasn't his fault I was a mess, especially where men were concerned. I hadn't meant to hurt his feelings. Or had I? Why was my throat so dry? "Can I have one of those?"

"Thought you'd never ask," he replied, scooting to the

left, making room for my sorry ass. He used his key ring to pop the cap off an IPA, then handed the bottle over.

"C'mon." I clutched the beer to my chest, snatched my handbag off the ground, and headed toward the backyard. "It's more comfortable back here."

Joe followed me through the gate, then onto the patio, where he had his pick of a lounger or a swing but settled next to me on the sectional, dropping his glorious ass right next to mine, our thighs playing rub-a-dub-dub.

Instead of complaining or moving, I took three long swigs of my beer, knowing I'd regret my indulgence in the morning. "This is good."

"I know how to pick 'em," was his simple reply.

He watched me take another drink, a lazy grin softening his features.

Joe smelled like he was fresh from the shower, and I forced mental images of his soapy skin from my thoughts.

He studied my lips, licking moisture from his own, then leaned closer like he wanted a taste. But instead, he asked, "How was work?"

Work? Four men had driven through the stand with their cocks on display. Nothing new there. One of them, however, had masturbated the entire time at the window and didn't tip. Nothing new, either, but I'd had enough and told the psychopath if he returned to any of my stands, I'd send the security video and his license plate number to the authorities. I would never do that, of course, but a man stupid enough to think any one of us baristas enjoyed watching while he choked his chicken was dumb enough to fall for my idle threat.

I told Joe none of that. "Good. How was your day?"

His smile faded, eyes glazed as if lost in thought. "Spent the day going through Alice's closets. Boxed clothes for donation, sorted through her collection of knickknacks." His breath hitched. He drank. Sighed. Hit me with a gaze so full of desolation that my own sadness faded into the shadows. "Some days, I really hate being in that house."

"I get lonely too," I blurted, sharing our mutual truth. Until recently, I hadn't been alone for eighteen years, and though I had my employees and my small circle of friends, the hollow in my heart could only be filled by one person.

"It's a good thing we're neighbors." Joe twisted his bottle between his fingers, the heartbreak he wore achingly familiar.

Silence lingered to the point of uncomfortable before he asked, "Was she happy? Did she live a good life?"

"Alice?"

He nodded.

"Oh, God yes. She was crazy and fun and smart. And that laugh... I miss that laugh so much."

The big man next to me blew out a breath and relaxed into the seat, his head falling back. "It was worth it, then."

"What was worth it?"

"Nothing." His eyes slammed shut. "She was happy. That's all that matters. That angel deserved nothing but the best."

Vulnerability made him all the more attractive. "Alice was the happiest, most gracious woman I've ever met. She was the kind of person that made you want to be better. And her joy was infectious."

He rolled his head to the side, meeting my gaze. "I'm glad she had you."

"She had a tribe, Joe," I assured him. "Everyone in the neighborhood loved Alice." Over the past couple of years, her memory had become less reliable, her behavior more eccentric, but she was well loved by the community. "We all watched out for her."

His warm hand landed on my thigh, those thick, strong

fingers curling, holding tight like I was his anchor. A furnace blazed under my skin. I missed being needed but hated how easily I softened under his touch. I sighed, fighting a shiver.

Joe broke the connection and popped the top off two more beers. We drank. We talked about Alice. When the sky darkened, we lit the firepit.

Conversation came too easy. Joe's laid-back persona was comforting, his laugh addicting, making me crave his smile, and shit, I hadn't thought of Dylan since we'd sat down. Oh, God. What was I doing? I was in danger of falling in like with my new neighbor, and that could not happen. "Thanks for the beers and the company, but I should get to bed."

A groan rumbled from his chest, deep and desperate. "Was it you who called the paramedics when she had her stroke?"

"No. I was out of town. Got back the next day. Mr. Slavic from across the street filled me in. She was having tea with her church friends when it happened. Why?"

Those blue eyes darkened, and Joe seemed lost in thought for too long before he cleared his throat and met my gaze. "I just wanted to thank whoever it was."

The pain he wore broke my heart, reminding me that I danced too close to the danger zone. I could not afford to care.

I rocked forward, ready to head inside. Joe plucked the empty bottle from my fingers and dropped it at our feet, the *clink* ringing in the night air. Before I could stand and flee to the safety of my house, he cupped my face and claimed my mouth. His kiss was fast and desperate, vicious and hot. Frantically, he groped everywhere, my breasts, my thighs, my ass, like he couldn't decide which part of me he favored. One second he was at my side; the next, I was on my back and he was over me, sliding his fingers under my waistband, searching for that sweet spot, stealing my sanity.

"Let's go inside," Joe growled, working me into a frenzy.

"No." I bit his lip, then pulled him closer, hooking an arm around his neck.

Men were not welcome inside my domicile.

"Have it your way." He chuckled, shifting his weight to one side to tug a condom out of his back pocket. "I'm fucking you here, then."

"No" would have been the correct response. No was not an option. Joe's strength and weight, his scent, those heavy breaths and desperate kisses, the contrast of his hard to my soft, the gravity of my need... If I sent him away, I would die. Combust into a billion shards of molten flesh. "Shut up and get naked."

Our clothes disappeared in a blink. Joe sunk into me, slow and smooth before finding his rhythm, his girth beautifully brutal, his words crude and demanding.

Clawing and clinging to his sweaty ridges, I bucked and writhed, a wanton woman desperate to feel desired, to feel anything other than the hollow ache that haunted my every waking hour.

One tiny corner of my heart still pumped healthy and vibrant. As flutters erupted in my belly, pain pricked my chest because what was left of that vital organ needed protecting, and everything about the man pounding into me screamed devastation.

As an orgasm tore through me, I pulled at his hair, mumbling profanities. Tears fell, and sweet coffee and cream, I'd never come so hard or wanted to cling to a man like I did Joe.

My head and heart were so messed up.

Ashamed and still riding the high, I held Joe through his

last orgasmic tremor and wallowed in his caresses until he rolled to my side. Only then did I kiss his cheek and whisper, "Thanks for the drinks," before leaving him naked in my backyard.

"Oh, my god. You did it again, didn't you?" Lilly clapped her hands and bounced on her toes, her breasts jiggling in the cups of her red sequined bikini top.

"Did what?" I bumped into the counter behind me, dodging her overly enthusiastic greeting.

"It!" she sang, throwing her arms around me and swaying, her vanilla-scented hair tickling my nose.

I wrestled my face out of her loose curls. "You're confusing me."

"You hooked up with some dude. Good for you, girl. Same guy?"

How did she know? I'd checked for new bruises. "None of your business."

With a hard slap to my ass, she stepped back, giving me room to breathe. "It's about time you have some fun."

Fun was the seed that had rooted deep and grown into the prickly weeds that infested my soul. A good time had led to me growing up too fast, bearing adult responsibilities, and making decisions based on need, not wisdom.

I shook a finger at Lilly. "You have enough fun for the both of us."

Brow quirked, hip cocked, she said, "Okay, seriously, twice now. You gotta tell me about this guy."

"How do you know I did anything?" I shrieked, throwing my hands up in frustration.

"I just know. And don't bother trying to lie. Look at you. You're beaming."

I'd never been a top-notch fibber, and Lilly was a freakin' human lie detector. The girl could work for the CIA.

"There's not much to tell." I turned, pretending to take inventory of the paper cups, and decided on a half-truth. "We had a few drinks. Talked. He kissed me. I sent him home. End of story."

Again, she captured me in an embrace, this time from behind, and rested her chin on my shoulder. "Come on. There has to be more. You gonna see him tonight?"

"I'll be seeing him plenty." I shifted free of her hug and turned. "But no more sexy time."

A deep sigh. "Explain."

I moaned, scrubbing a hand over my cheeks and putting distance between us. "He's gorgeous. And big. Muscles the size of Rainier. An ass you can bounce a quarter off of. He's hung"—I threw my arms out wide—"like a freakin' horse. The guy is clumsy as shit but eager to please. Like multiple Os, if you know what I mean."

Her eyes sparkled with mirth. "So, what's the deal?"

Lilly was my employee but also a good friend well acquainted with my history. I hit her with my severe glare, warning that we were done with the convo. "He's fresh out of prison." And for the double whammy, I threw in, "And he's my new neighbor."

"Oh. Wow," she whispered, arms dropping to her sides, concern settling into a crinkle between her brows.

"Yeah. Wow is about right." Wasn't much more to say on the matter. Bad boys were my weakness and the reason my heart was hard as a rock. I blame my sperm donor. He was gorgeous and charming and a frequent resident of many state institutions. I loved him to death, and he killed my carefree spirit.

Her gaze slid to the security monitor, then sliced back to me. "Oh, shit. Here comes Mr. Harper. Wanna hide?"

Outside, a spotless silver Escalade rolled up to the window. "No. I've got this." Sad truth? Men like Mr. Harper didn't intimidate me like they should. I snagged my sweatshirt from the closet, slipped my arms through the sleeves, and closed the zipper to my chin. His visits had nothing to do with coffee or naked skin.

Per his norm, Harper rolled to a stop nice and slow, waiting to lower his dark window until he shifted into park and knew he had my full attention. The glass rolled down, down, down, revealing his wrinkly tanned skin, over-bleached teeth, and silver beard trimmed to perfection.

"Morning, sunshine."

Gag. "Morning." I gave a halfhearted but sweet smile. "The usual?"

"Yeah, doll." His leer lingered on my chest. "Looking gorgeous today. How's business?"

"I'm sure you already know." I offered a playful wink, keeping things light.

Harper knew everybody's business. That's how he slew his dragons, collected his trophies, and stayed out of prison. Johan Harper owned every strip club in the area, several bars and restaurants, a chain of laundromats, several motels, and apartment buildings spread throughout south Seattle. Those were his "legit" business dealings, anyway.

"When are you going to come and work for me?"

"Never, I'm afraid." I turned to make his double espresso, but Lilly already had it covered, bless her heart. "Although, I do appreciate the offer," I lied, fighting a shiver.

"We'd make a great team, you and I."

Every time with the same back-and-forth, and the slime-ball was never clear about what, exactly, he expected me to do under his employ.

"Now, Mr. Harper. You know I won't change my mind. I'm a solitary woman. No teaming up with anybody. For any reason." Especially men who made my skin crawl.

He made a *tsk* sound, then poured on the charm, flashing those pearly whites enough to make his dimple pop, making him almost look like somebody's sweet grandpa. "You're breaking my heart, girl." He handed me a twenty.

I shooed his offering away. "Your money's no good here."

Lilly set the cup in front of me. I held it out to Harper.

After shoving the bill into the tip jar, he snatched the steaming drink from my fingers and winked. "See you next week."

"See you." I slammed the window closed and sucked in a hearty dose of oxygen.

Lilly offered a sympathetic smile. "Why are you so nice to him?"

"Can't afford to be on that man's bad side, my dear." My father had made that mistake. Landed in the hospital with a broken arm and a missing toe that he'd blamed on a bike accident. Let it be said that my father never owned a bike.

Honestly, I was surprised Harper hadn't tried to strong-arm me into compliance. Perhaps he was biding his time, or maybe he was only coming around to let me, or more accurately, my father, know he was paying attention, a way to keep my dad in check. Whatever his motives, I played along and gave him the respect he thought he deserved because I was rather fond of my toes.

CHAPTER
Six

"Those are some ugly-ass toes." I gave Frank a shove. "You should cover those. Seriously."

He huffed a laugh and looked down at his bare feet planted on the black-and-white checkered floor. "How did you talk me into this?"

"You'll be singing my praises in a few short minutes," I assured him.

Ly jetted from the back room, but her steps faltered when she took in the sight of us—two gargantuan men—standing inside her salon. "Hi, Joe."

"Morning, Ly." I nodded, then made introductions.

The salon owner was maybe five feet and couldn't weigh more than eighty pounds. What she lacked in size, she more than made up for in grit.

"You bring me new customer." Her delicate hand landed on my arm. "Good boy." Though her accent was heavy, her gratitude was unmistakable.

Ly sized up Frank before giving me a nod and gesturing to the black pleather massage chairs sitting side by side, where blue liquid already churned in the porcelain tubs. "You sit. Be right back."

Frank shot me a glance, shrugged, then stepped into the water. "Jesus. Fuck," he hissed. "That shit's hot." He dropped his ass to the seat and planted his heels on the edge of the basin.

I followed suit, sinking my feet into the bubbling water and settling into my chair. I rolled my head to the side. "Just give it a second. Relax."

Ly and Trudy hurried our way, both donning white smocks and blue masks. Trudy stood half an inch taller than Ly but was thinner. Ly's black hair was cut in a sharp line below her ears, and Trudy wore hers shoulder-length and stick straight. Besides their petite statures, the women shared wise, warm brown eyes with laugh lines at the corners—a beautiful mother/daughter team.

Trudy pulled a remote from the back of Frank's chair and hit the power button, engaging the magical kneading rollers.

"Dear God," he groaned. "I need one of these at home." He lay his head back and closed his eyes.

Yeah. Pedicures were the jam.

But that wasn't why I'd suckered my friend into joining me for my weekly visit. Across the street from the little strip mall where Emerald Glow Nails resided stood an ungodly bright red building in the middle of a square lot. A privacy screen covered the single service window, and security cameras hung from each corner. The roof was black, the trim too, and above the door hung an enticing neon sign.

Their logo was the silhouette of a busty female form bathing in a large steaming coffee mug.

Dirty Dreamz was famous, not for its excellent service, but for the nearly naked women who served the chain's mediocre drinks.

There was rarely a lull in vehicles waiting their turn for coffee with a side of flesh. However, on any given day, a rotation of four different cars were parked outside, not against the building, but along the property line shared with a Dairy Queen. To anyone who wasn't paying attention, they appeared to be customers of the fast-food joint.

But I paid attention.

Not because I gave a shit about the shady coffee franchise, but because the black Cadillac sedan, currently occupying one of those aforementioned spots, belonged to my uncle.

"You see what time the Caddy rolled in this morning?" I asked, nodding across the lot.

Ly shot a quick glance out the window, then focused again on my foot. "He here when I come in. They open early. Four AM. I come in eight thirty."

"Any new cars?"

She nodded, then lifted my ankle to scrub the bottom of my foot. "A large SUV. Silver. Last week on Tuesday. This week on Friday."

As I'd suspected, Frank kept his thoughts to himself, but I caught the flare in his eyes when he recognized Larry's CT6.

My friend waited a good minute before warning, "Don't go down this road, Joe."

I ignored him. "Thanks, Ly. I appreciate the info."

"I got license plate number for new car." She stood from her tiny stool and headed for the front desk, then rifled through some papers. She came back with a wrinkled grocery store receipt. On the back was a number scribbled in black ink.

"Ly. This is perfect. Thank you." The woman had earned herself a killer tip.

"You my favorite customer," she reminded me. "Maybe you take Trudy on date?" Every week with the same question.

Trudy, who up until that point had remained silent, made a pained sound. Frank chuckled.

I glanced at the blushing girl. She was beautiful.

She was not, however, the one woman I couldn't stop

thinking about. That emotional real estate belonged to my feisty neighbor for reasons I'd yet to figure out.

Trudy mumbled something to her mother in Vietnamese. Ly responded, tipping here head in my direction.

Trudy, who rarely spoke, cleared her throat and then stated, "Last week, I was here late. I saw two men lead a woman inside Dirty Dreamz. I was curious, so I stayed and watched." She shot a nervous glance at her mother, who nodded for her to continue. "Maybe an hour later, they dragged her back out. It was dark, so I couldn't see very well, but her hair was messy, and she could barely walk."

Frank sat straight, no longer relaxed. "You call the police?"

Ly huffed, rolling her eyes. Trudy shook her head no, gaze dropping to the floor. They were scared.

Frank didn't push but shot an icy glare my way.

Guilt raked jagged claws over my ticker. I never should have gotten these women involved.

I'd stumbled upon Emerald Glow Nails when I had followed my jackass uncle and needed to keep an eye on him while staying outta sight. Ly's nail salon had the perfect vantage point. But then I'd discovered the wonders of pedicures and decided weekly visits were in order. Besides, Ly and her daughter were great ladies, stimulating conversationalists, and also happened to be as sharp as fucking whips.

Frank ripped the receipt from my hand. "Don't need this. Everyone knows Johan Harper drives that silver Escalade and pulls the strings behind Dirty Dreamz." He waited, glaring at me, thick brows pinched. "You're clear of their shit. Stay that way."

I scrubbed a hand over my face. I would never be free of the Kaine legacy. "Larry was sniffing around Alice's wake. He's up to something."

"Joe." Frank shifted his ass and leaned in my direction, his voice lowering to a gnarly growl. "You know I've got your back, always."

I nodded.

"The devil's gonna get his due."

"He's in his sixties. That fucker's never paid for shit."

"Let the law handle Larry Kaine. Hell, let karma handle that crusty old bastard. Don't get involved." He pointed a finger my way, his dark eyes narrowing. "I'm telling you, I will not stand by again and watch you take the heat for that fucked-up gene pool of yours. Never again."

"Understood." Thick emotion clogged my throat.

Frank and Con had backed my story and stayed quiet while I'd served time for Bill's death. Not that they'd had a choice after witnessing the state of affairs that god-awful night. But still, they'd been reluctant accomplices, and I was forever indebted.

"Good," Frank huffed, scratching at his clean-shaven jaw. "Can we enjoy ourselves now?"

"Yeah. Sure." I leaned back, tried to settle.

A hard thump hit my shoulder before Frank warned, "You tell a soul about this"—he pointed to his hairy legs—"I'll gut you."

"But it's fucking awesome, am I right?"

Frank responded by closing his eyes and relaxing back into his chair.

I did the same and tried to ignore the knot in my gut.

Growing up, I'd done my damnedest to steer clear of the Kaine legacy. That family tree bore nothing but dirty, rotten fruit. The dark side had tempted me more than once, but between Mom, Alice, and my two buddies, I'd managed to keep my head on straight and my ass outta trouble.

Until that night, anyway.

Those ghosts would haunt me forever.

CHAPTER
Seven

"You're coming to opening night, right?" Bridget Cross asked, her tone harsh, the warning clear though unnecessary because she knew I would deny her nothing.

Con's sister, CEO of Cross Crew Enterprises, the company she ran with Connor and their father, had been the bratty kid sister Con, Frank, and I had tormented while growing up. Bridget had a great head for business and finances, and Con was a genius with the development and construction side of their mini empire.

"Wouldn't miss it," I said through a yawn, stretching my aching muscles.

The tomboy who had once followed us around like a shadow had grown into a force to be reckoned with. Killer blue eyes, wicked curves, and a keen business sense made for a deadly combination. Cross Crew Enterprises currently owned three successful neighborhood bars, two gourmet food franchises, and several small-scale entertainment venues. Her newest endeavor was a nightclub near downtown Seattle.

"Good." She sighed. "I've missed that ugly mug of yours. Oh, I've got a suit lined up. I'll bring it over later this week."

She ended the call before I could argue. Not that I would complain. Two Men's Wearhouse purchases currently hung in the closet, courtesy of Mom and her Joe-is-home shopping extravaganza, but they were conservative, cut for job interviews, not swank club openings. I harbored a strong disdain for shopping, so if a pretty lady wanted to dress me for a night on the town, God bless the angel.

I scrubbed a hand over my face and rolled to a sitting position, grunting through the pain. My back was a mess. My feet hung off the end of Alice's queen-sized, and the yellow floral pattern on her comforter clashed with the ink on my arms and torso. I doubted Alice had updated her mattress or her bedding since I'd hit puberty.

My to-do list grew daily. Purchasing a man-sized bed was the latest entry and torture that could wait another day.

I slipped into my shoes and limped downstairs, cursing myself for having added the extra weight on leg day when I hadn't been to the gym in weeks. I headed outside, inhaling the warm spring air.

Most people took checking the mail for granted. Me? I couldn't wait for the blue-and-white truck to pass every day. For one, when I was in the joint and the years following, I never received one fucking letter, and that was on purpose, but two? Well. The tin box sat across the street, meaning, after checking for any letters, I had an excuse to study Marley's house, and with any luck, catch a glimpse of her inside.

I had just slammed the metal door on the mailbox closed when a soft voice startled me.

"Hi, Joe."

Sweet hell. My nostrils flared. My chest pounded a sporadic rhythm. I took a moment to pull my shit together before turning to greet my neighbor.

Not that those measly seconds did any good. The sight of her scrambled my thoughts.

She wore cutoffs, green flip-flops, and a black wife beater with no fucking bra. I knew there was no undergarment because I could make out the shape of her puckered nipples through the thin shirt.

Lord have mercy. How was I supposed to keep my eyes at a respectful level? Marley had grade-A, top-shelf, major league tits. More than a handful. Soft but still firm enough they didn't droop or sway when she moved.

"Hey, neighbor." I pretended to look through my stack of envelopes before finding her eyes.

Marley smiled, then stuck her key into the lock, wriggling it a few times before the latch gave way. "How're things?" she asked, shoving both hands inside to gather her correspondence.

"Things are rolling along." I studied her ass while her back was turned. Those shorts hung so low and loose on her waist that I was sure the slightest tug would send them to her ankles.

She gathered a box and some envelopes to her chest before locking things back up, then gave me a once-over, her bright gaze lingering on my lips for a beat. "Hot today, huh?"

"Yeah." Hotter, suddenly, with her standing so damn close. "Haven't seen you around. Been busy?"

"Always." The skin under her eyes was darker than usual. "New truck?" she asked, nodding over her shoulder toward my driveway.

"Had her awhile." My pearl white Tacoma needed a good wash but even dusty from the long drive, she was a beauty. "Waited to bring her home until I found a home for Alice's Camry."

"What'd you do with Alice's car?" She shielded her eyes from the sun with a hand to her forehead.

"Single mom who lives a few blocks down took her off my hands."

Marley's face lit, eyes sparkling. "You gave it to her?"

I shrugged. "Wasn't a big deal. The woman needed a vehicle. I needed room to park my baby."

Marley stood silent, gnawing her lip, seemingly lost in thought.

"Everything okay?"

Her head shot up, eyes widening, like my concern had been a surprise. Or maybe she was offended? Either way, she shifted on her feet, then sighed.

"Everything's great," she mumbled. She turned and left but threw over her shoulder, "Good to see you," like we hadn't been intimate. Like I hadn't been inside her body, or she hadn't left claw marks on my back or scars on my soul. Like she was erecting a giant fucking wall meant only to keep me out.

Challenge accepted.

"You ever wanna talk, I'm just a few feet away," I said to her back, and yes, I took advantage of the view, soaking up the sight of those toned legs, the sway of her small hips, and the confident set of her shoulders.

Fuck. I wanted to follow her inside. Sink into that tight body. Get lost in her smell, her moans, or hell, even just trap her between my arms and hold her for a while.

Instead, I looked left and right before crossing the street back to my own front door. Then I looked left again because the white car with dark windows parked half a block down had caught my eye. The same 370Z NISMO I'd seen two days ago parked on the opposite side of the road.

Something about that rare beauty didn't sit right. Maybe I was paranoid, or bored, or perhaps dear ol' Dad, on the rare occasions he'd acted fatherly, had instilled in me the importance of paying attention to my surroundings.

I considered getting a closer look at the Nissan when another car caught my eye. A familiar black Caddy.

Crusty fucker. What was he up to?

My first instinct? Grab a rock and smash his window, the standard Kaine reaction to possible threats—crush them before they crush you.

Every cell in my body itched for a fight, or to at least scare some sense into my uncle, but I refused to cause a scene in Alice's neighborhood in front her friends. I wouldn't tarnish her name.

I looked down at the now twisted and crumpled mail in my hands and drew in a steadying breath.

I'd deal with Larry on his turf, not mine.

∘ ° ∘ ° ∘ °∘ ° ∘ ° ∘ °

The secured building had been easy enough to breach. One well-practiced smile and innocent lie to the sweet woman who'd returned from walking her poodle, and I was in.

She headed toward the elevator. I found the stairs and hiked to the sixth floor.

Number sixty-nine hung in gold letters above the peephole. I bit back a laugh while I banged with an angry fist.

Larry yanked open the door. "What're you doing here?" he grumbled, a grimace on his face, his thick gray hair slicked back and shiny.

"We need to talk."

His grip tightened on the doorknob, the veins on his arms popping. "'Bout what? I said my final goodbye the day you laid Alice to rest."

I shoved past the man and made my way inside. His modest apartment reeked of cologne and cigars. "See, that's the thing. Can't wrap my head around the fact you showed up at her funeral. Wondering why."

Larry slammed the door and avoided eye contact while

tucking his navy striped button-up into his jeans. "Getting on in my years, boy. People around me are dropping like flies. Gets a man thinking. Gets a man pondering his regrets."

"Regrets?" I snarled. "Bullshit." I glared down at him. "See, I think you showed up hoping Alice had the heart to leave you something in her will."

Nostril's flared, he hit me with an icy glare. "I knew better'n that. Alice never liked me." He pointed a shaky finger my way. "Funny. You made out well. How is it you inherited everything my brother left behind after what you did?"

Larry's hate for me was palpable. Couldn't blame him.

Since Alice no longer needed protecting, I could've hit Larry with the cold, hard truth about that night. But fuck that and fuck him.

Larry had been an active participant when Bill had conned Alice into marriage and had been more than willing to help siphon her five-million-dollar bequeathal.

"Only thing I know," my uncle continued, "is you were living under his roof, off his charity, and now he's dead."

Like he deserved, I left unspoken.

"Larry." My patience wore dangerously thin. "Why are you casing my home?"

"Bill's home," he snapped, lip curled in disgust.

"My fucking house!" I yelled, slamming a fist on the sideboard. His ashtray jumped, and his half-smoked cigar tipped off the edge and rolled to the floor. "My home!"

The old coot jerked back, stumbled, and fell into a ratty wingback chair. I towered over his weathered body, then bent low so he'd hear me loud and clear. "The only time Bill ever stepped foot in that house was to take Alice's money or beat the shit out of her. Now you're sniffing around, invading my privacy. For what?" I asked, throwing my arms out wide. "There is nothing there for you. Nothing of your brother's. Stay the fuck away."

The man held his chin high, gaze fierce. "You're crazy, just like that old bag."

Too many seconds passed with unspoken threats hanging between us. I backed off, standing straight.

Larry huffed. "Get outta my house, boy."

Yeah. Good idea.

Before I cleared the room, Larry shouted, "You don't want me as an enemy, kid. Watch your back."

That stopped me dead. Hmm. Larry had grown himself a pair of balls. Yeah, I couldn't let that little threat slip. "Whatcha gonna do, uncle? Kill me? Or maybe pay your buddy Harper to take me out?"

Larry's eyes widened, then narrowed before he dropped his head in false defeat. He said to his lap, "You wanna know why I was at the wake?"

Was he kidding me?

The man was a career lowlife, and as I watched the lie knit together behind his golden eyes, for a brief moment, I was tempted to play along.

Instead, I said, "Don't give two shits. Whatever you're looking for, it isn't at the house. Even if it was, never belonged to you in the first place."

"Wasn't yours neither," he grumbled.

It was then I knew. Larry shared the same suspicion I did. Alice hid something somewhere on her property, and he'd stop at nothing to claim what he believed to be his right.

I stormed out the door and damn near ran over a tiny little thing holding a covered casserole dish and wearing her weight in gold necklaces and bracelets. Smelled like garlic and herbs. My stomach rumbled.

"Excuse me, ma'am," I said, scooting out of her way.

"Oh, my. You're a big fella." She looked up and smiled.

Red lipstick bled into the crepey skin around her lips. Long, silver hair billowed over her bright pink blouse.

"Are you a friend of Larry's?" Such sweet innocence in her voice.

"No, ma'am."

"Family?" she asked, her arm shaking under the weight of her offering.

Seemed wrong to lie to the woman. "Nephew."

Her beady eyes narrowed. "The one who killed Larry's brother?" Her head bobbed, then her hunched shoulders straightened. "Are you here to murder Larry, too?"

Kill me now.

"No, ma'am. Not today. He's all yours." I reached around her petite frame and turned the knob, opening the door.

"Oh, good." Her crooked eyebrows bounced up and down. "It'd be a shame to waste this lasagna." She stepped inside.

Larry stood at his kitchen counter, gaze bouncing between the two of us in confusion.

The woman turned to close the door and shot me a wink, whispering, "If things don't work out with Lare-Bear, maybe you and I can give it a go."

CHAPTER
Eight

I slammed a foot on the plastic bumper of my mower, shouted, "Come on, baby," and yanked the pull handle with all my might.

The ancient contraption roared, teasing, then sputtered and coughed, giving up the ghost.

"Piece of shit!" I kicked the handle and fell to my butt. I'd neglected my yard for days, a cowardly attempt to avoid my neighbor for fear of falling into bed with him again or, heaven forbid, falling into like with the guy. Because Joe was undeniably, irritatingly likable.

I laid back in the cool grass, taking deep, measured breaths to calm my foul mood, and focused on the streaks of white suspended in the ocean of blue overhead. Sweet springtime air filled my lungs, soothing my agitation.

My pulse started to slow until I heard, "Sweet Jesus, Joe. You been keeping that lovely lady all to yourself?"

To which Joe replied in that deadly sexy voice, "Keeping her away from players like you."

I jerked to a sitting position and lost my breath.

Joe stood just on the other side of the hedges, shirtless, thumbs hooked in the front pockets of his jeans, gaze narrowed and aimed my way. His blatant regard was downright sinful.

My skin tingles and heart palpitations were simply shameful.

Next to Joe stood another beautiful man. Brutal edges, cocky stance, perfectly mussed blond hair, and a devilish panty-melting grin. Threesomes weren't my cup of tea, but those two standing side by side? Temptation dipped in chocolate, wrapped in gold, and coated with diamonds.

My peaceful bubble popped, the hot air expelled, and my sour mood turned acidic.

Joe's friend swiped hair from his face, biceps bulging under the sleeves of his linen button-up. "Need a hand, little lady?"

Little lady? "You can take that hand and shove it in your keister," I mumbled under my breath, pushing to stand.

"Hi, neighbor." Joe waved in greeting, a reluctant smile gracing his face. "This is my buddy, Connor Cross."

"Morning," I croaked, dusting off my ass.

"Wanna borrow mine?" Joe assessed me with sharp eyes, searching my face. For what? No clue, but I was sure he saw right through my bitter, guarded heart.

"Thanks, I'm good." Eager to flee all the unwelcome feels, I pushed the metal traitor toward the backyard.

"Marley." His voice dropped low, commanding.

Heart racing, gut swirling, I stopped and turned to give the devil my full attention. Pathetic, yes, but that deep tenor left me mindless. I needed to up my getaway game.

"I could take a look for you. See why it's giving you trouble," Joe offered.

Don't ogle his pecs. Do not ogle his pecs.

"Really. I'm good." My motto? If something breaks, fix it yourself. Don't know how? Learn. "It's probably the spark plugs."

If the damage was beyond my abilities, I had two mechanics on speed dial. Both of whom were older, happily married men with beer bellies and too much nose hair. I was in zero danger of lusting after either of them.

Joe's brows furrowed, and he shifted, rubbing his forehead with the back of his hand. "Suit yourself." He shrugged, then added, "Having a barbecue this afternoon. Wanna join us?"

Connor stepped forward, deep dimples popping, a practiced skill for sure. "Grilled steaks, cold brew, and excellent company."

"God, no!" I shrieked, then cringed at my outburst.

Joe plus Marley plus alcohol equaled Joe plus Marley having sex. Sex led to feelings, feelings to relationships, relationships to devastation.

Joe was a criminal. His friends were most likely felons, and I wanted nothing to do with any of them, no matter how gorgeous they were. Still, I knew better than to piss off outlaws by being a bitchy, ungrateful neighbor, so I blurted while forcing a grin, "Sorry. Didn't mean to snap. Have a hundred things to check off my to-do list today, the first being to buy a new mower." I tapped on the handle of my soon-to-be-trashed hunk of junk.

"Right." Joe's glare burned down to my toes, a dangerous mix of lust and aggravation. "Haven't seen you in a while."

He hadn't seen me because Operation: Avoid Joe was in full swing. "Yeah. I'm crazy busy during summer."

Head tilted, he raised his thick brows and inquired, "Where'd you say your coffee stand was again?"

Ah, shoot. Miraculously, despite our trysts, we had managed to avoid that topic. "I didn't say."

Connor coughed and mumbled under his breath, "Burn."

Be nice, I reminded myself. "I have three stands, all of them in the south end."

My spirits tanked. Next came the inevitable, uncomfortable conversation. Joe would ask the name of my business. I would tell him. While secretly judging, he'd pretend not to care that I served coffee in the buff. Eventually, I would tell him to go to hell. Same back-and-forth, different day.

Joe opened his mouth to speak, but thank the heavens above, my phone buzzed in my back pocket. "Sorry. I have to answer this. It's work."

Giving him no time to respond, I answered my call and retreated into my house. Away from Joe. Where I could think straight. Where I was not in danger of falling for another bad boy. Distance was crucial for the sake of my bruised and battered heart.

I pulled the pillow over my head and screamed at the clock, the numbers nine, three, and seven blaring at me like a million middle fingers. Sure, the night was young by ordinary people's standards, but my overworked, sleep-deprived brain considered the hour to be obscenely late. And any asshole, or in my case, assholes, who blasted country-pop through their lawn speakers while drinking and smoking a shit-ton of weed after nine PM on a weeknight were, quite frankly, douchebags.

Sleep was vital for the safety of my employees and my customers. I threw a sweatshirt over my cami, marched to the rowdy house next door, then released my frustration on the doorbell.

Connor whipped open the door, a happy grin brightening his bloodshot eyes, his dark blond locks a tousled mess. "Hey, neighbor! You decided to join us?"

"No." Jeez, he was pretty. "Where's Joe?"

His gaze drifted from my face to my chest, my bare legs, then bounced right back to meet my glare. Not a leer, but an observation. He stepped aside, gesturing for me to enter. "Backyard. Come on in."

I waved a hand and took a step back. "No, thanks. Just get Joe, please."

"Sure thing." The skin between his brows crinkled. "Everything all right?"

"Just need Joe. Please." I crossed my arms, a shield against the concern on Connor's face—Connor the con man, most likely.

He turned to call for Joe, but my man-beast neighbor was striding our way, a sight for sleepy eyes. Sage green T-shirt, khaki shorts that hung low on his trim waist. No shoes on big feet with high arches and straight toes. My God, the man didn't own an unattractive body part. My insides heated. And when he gave me a slow once-over, I swear my body hummed. I was so screwed.

"Marley." My name dripped like hot caramel from his lips. He leaned against the frame, crossing thick arms across his chest, mimicking my pose.

"This is a respectable neighborhood," I informed him, holding my chin high, ignoring the rampant body tingles.

"Respectable?"

"Yes. Meaning we're quiet. Respectful."

Connor slunk away. Good boy.

Joe quirked his head, brows raised, clearly waiting for further explanation.

"Meaning we keep it quiet." I threw my arms out in frustration. "We don't throw obnoxiously loud parties."

"Gorgeous, half the neighborhood is sharing a bowl in the rose garden." The bastard chuckled and moved to the side, allowing me a full view of the backyard through the glass slider.

Familiar faces, each and every one of them having a great time, judging by their smiles. None of them seemed concerned by the trouble they welcomed into our close-knit community.

Mrs. Collins, who lived three houses down, sang along to Eric Church's "Hell of a View" with eyes closed and a red plastic cup raised to the sky.

"You're the only one who turned down my invitation." Joe stepped closer, bringing a warm hand to cup my cheek. "Come on back. It'll be fun. I promise."

I jerked away, his touch heating my veins, that tender gesture too dangerous, habit forming—the very reason I couldn't join the fun. I could not, would not, get involved with another low-life, self-serving swindler. "No. But can you lower the volume a little? I've got an early morning tomorrow."

Joe didn't respond. Instead, he stared, long and hard, fighting a smile. God, his cocky sex appeal was a burr in my bikini briefs.

"Why are you looking at me like that?"

"You're sweet as pie when you're pissed."

"Shut up."

"Come join us." He pursed his lips, teasing.

That expression would've been cute if I wasn't so worked up.

"I grill a mean steak." He stepped back and gestured for me to enter.

I threw out the only defense I could muster. "I'm not gonna sit around eating and drinking with a bunch of criminals."

He stiffened. "Criminals?" That massive chest rose and fell. "That what this is about?"

"I can't get involved with people like you."

"Like me." He nodded, his jaw going rigid, those blue eyes arctic.

I'd sliced him with my judgmental blade. A low blow, but a necessary punch. God, how far would I stoop to protect my wounded spirit?

Joe's face reddened. He took another step closer, towering over me. "I take it back. You're not sweet. You're bitter like rhubarb. Bitter and sour."

I dropped my arms to my sides, fists clenched. "Turn the damn music down."

Inching closer, he sneered down at me. "Pull that stick outta your ass."

Bastard didn't know I wasn't easily intimidated. He could tower and glower all he wanted. When the time came to protect me and mine, my skin was plenty thick, my fuse short. "It's almost ten PM. City code says that's quiet time. Don't make me call the cops."

"That's precious. Call the police. I dare you."

Damn. Joe had me. I wasn't bitch enough to call the cops and ruin a night of fun for the rest of my neighbors. I scrambled for an appropriate comeback, anything to save face, but I had nothing, and judging by his smirk, he knew my spark had fizzled.

"Okay. Fine," I said, turning to retreat. "Party away. Have fun. Sorry I bothered you."

I made it to the bottom porch step before he caught my waist and pulled me flush against his tense muscles. Mouth to my ear, he threatened, "If I didn't have company, I'd throw you over my shoulder, carry you upstairs, and help you dislodge that stick the old-fashioned way."

Cue the prickly tingles. "Asshole," I mumbled, breathy and too damn soft.

Joe chuckled and backed away, leaving me cold, empty,

and angry. "Night, neighbor," he grunted before slamming the door.

I stormed back to my house, crawled into bed, and dialed Lilly.

She answered on the first ring. "Hey, boss. Everything okay?"

"Everything is fine. Sorry for the short notice, but can we switch shifts tomorrow? I have some things I need to take care of in the morning."

"Sure," she said without question. One of the many reasons she was invaluable.

"Thanks. I owe you one."

I ended the call. By the time my head hit the mattress, the noise level had decreased a few decimals at least. The party, however, continued on until the wee hours of the morning.

And that was fine. Gave me plenty of time to plot my revenge.

. ° . ° . ° . °. ° . ° . ° . °

Arms waved frantically from the other side of the privacy fence that divided our two backyards. Ignoring the bait for attention, I continued swinging my Ryobi, cutting weeds that weren't there. Missy Elliot blasted through my earbuds, louder than necessary but vital for keeping my mind in the game.

I whacked and whacked, hitting rocks and nicking the fence. I revved the motor, then killed the switch just so I could start the noisy gadget back up again.

A sharp sting hit my head. A pebble, most likely. That bastard. I ignored the pain.

Another hit my back. That one hurt. Still, I was a woman on a mission, so I shrugged off the annoyance.

When I'd weed-whacked all I could butcher, I sauntered back to the garage where my shiny new Honda waited, pulled the easy start handle, and got busy trimming the lawn.

I pushed the red machine to the end of the grass, gave her a turn, and nearly ran over a set of flip-flop-clad feet. Those size fourteens were too attractive for a man with a record. Clean nails. The perfect amount of hair. Too shiny, like they'd just been polished.

I dragged my gaze up the length of him. Black basketball shorts. Bare torso. Bare chest. Muscles twitching and flexing, biceps bulging, and... Oh, shit, arms flapping along with his lips.

I jerked my headphones off my ears and killed the engine.

"And who the hell mows their lawn at seven thirty in the morning? Christ, woman. Have some common decency."

I cocked a hip and quirked a brow. "I'm sorry. Were you saying something?"

Those dreamy eyes narrowed, red-rimmed and swollen like the first day we'd met. Only now, I was confident that lack of sleep and too much beer the night before was to blame.

"What's the matter, big guy? Bit sleepy today?" I tilted my head, pretending to study his face. "You're a little green around the gills."

"You did this on purpose." He huffed, hands moving to his hips, head shaking.

No sense in lying. I'd made my point. "Sucks having rude neighbors, doesn't it?"

Joe nodded, chin down. His full lips disappeared

between his teeth, and that solid, square jaw flexed, veins popping in his neck. Poor guy. Looked painful when he said, "Point made."

He turned to leave, then stopped. "What's your problem with me?" he asked over his shoulder.

Dear God, he was every bit as enticing from the back as he was from the front. My body fevered, sick with desire.

"I mean, fuck," he continued, turning back, coming face to face with me, his morning breath only slightly off-putting. "The chemistry wasn't my imagination, was it?"

My neck muscles betrayed me, moving my head back and forth. My mouth, however, stayed on track. "Listen, Joe. The sex was phenomenal. It's just. I. Um..." Jeez, I was tired of playing the same broken record over and over. Still— curse my stubborn will—I continued. "I've been with guys like you."

His whole frame slumped like a disappointed father. "There you go with the 'like you' crap again."

"Well, you're fresh outta the slammer." I threw my arms up in frustration. "You didn't get there by being a good guy."

"Know what?" He opened his mouth, closed it, released a loud breath, then threw up a hand. "Never mind." He backed away, his shoulders sinking in defeat.

"Listen. We're neighbors. We—"

Joe silenced me with an icy glare, one I'm sure he'd perfected in prison. "Save your breath, gorgeous. I can smell bullshit from a mile away." With that, he stormed off.

I'd won that round. Yay, Team Marley!

But why, oh why, did my chest cave in defeat?

My cell buzzed in my back pocket. Flustered, I paid no mind to the screen and answered, "Yeah?"

"Doll, it's me."

Warren. Ugh. I didn't have the energy.

I ended the call.

The phone buzzed again. Angry, more at myself than anyone, I hit accept and yelled, "Don't call me anymore. We have nothing to talk about!"

Silence.

"I mean it. I have nothing to say to you."

Heavy breaths. Buzzing in the background.

"I'm not giving you money if that's why you're calling." The man had some nerve. "Learned that lesson the hard way."

More erratic breathing.

Prickly tingles battered my scalp. Warren couldn't keep quiet if you cut off his tongue and sewed his lips together. Heart in my throat, grasping for straws, I asked, "Dylan? That you? Are you okay?"

Nothing.

"Please, come home," I pleaded, desperate, my heart crumpling under the weight of regret. "I love you so much, and I'm so sorry for everything I—" Everything I what? The only thing I'd been guilty of was loving too hard. "Please. Just come back. Talk to me."

More buzzing muted by heavier breaths. A low, unrecognizable voice growled, "Who's Dylan?"

An ice-cold chill permeated my skin.

Through my phone and out on the street, an engine revved.

"Who is this?" I asked, jogging to the side gate.

The call ended. Tires squealed. By the time I hit the front yard, there wasn't a vehicle in sight.

. ⁰ • ° • ° °₀ ° ° • ° ₀ °

Lilly tugged the seam of her red gingham bikini, dislodging the thin strip from her butt crack. "Hey, hey," she sang, turning to give me her full attention, her playful ponytail whipping the air. "How's my favorite boss?"

She spun me around, lifted my skirt, and smacked the bare skin on my ass.

"Ow!" I turned away from her wandering hands. "Dammit, woman. Stop that."

So inappropriate. Good thing I loved the girl.

Lilly laughed, her cherry red lips parting in a wide smile. "I had to check for fresh bruises."

"No new marks." I slapped a hand over my heart. "And, I'm happy to report, there will not be any more."

Those kohl-framed eyes rolled. "Ooohhkay."

"I speak the truth," I declared, chin held high despite the shift in my gut. "I will never, even if the fate of the world depends on our coupling, have sex with my neighbor again."

A depressing revelation, really, but my heart was worth the sacrifice.

"How's business this morning?" I asked, effectively and quite authoritatively nixing the subject.

"Been busy." She shrugged. "Minivan Guy asked to touch my boobs again. Offered me a hundred bucks."

Minivan Guy was a forty-something soccer dad who dropped his sons at school every morning, then hit our stand on his way to work. The man had a thing for Lilly, a plethora of dollar bills, and no shame.

"Ugh. Is he trying to get us shut down?"

"He's a sad, lonely single father. I'm irresistible. Give the guy a break. At least he hasn't shown me his dick." She shot me a wink, then opened the window to help the next customer in line.

I checked my face in the mirror, then reapplied my

lipstick—red to match my plaid cheeky skirt and black bustier. I tightened the ribbons tied at the end of my braids and mentally readied myself for another round of fake smiles, amped self-confidence, and megawatt flirting. As long as I kept my head in the game and not on my neighbor, tips would be bountiful, like my breasts.

"Did you get everything taken care of this morning?" Lilly asked, flipping open the lid on the ice machine.

"Oh, yes." I mentally high-fived myself for not jumping Joe's half-naked body during our earlier tiff. "Thanks for trading shifts."

"Anytime." She filled a plastic venti cup while I readied two shots of espresso. "Oh, hey. Prius Guy asked for you."

"What? He speaks?" Prius Guy never struck up a conversation, let alone asked questions. "What did he want?"

"He just asked, 'Where's the other one?' I told him you'd be in later today." Lilly finished with her customer and closed the window, turning to face me. "He took his coffee, gave me a weird look, and drove off."

"Hmm." I'd never given the man much thought. He was handsome in an understated way. Pale, clear skin always shaved baby-butt smooth. He wore his dark hair combed back. Strong jawline. White teeth. Dark brown eyes. Always wore a dress shirt and tie. No wedding ring.

"Anyway." She emptied the tip jar and started to sort the bills from the change. "You ready for the party next week?"

"Party?" I reached above the storage cupboard to adjust the air conditioner. Best to keep the small sweatbox cool. Nips equaled tips.

"Marco's birthday," Lilly scolded, dropping the change into our charity collection pouch and tucking the bills into her handbag. "Please tell me you didn't forget."

I forgot.

"No. no. I didn't forget. That new club in Belltown, right?"

"VIP section, baby," she hollered, dancing where she stood. "Heard it's amazing."

Cue the long-winded internal groan. "Can't wait."

"Good." She stepped behind the closet door and shimmied out of her costume. "We'll pick you up. Hired a driver so we can party like rock stars and not have to worry about getting home in one piece."

"You spoil him. You know that, right?"

"Yeah, but that beautiful man spoils me right back," she said, shoving her arms into the sleeves of her Henley. "Who knows, maybe you'll meet your Marco."

"No." I shook my head. "I'm an independent lady. Got my house. Car. Run a successful business. Own a top-of-the-line vibrator. Marley needs no man," I lied. I longed to experience an unconditional, unwavering, 'til death do us part kind of love.

"Everybody needs somebody."

"I have you. I have my Pink Sweets girls. I have Prius Guy."

"Not every man is gonna hurt you like Warren did."

Every important man in my life had hurt me. Warren had only been the first. Followed by Dylan Senior, Dylan Junior, and many others not important enough to mention. "Not gonna have this conversation."

"Fine. I'm running to the post office. Need anything?"

"No, but thanks."

"Be back in thirty." A quick hair fluff, and she snagged her keys and handbag, leaving me to my thoughts and an inventory check.

Three iced drinks, four hot black coffees, and two offers of kink into my shift, a familiar rumble caught my attention, making my skin tingle. The roar of engines was nothing new. One block north, a motorcycle repair shop thrived. Choppers of all shapes and sizes passed by during the spring and summer months. However, one machine roared louder, grumbled meaner than most—the bike belonging to my neighbor.

I squeezed my eyes shut and whispered, "Please keep driving, please keep driving," repeating my mantra until the rumble vibrated my window and I could no longer avoid my shit luck.

Sucking in a courageous breath, I forced my friendliest grin and offered a sticky-sweet greeting. "Hey, handsome. What can I get for you?"

Joe wore an open-face helmet and dark glasses. He hadn't looked my way, allowing me a long gander at his strong jaw and that talented mouth.

"Yeah, I'll have..." When he turned his head my way, he went silent for a long, irritating spell. I couldn't see his eyes behind his dark frames, but their heat scorched me none-theless. "Marley. Are you freakin' kidding me?"

I cleared the nerves from my throat.

Joe's head turned left, then right, like he was checking the perimeter for perps. "This is your place?"

I nodded. Crossed my arms. "There a problem?"

"Yeah. You have no clothes on."

Ouch. I'd dreaded this encounter.

I refused to be shamed by anyone, but especially Joe, for reasons I was not ready to analyze. "You don't like what you see, you can leave."

"Why the hell are you working in a place like this?"

"Why the hell you buying coffee in a place like this?" I countered.

His head snapped back. I wasn't finished.

Leaning closer, I warned, "Don't you dare judge. I make

an honest living. Something you wouldn't know anything about." Low blow, true, but apparently, wounded me had no scruples.

"You're naked."

Dear God, his voice was daunting and rumbly like his chopper. Dark and gritty like my temper.

"My naughty bits are covered," I shot back.

"Not enough."

Irritating prick. "Do you want coffee or not?"

"I want you to put on a sweatshirt or something so I can think straight."

"Listen, I've got work to do. Don't have time for your caveman bullshit. Order a drink or leave."

Joe's hands curled into fists on his thighs. His chest rose and fell. "Did Alice know about this?"

Alice had hated my career choice, but she also drove through the stand every time I worked a late shift and ordered coffee she never drank. She'd told me once that she liked to support local businesses, but I knew she was merely checking up on me. Our south Seattle neighborhood was small, but crime had been on a steady rise over the past five years.

But my relationship with Alice was none of Joe's business. And screw him for bringing her into our convo.

"Your aunt supported everything I did and sure as hell didn't make me feel like shit about my job. Too bad you weren't around long enough for her manners to rub off."

Joe mumbled something under his breath, then kicked the stand on his bike, fired her up, and raced out of the lot, dramatically blowing me off.

CHAPTER
Nine

JOE

"Blowing off steam?" Frank stepped between me and the mirror, breaking my concentration.

"You have no idea," I grumbled. The vision of Marley ninety percent naked was still fresh in my mind. No amount of bicep curls or miles logged on the treadmill was wearing that image down. I breathed through two more reps and lowered the dumbbells to my sides.

My rage was unjustified. Marley wasn't mine to shelter or protect, but men ogled her body daily, and I wanted nothing less than to gouge their eyeballs from their sockets.

"Need to get laid?" Frank interrupted my dangerous introspection. "Cyn's got a few single friends who would be more than—"

"Jesus. No!" I racked my weights. "Don't need help in that department." Only one woman I wanted my hands on. Me and every fucker she serviced, I suspected.

I needed to cool my shit.

Before Frank could argue all the reasons I needed a woman in my life, I scolded him. "You're twenty minutes late."

"Traffic." He smacked his gum, shrugging his shoulders, and followed me to the bench press. "You find anything yet?

"Not a damn thing."

We loaded the bar. I lay down first, situated myself, then tested my grip. "I've searched just about every room."

"Maybe you're wrong about the letter." Frank took his position over the bar.

"It's possible." I powered through my first set, then continued. "Attic is stuffed with boxes full of God knows what. Hitting that next."

"I can help. Con, too."

"Nah." I struggled through my second set. "This is my mess, my problem."

"Your problems are my problems, brother. You know that." He clapped my shoulder. "How 'bout we get started tomorrow? Then head to the Ram for a bit. We haven't been out since you came home."

The Rusty Ram, our old haunt back before we'd become responsible adults. Crowded bars weren't my jam, but I'd take drunk and horny dickheads over solitude any day. "Yeah. Sounds good."

"Great! I'll give Con a heads-up." Frank clapped his hands and rubbed them together, his grin sinister. "This'll be great. Look at you. You're a beast. You'll have more pussy than you know what to do with."

Some things never changed. Frank was not content unless he believed Con and I were getting laid as often as he was.

"You talk like that around Cynthia?" I asked, gripping the bar for my last set.

"Joe, you poor, clueless bastard. Getting you laid was her idea."

I believed him. His fiancée was a sweetheart. Last week, she'd confided that she couldn't wait for Connor and me to settle down. Cynthia figured if we had girlfriends, we'd occupy less of Frank's time.

"Not interested in a hookup," I breathed through my reps.

Frank chuckled. "Yeah. I heard there's only one lady you're interested in right now."

No surprise Frank knew about my neighbor. "Con can't keep his mouth shut," I grunted, my arms trembling on the last push.

"Says you can't keep your eyes off her." Frank helped rack the weight.

I rolled to a sitting position, my energy depleted, my head still a mess, images of Marley and all that smooth, sweet skin fresher than ever.

The woman was deadly gorgeous. Independent. She had grit. A warrior's spirit like Alice. Maybe that was the root of my attraction. My aunt fought from her heart more than her head. Damn, how many times had I come to her rescue? Thing was, I loved Alice fiercely, and whether she'd been right or wrong in her convictions, I'd always backed her up. She'd had nobody else to fight for her, and though I'd known Marley only a minute, it seemed she had no one to fight for her either.

"Doesn't matter. Marley made it clear she wants nothing to do with me."

"How so?" he asked, shoving me off the bench and settling in for his set.

"Alice told her I was in prison."

"But she doesn't know the reason." He wrapped his massive hands around the steel.

I stepped behind his head and settled my weight to spot. "And I can't tell her. So where does that leave me?"

Frank grunted through eight reps. When finished, he said, "If you like this lady, Joe, give her time." He laughed, then shook his head, brows pinched. Hitting the ceiling with a stern glare, he asked, "Hell, is she even worth your energy? Seems to me she labeled you a monster before getting to know you. Is that the kind of woman you want at your side?"

Frank had a point. Then again, what woman in her right mind would date an ex-con she believed was fresh outta lockup? If I were anyone else, I'd warn her away from me. Still, his observation grated my nerves. "She's got some walls up. That's all." Barriers I intended to breach.

Whether anything came of us or not, I wanted to peel away her layers of pretense and discover what made the feisty woman tick.

Exerting far too little effort, Frank pumped through eight more reps. "Walls, huh? Sounds to me like she has a stick up her ass."

Funny. I'd told Marley the same thing. "More like a branch."

Frank laughed again, breezed through his last set, and we moved to the incline bench.

"Seriously, bro," he huffed, adjusting the back of the chair. "You got it bad for this lady?"

I stacked a forty-five pounder onto the bar. "I got something. Not sure what to call it." Blue balls, maybe. Christ, I couldn't think about Marley without getting hard.

Frank loaded the right side. "Invite her to opening night."

"Like I said, she wants nothing to do with me." I shook my head, adding another forty-five.

"Listen. There's one thing I know about women—they want to be wanted. They just don't think we've figured that out. You want her, let her know. Make her feel you"—he pounded a finger into his chest—"right here, no matter how hard she pushes you away. Fill her so full of you that other fuckers don't have the opportunity to weasel their way in." With that, he dropped his ass to the bench, planted his feet, measured his grip, and killed his first set.

Whatever, I thought, mostly ignoring his *fill her so full of you* bullshit.

I held back my snort. She'd had her fill of me all right— between her legs, between her lips, even her tits. Marley and I were in for one hell of an explosive adventure if our sexual encounters were any indicator of what a relationship would entail.

That was if she'd lower those walls and let me in.

. ° . ° . ° . °. ° . ° . °

The skeletal remains of a spider were stuck to the dusty packing tape of a box labeled *Fragile*. But just like the first four I'd pilfered through, the cardboard housed not one breakable item.

The first three had contained stacks of old bills and invoices. Box number four included a mix of old photos, handfuls of dried-up pens, a collection of ancient holiday and birthday cards, some still unopened, some containing unused gift cards and notebooks.

Frank and Connor had helped me transfer thirty-six boxes from the attic to the garage. I'd sent them away shortly after. My emotions regarding Alice were unreliable, and though there were no secrets between the three of us, I wasn't ready to expose my raw feelings to my two closest friends.

I pulled the blade of the cutter through the seams of box number five and lifted the flaps, the musty scent of decaying paper hitting me hard. Inside, resting on top of what appeared to be more unopened bills, sat a blue box. I lifted the small package, its weight substantial.

Outside, cars passed. Down the street, a lawnmower

roared to life. An airplane flew overhead, the jet's rumble temporarily muffling all other noise. Something shifted in my chest. When I was younger, Alice had often sat in the backyard, trying to guess the destination of passing planes, too many times making me join her while she sipped tea and stared at the sky.

Deep down, I'd known she wished to reach up, grab one of their wings, and be carried to some faraway adventure. But stubborn Alice was a fighter, if nothing else, and though she'd unknowingly married a monster, she was faithful, and despite the bruises, the torment, and all the shit Bill put her through, she never gave up hope that one day her husband would see the light and change his ways.

He never did. He never would have. And by the time Alice had realized money was his mistress and would always come first, it'd been too late to save his soul.

I popped open the lid of the blue box and found three identical thick-band gold rings and one heavy, braided gold chain. Strange. I couldn't remember Alice or Bill ever wearing much jewelry.

I set the gold aside and rifled through the remaining contents. More bills, many of them with *Late Notice* stamped on the top. Beneath the envelopes lay more photos, scattered like they'd been tossed carelessly to the bottom.

One stood out. A picture of Bill, Larry, and Alice. Alice stood between the men, wearing her gardening gloves and hat, a new, unplanted rose bush at her feet. An apology plant.

Bill stared straight ahead, arm slung around Alice's shoulders, a smug, crooked grin cracking his face. With his free hand, he pointed at the rose bush. Alice's gaze seemed to be aimed to the left, her smile unconvincing, her lip swollen, the brim of her hat not long enough to hide the purple mark on her cheek.

"Fuck!" I threw the box across the garage, knocking a pair of pink shears off their hook, then hopped to my feet and stormed outside, desperate for fresh air.

Marley stood at her car about to get in, and my wave of rage receded. Suddenly, all that mattered was unloading the heavy regret I'd carried for too many days.

Our eyes met, then locked. I jogged her way, never breaking that connection. Marley stood in wait, clinging to her purse strap with one hand and tapping the roof of her car with the other. I deserved that apathetic look, but damn, her lack of giving a shit stung.

Clearing the emotion from my throat, I mumbled, "Hey."

"Hi," came weak and forced. Clearly, she hadn't forgiven me for being a jackass about her job, and as she turned to grab the door handle, I decided a sincere grovel was in order.

"I'm sorry about the other day," I blurted before she could escape inside her Subaru. "I was taken by surprise." Shit. I was about to make excuses for my behavior. There was no excuse. I was solely responsible for every word that came out of my mouth. "You know what? I'm just really fucking sorry. My behavior was uncalled for."

She paused, her back to me. Dark jeans hugged that magnificent ass and clung to every curve from thigh to ankle.

Marley turned and stared at my chest before hitting me with a harsh glare, a million chaotic emotions swirling through her hazel eyes. "You're forgiven."

Too easy.

"That's it?" I laughed, confused.

"That's it."

Gesturing between us, I asked, "So, we're good?"

"Sure." She nodded toward the garage. "Everything okay? I heard some commotion."

Arms crossed, I studied the concern in her gaze, then lingered on those freshly moistened lips, pink and ripe. "Just clearing the attic."

"Find something you didn't like?"

"You could say that."

Marley dropped her purse on the car seat. "I'd offer to help, but I'm on my way out."

"To a game?"

She looked down at her Mariner's shirt, then back to me, crossing one Nike-clad foot over the other and shoving her hands into her back pockets. "Yeah."

"Date?"

Brows pinched, she said, "No. Not really."

"Not really?" I chuckled, hoping to hide my ire. "What's that mean? It's either a date or it isn't."

"None of your business." The woman hit me with a feral glare, ready for a fight.

Murder crossed my mind. I wanted to hunt down and end the man who would sit next to her in the stadium, date or not. God, had I always been a possessive asshole?

I rubbed at the throbbing vein in my temple. "You're right. Sorry. None of my business."

We shared a moment of silence, gazes locked, hers slowly softening. With a nod, Marley turned back to her car and said, "See ya 'round, Joe."

Frank's *make her feel you* speech suddenly made sense, and though I had no right, I could not let my gorgeous neighbor leave on a possible date without filling her to the brim with all the confusing shit in my head and chest.

Slamming a hand around her neck, I pulled her to me, her gasp an opening, and I captured that sweet mouth with a kiss that left no doubt about my intentions. Our tongues tangled, wrestling. Her body stiffened before melting against my vibrating muscles. I dug my fingers into that tender skin below her hairline, gripping tight, then coiled my other arm around her waist, holding her steady. Sweet Jesus, the woman moaned and damn near clawed through my shirt.

And as quick as I'd claimed her, she shoved me away, her strength mighty despite her size.

Lips parted, chest rising and falling, the red-faced woman hit me with a slap that made me see stars.

There she was, my little fighter.

Gloating wasn't my nature, but I'd made my point, and I couldn't help but smile despite the throbbing pain in my cheek.

Marley shook her hand and cupped it to her chest, bending at the waist. "Dammit! Ow. Is that jaw made of steel?"

I only laughed. Wasn't the first time a woman had hit me. Was the first time I'd wanted more, though.

"What the fuck was that?" she asked, pink lipstick smudged.

"Have fun on your date." I chuckled, turning to leave.

No way in hell she'd be touching another man without thinking about that lip-lock. I was in. Our kiss would rattle around that crazy brain of hers all night.

What a marvelous goddamn feeling.

. . . .

Shopping sucked, seriously. Lock me in a room full of sugar-fueled toddlers or drop me naked into a pit of starved lions, but a busy supermarket? No, thank you. Unfortunately, a man needed food and the basics, so the earlier I got the unpleasant excursion out of the way, the better. Six AM was prime time.

My game plan? Get in. Get out. Don't waste energy on pleasantries or eye contact. If Mrs. Cataract Surgery with dark glasses cut me off on aisle nine with her motorized cart? No problem. Turn around and get on with business. Canned soup could wait 'til next week.

However, I'd been in a mood since I'd planted that kiss on Marley. Add to that the stress of digging through Alice's nonsense, and—kill me please—discovering that Marley starred in perverted coffee fantasies of countless men, best to steer clear of the general population. And because my ill temper was a danger to those around me, I was also in the zone, meaning zoning everyone out, which was why, when I turned the corner to the toilet paper aisle, I crashed into an unsuspecting shopper.

My emotional state flipped from dark to brilliant in a blink.

"Oh, jeez," Marley blurted, her gaze glued to my chest. She swallowed, then lifted stormy eyes to mine.

"Hey, neighbor." Yeah, that greeting might've come out too loud, my voice an octave too high, but the woman knocked me off my game. "Sorry. Wasn't paying attention."

"Obviously." She backed her cart away and moved to go around mine, her chin held high, shoulders set in defiance. Clearly, she was upset with yours truly again.

"How was the date?" I teased because, apparently, I was twelve.

Marley stopped, her shoulders going rigid. Slow and steady, she turned to face me, and shit, if looks could kill, I'd lay dead next to a row of Charmin.

"You didn't tell me I had lipstick smeared all over my face. I went through security, walked past hundreds of people on the way to my seat, wondering why I was getting funny looks." She squeezed the handle of her cart with one hand and planted the other, fisted, on her hip. "My girl-friend laughed so hard she ruined her own makeup. Then I had to explain to everyone why I looked like a toddler who'd stolen Revlon outta her mamma's handbag."

I bit my lip to keep from laughing. "Be honest, you were thinking about my mouth and tongue all night." Not the least bit sorry, I taunted further. "You woke with a lady boner thinking about me, didn't you?"

"God, you're so..." She fought a smile, shaking her head. "Such an asshole."

Shrugging, I conceded. "I'm sorry for not telling you about the smudged lipstick." I stepped closer because I had no choice. "Figured you'd check yourself in the rearview at some point."

"Whatever," she huffed, moving away, the swing of her hips making me dizzy.

"It was a great kiss, though, right?" I yelled after her, then when she didn't respond, I grabbed my two-ply and continued checking shit off my list. Only, fuck, I couldn't stop grinning.

When I reached the deli counter, I found Marley in line behind a woman with purple hair, facial piercings, and ink from collarbone to Doc Martens. The artwork would have been worth a good gander had I been able to tear my gaze from my neighbor.

Sidling next to Marley, I cleared my throat and braved the question, "So, if you're over being mad, I have a favor to ask."

"Sure." She stared straight ahead, though her body leaned in my direction. "What is it?"

"I have a function to attend tonight. Lotta people. I

don't do well in crowds. Would you be my plus-one? I promise I won't mess your lipstick."

She stepped back, her ass bumping the cart behind her. "Oh, sorry," she said over her shoulder.

A man with dark hair and darker eyes scanned the length of her, his assessment predatory. "No worries."

The guy clearly thought I wasn't a threat, judging by how he pretended to be busy with his cell but braved leers at her ass.

"Why do you have trouble in crowds?" she asked, face now lifted, focused on me with a curiosity I hadn't expected but cherished nonetheless.

And although she ignored my question and zeroed in on my vulnerability, I didn't feel attacked or rejected but was instead forced to ponder an issue I'd never given much thought to. Before "serving time," I'd had no problem with social settings.

"The whole prison thing, I think," I answered, loud enough for the dipshit behind us to hear. My intention hit the mark, drawing his attention from her luscious ass to the tats on my arms.

"The prison thing." She gnawed her bottom lip, nodding, her gaze losing focus.

Shit. Wrong move. Why the fuck had I mentioned lockup?

"I, um..." She hit me with a sweet smile. "I have plans already. I'm sorry."

"Oh." I nodded. "Another date?"

"A birthday celebration."

Purple hair stepped to the counter and recited her order.

Marley and I stepped ahead in sync.

"That's too bad. Maybe another time."

"Probably not," left her lips like rejection was her practiced response.

The dead man behind me snorted.

Marley and I stood side by side in silence, waiting our turn. Every Y chromosome that passed did a double take, and who could blame them? Marley was irresistible. Tight jeans hugged her bubble-gum ass and thighs. Her white shirt was loose but did nothing to hide the breasts underneath. And those fuck-me lips were shiny and inviting.

She must've spent time in a tanning bed recently, because the Seattle sun didn't allow for that kind of glow. Then again, I supposed sun-kissed skin was required for a job as a nearly nude barista.

Fuck. Irritation crept up my spine. I stepped closer. We weren't together, but I could make it appear that way, you know, for all those hungry leers and perverted imaginations.

"What are you doing?" she asked, standing her ground, not budging when our arms pressed together.

I stared down at her, and Christ, those eyes, so wild and full of life, and she smelled like vanilla. My stomach growled. I should've had breakfast before leaving the house.

"Stop staring." Brows pinched, she glared up at me. "Why are you looking at me like that?"

So many fucking reasons, I thought, my libido in high gear. "You smell good."

Her cheeks darkened.

I was seconds from bending down to taste her lip gloss.

"Next," the man behind the counter bellowed. His demeanor morphed from blasé to stoked at the sight of Marley. I silently chuckled. *I feel you, buddy. I feel you.*

Marley stepped forward. I stayed behind. When finished, she passed by and offered, "Good luck with your shindig tonight," pretending to be unaffected by my presence. But damn, that woman felt me deep. I knew by the weight of her gaze, her blush, the pucker of those nipples under her thin shirt, and by the way she paid no mind to anyone else, Marley Masters was into me.

"Hey, neighbor!" I called after her because I hadn't gotten my fill.

Marley looked over her shoulder, slowing her pace.

"You didn't say if you had a date for your party tonight."

The beauty laughed, shook her head, and said, "No date," before flipping me the bird.

"Good answer, neighbor!" I shouted. Didn't give a shit who was in earshot. "Good goddamn answer."

Then, as I turned toward the counter, I caught the man behind me watching her retreat, and I didn't say a word. Couldn't blame him.

She looked good enough to eat.

CHAPTER
Ten

"Damn, girl, you look good enough to eat." Dressed for a night on the town, Marco stood outside the stretch limo and blew a low, appreciative whistle, his smile and stance that of a man who knew his worth.

Wobbly on my new stilettos, I shimmied into his strong arms, careful not to get makeup on his silk shirt. "Happy birthday, beefcake."

"Thanks, Marls." The birthday boy spun me around once before setting me back on my feet.

I kissed his cheek, then folded into the back of the black car. Lilly waited at the other end of the buttery leather seat, wearing a grin that out-sparkled her shimmering silver minidress.

"You ready for a night of debauchery?" she asked, a mischievous twinkle in her eyes.

Drinking, dancing, and harmless flirting with men I would not be having sex with, who did not live next door, and who definitely did not get off on stealing kisses that left me dizzy and wanting more. "Debauchery, drunk and disorderly, let's do it all."

"That's my girl." Lilly flashed a megawatt smile, offering her palm for a high-five.

Marco settled into the seat opposite us, laser-focused on Lilly's cleavage. "I might just be the luckiest guy alive tonight."

"Why's that, hot stuff?" Lilly asked.

"Spending my thirtieth birthday with two of the hottest ladies in Seattle," he said to her chest, then chuckled and shot me a wink.

Lilly's boyfriend was cover-model handsome. Dark, wavy hair, perfect amount of scruff on his chiseled face. His best attribute, though? Never once since they'd met—at church of all places—had Marco judged Lilly's career choice or asked her to give up her job.

"I'm not into threesomes if that's where you're going with this flattery," I teased. "But I know a few girls who are. I could hook you up."

Lilly slapped my thigh. "No way. Yuck. I don't share." She blew her man a kiss. "Besides, I'm more than enough woman for you, baby."

"Don't I know it." Marco shook his head, stretching his arms across the back of the seat.

I'd never tire of watching the two of them blush around each other.

Lilly opened the built-in console set between us and pulled out three chilled tumblers and a bottle of Kaniche rum. She poured, and we toasted first to Marco, then to love, and finally, to growing wiser with age.

By the time we'd rolled up to the private entrance of Misled, we'd finished our second drink. My stomach floated, the weight of my day evaporating into the sticky night air.

We bypassed the line, Lilly gave her name, and a man dressed in black from his tie to the tips of his shoes escorted us to our table in the far corner of the second-floor lounge. We had a full view of the bar and dance floor from our position.

Marco's friends, Singleton, Tye, and Shawn, were already seated but rose to greet us with hearty hugs. Singleton wore his wavy hair slicked back. His white dress shirt was open at the collar but tucked into a pair of gray herringbone cropped suit pants. My favorite part of his outfit, however, were the thick-soled, patent leather oxfords on his feet. The polished buckle strap was fun, but add to that the spiky studs jetting out from the heel? Singleton in a nutshell. Suave and sophisticated at first glance, carefree and kooky upon further inspection.

Tye and Shawn were both dressed to impress, too. Shawn looked edible in a gray suit that complimented his dark skin and hugged his lean, fit physique. His buzz cut, I'd decided, was the perfect style to showcase his dreamy brown eyes, thick brows, and full, cushion-soft lips. Tye, though shorter and stockier than the others, wore his blue suit with the grace of a prince. His inky black hair looked freshly cut and styled into a gelled comb-over. His emerald eyes and thick black lashes never failed to make me swoon.

Our private waiter took drink orders, then disappeared behind a black curtain.

The party had to have cost a pretty penny. Misled had the look and feel of a members-only, *unleash your best jewelry from the safe* type of establishment. The walls and floor were dark, and crystal chandeliers hung from high, tiered ceilings and sparkled like diamonds. Varying shades of blue lighting accented the dance floor and bar areas. The ambiance was an aphrodisiac—sexy, mysterious, and forbidden.

"I'm ready to dance," Lilly announced, scooting out of her seat. She grabbed Marco's hand and asked, "Boss, you coming?" then hooked her free arm through mine and pulled me along.

Every size, shape, and pronoun filled the dance floor. I shimmied through the tangling limbs and found a free spot in the center of the gyrating horde, where I lost myself to the heavy beat and the hypnotic pulse of flashing lights. I drowned my cares in the wave of movement. Men and women moved with me, against me, sharing a cathartic release, purging, or perhaps unleashing, their demons.

The DJ took a break. Sweaty and amped and feeling lighter than I had in ages, I made my way back to the table, where bottled water and shots of amber liquid waited.

I parked my butt next to Singleton and rested my head on his shoulder. "Who ordered these?"

"Compliments of the house." He twisted the lid off an Evian and made me drink.

After another round of shots, our server brought the cake. We sang. We toasted the birthday boy. True to her nature, Lilly decorated Marco's face with purple frosting, then cleaned his mouth with her tongue. Singleton pulled me back onto the dance floor, and again, the music filled my soul. He soon disappeared into the crowd with a raven-haired goddess. I didn't mind. For the time being, I was a carefree, sensual female. On the dance floor, I was the woman I could've been had life not stolen my youth.

Large hands rested on my hips, gripping tight, and the heat of a body pressed behind me.

He moved.

I swayed.

The crowded space left little room for much else.

I chose not to look at the stranger but moved with him like our bodies were lifetime friends. The beat grew heavier, the crowd thicker, the man's hands wandered, one pausing under my breast, the other my abdomen, keeping me steady, holding me captive.

Warm lips pressed against my neck, sending waves of euphoria over my lowered walls. When he teased his tongue across my sweaty skin, my defenses dropped completely. Shameless and so turned on, I arched for him, offering more. I closed my eyes and imagined Joe's hands and soft lips. I danced against the man behind me, his body a mere vessel for the fantasy.

Whiskey-laden breaths amped my fire, searing my skin, the heat racing through my veins to settle, molten, in all the right places. Our private dance continued. Grinding. Touching. Panting. I dripped with need, the ache driving me mad, the memory of Joe's hands and lips, his grunts and thrusts, fueling my wanton frolics.

"Goddamn, sweet thing." He groaned. "Let me take you somewhere private."

"No." I needed one man and one man only.

My ass bumped against his hard cock, and I pulled away.

Strong arms yanked me right back. "Why?"

"Because I'm unavailable." Because I wanted those hands, those arms, those lips to belong to Joe, the man I was trying so hard not to like or need or crave.

He pulled me flush against the length of him, ensuring I felt every hard bump and powerful plane. "Good answer." A sharp sting bit my backside, and the stranger rasped in my ear, "Good goddamn answer, neighbor."

My fevered body cooled to frigid. I whipped around, but the man was gone, swallowed whole by the throbbing mob.

Knees weak, heart rate turbulent from the erotic dance floor encounter, I stumbled back to our group, fell into my seat, and slapped the table. "What'd he look like?"

"Who?" Singleton asked, his thick, flaxen hair rumpled, his shirt askew.

I dipped a napkin into a glass of melting ice, then used the wet cloth to rub cherry red lipstick off his chin. "The guy who brought our drinks."

"Dunno." Singleton shrugged. "Big guy. Dressed nice."

"That's it?"

"Wasn't paying much attention. Figured he was management." His thick lips spread into a quirky grin. "He did ask if you and I were together."

"What?"

"Yep." He closed his eyes while I finger-combed his unruly hair back into place. "He knew your name."

"Dammit, Singleton, you could have led with that piece of evidence."

He turned his body toward mine, our faces close enough I could smell the alcohol on his breath. "Evidence?"

"Yes. What did you tell him?"

"Told the truth." He leaned closer, then grumbled as if painful to admit, "You are off limits. I'm partial to my balls, so I keep my hands to myself."

"Partial to your...? Keep your... what?"

"Marley." Singleton laughed, then eased back. "Seriously. You don't know?"

"Obviously not."

"Here." He passed a shot glass my way. "I've had a thing for you since Marco introduced us years ago. All the guys do. But you're Lilly's girl, and she's Marco's girl." His brows lifted while he waited for me to catch on.

I didn't, so he continued. "Marco threatened our manhood if we were anything other than brotherly toward you. And believe me, Marco is a man of his word and one man I know better than to tangle with."

I threw the shot back, not tasting a thing but going straight for the kill, as in killing all the feelings, then reached for another. I'd always believed that Dylan was the reason none of Marco's friends had made a move. Would I have dated them? Maybe. But, damn, I'd pegged all of them wrong by assuming white-collar workers wanted to avoid getting involved with the likes of me.

"You should slow down, Masters." Marco's warning came over my shoulder. "Want you to enjoy the celebration, not end up in the ER with alcohol poisoning." He scooted next to me, bumping hips.

"Ah, Marco, you're just jealous because I can drink you under the table." I spoke the truth. Thanks, Dad, for those genes. "Where's Lilly?"

"Ladies' room."

"Good idea. Scooch over." I made my way out of the booth and toward the VIP Ladies' Lounge, swaying on my heels. The railing attached to the wall in the hallway was a freaking lifesaver. I'd have to mention that often overlooked but brilliant detail on my Yelp review.

I threw the door open. "Lilly, where are you?"

"I'm here," she said from behind a hand-carved door.

"This lounge is roomier than my house." Lordy, I was enjoying my buzz.

"I know, right? Think they'd notice if we moved in?"

"They'd never find us in here. My voice is echoing."

"I thought that was in my head. You hear it, too?"

We laughed hard belly laughs. Then I pushed open another fancy door, locked myself inside, and took care of business. "This stall is bigger than my bedroom."

"I'm telling Marco to build me a bathroom like this."

"If he does that, I'm moving in with you."

We met at the sink and primped.

"Did Marco tell his friends to keep their hands off me?"

"Yes. Years ago." Lilly turned to face me, one hand on her hip, the silver dress clinging to her every curve, her long, toned legs on full display. "They're all players, and Marco didn't want them hurting you. Oh, my God. Did Singleton try something? That fucker is dead."

"No. Jeez. Singleton has been a perfect gentleman." I dried my hands, tossed the towel into the basket, and headed toward the exit.

"What would you do if he made a move?" Lilly asked, holding the door open for me.

"Nothing." I blew a raspberry, waving a dismissive hand in the air. "He's not my type."

"Who is your type?" she asked.

My rough-and-tumble neighbor came to mind. "The wrong type, apparently." I turned to face her, backing into the hallway.

Lilly's eyes widened at the same time my foot landed on something foreign. My ankle turned, and my drunk body careened sideways. Someone caught my waist, setting me straight. Someone quick on his feet and scary strong.

"Christ, woman. Those are deadly heels."

A giggle erupted. "I'm so sor—" I looked over my shoulder, then up, up, up to find a set of angry eyes. Turning in his arms, I whispered, "Joe?"

"Neighbor."

He wore a blue dress shirt that slipped beneath my fingertips like warm butter and a tie that complemented his steely eyes.

Lava flowed under my skin. "What are you doing here?"

His roguish gaze dropped to my chest, then his nostrils flared before he hooked an arm around my waist and spun me until I landed between him and the wall. "Jesus. Cover yourself."

I looked down and, yep, my dress had twisted during my almost fall, and there was boobage, a full nip peeking out.

Personal boundaries be damned, Joe groped the exposed flesh and stuffed the naked tit back into my halter.

"Hey. Hey. Hey." Lilly smacked at his arm. "Hands off my girl. Don't make me call—" Eyes widening in recognition, she stepped back and pointed. "Oh, it's you. Motorcycle Guy."

Joe didn't bother a glance her way, his ire aimed at yours truly. "Isn't there some kind of magic tape you ladies use to keep those things covered in a dress like that?" He continued straightening and tugging, his gaze bouncing from my chest to my waist to my hips. "I mean, seriously, why you gotta show so much skin?"

His comment snapped me out of my *oh, my God, Joe is here* trance.

I slapped away his wandering hands. "Stop touching me. Get off."

The man eased back, only enough to allow breathing room, but certainly still blocking me from any onlookers, not that there were people in our private hallway that led to our supposed private restroom, which reminded me...

"What the hell are you doing back here?"

"Checking on you."

Sidling up to me, Lilly looped her arm through mine and asked, "You know this guy?"

"Lilly, this is my neighbor, Joe."

"Ohhh..." Her voice trailed off, her head bobbing as she connected the dots. "Nice to meet you." She offered a hand.

Joe appeased her with a quick shake and a tight smile. "Lilly. You mind giving us a minute?"

Her grip tightened, a show of support. "Nah, I'm good. I'd like to know what you're doing back here, too."

God bless her.

"Fine." Joe inched backward, giving us space. "I saw

you stumbling away from your table and wanted to make sure you were okay."

"I knew it." I poked a finger in his chest. "It was you bumping and grinding against me out there."

"You were showing the whole club your goods. Men were leering. I couldn't let—"

"Showing my goods?" I shrieked, my buzz wearing off.

He gestured to my chest, then my thighs, quirking his brows.

Yes, my dress was short. Yes, the neckline plunged halfway down my abdomen, but the clingy skirt had a little boom-chicka frill at the hem, covering all the scandalous parts. I was certainly not showing any more flesh than any other lady at the club. Seriously. In Vegas, my getup would be considered prudish. And yes, he'd been right; we ladies used magic tape to hold our garments in place. Mine, apparently, had failed. Good thing I had an extra strip in my handbag. But that was beside the point. The point was... "So what? You were protecting me from all the big, bad men?"

"No, goddamnit." He rubbed the back of his neck. "I just... Well, yeah. Shit." He dropped his arm and hit me with a direct glare. "I couldn't stand by and watch while other men touched you."

His epic confession knocked me back a step.

My traitorous heart stretched her wings.

Joe didn't want other men touching me. Well, damn me to hell, I didn't want other men touching me either. What a stupid, dangerous revelation.

My best defense against the rising feels? Bitch mode. "Seriously, Joe. We fucked. Okay. That doesn't make you my boyfriend or my guardian." I pushed from the wall and grabbed Lilly's hand. "You don't get to lay claim. And you do not get to corner me in a dark hallway and tell me to cover myself."

Lilly snorted, clearly entertained, but then, as if sobering, she stepped between Joe and me, hands to hips, and asked, "This is a private hallway. How did you get back here, anyway?"

"He's a criminal, Lilly." The words shot from my lips, nasty, spiteful, and self-preserving. I cringed at my cruel outburst, the regret white-hot and immediate. My ugly had spilled, and there was no mop in reach.

"Again with that shit?" Joe took one heavy step back, then another. His chin dropped and his heated stare fell from my face, aimed at the floor.

Soured liquor swirled in my stomach. "Joe, I'm—"

"Save it." The venom in his voice paled in comparison to the disgust on his face. "Why the fuck am I wasting my time? I've never met such a bitter, judgmental woman in my life."

"What the hell did you just say?" Lilly came to my defense, but she was too late.

Joe was gone, disappeared down the dark hall.

. ° . ° . °. ° . ° . °

Bang. Bang. Bang.

My antique mirror rattled under the excessive force of the knock.

Unexpected visitors were the worst. I considered my state of undress and sunk deeper into the couch cushion.

Bang. Bang. Bang.

A quick stretch to my left, a tug, and I turned off the table lamp.

Bang. Bang. Bang.

The only other person with a key would never knock, just let himself in and make himself at home. I hoped and prayed that a visit would come sooner rather than later, but deep down, I knew that the guy who owned my heart and soul was not on the other side of my door.

Tucking pink, fuzzy-clad feet under my butt, I raised the volume on the television, hoping my mystery caller would take the hint.

What kind of monster came to visit after dark?

"I know you're in there. Open up."

Monster. Crazy neighbor. Tomato. Tomahto.

Rap. Rap. Rap.

He was losing steam.

"C'mon. Let me apologize." *Tap. Tap. Tap.* "I'm an asshole."

Cheers to that. I raised my glass to my lips and finished my wine in one long swallow, washing my ire down to the pit of my stomach. The sad truth was that I owed Joe an apology, not the other way around. Yet, there he stood, the bigger man, making right the wrong I'd instigated.

"Please, neighbor."

"Ugh!" Why did he have to be so freaking nice? I kicked my legs out from under me and stormed to the door, led solely by my guilty conscience.

When I opened, Joe fell forward, nearly knocking me over in the process. When he caught me by the shoulders to steady himself and that familiar heat flooded my veins, I knew I was toast.

"Shit. Sorry." Joe straightened and braced a hand on the doorframe, the muscles in his arm bulging and flexing, the sight making me giddy.

Dear Lord, he smelled good, like spiced rum and leather, which made no sense because the man wore jeans and a Metallica tee. No leather anywhere on his person. Oh, wait. Yep, there it was. A leather bracelet. Black. Studded. Well worn. God, look at that solid wrist. Huh. Thick. Like his...

I winced, shaking the thought away, regretting my decision to open the door, especially in my floaty, borderline-inebriated state.

I cocked a hip, feigning indifference. "Say what you gotta say, Joe. I'm listening."

He released a long breath, his cheeks puffing, then shrinking. "I was a jackass again. I'm sorry."

Joe's eyes held no secrets. I studied them, searching for a reason to slam the door in his face, lock all thoughts of him away in my mental filing cabinet alongside my last dating mistake, the abusive, narcissistic drug dealer. I found only regret and shame in Joe's baby blues, and the man appeared sincerely repentant.

I hadn't the heart or the energy to turn him away.

Slumping in defeat, I mumbled. "You're forgiven." Then I cleared my throat and shocked myself by blurting, "I'm sorry, too."

Seconds ticked between us, ripe with possibilities. I was about to say goodnight when he asked, "What're you drinking?" followed by, "Can I join you?"

Good Lord, the guy was killing me. "I can't have a drink with you."

He smirked, highlighting a dimple. "Why not?"

"Because we always end up naked."

"That a bad thing?" he asked, gaze roaming my body.

My thin cami and ruffled sleep shorts may have well been a lacy bra and thong panties.

Rolling my eyes would have been rude, true, but doing so also would've made me dizzy and exposed my lack of sobriety. Instead, I lowered my gaze. "Good sex is never bad. I just don't want this to become a habit."

"You're staring at my crotch, neighbor. Makes me think you do want this to become a habit."

Damn! Stupid wine.

I pondered my predicament. Mind-blowing sex was an excellent way to de-stress, but definitely not with the man who caused said stress. Definitely not on a night where I had nursed a bottle of Petite Sirah to forget the hunk who currently towered over me with nothing but lust swirling in his gaze.

That look could very well be the death of me.

Joe needed to leave. I needed to go to bed.

"One drink," he argued. "No touching. Then I'll head home."

"Fine," I conceded, then ordered, "Sit." I pointed to the front step of the porch before closing the door.

Joe inside my four walls? Not for a million dollars. As a matter of fact, no man entered my domicile.

After tugging a long cardigan over my bare arms, I headed to the kitchen to grab a goblet. I swigged straight from the bottle, filled his glass, then joined him outside in full view of the neighborhood, zero risk of losing my clothes.

Joe sat on the top step. I handed him his wine and sat, too, the gap between us slight but a buffer nonetheless.

I ignored his chuckle.

"Comfy?" he asked, lifting the drink to his nose for a sniff.

"Yep."

Joe scooted closer, bringing us shoulder to shoulder.

"What are you doing?" I yelped, desperate to flee but with nowhere to go.

He stretched his arm behind me, resting his palm on the

cold cement at my rear. "Enjoying a glass of wine with my neighbor." He sipped from the goblet, his large fingers wrapped around the skinny stem in a ridiculous display. "This is good shit."

"You strike me as more of a beer man."

"Ah, the drink doesn't matter. Company's what's important." He took another long swallow before placing his drink out of harm's way, then dropped elbows to knees and sunk into the weight of both arms, rolling his head to catch my gaze.

Oh, Lordy, there he was, a mountain of sinful temptation, staring down at me with dubious intent. The scent of virile man enveloped me, warm and heady. He must've worked on his truck or motorcycle at some point during the day, because I also detected a hint of old motor oil and degreaser.

When he asked, "How was your day?" the simple words struck me by surprise and took too long to register. When was the last time someone had asked me, "How was your day?" and actually gave a shit?

A smirk twisted those full lips while he waited for my response.

"Busy," I said to his mouth because if I looked up, met his gaze, I ran the risk of exposing my soul. "One of my girls quit after her uncle drove through the stand. He didn't know she worked as a bikini barista, and the poor guy lost his shit. There was a lot of yelling and tears, and I had to pull out my baseball bat—"

Warm lips quieted my rant, surrounding me in heat and need and that dangerous spark of hope—that blind faith that only led to disappointment. Only with Joe, the fire burned hotter and desire rooted deeper, the ache to be wanted intensifying with every sweep of his tongue, every brush of his fingers, every throaty moan and heavy inhale.

Joe kissed like I was a lifeline, his only tether to humanity. My body responded by going soft, relaxing, like he was a hot bath after a long hike in the rain. His arms were too assuring, his lips too promising, the potential for disaster too blaring. I shoved away, struggling for breath, desperate for a moment of sanity.

"Been thinking about kissing you all week," Joe rasped, lips parted, chest rising and falling in barely controlled bursts.

"You promised no touching." I tried to stand, but he caught my wrist.

"Tell me you don't feel what I feel."

There was no hiding my state of emotions. My cheeks burned, my skin tingled, and my nipples hardened to pleading peaks. Joe needed to go and leave me be. I had to make him hate me.

Reclaiming my arm, I stood, snatched his glass, moved to the door, and blurted over my shoulder, "You're not my type."

"Not your type?" He was on me in two steps, his chest to my back, fingers claiming my hips, his breath in my hair. "Tell me then, gorgeous. What is your type?"

Well, wasn't that the question of the week? The answer was obvious. Joe. Unfortunately, my type broke my heart, over and over and over again. I forced the lie, "Extraordinary. Driven."

"What do you see when you look at me?"

"I see..." A criminal. An ex-con. "I see..." A man who would make me love him, then leave me broken. "Average."

The weight of his hands, his warmth, disappeared. "Average. Ouch."

I hated the pain in his voice.

"Listen," I said, hand on the knob. "You don't want me, anyway. I'm a mess. I work too much. I've been a terrible bitch to you." I'd been horrible, but how else could I protect myself? "But like a lost little puppy, you keep coming back for more."

"I like you." The hurt had left his voice, rage now taking the lead. "Is that so hard to believe?"

Angry Joe was easier to reject than Sad Joe, giving me the courage to turn and face him once again. "You're just lonely."

He huffed, backing away, two steps, then three, hands sliding into his pockets, shoulders slumping. "True. I get lonely." His eyes lifted to mine, the fight gone, the desire snuffed.

I'd hit my intended mark. I hated doing so, but still, I finished with, "I can't fill that hole for you. You should get a dog."

"A dog?" His sneer twisted my guts.

Conscience be damned, I drove the knife to the hilt. "I hear pets are the best cure for loneliness."

Mom had raised me to be kind and forgiving. Warren Masters, and every man after him, had swung their hammers until they'd forged all my soft and sweet into hard, mean grit. Still, that didn't stop the shame and embarrassment from weighing me down as I left Joe, alone, on my front porch.

॰ ॰ ॰ ॰ ॰ ॰ ॰ ॰ ॰

Yap. Yap. Yap.

I forced my eyes open, lids heavy with exhaustion.

Yap. Yap. Yap.

Ugh. Not even my pillow blocked the noise.

Yap. Yap. Yap. Yap.

I performed a full-body spasm, kicking off my sheet in the process, fuming at the audacity. Only terribly rude people allowed their dogs to bark at such obscene hours of the night.

Yap, yap, yap.

Cursing into the darkness, I hopped to my feet and tore open the curtain, revealing an inky, starless sky.

Aiming my ire toward Joe's open bedroom window, I waited.

Yap. Yap. Whine.

His shades were drawn, the room dark, but I could swear that awful noise came from inside his home. But that was crazy. Joe didn't have a dog.

Ears on alert, I watched for any signs of life. After five minutes of no barking and no movement, I fell back into bed, squeezed my weary lids, and drifted again into dreamland.

Yap, yap. Whine.

When I woke again, I blinked against the hazy rays of sunshine peeking through my curtains. Had I even slept? How was the sky so bright already? And why, why, why, could I still hear that damn dog?

I lay silent, listening for the offending sound, breathing deep to keep my heart rate at a steady pace. No barking. Perhaps I'd been dreaming. I stretched. Checked the time. Tried to go back to sleep.

At six-thirty, I gave up my quest for slumber and ate a quick breakfast of peanut butter toast washed down with a large mug of coffee before dressing in my yardwork attire— comfy sweats, black sweatshirt, and work boots.

I'd looked forward to my day off all week. There were weeds to be pulled, a mucky gutter that needed cleaning, and a lawn that was three days overdue for a trim. Mother Nature and I seemed to be on the same page since the sun was bright, the clouds nonexistent, and the air cool and dewy. A perfect spring morning.

Earbuds situated, I started the yardwork playlist on my phone and headed to the privacy fence dividing my backyard from Joe's. I dropped to my knees and tore at the weeds that thrived under the weathered pine boards.

Eminem spilled his guts about drug addiction while I ripped bluegrass roots from the soil. I was tugging on a pesky clump when something fuzzy touched my fingers. As the weed disappeared under the fence, I jerked back, startled, watching the earth shift under the fence line. Two tiny, fuzzy brown paws clawed at the dirt like mini excavators, de-rooting the damn weeds faster than I ever could.

I should've shooed the rodent away but instead sat back on my heels, enthralled with the scene. Before long, a tiny black nose appeared. Soon after, a dirty brown snout.

Tearing the buds from my ears, I watched. Waited.

Dig, dig, dig.

Huff. Huff. Huff.

The little guy was persistent, and I hadn't the heart to scare him away. Besides, he was probably lost, and if I let him dig his way under the fence, he'd be easier to catch. He wasn't the first stray that'd wandered onto my property, and I had the number for a local dog rescue on speed dial. He was the first, however, who'd tried to make his way into my backyard. For that alone, I'd cut the guy a break.

Dig, dig, dig.

Hug. Huff. Huff.

Come on, little guy. You can do it.

Five minutes later, a scruffy head poked through the hole.

Dig, dig, dig.

Huff. Huff. Snort.

He hadn't noticed me yet, too focused on his task.

God, the poor thing looked ragged. Needed a good meal, no doubt.

Another few moments, and he'd pulled his body halfway through the hole.

I held back my laugh, sitting silent, waiting patiently for the creature to discover my presence. A few hard kicks and grunts and the tiny, mangy mutt sprang to all fours, shook the dirt from his fur, and smiled up at me. Yes, smiled. Tail wagging, one gnarly tooth that looked too large for his mouth stood tall amongst the others.

I hated to call a dog ugly. But the little guy was... well, ugly. Wiry black-and-brown coat, bulging eyes that didn't seem to focus, and a tongue that lolled out the side of his mouth.

He couldn't have been taller than eight inches or weighed more than five or six pounds.

Poor thing.

"Hey, little guy." I slowly offered my hand for the creature to sniff.

He gave me a lick but then took to following a scent through the grass, ignoring me altogether.

A red collar adorned his neck, a small metal tag hanging from the clasp. The mini monster didn't protest when I scooped him up to inspect the engraving for an address.

"Oh, for the love of..." I grumbled.

I knew that residence by heart.

My cheeks heated.

A loud whistle came over the fence. "Ginger." Another whistle. "Come on, girl."

The dog, a female apparently, wiggled in my arms, tail spinning like a propeller on a boat engine.

"Hey, girl. Where'd you go?" Joe's voice rose an octave. "Come on," he sang. "Breakfast is ready."

The mutt wiggled harder, and I set her on her feet. She

ran to the fence, butt shaking something fierce, that tiny tail a blur. She crouched at the hole, nose to the ground, rear in the air, and barked.

"Aw, fuck." Joe's voice came closer. "Shit!" He patted a hand in the hole. "What'd you do? Neighbor lady's gonna kill me." He whistled again. "Come on, Ginger. Come."

I covered my mouth, stifling my laughter.

Ginger barked louder, pouncing at Joe's fingers, enjoying the game.

"Come on, sweetie, cut me a break. Our uptight neighbor hates me enough already. Let's not give her another reason."

Uptight neighbor? Ouch.

He grabbed at the dog, and she only yapped harder at his hand.

"Fuck!" he shouted.

"Morning, Joe," I said, scooping Ginger off the ground again. "Lose something?"

A mumbled "Shit" sounded through the fence. "Uh, yeah. Sorry about the hole."

"You can fill it later. I'll bring her over."

"Uh, thanks."

I made my way around front where Joe waited on his porch, shirtless, sleepy, and scrumptious.

I would not stare at that chest. I would not. "You got a dog."

He met me at the bottom step. "A wise lady once told me a dog would cure loneliness."

Sadness haunted his features, stabbing me in the chest, and I ached to reach out and caress his scruffy cheek. Jeez, I was such a sap.

I hadn't seen Joe in over a week, although, according to Lilly, he'd been through Pink Sweets daily, conveniently when my shift was over.

I shoved the wiggling fuzzball into his naked arms. "Well, she's just about the ugliest dog I've ever seen."

Those big, beautiful eyes sizzled. Joe curled Ginger into his neck, rubbing his cheek against the dirty fur. "Yep. She's perfect." He kissed her, his full lips pressing against the top of her head. I could swear the puppy swooned and sighed.

I knew how she felt. The man had beautiful lips—talented, too.

Who turned up the heat? Gah, my throat was parched.

"Well, keep her out of my yard, please. And for crying out loud, don't let her yap all night. Or at least be decent enough to close your window."

"Naughty girl," he said to the dog. "Did someone disturb our neighbor's beauty sleep?" He held the pooch in both hands and nuzzled her snout.

My ovaries threatened to explode.

"I was about to shoot a hole through your bedroom window last night," I warned. "Keep her quiet, please."

"Neighbor lady's violent, too." Nuzzle. Nuzzle.

Dear God. Baby talking to the puppy. A cold shower was in order.

"You have no idea." I flashed my best angry face, but my forced crossness landed in pieces at my feet when he laughed and kissed the dog on her head again.

Joe turned, retreating through his open door. "See ya 'round, neighbor." The door slammed in my face before I could respond.

My chest deflated.

How pathetic. I was jealous of that little bitch.

CHAPTER
Eleven

"Bitch, put your feet in the water." I laughed, giving Con a hard smack on his shoulder.

"That shit's hotter than Hades," he whined, his hairy toes dangling above the swirling blue liquid.

Frank shook his head, already adjusting the settings on his chair's vibrating feature. Trudy watched, her eyes crinkled at the corners, a smile hidden behind her mask.

Ly slapped a hand on Connor's knee with a huff and forced his foot into the basin. From her little chair on wheels, she chastised, "Don't be a baby. You like this. I promise."

Con lowered his other leg, his face turning a shade of red you only see in cartoons.

"You'll thank him later. Trust me," Frank assured him, then winked at Trudy and closed his eyes.

"Any more action at Dirty Dreamz?" I asked the ladies, strolling to the window to get a better view of that damn coffee stand.

Two cars sat side by side at the edge of the lot, neither belonging to Larry.

"I'm sorry, Joe. Nothing new," Ly said, lifting Connor's size fourteen and placing it on the toweled footrest.

"That silver Escalade come back?"

"No," she replied. "Not since you ask last week. Trudy? You see that silver Escalade?"

Trudy shook her head in the negatory.

"Wait a minute." Connor sat up straighter. "You're doing this girly shit once a week?"

Frank twisted, yanking his cell from his back pocket. He snapped a pic of Con, and with a lazy grin, said, "You tell a soul, I'm plastering that photo all over your social media."

"Prick." Con white-knuckled the armrests and sucked in a sharp breath when the grooming tools came out.

Ly stood from her chair, shaking her head, and pulled the massage control from its perch to set the rollers in motion. Patting Con's shoulder, she said, "You shush. I take good care of you," then sat back down.

Con grumbled but did as told.

"Joe." Ly turned my way while she scrubbed Con's heel. "You no take Trudy on date. Frank no take Trudy on date. Maybe this one?" She lifted her chin toward Connor.

Trudy grumbled, shaking her head.

"I'm sorry, ladies." Con cleared his throat, then let Trudy off the hook. "You're beautiful, but I'm not dating material."

"I've got a lovely woman at home." Frank chuckled. "And one woman is all I can handle."

"And Joe, here," Con added. "He's hopelessly in love with his neighbor."

Jesus. These guys.

"How's that going, by the way?" Frank asked, raising his head to shoot me a brow wiggle.

"It's not."

"She still mad you assaulted her outside the ladies' room at the club?" came from Con.

"I didn't assault her."

Franked chuckled. "You kinda did."

"Doesn't matter. Marley looks at me and sees a criminal." I rubbed at a twitch in my eye. "Wants nothing to do with my dirty life."

Maybe the time had come to move on and give the dating scene a try. Most men would've thrown in the towel after the first rejection. Hell, after the third or fourth. What was my hang-up? Easy. I couldn't get Marley out of my head, and I spent too many hours dreaming of ways to light her fire.

"Why would you wanna be with a woman who serves coffee in her lingerie, anyway?" came from Frank.

He obviously hadn't seen her in her work attire.

"True," Con added. "If I'm with a woman, her body is for my eyes only."

"I dated an exotic dancer once," Frank chimed in, having way too much fun at my expense. "Nothing but drama."

"I know you dickheads are trying to rile me up, but for fuck's sake, can we stick to the task at hand?"

"Which is what?" Frank grumbled.

"I dunno. My uncle." I grabbed the nearest chair and dropped my ass into the cushion. "Something isn't sitting right. Something's up. Can feel it in my gut."

Why I wasted time worrying about what Larry was up to was a mystery. That old cranky ass could be Lucky fucking Luciano for all I cared as long as he stayed clear of me and mine. But, like I couldn't quit Marley, I couldn't shake the feeling there was unfinished business with my uncle.

"You would've made a great cop." Con hit me with a hard stare, his voice low and gruff.

Frank grunted in agreement.

Fucking shame. Frank and I had planned on attending the academy together. Then the whole "murder" thing happened, and my dreams of being the next John McClane were snuffed.

Worth it, though. Every miserable second. Except for the part where I didn't get to see Alice enjoy her freedom.

Frank huffed. "You'd be putting away real criminals, not obsessing over a washed-up thug."

Trudy cut in, her sweet voice stronger when she spoke English. "You know what would be nice?"

Con, Frank, and I shared a glance.

"It would be great if you grown men could sit back, enjoy the service my mother and I provide, and quit pretending like you're coming here for some big, bad stakeout." Born and raised in the United States, Trudy had no accent. "You like pedicures. So what? There's nothing wrong with that."

She dropped Frank's foot and turned to face me. "Seriously. Why don't you just walk over there, knock on the door, and see what's up? What are they gonna do, shoot you at eight-thirty in the morning on a busy street?"

I shook my head no.

She wasn't finished. "You don't like your neighbor's career choice?" She shrugged. "Too bad. What do you do, anyway? I've never heard you mention a job."

Feeling all of two inches tall, I opened my mouth to answer, but she continued.

"You have no idea how hard the service industry can be. Having to smile and be nice when people are being rude, or having to pretend you're happy to be working when you have a bad cold or severe cramps or you're just in a terrible mood." She pointed her loofa my way. "Before you judge what that woman does or does not wear to work, open your own coffee stand." She laughed, shook her head. "Shirtless men. I'd pay twenty bucks for a latte with a side of beefcake. Women can be just as dirty as you boys, for fuck's sake."

She winced and said, "Sorry, Ma," then continued. "Beautiful men and coffee? What could be better?"

Ly dropped her nail buffer and clapped her hands together. "See, Joe. My girl smart. You date her, you be happy."

"Ma. Stop," Trudy hissed. "I have a boyfriend. And Joe has a girlfriend. And he's too old, anyway."

"She's not my girlfriend," I mumbled, ignoring the "too old" comment.

Silence hung in the air a beat past comfortable before my brothers burst into hysterics.

"Yeah, right. Joe serving coffee in the buff." Con slapped his knee. "Can you imagine?"

"At least he wouldn't be a thirty-something unemployed loser," Trudy countered, eyes smiling.

Excruciating minutes later, the ribbing and chuckling subsided.

Con's eyes sparkled as he looked down at Trudy, then back up to me. "It's true, man. You taking that waste management job or what? You can't live off your savings forever."

Thanks to the money I'd put aside while working for dear ol' dad, there was no rush, but I wasn't a man to sit idle. I needed to make an honest living. Earn my way.

When Frank's pedicure was finished, I took his place in Ly's chair. We slipped into a comfortable conversation, Trudy going silent once again. After my feet were scrubbed and my nails buffed, Ly asked, "So, same time next week?"

"Yep," Con said without hesitation.

"Please, ma'am." Frank pulled a stack of bills out of his wallet and handed it to Ly without another word.

"Thanks, ladies. See you next week." I laid my cash on the counter and followed my buddies into the cool morning air.

CHAPTER
Twelve

*J*OE

"Morning, beautiful." With a groan, I rolled to my side, body aching something fierce thanks to the new hiking trail Ginger and I braved the day before.

I reached over and gave her butt a pat. "Breakfast?"

Sleepy brown eyes lifted to mine before the beauty stretched, then snuggled into her nest of bedding.

Sharing my bed was a novelty, but I had no complaints as far as my new sleeping partner went. Ginger kept to her side of the mattress, snored, but the sound was fucking adorable, and she wasn't a blanket hog.

The bonus? My new girl didn't talk back, and there wasn't a judgmental bone in her body. The exact opposite of my neighbor, whom I hadn't seen in days.

"Get your beauty sleep. I'll be downstairs." Despite the heat, I wrapped a blanket over her tiny body, then stumbled to the restroom.

By the time I reached the kitchen, my muscles had loosened.

A soft rap hit my door. I peeked around the corner. Marley's form filled the window, and good goddamn morning, my weary bones sparked to life.

I considered my mostly naked state, contemplated jogging upstairs for some pants, then thought, fuck it. I'd never get enough of the way she blushed or struggled to keep her eyes from roaming the stretch of my skin. A man could jet to Saturn from that ego boost.

Another knock, then the doorbell chimed.

I waited for the coffee machine to finish filling my cup, hooked my finger through the handle, and sauntered her way.

Our eyes met through the glass, and her gaze heated my skin like a third-degree sunburn.

I pulled the door open and waited while she made her appraisal, those cheeks growing rosier by the second. No better way to start the day.

"Do you ever wear clothes to answer the door?"

"Nah." I smirked, lifted the cup to my lips, and drew a slow sip. "That bother you?"

"Respectable neighborhood." She pointed a thumb over her shoulder. "Remember?"

"No one can see me but you."

We shared a weighty glare. My boxers failed to disguise the swelling bulge.

"What can I do for you, neighbor?"

Her long hair fell over her shoulders, wavy, the ends wetting her pale yellow shirt. Baggy shorts hung low on her hips, the denim frayed at the hems. She held a key between her thumb and forefinger. "This isn't my spare."

"It's not?"

"I tried it last night. Doesn't fit my lock."

"Hmm." I opened the door wider and gestured for her to enter.

Like she owned the place, Marley headed to the kitchen, opened the cupboard containing Alice's teacup collection, rose on her toes, and reached into the far corner.

Sweet Jesus, those tone legs and tight ass. Flawless. Delectable. My stomach growled, and all the blood in my body raced toward one destination, my uncomfortable morning wood breaching the point of excruciating.

"It's not here." With tender care, she inspected each dainty dish. "They're all empty." She reached for the second shelf but came up shy.

"Here, let me help." I moved behind and reached over her head, my arousal pressing against her backside because, shit, there was nowhere else for the damn thing to go.

Marley stiffened. I didn't move. Was I a jackass? Sure. But I loved to fuck with her, and that sweet body was warm and inviting, and...

What was I doing? Marley didn't want me; she'd reminded me time and time again.

Only, that slight arch in her back told a different story. The little firecracker felt me. Deep. Were I to caress a tit or venture lower between those gorgeous thighs, she wouldn't ask me to stop.

My hips rolled, seeking the friction, and her head fell back against my chest. Sweet hell.

A thump sounded upstairs, followed by the patter of tiny paws overhead, then the click of nails on the staircase.

Marley whipped around, nudging me out of the way, and I'd bet my life that was a moan of frustration that fell from her lips.

A whimper came from the hallway before Ginger barreled our direction, tail spinning, paws seeking purchase on the smooth floor.

"There's my lazy girl," I cooed. "Finally decided to roll outta bed?"

Marley's laugh set my soul at ease, and when she squatted to catch my wriggling little furball, I turned back toward the cupboard, willing my dick to deflate while biting back my smile.

Marley wanted me despite demanding the opposite. My

spirits rose to the sky. I'd just been cock-blocked by a mutt, but I'd never been happier.

One by one, I checked the first row of cups. All of them came up empty. I started on the second row, sliding a finger across each bottom of the smooth glaze. Nothing.

I had no clue why anyone needed a full cupboard, four shelves high, full of teacups. The collection of fine china was one part of the house I'd yet to disturb. They'd been Alice's treasures, some of which I'd gifted her over the years. Seemed wrong to upset their resting place.

"Wanna grab that stool?" I asked, but Marley was ahead of the game, setting the unfolded stepladder at my side.

Couldn't help my chuckle. "You must really want that key back."

Even her eye rolls revved my engine.

She set my wiggling pup on the floor and leaned against the counter. "I can make a hundred spares at the hardware store, but I figured I'd return this one. It has to belong to a door or lock somewhere here."

I climbed higher for shelf number three. Inside the first cup, I found an old gold pin—two birds with long tails, their feet and wings tangled in a fight or passion, I couldn't be sure. The trinket was heavy and nothing I'd ever seen Alice wear, not that I had paid much attention back then.

"Funny place to store jewelry." I handed the piece to Marley and continued my inspection, amused to find each cup contained one or two pieces of, in my opinion, ugly and probably ancient broaches, earrings, and necklaces, some gold, some silver, or pearl. A few with stones of varying colors inlaid.

"Joe," Marley whispered. "These have to be worth a fortune." She held another broach in the air, inspecting its underside. "There's a name stamped on the back, but I can't make out the letters."

"They're probably junk." I frowned down at her from my perch. "Alice wouldn't keep this shit in cups on a shelf if they held any value."

"We both know Alice was an oddball, bless her heart. Trust me, you need to get these appraised."

I climbed onto the next step and started on the top shelf. First cup in, my gut knotted. The rose-pattern porcelain was filled with plain gold rings almost to the brim. The next cup was filled with much the same, only gold with diamonds.

By the time I reached the fourth, I was slick with sweat. What had Alice done? Gold rings, diamond rings, diamond bracelets, earrings, necklaces.

The shit must be hot. Had to be the work of a Kaine man. Alice never would've been involved in my uncle's illicit shenanigans.

"What the hell do I do with this?" I mumbled, mortified that Marley was a witness to the Kaine circus. She'd never believe I wasn't a criminal if she knew whose blood I shared.

Marley laughed.

But I found no humor in the situation. If the jewelry was stolen, I wanted my neighbor far away from the threat of implication.

"You need to leave." My feet hit the floor.

"What?"

"I'll find your key. But you need to go."

"Joe. I don't care about the—"

Before she finished her sentence, I hoisted the sweet-smelling sack of curves over my shoulder, stomped to the front door, and deposited her on the porch. "Don't tell a soul about what we found today. Let me get this sorted first." My intended command sounded more like a desperate plea.

Brows knitted, she whispered, "What's happening?"

I closed the door, knowing I'd likely ruined any chance

of having a relationship beyond friendly with my neighbor. The ache in my chest and knot in my gut forced me to double over. Three deep breaths, then I straightened and headed for my phone.

Bill Kaine had ruined me once. Now he threatened to hurt me from his grave? Fat chance in hell.

CHAPTER
Thirteen

Connor wrenched the nut one more time, then contorted to free himself from the small space under the sink. "There is no possible way Alice was involved."

"I agree, but how'd that jewelry end up in her cupboards?" For the fourth time, I pulled Ginger out of Con's way. The nosey little furball, determined to help, grunted when I scooped her off the floor. I deposited her outside the back door, her legs spinning before her paws touched the ground.

Con dropped a glob of soggy shit into my hand and tossed his tools onto the counter.

"What the hell is this?" I shook the muck into the trash.

He ran the faucet to test the drainage and answered over the running water., "Looks like your aunt was shoving her stogies down the drain."

"Jesus," I huffed, rinsing my hand. "That woman was nuts. Gold in the teacups, cigars in the sink. What else am I gonna find?"

The front door opened, then closed. Heavy footsteps came our way. Frank entered, dropped folders and a plastic box on the kitchen table, then lowered with a grunt into a chair. "You, my friend, are one lucky bastard." He scratched his chin, fighting a grin.

He'd taken the stash off my hands over a week ago,

convinced, as was I, that the teacup trinkets were of illegal gain.

"Half that haul was from a rash of jewelry store smash-and-grabs from six years back," he stated.

"Larry and Bill." My knees buckled under the hefty weight of Kaine absurdity. "Fuck. That would explain why Bill was here that night. Why he and Alice were..." I couldn't finish the thought. Revisiting those memories would spoil my mood for days.

Frank finished for me. "He wanted to hide the jewelry here, and Alice must've fought back."

"Makes sense," I mumbled. "But why didn't Alice turn it in afterward?"

"My guess?" Con piped in. "She was protecting you. Didn't want you tied to any other crimes involving the Kaine men."

Nodding, Frank said, "That'd be my guess. And on that note, your dad's lawyer did a great job keeping your name in the clear."

Another favor I owed my father. The kicks just kept coming. But thank fuck I'd had my pops on speed dial.

"What about the other half?" Con joined Frank at the table.

Frank laughed, then tapped the plastic box. "This old stuff? Family heirlooms would be my guess. Took the liberty of having a few pieces appraised by an acquaintance of mine." He leaned forward, elbows to the table, hands clasped, a grin cracking his face. "That ugly pin with the birds who look like they're mating? That hunk of metal alone could go for over thirty grand at auction, my friend."

"You're fucking with me."

"Dead serious."

Fist to his mouth, Con laughed. "Holy shit, dude. There are, what, thirty pieces of jewelry in there?"

"At least." My legs could no longer hold my weight, and I claimed the chair between my buddies. "This can't be the treasure Alice hinted about in her letter, can it?"

"Who knows." Con pointed a finger first at me then at the heirlooms. "But man, I'm telling you, hide this shit somewhere safe. Today."

The doorbell sounded, raising my hackles, the chime loud and out of tune. I jogged toward the door. Halfway through the living room, I slowed to enjoy the scene. Marley cradled Ginger in a football hold, dirt on both of their faces. Ginger's tongue hung loose, a smile on her furry face. Marley wore a scowl that erased all the unease I'd suffered only moments ago.

Damn, that woman wielded some mystic voodoo power.

I forced my grin straight, going for calm and collected, and pulled open the door. "Hey, neighbor."

"Seriously," she huffed, dodging a lick. "You have to do something about her digging."

I snatched my dog free of Marley's hold, and hell, I deserved an award for not laughing at the amount of dirt covering her chest. "Sorry about that." I kissed Ginger's head to hide my grin, ignoring the earthy stench and gritty fur.

"Can you fill that hole today? Please?"

"Just about to head out, but I'll take care of it first thing tomorrow."

Marley looked down at herself, mumbled, "Dammit," then brushed at the soil on her tee, spreading the stain. "Do something about her digging. I mean it. What if she got out to the street?" Her disappointed mother expression was spot-on.

Consider me chastised.

She pulled at the hem of her shirt and grumbled, "It's ruined."

"I'll buy you a new shirt."

"You don't have a job." Angry eyes snapped to mine, her smile anything but friendly. Shit was about to get nasty. "What are you gonna do, steal me a two-bit rag from the thrift store?"

"Low blow, girl," I warned, though I was anything but offended. Turned on? Without a doubt. Eager to spar? Hell, yes.

When I should've sealed my lips, I couldn't help but throw gas on her flame. "I'm sure you didn't buy that tit hugger at Goodwill. A high-class business owner like yourself can certainly afford to shop at one of our city's finer establishments. Nordstrom Rack, maybe?"

"That wasn't a low blow." Hands to hips, she went off at me like a dollar store firecracker. "Did I lie? Do you have a job? Or a clue what it's like to work a steady nine-to-five? Or work your ass off twenty-four seven to try and make something meaningful or successful out of nothing?" She stepped closer, her heat scorching my soul. "No. You've probably wasted your entire life taking from those who do." Eyes glassy, she scolded, "Don't you dare mock me, you criminal lowlife burden."

And then she unwittingly threw down a challenge by adding, "You couldn't run a business even if you had Jeff Bezos for a partner."

With that, she turned and left, her fine ass jiggling as she hurried down the porch steps. When she hit the walkway, she threw over her shoulder, "I'll fill the damn hole myself."

I watched until she was out of sight, then turned to find my buddies standing behind me, faces wet with tears of laughter.

Good God, the buzz in my veins. Addicting. "She's fun, right?"

"Oh, you're in trouble, my man." Frank slapped me on the back, then headed out the door. "Catch you two later."

"Thanks for the help. I owe you, big time."

Back in the kitchen, Con helped himself to a San Pellegrino. "What are you gonna do with this windfall?"

I couldn't contain my smile. "I have an idea."

Marley would be pissed, but ah, hell, what fun I'd have ruffling her feathers.

. ° . ° . °. ° . ° . °

"A coffee stand?" Bridget asked, her sun-kissed nose crinkling as she headed toward the sink.

"Yes."

She ran her empty mug under the water and gave it a good rinse before facing me again. "There's a coffee stand on every corner."

True. But none like I had in mind.

I downed my last sip of coffee and gave her my practiced smile, the cheesy grin she'd never been able to resist. "Can you please do some research? Let me know what's involved. Risks?"

"Tell you what." She stalked closer, clearly immune to my charm, judging by the tight pull of her lips and the weight of her glare. "I'll pull some numbers, but you"—the little shit stabbed my chest with a shiny red nail—"do the research. Do you even know how to make coffee?"

"Seattle is home to one of the best barista schools in the country." I slid the file folder to the end of the table. "I've got nothing but time. I need your brilliant business brain. Let me know if this is an insane idea."

She studied me long and hard, her heel tapping a slow

rhythm on the linoleum before she tucked the folder into her leather bag and slung it over her shoulder. "I'll dig in tonight. But know that I'll be brutally honest."

"Thanks, kid." I stood and pulled her into a bear hug. "I'd expect nothing less."

"Enough with the kid crap. I'm only two years younger than you assholes."

Bridget was not my sister by blood, but I treated her as my own. Between Frank, Connor, and I, the poor girl never had a moment's peace or a chance at teen romance. We'd even prearranged her prom date with a thoroughly vetted and discreetly threatened member of the chess club.

"But you'll always be my kid sister, Bridge." I swayed, rolling her side to side, her cheek smashed against my chest, her arms pinned at her sides. "Just let me have this. I've missed you."

The doorbell chimed. Bridge wiggled free and laid a palm on my heart. "You want my honest opinion? That waste management job has great benefits. The pay is not awesome to start, but it's enough for you to be comfortable. And it's secure. Low turnover rate. High employee satisfaction ratings. The fact that they're willing to hire you, given the circumstances, says a lot. Running your own business, that's not easy. And there are risks."

"And you'll list every single one of them for me." I kissed her cheek and turned her toward the door, urging her forward. "And I'll buy you a fancy-ass dinner as a thank you."

"I'll hold you to that."

A *bang, bang, bang* came from the door. Through the gap in the curtain, I was pleased to see Marley until I noticed Ginger in her arms. Shit.

"Oh, who's the lovely lady?" Bridget asked, a sly grin gracing her face.

"My neighbor."

"She's pretty." She reached for the door handle before I could get there and tore open the door. "Hi!" she said to Marley, then turned and planted a kiss on my cheek. "See you later, Joseph." She skirted past Marley, flitted down the porch steps, and sashayed toward her car.

"Hey." I met a set of angry peepers.

Marley held Ginger in outstretched arms, the poor little mutt's bottom legs dangling, and said, "She dug a new hole under the fence. Found her on my back deck with a dead rat in her mouth."

She was pissed, and curse my sadistic heart, I liked her fire, but I loved being the asshole who stoked those flames. "Sounds to me like you have a rodent problem."

Shoving the pup against my chest, she growled, "Keep her out of my yard."

I kissed my little fleabag on her scruffy head and teased, "Ginger is only trying to help."

That heated gaze bounced from Ginger to my lips and back and forth before she blinked and found my eyes. "I want that hole filled today," she ordered, clueless to the images she conjured every time she said she wanted her holes filled.

"I'll fill your hole." I laughed—couldn't help myself. "Or maybe we should cut a little door in the fence. You know, in case more rats breach the perimeter. She's a great guard dog. I don't mind sharing."

"Keep your ugly mutt out of my yard, *Joseph*." My name escaped her lips, growly and snide.

Huh. The woman was jealous. Good to know.

I covered Ginger's ears, expelling an exaggerated gasp. "This mutt is beautiful. And she's sensitive. Watch how you talk about my girl."

"Oh, for fuck's sake." Marley threw her hands in the air, her head falling back on her shoulders.

I took the opportunity to drink her in, that tight tank top that barely covered her stomach, the swell of her breasts, the way the leggings hugged her killer legs. My cock was rock hard, and I didn't give two shits if she noticed. That beauty could ogle and drool all she wanted.

"Should I come fill your hole now? Or maybe we could have a drink first. You seem a little uptight."

Her glare dropped from my eyes to my crotch, and oh yes, that blush made me proud. My cock was magnificent; she'd said so herself more than once.

No surprise, Marley didn't take advantage of my impressive boner. Much to my disappointment, she stormed away, a torrent of emotions stirring the air behind her.

Laughing, I carried Ginger through the house, out the back door, and set her down outside the shed. I found the shovel, filled Marley's hole, packed the dirt nice and tight, then stacked large rocks against the fence so my mangy little princess couldn't dig in that area anymore.

I whistled. "C'mon, girl. Let's go for a ride."

I searched to my left, then my right, just in time to see a tiny brown tail slip under the fence.

"You have got to be fucking kidding me."

CHAPTER
Fourteen

MARLEY

"You have got to be kidding me." I stared, disbelieving, at the pile of charred rubble that used to be my coffee stand in the South Park neighborhood.

A few skeletal remains stood, one corner of the frame pointing skyward like a middle finger to the rising sun. Firefighters loaded gear back onto their truck.

The place had been engulfed in flames when Jessica arrived for her shift, and she'd called 911, then me. Already fifteen minutes into my own shift, I'd had to wait for Lilly to arrive, which she did in record time, thank you, Jesus, before I made my trek to the scene.

"Nobody saw a thing?" My voice quivered, and my hands shook.

"No, ma'am." Officer Watson jotted notes on his pad, then nodded over his shoulder. "Property across the street has security cameras, but they've been down all week. Owner said somebody messed with the connection." He shifted his weight from one hip to the other. "I understand you had cameras?"

"Yeah," I mumbled, staring, vision blurry, into the destruction.

"Would like a look at that feed."

"Sure." I nodded. "Of course. I can view the recording from my home office."

Jessica kicked at a pile of charred wood. "We already know it was that strip-club pervert."

The cop caught my glare. "Something you wanna tell me?

I shook my head too fast and too hard. "Harper wouldn't stoop this low."

"Johan Harper?" the cop asked, wrinkles forming between his brows.

"Yes," I mumbled, not surprised that Harper was on the SPD radar.

"Nothing is beneath that man." He scribbled a note, then shoved the pad into his breast pocket. "What's your connection to Harper?" he asked, crossing beefy arms across his chest.

I sighed, knowing the conversation was futile, but playing along nonetheless. "He comes by once a week. When I'm not here, he tries to recruit my girls. When I'm in, he insists we go into business together."

Officer Watson cleared his throat. "Doing what?"

"I know better than to ask."

He nodded, his blue eyes brightening as if in approval. "Has he threatened you?"

"No." Not outright. "He's just persistent in offering a partnership."

The cop studied me, not wholly convinced. Though he remained stoic, the judgment was there behind his eyes— nothing I wasn't used to seeing. People assumed the worst about me and my girls. What kind of woman would run a sexy coffee stand, let alone work at one? I'll tell you who—a girl who had no other choice. People could keep on wondering. My reasons were nobody's business but mine.

I held the officer's gaze, forcing my chin high, feigning confidence.

"All right, Miss Masters," Watson conceded, pulling a

card from his pocket. "I'll be in touch about that feed. Here's my contact info. Call if you have any questions or need anything in the meantime."

"Thank you," I squeaked, my throat dry.

Jessica leaned into me, and I wrapped an arm around her shoulders while we watched the officer settle into his car.

"Don't worry," I assured her. "You can take my shifts at the Burien stand until we get this mess sorted."

"That's the thing, Marley." She splayed her fingers over her lower belly. "I'm pregnant."

"Oh, Jessica. That's wonderful news. I'm so happy for you." I silently hoped for a girl because boys turned into men, and men sucked.

"I know this situation is shitty"—she waved a hand toward the smokey rubble—"but the timing is perfect. I would've had to give my notice soon anyway, and I was nervous about telling you. And..." Her face scrunched with emotion.

Several industrial business complexes surrounded the South Park stand. Jessica had a loyal group of customers, her boyfriend of two years being one of them.

I pulled her into a hug. "I sensed something off with you but couldn't put my finger on it. God, I should've noticed the signs."

"Quinton accepted a promotion, and they're moving him to Boise to run the Idaho division." She pulled away and wiggled a diamond-clad finger at me. "He proposed last night."

"Oh, sweetie. I'm so happy for you."

"With his new salary, I'll get to be a stay-at-home mom, Marley."

"You'll be the best mother," I told her, smiling, though my heart blackened with jealousy.

My cell buzzed. Distracted, I answered without checking the caller.

"Hello?"

Silence.

"This is Marley," I sang into the phone while grabbing Jessica's hand to study the mammoth diamond.

"Do you like my gift?" asked an emotionless male voice.

Still preoccupied, I answered, "Sorry, you must have the wrong number," then ended the call.

My phone rang again seconds later. I didn't recognize the digits and figured the same person had misdialed, so I didn't answer.

After sending Jessica on her way, I waited for the fire department to finish their inspection before tucking back into my Subi, where I sat in contemplation.

The morning's events should've crushed me with worry. Funny, though, the weight on my shoulders lightened by at least a hundred pounds. I owned three stands. Sex sells, I'd learned, and I had reaped the benefits of my employees' good looks and hard labor. I'd paid off the loans for all three of my locations within their first year of opening. The income was hard-earned but substantial. But I could live comfortably on the earnings of two. I had no debt, and I no longer had two households to support. And now, I had one less employee. Yes, I could manage. Everything would be hunky-dory.

Heck, college no longer seemed out of reach. Maybe the fire was a blessing in disguise—a gift from above.

Do you like my gift?

My stomach churned. Couldn't be related. I looked at the number on my phone, pressed *Call*, then hung up. "You're being ridiculous," I mumbled to myself.

But was I? The timing had been perfect.

Do you like my gift?

Oh, jeez. My curiosity would come back to bite me in the ass, but still, with trembling hands, I pressed *Call* again.

Three loud beeps sounded in my ear. "You have reached a number that is no longer in service—"

I hung up, shook off the funky vibes, then headed home to contact the insurance company and hunker down with a mountain of paperwork.

⠂⠐⠂⠐⠂⠐⠂⠐⠂⠐

I rolled into my driveway, nerves vibrating. At the same time, a mammoth Silverado muscled into Joe's driveway, engine purring, chrome blinding under the sun's command.

Mentally ticking off my to-do list, I headed up the walkway, then stopped short when the door of the Chevy opened. Two heavy boots landed hard on the cement, and a thick voice shouted, "Hey, neighbor."

The man strode my direction, two hundred plus pounds of rolling muscle, olive skin, and piercing gaze. I recognized him from Alice's funeral, though we hadn't been introduced.

"Um." I tossed a look toward Joe's front door. "Hi."

Faster than I could flee, he hopped over the shrubbery, crossed my lawn, and stood before me, his soft, citrusy cologne a pleasant sensation, his appearance crisp and clean and oh so easy on the eyes.

"Wow." He held my gaze, no leering, which I appreciated, until he spoke again. "Joe wasn't lying when he said you were a looker."

"A looker?"

"Sorry." The guy scratched the back of his head,

shifting on his feet. "His exact words were, 'She's the prettiest woman I've laid eyes on in ages.'"

My insides heated. The shit on my plate was stacked a mile high. I couldn't handle Joe's shenanigans. "Yeah. Well, considering where he's spent the past few years, can't say that's much of a compliment." I shimmied my key into the lock.

Hearty laughter boomed from his chest. "He said you were feisty, too."

"Is there something I can do for you?" I snapped, turning again to face the annoyance at my back.

Lordy, he was gorgeous. The man was clearly into grooming. His thick, dark hair was cut tight and to perfection on the sides, while the top, slightly longer, was held in place with product. His brows were too perfect to not have been waxed and trimmed. He studied me with golden eyes that'd seen too much of the world's underbelly. Square jawline. Sculpted bulk that stretched the seams of his navy V-neck.

"Heard you had a little trouble this morning." His friendly smile withered, most likely in reaction to my grimace.

Ire prickled my skin. Still, I forced calm into my voice. "How do you know about my troubles?"

"Fuck. Sorry. I didn't introduce myself." He shoved a hand at me. "Officer Frank Garcia."

Like that explained anything.

"You're a cop?" I asked, giving him one good shake.

He stood taller, smiled wide, proud, and answered, "Yes, ma'am."

"Oh. You must be Joe's parole officer."

His snort was adorable. "No, ma'am."

"I'm Marley. You can drop the ma'am crap. And you still haven't told me how you know about my morning."

"Right." He wiped his forehead with the back of his hand. "Officer Watson and I go way back."

News traveled fast. Loose-lipped Watson would get a stern talking to next time we met.

"Listen." Frank tugged a wallet out of his back pocket, pulled a card from inside, and shoved the little white offering into my hand. "You call me if you have any trouble or questions. Anything. We'll get to the bottom of that fire. I promise."

We'll get to the bottom of it? "Frank. Thank you, really, but that's not necessary. I'm sure it was just an electrical malfunction or something."

I should've been scared or, at the least, worried. But more than anything, I was annoyed. I'd bet my life an electrical malfunction was not the cause. I'd hired the best electrician in south Seattle, and though I suspected foul play, Harper was not my number one suspect. Stupid kids out for a thrill would be my guess.

"You're Joe's girl. That makes you family, and we take care of our own." Frank stepped closer, all whimsy wiped from his expression. "So don't worry. We got you."

Seriously? Was the guy for real? "I'm not his girl! There's no getting to be had—"

A whistle came from across the yard, cutting my argument short.

Joe stood next to Frank's truck, Ginger tucked against his naked chest, jeans hanging low on his waist. I hadn't seen him in days, and the sight, as always, stole my breath.

"We're just neighbors," I mumbled, throat tight, heart aching for something I swore I'd never want.

Joe stared at me, lifting Ginger to drop kisses on her snout.

"Oh?" Frank laughed, the sound deep and hearty, the kind of chuckle that made you want to put your head against his chest to feel the vibrations. "If liars were tires..." he started, then dropped his chin and scratched the back of his neck. "If liars were... wires? No, that's not it." Again with the laugh. "You know what I mean."

I hadn't a clue. "What?"

"Never mind." He shook the thought away and hit me with twin dimples and dazzling white teeth. "Joe's as good as they come. Want my opinion?"

"No, not—" I started, but he didn't let me finish.

"Give that guy the benefit of the doubt. You think you know him based on a few facts. But that guy next door? He's the best man you're ever gonna know." He cocked an eyebrow in challenge, then scuffed a foot and chuckled. "Besides, any fool can see you're a match made in—"

"Hell?" It was my turn to interrupt.

With a huff, he looked over his shoulder, waved to Joe, then met my glare, his brows quirked in a cocky, *you know I'm right* expression. "Bye, neighbor."

"It's Marley," I grumbled. "And tell Joe to keep his mutt out of my yard. I've had to fill three holes under the fence this week."

Frank shook his head and left me to stew on my porch. I watched, seething, while he greeted Ginger with a pat and the two men made their way inside Joe's garage without another glance my way.

"Good riddance," I mumbled, the insult falling flat at my feet.

I grabbed my phone and laptop, headed outside with a new box of Milk Bones, then snagged the rubber ball because it was only a matter of time before my new bestie scrambled under the fence to play.

The chip in my Black Onyx nail lacquer, though annoying, served as a welcome distraction and an outlet for my nervous energy. Fleck by fleck, I picked, focused on the mindless task instead of worrying myself silly over life's more significant issues.

"Marley!" Marco shouted, jerking the wheel left, then right, throwing me side to side, shaking me from my introspect. He laughed, then asked, "You okay? You're awful quiet this morning."

I studied the man to my left. In Lilly's eyes, Marco Vicente was perfection. I couldn't disagree. I'd yet to find a flaw, but, as I knew too well, some imperfections took longer to surface.

"Thanks again, Marco. This means everything to me."

A smile cracked his face. "No worries, Marls. The guys were happy to step up, especially since you offered free beer and pizza." Marco rested one hand over his coffee mug, the other on the steering wheel. "Besides, Lilly would have my balls if I didn't help."

I laughed. "Well, that's true."

Investigators had given me the go-ahead to clean up the rubble, and the guys were to meet us at ten, dressed for demolition and disposal. We turned the corner and pulled into the lot where Pink Sweets used to boast a steady line of patrons.

"What the hell?" I leaned forward to get a better look, my heart rate spiking.

Nothing remained but charred marks on the pavement.

Singleton, Tye, and Shawn stood in a circle engaged in animated conversation.

I hopped out of the beat-up Ford and sighed a breath of relief. "You've finished already?" I pulled Singleton into a hug, not because I wanted to hug *him* necessarily but because I was so damn surprised, grateful and, well, happy. "I can't believe this."

"Done?" Singleton's arms tightened around me. "We just got here. Place was emptied."

Though tall and fit and definitely handsome, Singleton had zero effect on my libido. The embrace we shared was lovely but innocent in every way.

Two large motorcycles turned the corner, coming our way, one of which I recognized. At that familiar, rumbly sound and the daunting form commanding the metal beast, my body tensed, my skin shrinking around my muscles like a warm hug. A familiar Chevy followed and parked in the far corner.

I turned, still in Singleton's embrace, as Joe cut the engine and dismounted. His booted feet planted on the pavement, his stance solid and intimidating as he raised those glorious arms to remove his helmet. Swear to the caffeine gods, he singed me with a glare so volatile my insides revolted, tightening into an unforgiving knot.

Officer Frank Garcia hopped out of the Chevy, his thick-soled Danners hitting the pavement like thunder.

Singleton backed us away. If out of possession or fear, I couldn't tell. Joe detected the shift, his death glare aimed at our joined bodies. What a morbid thrill to catch him noticing, but what a betrayal the way my insides buzzed and hummed. I clung to Singleton but was one hundred percent tuned in to Joe.

"Hi," I managed to rasp. "What's up?"

"Hi, neighbor," he grunted, tucking his helmet under

one arm, wiping his brow with the back of his other, his severe glare bouncing between Singleton and me. "Heard they were done with the investigation. Guys and I thought we'd clean up this morning."

"You did this?" It took some maneuvering, but I managed to wiggle free of the arms cinched around my back.

"We did." Frank came my way, his grin tight. He, too, seemed to have issues with my proximity to Singleton, his shoulders straightening, chest puffed, gaze assessing.

Joe's friend Connor dismounted his bike and settled next to Frank. "Hey, little lady." He offered me a curt nod, then sized up Singleton, wrinkles forming between his brows.

Jeez, these men. "Hi, Connor."

Joe stepped closer. Whether conscious or not, Singleton took a step forward, too, positioning himself between Joe and I, effectively putting himself in danger, judging by the scowls coming from my neighbor and his posse.

Two steps closer, and Joe towered over my friend, offering a hand but asserting his dominance. "Joe Kaine."

"Isaac," Singleton offered.

The men shook hands, lingering, tension vibrating between them.

"Uh, Joe." I bumped Singleton out of the way. "You didn't have to go to all the trouble. I had everything under control."

"I see that." His attention darted from man to man, landing on Marco. "Who're your friends?"

I made introductions. When the testosterone cloud dissipated, I said, "I promised these guys beer and pizza for their hard work. Now they've got nothing to do, and it's a little early for pizza."

"Never too early for pizza," came from Tye.

Marco chimed in, "Or beer."

To which Singleton replied, "I'm famished."

"Woke up this morning thinking about sausage and pepperoni." That came from Connor.

I chanced a glance at Joe, who only shrugged.

"All right then. Pizza it is."

Singleton leaned back, stretched his arms wide, then rested one across the back of my seat, brushing my shoulder with warm fingers. "Thanks, Marls, you're the best."

Joe stiffened, shifting, his thigh falling against mine on my other side. A low rumble vibrated his chest.

Singleton chuckled. Bastard.

My body warmed, face heated. Mere seconds ago, the vibe had been chill, conversation entertaining. Suddenly, the air was ripe with the stink of male ego and unvocalized warnings.

Marco snagged the last slice of Hawaiian, eyeballed Joe, then shot me a wry grin. No doubt, he'd defend his friend if necessary, but he wouldn't enjoy being put in that situation.

To diffuse the ticking bomb, I said, "All right, boys," then pushed from my chair. "Enjoy the rest of your day. I need to get going."

"Give me a sec, Marls. Gotta hit the head, then I'll drive you home." Marco shoved the last two bites into his mouth.

"I'll take her." Joe shot to a standing position, his chair clunking into the empty table behind us.

"No. No. It's fine." I waved them off. "You boys finish eating. I'll Uber."

"No, you won't," Joe huffed. "I'm ready to go now."

"You're on a motorcycle," Singleton piped in, and I could swear his intention was to rile Joe.

Joe shot back, "I've got an extra helmet."

"I'm not getting on the back of that thing," I interjected.

To which Frank replied, "Joe's the best rider I know. You're safer on the back of his bike than in a tank."

"You're my next-door neighbor." Joe curled his fingers around my elbow. "Makes sense that I drive you."

"Fine. Fine." I threw up my arms, clearly the underdog in the argument. "Thanks again, guys. I appreciate your help so much." I blew kisses around the table.

Joe grunted, then grabbed my hand and stomped toward the exit.

Caveman move, for sure.

Our hands fit like a plug into a socket, tight and right, and oh jeez, I was energized.

Still, I wiggled free of his grip, grumbled, "I can walk on my own," then pushed past the man-beast and led the way to his Harley, squinting against the blinding reflection of the chrome.

While Joe worked on freeing the helmets from their locks, I drew three deep breaths, trying to slow my racing pulse, the anticipation of the ride almost unbearable.

"Turn around. Let me get you situated." While he settled the smaller of the two on my head, our breaths mingling, his eyes burning and bright, he said, "It's a beautiful day. Wanna go for a ride before we head home?"

"Yes," escaped my mouth before I had time to strategize, gather my bearings, or form a defense.

His chuckle hit me in the gut, warming my insides. "I hoped you'd say that."

He'd brought extra head protection for what? Just in case he bumped into me? Who did that?

He adjusted his own helmet, straddled his bike, then gave me the okay. "This your first time?"

"On a bike?" I swung my leg over and scooted close, happy to find wide rear floorboards to settle my feet. "No. But I was a kid, so I'm a little rusty."

"Don't worry, gorgeous. I'll take it easy on ya." The bike growled to life, and I cinched my arms around his waist, thankful for the face shield to hide my widening grin.

Before rolling into traffic, Joe said over his shoulder, "We won't go far. You're not dressed for a proper ride."

Go far? Who cared? My arms were around a gorgeous man, a rumbling machine between my legs. Open road. Pure, unadulterated joy. Five hours or ten minutes. Didn't matter. Heaven had stretched her arms and wrapped me in a hug.

Joe headed south, then cut through several residential streets until we were winding down a hidden road that led to Puget Sound.

The secluded stretch of beach was empty of humans. A wet dog chased a crow into the water, then trotted back to the sand, shook his long black fur, and then disappeared into the tall grass leading to a cluster of homes on the hill.

We dismounted. Joe helped me out of my helmet, took my hand, and led me to a weathered log. He sat, and I stood. Barges trolled through the water, and in the distance, two sailboats looked as if they'd collide, only to pass each other and continue in opposite directions.

"This is a great spot." I turned to find him staring up at me, a tinge to his cheeks. "Come here often?"

"No. Found it on my way to pick up Ginger from her foster family."

Our gazes locked, and my chest expanded against the rapid knocking. Stupid, traitorous heart.

Joe was, quite simply, beautiful.

"It was really great of you and your friends to help me out today."

With a shrug, he said, "Neighbors take care of each other."

"You remind me of Alice, ya know?"

"Yeah?" His lips tilted in a heartwarming grin. "How so?"

"She watched out for everyone, too." I could no longer tolerate the white-hot lick of his attention and turned again to take in the scenery.

"She was a great woman." He grunted, standing, then stood by my side. "Helped raise me."

"Really?"

He nodded, shoving his hands into the front pockets of his jeans. "My mom worked hard. Two jobs most of the time. Alice drove me to school every day, kept me off the streets and mostly out of trouble."

"Single mom?" I asked, hungry for more, ignoring the alarm bells in my head that clanged and donged their warnings of oncoming heartbreak.

I could not fall for Joe, but, Jesus save me, I liked him.

"Yes." His eyes warmed. "Great lady. Good mom." He plucked some rocks off the ground and moved closer to the water. "She married after I graduated high school. Moved to Spain."

He threw a stone, watched it arc, then fall.

I followed suit, grabbing a handful of pebbles. "And you stayed in Seattle?" I threw, but mine landed only half as far as Joe's.

He continued. "Moved in with Alice. Planned on staying through college."

"College?" escaped my lips with a tone of disbelief.

"Don't look so surprised." He chucked another stone,

then dropped the remaining rocks at his feet and dusted his hands together. "Finished my first year with honors."

"Sorry." A large fly bounced around my Keens, then landed on a piece of driftwood, its purple-and-green wings catching the sun's rays just right. I couldn't look Joe in the eye, ashamed of my judgmental wall. "What about your dad?"

Joe looked over his shoulder toward his bike, fists clenched. "That's a convo for another day."

"Sure," I conceded, understanding one hundred percent. My father was the sorest of subjects.

Joe and I walked along the shore, conversation light. He pointed out the three-story house where he'd fallen in love with Ginger. On our way back, he asked, "What's the deal with Singleton?"

Oh, jeez. I laughed. "You've been chewing on that question for a while, haven't ya?"

Joe frowned, but I'd grown tired of making him scowl. Something shifted inside my rib cage, a little painful at first, but then, as I stared up at the man who'd been patient and persistent despite my ugly behavior, my chest loosened, allowing me room to breathe, feel, and maybe, God forbid, let somebody in.

"Just friends," I assured him.

"Good answer," was his reply.

And I couldn't help myself from teasing, "We could never be more than buddies. He doesn't have a motorcycle. And you know how chicks dig bikes.

CHAPTER
Fifteen

J*OE*

Chicks dig bikes.

That's what they say, anyway.

The chick on my bike? That woman dug me. Hard. Me and my bike. How did I know? Because every time I hit the throttle, she howled, "Whoo!" Twice, her chest bounced in laughter against my back. Each time we came to a stop, those soft fingers remained splayed against my abdomen, our bodies fused.

Had I known a ride was all it'd take to loosen her up, I'd have offered weeks ago.

Fuck. The way she clung to my waist, her breasts smashed between our bodies, thighs gripping my hips, the way she leaned into every turn, moving with me like we were well-practiced partners. For that short ride, Joe Kaine, unemployed ex-con, was the fucking man.

I turned the corner for our street, and as I approached our houses, a white Z rolled past, the window half down. The driver wore dark shades, his face aimed our way, hair thick and dark. The guy did a double-take, then hit the gas.

I parked in my driveway, dismounted after Marley, and watched, grinning, while she removed her helmet. The fiery little shit gnawed her lip, fighting a smile and failing to hide her joy.

What a great goddamned sight.

"Did you see that Z?" I asked, nodding down the street.

She looked over her shoulder. "What Z?"

"Just passed us?"

"No. Why?"

"Seen that car before. Parked across the way from you and also two houses down. Just wondering who it belongs to."

"People park on these side streets and walk to the bus stop around the corner all the time." She waved my comment off like I talked nonsense.

Maybe I did.

I let my suspicions drop. Marley had worried enough the past few days.

She lifted the helmet in my direction. "Thanks for the ride."

"You had fun." I tucked my own helmet under my arm and snagged hers from her fingers.

"I did." Shoving her hands into her back pockets, she rocked back on her heels, fighting a grin, then nodded toward her house. "I should head in. Got a lot of work to catch up on."

No surprise—we had a good time, and she wanted to bolt. Fine. I'd let her go. Baby steps and all. But first... "Got a minute? I have something for you."

"My key?" she asked with too much enthusiasm.

Ignoring the jab, I led her inside where Ginger sprung from her perch on the couch and danced on her back legs at my feet, her front paws boxing at the air.

"Hey, girl." I scooped the fuzzball up and kissed her nose, heading for the back door. "Need to potty?" I gave her another kiss before opening the slider and setting her free to do her business.

I turned to find Marley biting back another grin.

"What?"

"You," she said, then cleared her throat. "With her."

Waving her hand between Ginger and me, she rasped, "It's too much."

"I don't understand."

"Well. You're"—she gestured up and down the length of my body—"huge, scary, and kinda intimidating, but then you baby talk to the ugliest creature I've ever laid eyes on. Seriously, it's freaking hot."

Yeah. Marley was into me, and she loved Ginger despite pretending otherwise.

Still, that insult to my pup would not go unpunished. The name-calling was only a poke at me, but I loved poking back. "Last time I'm gonna say this," I warned. "Ginger is not ugly. She's gorgeous. She's got nobody else in the world but me." I moved closer, pulled by that invisible force between us. "I'm gonna kiss the hell outta that little ragamuffin for the rest of our lives. Call her ugly again, and I'll throw you over my knee and spank all that nasty name-calling right outta your pretty ass."

If her cheeks had been hot before, they'd gone molten.

Marley's mouth dropped open, then snapped shut, her brows pinching. I'd caught her off guard. No doubt I'd be in the doghouse when she collected her wits.

Until then, I stalked closer, my blood pumping something fierce.

Marley backed away, her eyes going wide when her butt hit the dishwasher. I made my move before her demon tongue caught up with the rage exploding in those fiery eyes.

Hip to hip, I pinned that little firecracker where she stood and bent low, forcing her to lean back and arch her neck, our lips dangerously close. "Don't worry, neighbor. I'm not into kinky shit. Won't spank you unless you ask for a good hard smack."

Marley's lips parted on a gasp, or maybe a pant.

For fun, I slid my palm down her hip, then around to rest on her tight ass, giving her a firm squeeze. "Please be nice to my dog. She's had a rough life, and I need to make sure the rest of her years are nothing but love and cuddles."

I pressed my lips to her forehead, hoping to soothe the wrinkles that'd formed between her brows.

My cock was rock hard. Marley was primed for either a good fight or a good fuck, her chest rising and falling, her skin a delicious heat beneath my touch, but that wasn't the reason I'd brought her inside.

Okay. Lie. But I had another agenda.

I stood straight and opened the cupboard to my right. "I have no use for teacups. Thought you might like your pick before I pack these lovely ladies up for donation."

Marley released her death grip on my waist, turned, cleared her throat, and sighed, "Oh, Joe."

"You can have them all if you want."

Liquid eyes met mine. "Alice loved tea parties."

"She hid the most expensive sets in the back of her closet. Took them out maybe once a year to enjoy. Those are yours, too, if you want them."

Nodding, Marley said, "She shared them with me once. We had a tea party in the rose garden with some of her friends. She insisted I wear a dress and hat, but since I only own baseball caps and beanies, I borrowed one of hers." She ran a hand down the length of her hair. "It was this ridiculous teal and lace monstrosity." Marley laughed. Her eyes widened, and she sucked in a breath as if struck with an idea. "If it's okay with you, I'd like to share them with her friends. I think that's what she would've wanted, don't you?"

If I could've plucked my heart from my chest and served it to Marley in one of those porcelain fancies, I would have, because that woman owned me. How that happened, and how it happened so fast, was a mystery, but one I didn't care to solve.

"Perfect idea."

Marley turned her attention to the shelves of teacups. "She loved these so much."

A lifetime of memories sat on those shelves. Those cups and saucers reminded me of happier days, and to be honest, getting rid of them would sting. "You know, when I was younger, Alice tried to make me drink tea. I hated that shit." I laughed despite the heavy ache in my ticker. "But, damn, I'd kill for a cup of Earl Grey with my aunt right now."

"Me, too," she whispered, then sniffed.

God, how I wanted to pull her close, kiss the sadness away.

Marley beat me to the punch, burying her face in my chest, hugging my middle. Into my shirt, she mumbled, her voice cracking, "Thank you, Joe. This gift means the world to me."

Little did she know that in that small confession, her little gesture of thanks, her trust and welcoming my embrace, she'd given me the world, the moon, and all the fucking stars, too.

. ° . ° . °. ° . ° . °

I nudged the laundry basket aside, aware of the stench from my workout gear. If Marley noticed the aroma, she hid her reaction.

"The room looks..." She ran a hand over my black comforter, took in my surroundings. "Masculine."

Gone were the doilies and floral prints. Gravity gray paint covered walls once adorned with hideous floral-striped wallpaper. Alice's squeaky ancient bed ensemble, now laid to rest, had been replaced with a simple, sturdy black platform frame. Antique furniture no longer lined the perimeter. New nightstands and dressers occupied the space, industrial steel and repurposed wood. Not polished, but rugged and indestructible.

"Masculine, huh?"

Marley offered a slow smile. "Suits you."

The woman had no clue the depth to which those words pierced me or the heights they boosted my ego. She stood an arm's length away, smelling sweet and looking edible. Took all my strength to stay firmly planted instead of tackling her to my bed and demonstrating my manhood.

I turned to the closet, cleared my throat, and drew a cleansing breath. The old, heavy door stuck in the top corner, so I had to twist and yank the refurbished knob. Inside, the narrow space left little elbow room. I dug in, clearing clothes, shoe racks, and plastic containers to get to the box labeled *TEACUPS* buried in the back corner.

Marley helped stack items on the bed.

"Who's this?" she asked, holding a framed photo, the box next to her having lost its top.

I set the container I held on the bed and snagged the pic from her hand. "That's Bill." Rage welled, but I tamped that shit down tight.

"Bill?"

"Alice's husband." I tossed the frame back into the open container of old pictures. "My dad's brother."

"Weird." She dropped her butt onto the mattress. "This is the first time I've seen his picture. I knew she was widowed, but she didn't have photos out. She rarely talked about him."

"That's because he was a piece of shit, cheating bastard," came my clipped reply. Arms crossed, chest tightening, I leaned against the doorframe. "Though, honestly, nobody cared he shacked up with other women. Didn't hit her when his attentions were focused elsewhere."

"Hit her?" Marley clapped a palm to her mouth, her liquid eyes melting my insides. "She was so vibrant. So strong," she muttered, shaking her head. "It's hard to imagine she'd been hurt that way."

"Bill was a con man. Married Alice for her money." I stood straight, bracing for the weight of my confession. "Unfortunately, she figured that out too late. Alice didn't believe in divorce, but she did move into her own home."

Ginger trotted into the room and claimed her pillow.

"Money?" Marley whispered, staring through me, her eyes unfocused as if working something out in her head. "She barely scraped by these past few years."

There'd been little cash left in Alice's bank accounts when she passed, which made no sense. She'd lectured me for years on the importance of saving.

"She inherited over five million when her grandfather passed. Married Bill shortly after." I fought against the sting in the backs of my eyes, blinking, swallowing the lump in my throat. "She was nineteen, he was twenty-two, and from what I've heard, a charmer, though I never found a redeeming quality in the man."

"I had no idea." Marley pushed to stand. "For the last three years, I paid most of her bills." The look on her face reflected utter confusion.

"What do you mean, you paid her bills?"

Marley stared long and hard over my shoulder, unblinking. Her chest rose and fell, and she seemed resigned by the time her eyes met mine. "Never mind. It doesn't matter."

Yeah, she wasn't leaving that comment to hang in the air. "Matters to me."

With a huff, she conceded, "She left mail laying around

all the time. Shut-off notices, late notices. I asked about them once. She assured me everything was under control, but the bills kept coming." She shrugged, her voice going soft. "I knew she wouldn't accept my help, so when she wasn't looking, I snagged them and made sure they got paid."

My heart swelled. Yeah, Marley wanted the world to see her cold, hard, jagged edges, but inside, that woman was nothing but fluff.

"Stealing mail?" I teased, a pathetic attempt to cut the tension. "You little thief."

Unamused, Marley asked, "Joe?"

"Yeah, gorgeous?"

"Why did she keep all of this from me?"

God, I wanted to kiss that pout away. "Alice was a proud, stubborn woman." Unable to stay my distance, I edged forward, closer to her. I cupped that sad face and caressed her soft skin because I needed the warmth of her flesh under my fingertips. "Obviously, my aunt was bonkers. I mean, jewelry in the cupboards, unpaid bills when she had always been a whiz with her finances. Always digging up and replanting those damn rose bushes. I found half-smoked stogies shoved down the sink. Yards and yards of PVC pipe in the basement."

Dewy eyes met mine. Marley released a soft laugh and dropped her forehead to my chest. "PVC pipe?"

"What the hell, right?" I chuckled. "I'd give my left testicle to hear Alice explain that purchase."

"She used to make late-night trips to Home Depot. I caught her a few times, tried to help her unload her car, but she shooed me away like she had a big secret."

Delightfully eccentric, my aunt. "God, I loved that woman."

"Me, too." Marley gave me one last squeeze, then

stepped away, my chest caving with every inch of distance that came between us.

"Marley," came out of my mouth, quick and desperate. I pulled her back to me, then caught her chin.

I wanted so much from this woman. Conversations. Laughter. Smiles. Her tears. I wanted to be the man who made her moan, the reason she was happy to wake up in the morning. I wanted more Alice stories.

I did not want her to leave.

Her head tilted up, mine down. Mere breaths separated us and, sweet temptation, her mouth was parted, those lips soft and edible, her minty breath a tease and an invitation.

"I should go," she said on a soft exhale.

Her half-mast lids and the glow on her skin told me she wanted a kiss as much as I did. She wanted me. Still, she held back, but not because she believed I was a criminal. Deeper, darker issues lurked behind that lusty gaze.

To test my theory, I dipped closer. Marley did not disappoint. Her lids fell closed, and she readied for a taste, but I didn't follow through. I caressed her dewy lip with my thumb, then slid my hand to the back of her head, tangled her hair in my fingers, and I held her there, wanting. But I wouldn't take, not this time. The next move was hers to make.

Freed from the spell, her eyes snapped open, the lust morphing into that scowl I craved.

Sweet torture.

"Marley, Marley, Marley. What am I gonna do with you, huh?"

"Jerk." She slapped my chest and pushed away, and hell, her lips quivered, fighting a grin again. Yeah, she wanted me.

Too bad she hadn't figured that out yet.

I retrieved the fragile cups from the closet and headed

downstairs, silent but satisfied. Marley opened the front door. I carried the box to her house, waited for her to open up, then slid the container into her arms. "Come get the rest whenever you're ready. I'll box 'em up."

"Thank you, really. I can't tell you how much this means to me."

It didn't go unnoticed that she blocked the entrance, but I wouldn't push. A woman needed to feel safe in her space.

"See ya 'round, gorgeous."

"Bye, Joe."

I jogged across the yard, then marched upstairs to take care of my boner.

Wednesday was garbage day. Much like every other day of the week, I rose around seven, stumbled through my morning routine with Ginger under my feet, and planned my day while sucking down a hot mug of dark roast. I finished my second cup of coffee, waiting for the clatter and bang of the Waste Management trucks to pass before heading outside to collect the emptied bins.

Cold cement bit my bare feet while I padded down the driveway, my attention focused on the house next door. I knew Marley wasn't home, because like every other morning, I stood at my window while she warmed her car and watched until she pulled out of the driveway. If I couldn't personally send her off with a kiss while kneading that spectacular ass, at least I could make sure she traveled from her front door to her Subi without running into danger. As I headed back up the drive, movement caught my eye, a large figure slipping behind Marley's house.

"The fuck?" Barefoot and bare-chested, I jogged across her lawn. The man—and I knew the perp was male by his stature—slipped through her back gate as I rounded the corner, his head covered in a black beanie, face and neck shielded by a blue mask, hammer dangling from his gloved hand.

Blood-red mist clouded my vision.

Sprinting, I shoved through the gate, dead set on immobilizing the bastard. I reached him mid-strike, hammer raised to the glass, and tackled the stranger away from her back door. The weaselly fucker knew how to wrestle, but between dodging blows and trying to stay upright, I landed three good strikes to his gut.

On the third, he wheezed and stumbled backward, the mask around his face askew. Our eyes met briefly before he ran the way he'd come. I gave chase but quit before I hit the gnarly pavement of our street, the pads of my feet already throbbing in protest.

I limped home after closing her gate, curled Ginger to my chest, and called Frank.

Twenty minutes later, I gave my statement. Fifteen more, and Marley sped into her driveway, slammed the brakes, stormed my way and, more animated than necessary, got up in my face.

"Did you see him?" was the first question she asked. "What did he look like? How tall was he?" She studied my eyes as if she could pull images of the guy from my pupils. "Young or old? Dark hair?"

Hell, the woman appeared excited, which made no sense. Still, I answered, "Only thing I know for certain was he had blue eyes, pale skin. Five-ten, five-eleven maybe."

One of the cops, Officer Watson, took Marley aside and spoke to her in private. She shook her head, gnawed her thumbnail, talked in whispered tones. A piece of lace, white and sheer, hung out between her baggy pink sweatpants and white hoodie. Clearly, her work costume.

My blood heated. Fuck. Did those cops know what she did for a living? Did they picture what she wore underneath that heavy cotton?

Watson stood a respectful distance away, maintaining eye contact except when he jotted notes on his pad, while the other officer—Hayes, Haynes, or Heims, I couldn't remember—bagged the hammer. Both of them remained strictly professional, thank fuck, because with the adrenaline pumping through my veins, who knew how I'd have responded had they looked at my girl the wrong way.

Heh. My girl. I chuckled, then shook the thought away.

I needed them gone, wanted Marley to myself. Her familiarity with that Watson character raised my hackles.

When the blue Ford sedan finally rolled away, Marley made her way to where I'd settled on her patio lounger, my legs outstretched, my dirtied feet crossed at the ankles. Ly would have a few choice words at my next appointment.

Arms crossed, she stared down at me. "You sure he had blue eyes?"

What the hell? "Why you stuck on the eye color, Marley?"

The woman closed her eyes, drew in a long breath. "Never mind." Those gorgeous peepers, framed in dark liner and shades of golds and browns, opened, spilling a thousand tales of heartbreak. "Thank you, Joe," she whispered. "What would I have come home to if you hadn't seen that guy?"

I fought a shiver. The thought of Marley injured, or worse? Fuck. I wanted to drag her into my castle and lock her away from every threat in the world.

Bruises and cuts marred my skin from head to hips. I

clapped the sides of my feet together. "If I'd had shoes on, that guy'd be six feet under Alice's rose bushes by now."

She didn't laugh, but she stepped closer, brushed a fingertip over my swollen lip. "You want me to drive you to the hospital? Make sure you didn't break any bones or damage that giant ego of yours?"

Only one thing could dull my aches. I lunged forward, hooked that slim waist, flattened her against my chest, and took what I'd needed since the last time we'd been together.

Palms to my chest, she pushed, but she parted her lips and let me in, and damn, the contact hurt like a mother. I didn't care. Nothing mattered but her body against mine, the taste of her minty gloss, the heat of her jagged breaths.

Marley wiggled, and I tightened my hold because, fuck no, she wasn't bolting. With a sigh, she shifted, straddled my lap, and broke the kiss.

"Joe"—she shook her head, eyes glazed—"I can't."

"Shut up." I jackknifed forward, thrust my hand under her heavy sweatshirt, and palmed her fabulous breast. "Stop pretending you don't want me," I grunted, pinching an already tight bud through the lace of whatever getup she wore under her sweats.

Her back arched, pressing her pussy harder against my growing erection. "I need to get back..." Her voice trailed off, her hips rocking as I worked her breasts.

"I almost died today defending your home." Between her legs, my cock swelled to throbbing, scalding steel. "You wanna thank me. I can tell."

Her laugh fizzled when I claimed her mouth. While our tongues tangled in slow seduction, I worked on removing her annoying cotton barrier, tugging the hem up, up, breaking the lip-lock to pull the shirt over her head.

Sweet Jesus.

Lace clung to her chest, see-through except for her

nipples, but loosened at the waist. I explored, shoving a hand down her backside, thrilled but also appalled to find nothing but a string ducking between her ass cheeks. The view was a privilege, and none of the men she'd served today deserved this gift. Lucky fuckers. All of them.

A single word played on repeat in my head. More. More, more, more. Desperation made men weak and foolish. Color me stupid because I needed, more than air, to be inside my beautiful neighbor. Claim what was mine. Mark my territory. Make her moan and scream and beg. Fill her so full of me she had no doubt that I alone was created to worship her body.

Sweet heavenly torture, I was about to explode. "Let's take this inside, gorgeous." I hooked a finger around that string of lace and tugged. "Wanna see you in these panties. Strip them down your thighs with my teeth, then fuck that pussy with my tongue."

The color of her cheeks was sensual enough, but when she pressed down hard against my erection, then dragged her cunt over the length of me, the euphoria damn near knocked me unconscious. I hissed, my body jerking.

Marley didn't stop. The woman slid one hand around my head, fisting my hair. The other held my shoulder tight, and she rocked and rocked, kissed me, then bit my lip. She slapped my hands away when I tried to touch her breasts or pull her close.

"Don't move, Joe," she panted before biting my earlobe. "Let me give this to you."

When a woman like Marley says, "Let me give this to you," you fucking hand over the reins. I sunk into the cushion and gripped the sides of the chair with deadly force. But fuck, with those tits in my face, the friction where she rubbed me, the noises she made while chasing her release, the scent of coffee mixed with her shampoo, or lotion, or whatever girlie shit she wore? Every ounce of willpower I possessed stretched to the breaking point.

We were nothing but sex and flesh and the thrill of the chase. Marley rocked while I thrust in response. We could have taken seconds or hours—who cared when we were lust drunk—but when Marley tossed her head back, mouth open in a silent scream, I blew my load inside my Calvin Kleins, and that shit just kept coming.

Marley fell against me, yet still, I quaked through the intense release, my arms around her once again, muttering, "Fuck, fuck, fuck," into her neck because that was the only word I could form.

When the rise and fall of our chests slowed, Marley dismounted, tugged the sweatshirt back over her head, and smiled.

"I need to get back to work," she rasped before turning to saunter away. She threw over her shoulder, "Oh, and thank you for being my hero today," then left me alone in a sex coma on her patio.

The woman would be the death of me.

And I would die with a dopey smile on my face.

CHAPTER
Sixteen

MARLEY

There he stood at my door with a dopey smile on his face. Warren. The last man I ever wanted to see.

Bile rose despite his beauty. Thick, wavy hair fell over bright eyes that sparkled no matter his mood. Deep dimples gave a false sense of warmth and sincerity. Women all over the country had fallen for his magnetism. Me? I'd numbed to his charm years ago.

"Hey, girl." His deep, rich timbre still made my heart gallop like a herd of wild horses running to their doom off the edge of a cliff.

"I told you never to come here." I gripped the door with one hand and the frame with the other, blocking his view of my personal space. "I don't want to see you."

He looked past me, sniffed, and nodded before meeting my glare. "You're my girl. We need each other."

That was true once upon a million heartbreaks ago. "I don't need you."

"I've changed."

Changed? Heaven help me.

"How many times have I heard those words?" I roared, knowing the point was moot. "They mean nothing."

The man flinched, then set his shoulders straighter. "Your heart is hard as a rock, baby, and I get that's mostly my fault, but someday you're gonna have to let me in."

"Just go. Please."

When I moved to shut the door, he threw out the old classic, "I miss you."

Those words—I miss you—used to mean something. They'd given a young, foolish girl hope. Hope, sometimes, was more destructive than heartbreak.

Pissed and so done with Warren and his games, I opened the door wider and seethed, "Good. You should miss me. I hope it hurts." He could never suffer enough in my opinion. "I hope you feel hollow inside. I hope the guilt of being a shitty person eats you alive from the inside out."

"You don't mean that." He studied me head to toe, then faked a warm smile and took a step closer. "You look good, sweetheart."

No denying, the man was handsome. Seemed the full package at first glance. It would've been so easy to fall into his arms, absorb his words and attention, pretend that he loved me like he should, and let him back into my life so he could rip my heart to shreds all over again. Destroy me. All over again. I'd been caught in that trap for too damn long. Lesson learned.

I loved him. I hated him.

"Get off my property." I shoved hard at his chest, pushing him away. "Don't come back. Do you hear me?"

"I'm not leaving." He threw his arms out wide, that cocky arrogance spilling through the glint in his eyes and the lift of his chin. "You can't get rid of me. I'm staying right here until you talk to me."

"The lady asked you to leave."

I jumped at the gruff tone. Warren turned to face the intruder.

My big, beautiful, terrifying, angry neighbor came up the steps, slow and calculated, a man ready for battle. "You'd be wise to do what she asked."

Joe had the intimidation factor dialed to deadly—his

stance set for a fight, a brutal lock to his jaw, a fierce glare that made me back away in self-preservation.

I swallowed the lump in my throat and managed to whisper, "I've got this, Joe."

Now standing toe to toe, neither one of the men paid me any mind, staring each other down like fighters waiting for the go-ahead to pummel each other. Their size difference was laughable. Joe stood at least a foot taller and fifty pounds heavier than Warren.

Bless Warren's poisonous heart, he didn't back down. I was morbidly proud of the man because there was no way, if provoked, Joe wouldn't pulverize the guy.

Excruciating seconds passed, my ticker hammering for reasons I did not want to contemplate.

Finally, Warren broke the tension, shooting me a quick glance. "Marley?"

He wasn't seeking guidance on how to handle the situation. He was questioning my relationship with the other man on my porch. He had no right to be concerned.

No doubt, if given the okay, Joe would throw Warren off my property, and by the look on his face, he'd find the most unpleasant way to do so.

I hated Warren, but I didn't want him bloodied or dead. "Just go."

Warren released a breath, his shoulders dropping. "Fine, baby girl. I'll go for now, but we gotta talk." Avoiding my glare, he ducked his head, shoved past Joe, and trotted down the porch steps.

Joe blocked my view of Warren's retreat, arms crossed over his chest. "This guy gonna be a problem?"

Heavens, he smelled good, like fresh laundry and an overload of testosterone.

"He's been a problem for a very long time." I rubbed at

the ache in my temples. "My problem. And thank you, but I can handle him."

Joe huffed, then stepped back, giving me space I hadn't asked for but needed desperately.

His assessment stripped me raw so that every naked, vulnerable nerve was exposed. His eyes softened, betraying his concern. "You look like you need a drink."

He looked like a puppy waiting for a treat.

He'd had my back, and though I didn't need his white knight gesture, he'd been there, and that meant something. Still, defenses always up, I reminded him, "You know what happens when we drink."

Joe nodded, his gaze dropping to the floor between us. He gnawed his lower lip, fighting a smirk, then lifted his eyes to mine. "How about we go for a ride instead?"

"No" fell from my lips on instinct.

My false bravado didn't fool him. "Nothing clears your head better than the open road. It's a gorgeous afternoon." He took another step back, giving me more space to think clearly. Hand to his chest, he promised, "I'll be a perfect gentleman."

Wouldn't be a terrible thing to get out of my head for a while. Plus, he smelled amazing. "Okay," I conceded.

"Yeah?"

Jeez, that smile. Too youthful for a man so dangerous.

"Sure." I stepped deeper into my house, fearful I might jump him on my front porch. "Why not?"

"Great. But you'll need to change into jeans and a warmer shirt. Boots, too, if you have them."

"No problem."

Joe clapped his hands together, turned, and jogged down the steps, then shouted over his shoulder, "Meet me out front in ten."

Though hard and full of splinters, the worn wooden bench was a reprieve from the bike's vibrations, and the aroma from the food truck had my mouth watering and my stomach grumbling.

Joe had been right. My head was clear.

My heart, however, ached something fierce. I'd been fighting tears for hours despite the wonderful ride.

Joe strode my way, balancing four plates, his heavy boots kicking up dust. He set the food down, then straddled the bench and scooted close, blocking my view of the patrons lined up for the famous fish tacos. The setting sun hit the shiny tin kitchen on wheels, and I suspected Joe was protecting me from that blinding glare as well. That was Joe, I realized. A guardian.

He placed one hand on my neck, rubbing his thumb in a slow circle, and his other on the table. "Wanna talk about that guy who was at your house earlier?"

I picked at my thumbnail, resenting the ache that was left in my chest every time Warren showed up. I didn't want to talk about him, but sometimes, talking about the ugly things made them a little less heavy.

Joe dropped his arm as if sensing I needed space.

"Not much to say, really. The man crushed me." I sucked in a long breath for courage, allowing time to choke down the emotion. "Took too many years to wise up and cut him out of my life." I lifted a taco from the plate, brought it to my lips, and said, "He keeps coming back for more," before taking a bite.

Joe waited a few seconds before turning to grab his own

food. "Can't say I blame him. You're a hard girl to give up." His tone left no doubt about his sincerity.

"Why do you say that?" I nudged him with my elbow. "You hardly know me. We've had sex. Had a few great conversations, some not-so-great conversations, and I've mostly been horrible to you."

"Yeah." He smirked, shooting me a sideways glance. "We've fucked. Fabulous fucking. Hands down, the best I've ever had, so there's that." He took a breath, his head bobbing. "You're funny. You're explosive. Smart and head-strong." He shoved a taco into his mouth and chewed, making me wait. "You make a killer cup of coffee. And you are, by far, the prettiest woman I've ever laid eyes on."

I was no stranger to compliments. In my line of work, flattery hit like a hailstorm, hard and fast, bouncing off my thick skin, leaving me cold and annoyed. Compliments from Joe were like the first hint of sunshine after a long stretch of damp, gray days. I wanted to stand naked under the blue sky and bask in the warm glow.

Uncomfortable with the heat rolling through me, I busied myself with a long swig of root beer.

Joe cleared his throat, wiped the grease off his fingers, then wadded the napkin in a tight fist before turning to face me again. "I see you, Marley. You're trying to hide from me, but I see you."

"Yeah?" I asked, studying the graffiti on the building across the street. "What do you see?"

"A hard shell protecting a bruised heart."

Me in a nutshell. "You're not wrong."

"I'm not a bad guy, and I'm not someone you need to protect yourself from."

I turned to straddle the bench and stared at Joe's massive chest before meeting his earnest gaze. "Despite what you think or how I act around you, I'm not unhappy. I like my life."

Warm eyes studied me, a soul-deep probe. With a sigh, Joe asked, "You ever been married?"

"No."

"That guy who was at your house earlier, he a boyfriend?"

"Oh, God no." I scrubbed my hands over my face, a laugh erupting. "That sorry excuse for a man is my father."

"He's your dad?" Joe jerked back, sitting straighter. "I should've shown some respect."

"He doesn't deserve your respect. Trust me."

"I see." Joe stared long and hard, then cleared his throat before saying, "Daddy issues."

My wounds ran deeper than the damage my father had inflicted. True, I had a history of looking for love in all the wrong places and, yes, I had one hundred percent blamed my father until I'd realized dads weren't the only assholes who left. All men left. At least, the men in my life. Unhealed wounds started to ache, and tears threatened to fall.

Joe laid a hand on my thigh and gave a gentle squeeze. "He really did a number, huh?"

I blinked against the burn behind my eyes. "Can we not talk about Warren anymore?"

"Not a problem." He smiled and grabbed the last taco off the plate. "You want this?"

I shook my head no.

He finished his meal in three bites, pure bliss on his face. Jeez, the man was striking. My stomach fluttered. Not only because he was so attractive, but because, dammit, I really liked Joe Kaine.

"Can I ask you a personal question?"

He wiped his mouth with a napkin. "I've been inside you. Multiple times. Doesn't get more personal than that."

"What were you in for?"

"Ah, shit." He scratched his forehead, then dropped his gaze to the space between us.

"That bad?"

Chin down, he lifted his eyes to mine. "You really wanna know?"

"I do," I blurted before considering the consequences. But did I? Knowing the truth might forever change our twisted dynamic. "I don't." I shook my head with little conviction. But then curiosity would eat me alive. A nervous laugh escaped, and I admitted, "I don't know."

Joe assessed our surroundings, I assumed to make sure no one was in earshot. He leaned close and whispered, "Killed a man. It was an accident," then leaned back again, eyes worried, waiting for my response.

"Oh." That was far worse than the criminal shenanigans I'd imagined. "Ohhhh." I'd lost my ability to speak.

"Not proud of what I've done." He grabbed my hands and held them tight as if afraid I would flee. "Paid my dues."

"Hmm."

"That all you've got to say?"

He'd taken a life. That had to be a complicated, painful truth to live with. "Wow. Murder."

He dropped my hands and stood, clearly not at ease with my response. "An accident," he snapped, his tone bitter. "I'm not a bad guy. You can check my records. Not a mark against me."

"Except one," I blurted because, shit, I couldn't help myself sometimes, always on the defense, building those walls.

"Just one," he mumbled, gathering our trash.

"One big mark." *With a capital M*, I left unsaid. I stood and grabbed our empty cups.

"My best friend is a cop." He headed to the trash can.

I followed. "Yeah. Met Frank. Nice guy." I knew from experience that not all cops were on the up and up. "Are you trying to convince me of something?"

He held open the dirty lid to the recycle bin while I deposited our paper cups. "I like you, Marley, and don't want my past to ruin our friendship."

With that, we headed back to his bike and he helped me with my helmet, not another word shared between us.

. ° . ° . °. ° . ° . °

The ride home ended too soon. There hadn't been enough time to process Joe's confession, my reaction, or my guilt over the way I'd treated him since we met. Warring emotions had my guts twisted and my head fuzzy. True, my neighbor was an ex-con. But he wasn't a career criminal like I'd assumed. Joe was not the man I'd accused him of being for the sake of protecting myself.

Still, he'd killed another human being, and taking another's life had to mess with someone's psyche, right?

Joe parked in his driveway and walked me to my door, his tension palpable.

Before inserting my key into the lock, I turned and raised my chin to meet his sullen gaze. "Thank you for today. You were right. The ride and the company were exactly what I needed."

A low groan rose in his throat, his usual swagger gone. My heart bled for him. One hand planted on the door above my head. With the other, he pulled a strand of my hair through his fingers, his gaze tender.

"Please tell me I didn't scare you away." Regret laced his voice.

"I'm not scared." I drew a deep breath. "I appreciate honesty. Even when the truth sucks."

With a huff, he dropped his arms and gave me space. "The truth sucks, and I wish you didn't have to know. I wish you could've known me before..." He laced his hands behind his head, staring long and hard over my shoulder before focusing on me once again. "Just before." He waited for me to respond.

But words failed to form. Instead, pain lanced my chest. I'd given the man every reason to fear telling me his truth.

Joe wasn't the dangerous soul in our friendship. I was.

Tucking his hands into the front pockets of his jeans, he shrugged. "I like you, Marley, and I want the chance to get to know you better."

Cue the weak knees and sweaty palms. And, suddenly, I needed to protect Joe. From me. From my bitter, broken heart.

"Joe. I'm not good at..." I couldn't finish the sentence, my racing heart at odds with my common sense.

"Relationships," he stated, no judgment in his tone.

"Getting close to people," I corrected him, the words sour on my tongue.

Joe stared for a long moment before settling back on his heels and crossing his arms. "You have no problem getting close to people. I've seen you with your friends. Letting them in is where your trouble lies."

Unsettling how well he knew me. I nodded because he wasn't wrong.

Finally, he shortened the distance between us. "How do I get in? Tell me what I need to do."

Damn my traitorous heart. The man had already burrowed halfway through my wall. I couldn't afford to give him all of me. But I was tired of pushing him away. I liked him too much.

The porch light flickered above us, drawing my attention away from his heated gaze. A moth bounced around the bulb, casting a large shadow. I wasn't brave enough to face Joe when I said, "Okay. You have needs. I have needs." What was I doing? "How about we help each other out with those needs?"

Joe laughed. "Fucking."

I cringed.

"If that's what you mean, just say it. You wanna keep fucking me."

"You are ridiculously attractive." Damn my rapid heartbeat. "And talented in the... fucking department."

"Yeah?" He moved closer, his chest bouncing in amusement. "I got skills? Wasn't so sure with the way you disappear every time."

My smile faded under the weight of shame.

Joe tucked a knuckle under my chin, tilted my head up and, oh, Lordy, he licked his lips and smirked. "So, you're asking me to be your fuck buddy? No strings?"

"Yes," I rasped, then cleared my throat. "At least until you find someone who can give you a relationship."

"I won't."

"You don't know that."

"I know." He dropped a soft kiss on my forehead.

My heart skipped at least three beats. "If we do this, there's no one else. If someone else comes along, we let each other know and make a clean break."

"Mmm," he groaned. "Sounds like a relationship."

"It's just sex."

"Right." His hand moved to my hip, those soft lips hovering over mine.

"Mutual pleasure," I stated, though my tone held no authority.

"Mutual orgasms. Got it." He moved closer, his feet now bracing mine.

Through labored breaths, I managed to ask, "We gonna do this?"

"Absolutely."

"Starting now?"

His erection swelled between us. "All that power between your legs got you hot and bothered?"

"That," I agreed, "or maybe the fresh air."

"So it was the bike and the fresh air, not my lethal charms?"

"Never mind." Palm to his chest, I pushed him back and teased, "You've ruined the mood."

Joe attacked with raw, lustful determination, grabby hands, hungry lips, and that iron-hard cock rubbing between us. First, he bruised my lips, then went for my neck. Under the waning light of my porch, he took his fill, basting my skin in kisses and nips, marinating my soul with moans and dirty promises. Oh, shit, my skin was amped, my body tenderized, and that glorious space between my thighs was wet and swollen and aching to be pummeled.

Never had a man put so much effort into making me feel, to making me smile, to making me... his.

Everything about Joe was extraordinary. From his rugged good looks to the way he cared for people, for Ginger, for his neighbors. His hard spots. His soft spots. His persistent attempts to make me like him. His laugh. His moans.

"Oh, yes," I whimpered.

Joe pulled away, his grin salacious, then dropped his forehead to mine. "Mood still ruined?"

"Hell, no. Do it again."

"Damn, you're sweet." He kissed my nose. "And so fucking into me." He nipped my ear. With another sexy moan, his hands slid down my waist and rested on my backside. "You can't get enough of me. Admit it."

"Never." God, I was screwed.

A sharp sting hit my backside.

"Ow!" I laughed. "What was that for?"

"Because you drive me fuckin' crazy," he rasped before attacking my neck again.

Ginger's muted bark sounded from inside his house. We both turned our heads. Her gnarly, happy little face peeked through the curtain of the side window, and she yapped something fierce. She had to have climbed on top of the side table to see out the window.

Joe growled, pulling me tighter between his arms. "That dog is not cock-blocking me right now."

"She is." I wiggled free. "Go let her out. I'll take a quick shower and meet you over there."

"Fine," he grumbled, letting me go. "You're not at my door in ten minutes, I'm coming after you."

"Give me twenty," I said, turning to put my key in the lock.

Joe backed away, and before slipping through the door, I said, "I hope you're not expecting me to spend the night."

To which he replied, "Only one woman sleeping in my bed, and she's six and a half pounds of ferocious when it comes to sharing." His smile put the setting sun to shame.

CHAPTER
Seventeen

What a shame. Morning sun oozed through the curtains, and I lay alone with painful morning wood, craving a soft body to sink into. Marley's, to be specific.

Body aching, I rolled over and nuzzled Ginger's snout. "What's with that woman?" I asked my bed buddy. "She's clearly into both of us. Why won't she stick around?"

Seriously, Marley studied me like I was a work of art and fucked me like I was her favorite rock star, yet, after she'd come twice on my face and once on my dick, she'd bolted again.

Daddy issues were shit. Knew that better than anyone. But Marley's emotional well ran deeper than suffering a deadbeat dad. How many ghosts of boyfriend's past did I need to expel before she'd trust me?

Only thing I knew for sure was I hadn't slept a wink, and six AM was too goddamned early to figure anything out. Then again, maybe I'd never know. Women were puzzles, and mind games weren't my jam.

I jogged down the stairs, brewed coffee, then headed to the front door for a peek outside. The neighborhood was quiet. Two squirrels played chase up and down the telephone pole, then scrambled across the fence and down the alley.

Across the street sat the same white Nissan I'd seen

more than once. The NISMO. White with black tinted windows—darker than legal. New tires. She was a beauty.

The coffee pot sputtered, squeezing out the last drops of java, dragging my attention away from the view. I was about to turn around when the driver's door of the suspect car inched open.

A man stepped out, by no means in a hurry, clinging to the roof and top of the door, head bowed as if in prayer, either that or an extreme bout of psyching himself up. A Mariner's cap covered his head, but long, dark hair covered the back of his neck, and he wore a dark hoodie and jeans.

He stared at Marley's home for half a minute, his hip resting against the car before he shut the door, walked toward her house, then stopped at the end of the driveway, hands fisted at his sides.

I willed the guy to keep going, to make one wrong move so I had reason to step outside and bloody my knuckles. He stared at Marley's house while agonizing seconds ticked away on Alice's old rooster clock. Tick. Tick. Tick.

Thump, thump, thump beat my ticker against my rib cage.

The guy's chest rose and fell. He took another step forward, shook his head, then dropped his chin before retreating back to his car, shoulders slumped in defeat.

The perp was tall. Thin. Carried himself like a man yet to reach his full potential. Tucked back into his Z, he rolled away, quiet and too damn slow.

"What's your deal?" I mumbled to the window. The guy didn't seem threatening, but who was he to Marley?

Friend? Ex?

Stalker?

Shit. Who really was the creeper? Me. Standing in nothing but boxers, peering through the half-open shades like an old biddy.

Ginger agreed, yapping and snapping my attention back to where it belonged—her empty food bowl.

Exhausted from last evening's erotic workout, I zombied through my morning routine, then hauled Ginger to the backyard to talk to the roses.

The garden had been Alice's refuge, her babies, her fuck-you to my uncle. For me, these thorny beauties had become a sounding board, much like Alice had been. I supposed, in a way, taking care of them made up for the years I'd missed with my aunt. For Alice, I would keep her roses not only alive but thriving.

That was if I could keep my little princess from digging them up.

"Ginger!" I blew a whistle. "Leave it!"

Excavation paused for five seconds before she huffed and continued on her mission. Little shit.

"Girl," I warned, stalking her direction.

The pup bounced away, then attacked a stick twice her size before frolicking after a wayward bee.

Fucking adorable, that little troublemaker.

Seemed I had a thing for spirited females.

⁕ ⁕ ⁕ ⁕ ⁕

Ginger shivered in my lap, her head resting on tiny paws, her wiry fur rough but soothing under my calloused fingertips. The rhythm of my racing pulse slowed to match the slight rise and fall of her body.

Marley was usually home by six, and my cell told me it was eight forty-five.

Connor threw back the last of his IPA and tossed the

empty into the paper bag between our feet. "What's eating you, bro?"

"Nothin'," I grunted, staring at the orange flames dancing in the firepit, the grass beneath my feet freshly cut and cool, but not cool enough to soothe the current of unease under my skin.

"Looks like you're working through some shit."

I nodded.

"Give it to me." He settled deeper into his lawn chair and stretched out his legs. "I'm a good listener."

True. Con loved a good heart-to-heart, especially after a beer or two. Pathetic as my concerns were, I told him, "Marley's not home yet."

His right eyebrow hitched. "And?"

"She's never home later than six. I drove by Pink Sweets today, and they said she'd taken the day off."

"Are you her daddy now?" he teased, crossing his arms over his chest, wearing a smirk. "She break curfew?"

The mental image of Marley riding my cock and calling me "Daddy" made me chuckle. "No."

"So, what's the deal?"

When I shifted in my chair, Ginger grunted her disapproval. "Someone tried to break into her house the other day. This morning, I watched another guy creeping onto her property."

"Get a look at his face?"

"No. Sun was barely up, and he wore a cap."

"Get his license plate?"

"No."

Con perched an elbow on his armrest, leaning closer. "What are you thinking?"

"You know what she does and what kind of men frequent her stands."

"You're worried some psycho is stalking her."

Bingo. "Something like that."

Con sat back, then said to the sky, "I get the feeling you're the only asshole she needs to worry about."

"You're a terrible therapist."

"Maybe." My friend laughed. "But you're whipped."

Ginger's head popped up, and she lunged off my lap and ran around the corner of the house.

"I need another beer." I snagged a bottle out of the cooler and popped the lid.

"Got one for me?" That voice, though sloppy, set me at ease. I turned, and my muddy heart pumped harder, clearing the sludge from my veins.

Something was off, and while I wanted to spring into action, wrap my arms around my girl, I played it cool because she wasn't really my girl. Not in her mind, anyway. Also, she wore nothing but a long T-shirt and one shoe. A million scenarios explaining her state of undress raced through my head, leaving me dumbstruck.

She took my offered beer and dropped her ass to the grass beside my chair. Stringy hair hung in her face, and though it was dark, the fire lit her profile enough to show she was a mess: red, swollen eyes marred with streaks of black, lips chapped and raw, skin blotchy.

"Hey, neighbor." Connor leaned forward and shot me a worried glance. "We were about to send out a search party."

Marley huffed, then lifted the bottle to her lips and tipped it back, where it stayed while I watched her pull swallow after swallow into her gut.

Shit.

"Why?" she asked, dropping her bottle to the ground before tucking her knees to her chest and hugging her legs.

"Isn't it obvious?" Con teased. "This big lug has it bad for you. He hasn't smiled all fucking day, and he's been counting down the minutes until you pulled into your driveway."

"Bullshit," Marley muttered, staring into the fire. "You fucking men are all alike. Don't give a shit about anything but pussy." She swayed, caught herself with one arm, then assumed her original position. "You get what you want, and you leave. Always leave." She laughed, then tried and failed to lift her head. "I'm gonna leave this time. Gonna fuck you good, and then I'm leaving."

Shit-faced.

Sloppy drunk.

Not attractive, but breaking my fucking heart. I hoped to God she hadn't driven home.

"Yeah." Con pushed to his feet, shot me a worried glance. "Time for me to ghost." He clapped my shoulder. "Need help getting her to bed?"

I shook my head. "Thanks, brother. Talk tomorrow?"

"Yep." He headed into the house but turned before disappearing. "Hit me up if you need anything."

Ginger sprinted around the corner and followed my friend inside, leaving me alone with the night sky and the tormented woman at my feet.

I rocked out of the chair and squatted in front of her. "You been out drinking all day?"

Dear God, the woman reeked of dive bars, cigarettes, and cheap alcohol. I fell on my ass and caged her legs with mine. "Wanna talk about it?"

"The hell is talking gonna do? I came to fuck. Let's fuck," she said to the ground.

"Marley. What do you need? You need to drink until you pass out?" I cupped her face, hoping to help her focus. "Need food? A shoulder to cry on? How can I help, gorgeous?"

"Birthday cake," she slurred, her words barely audible. "Candles. Stupid expensive presents."

"Is it your birthday?" What a jackass. I didn't even know her age.

"Not mine. His." She pushed at me but fell to her side to lay in the grass, one hand under her cheek, the other fisting the blades. "He's gone," she sobbed. "Men leave... I can't say happy birthday... I miss him. I miss him so much I can't breathe."

I stood guard while she purged, confident the neighbors could hear her grief spill into the night.

"He's my whole life. Gave him everything," she cried into my lawn. "And he left."

Her pain gutted me, but her words? Fucking hell. I had my answer. Understood, with sobering clarity, her reluctance to be with me.

Marley's heart belonged to another man.

A guy who'd left her to bleed out.

Every day, this woman got out of bed and pretended to be okay. While Marley was twisted in knots over some piece of shit, all I would ever be was her fuck buddy.

Fighting a wave of rage, I lay down at her side and pulled her to my aching chest.

Marley bawled, dragging me back to the first time Dad had left me and Mom standing on our front porch. I'd never heard my mother cry so hard, and I'd feared she'd never stop. But weeks later, that strong, beautiful woman dragged herself out of bed, and day by day, she'd cried a little less, smiled more, and fucking pretended to be okay until, one day, she was.

When Marley's sobs faded to whimpers and her hitched breaths steadied, I carried her upstairs, ditched her wet clothes, covered her in one of my shirts, and laid her in my bed.

When I woke five hours later, she was gone.

.˚.˚.˚.˚.˚.˚

I pulled up to the covered window, cut the engine, and waited, palms sweaty, guts twisted over a damn woman like I'd never matured past middle school.

Five minutes later, the neon *Open* light flickered then illuminated, the privacy curtain lifted, and Marley stood before me, tits spilling out of a red satin bra covered by a scrap of red flannel pretending to be a shirt.

Bare torso.

Denim shorts hit below her hip bones and barely covered her crotch.

No doubt, when she turned around, her ass cheeks would be on full display.

Sweet, beautiful Jesus.

Marley made me hard as a fucking diamond, but still, the visual messed with my head. Other men got off on her outrageous body, and I took great personal offense to that injustice.

Marley broke the silence, drawling, "Mornin', Joe," getting into her farm girl character. Her makeup was flawless, but her smile was forced and her eyes didn't shine. No, those peepers, dull and weighted, hid behind heavy eyeliner and thick lashes.

After an all-day bender, that woman had managed to rise, get to work looking downright edible, and pretend to be okay when she had to be dying inside.

Respect.

"Morning, neighbor." When my voice cracked, I cleared

my throat of the morning junk. "Came by to check on you. See how you're doing."

Facade crumbling, her shoulders dropped. As fast as she broke, she pieced her shell back together, then hit me with a sweet smile. "I'm fine, Joe. Thanks for worrying."

Headlights shone behind me, but Marley never strayed her gaze, a million apologies shining in those hazel beauties, each of them unnecessary.

"I washed your clothes. Found one of your shoes on my front porch and one in Ginger's bed. She chewed through the laces."

"Oh, man." She laughed, more embarrassed than humored. "I was a mess. I'm sor—"

"Don't apologize," I interrupted, raising a hand. "Don't. I mean it. We're friends. We take care of each other. Got me?"

Marley nodded, pulling a red-stained lip between her teeth. Her eyes liquified, but she blinked the emotion away. "Coffee?"

"Please."

"Americano, black, no sugar," we said at the same time.

I nodded, and she turned to make my drink. Damn. I'd guessed right. Her ass was on full display. Won't lie. I took a good, long gander.

More headlights hit my rearview, and I looked back. Two cars waited behind me. A Prius and a Honda. More shitheads who didn't deserve her smile.

When she returned with my drink but refused to take my money, I shoved the twenty into the tip jar, then begged, "I'll pay you a thousand dollars right now to close shop and let me drive you home." Meant every word, too.

Marley didn't miss a beat. "Do you have any idea how many times a day some well-meaning asshole says that to me?"

"Fine. Two thousand if you put on a sweatshirt or something."

"Ha. Funny."

Through the rearview, the guy in the Prius drummed a rapid beat on the side of his car, seemingly agitated, and though I couldn't see his eyes, I felt the burn of his glare.

I wanted to kill the man.

Instead, I asked my neighbor, "Will I see you tonight?"

Marley tugged at her bra strap, then adjusted her boob. When satisfied, she said, "Not tonight. I'll probably crash the second I get home."

Wrong answer. "I'll make dinner, we'll eat, then I'll tuck you in, nice and early. No hanky-panky."

She started to shake her head no, so I threw in, "I'll bring food to your place tonight."

Her eyes widened. "No! Not my place. Not tonight. But thanks anyway."

Knife to the chest.

I had yet to see the inside of her home. I'd never pushed, but it had become clear that she had something to hide.

A horn honked behind me.

Marley rolled her eyes and shooed me away. I leaned out my window and turned to the car behind me. The man glared hellfire in my direction. I huffed a laugh, shifting my truck into drive, and asked, "What's his deal?"

"He's my first customer every morning, and he's probably upset that you beat him to the window."

My jaw ached from holding back profanities.

"Want me to talk to him for you?" I teased, flexing my arm and shooting her a wink.

She laughed, waving me off again. "Joe. Go."

"Fine. See you at six. My place. Dinner." With great effort, I rolled away before she could deny the invite.

Hackles raised, I drove around the block and parked in

the alley, where I had a full view of her stand. The Prius was gone, though four different cars filled the space.

Past the lineup of eager cocks, across the intersection, a vehicle caught my attention.

An Escalade. The same silver Caddy that'd been parked outside Emerald Glow Nails. Like me, the SUV that belonged to Johan Harper was parked in the shadows, where he had a full view of Pink Sweets.

What the fuck?

I settled into my seat and lifted the coffee to my lips. Scribble on the cup caught my eye. *Thank you for last night.*

The knot in my gut loosened but didn't give.

For thirty minutes, I spied. The line cleared, filled again, cleared, filled. One of Marley's employees joined her, and the line dissipated once more. Harper chose that time to make his move, rolling up to her window.

Funny thing, Marley greeted him wearing a pink sweatshirt zipped tight.

She smiled. Talked. Laughed. Handed the goon a drink without taking any money. When Harper drove away, she tipped her face to the sky, took a deep breath, then turned and disappeared.

My blood boiled. Johan Harper and Marley appeared too friendly for my liking. How much prison time would I get for shaving a man's flesh from his bones with a potato peeler? Would the rose bushes be the first place they looked for his body?

Ha. I chuckled. Burying a man in my backyard wouldn't fly; Ginger would have him dug up in a matter of hours.

Shit. I scrubbed a hand over my face. My need to protect Marley had me contemplating murder. Mom and Alice had always teased me about being overprotective, and old habits did, indeed, die hard.

Good thing I'd had no plans for the day. Under the guise of watching out for my girl, I followed Harper.

His first stop was Pink Sweets in the Georgetown neighborhood, where he talked too long with the barista. Next, he headed to the first of many Dirty Dreamz locations, Marley's competition, where he went inside carrying a paper bag, stayed fifteen minutes, then came out empty-handed. That fucker made his rounds for the next two hours, the same routine at each.

His last visit took us to the Dirty Dreamz across the street from Emerald Glow Nails. When Harper didn't come out after thirty minutes, I headed home, cursing myself for wasting time to confirm what I already knew. Johan Harper was a low-rent mob boss, and the scantily clad women of Dirty Dreamz were under his thumb.

◦°◦°◦°◦°◦°◦°

Marley brought the bottle to her lips, staring into the dark kitchen while she curled her fingers through the scruff on Ginger's nape, lost in thought or, knowing her, devising an escape plan for the evening. Food and drink had softened the furrow between her brows, and I now hoped they would loosen her tongue.

Heh. That tongue.

With great restraint, I stayed on my end of the sofa. If things went my way, the only activity involving tongues would be talking. My plan was to get the woman to open up, trust me enough to share. Hence, my kitchen was stocked with every manner of alcoholic beverage. I'd even made a trip to the cannabis shop in case weed was her go-to unwinder after a hard day's work.

She'd arrived freshly showered, no makeup, hair knotted, wearing clothing that hid her shape—gray sweats two sizes too big, a men's-cut baggy white tee with the letters FTP over her chest.

If I had to guess, she'd tried to look as unappealing as possible, not that she was unattractive by any means, but Marley doubted my sincerity about wanting to know her better, and maybe her attire was a test. Maybe she just liked loose clothing after wearing her skin-tight, next-to-nothing work costume all day. Perhaps she was trying to turn me off. Who knew? What she didn't understand was that she could shave her head bald, wear a damn knapsack, and not shower for weeks, and I'd still be the unemployed big lug who was head over heels for his neighbor. I finished my Fat Tire, cleared my throat, and said, "We need to talk."

Marley swallowed, set her bottle on the coffee table, Ginger on the floor, then turned to face me and whispered, "Okay."

The woman was too far away. "C'mere." I offered my hand.

Much to my pleasure, she obliged, crawling across the couch, straddling my hips, then settling, ass on my thighs, hands on my chest, our faces close, and fuck, my brain glitched, everything going fuzzy before coming back online.

With Marley in my lap, an eternity could pass, and I'd be none the wiser. No man stood a chance against that sugary sweet, fresh-baked cookie scent she wore.

I gripped her waist and held her steady. "I could eat you alive right now."

"Then do it," she commanded.

I stopped her hand's descent to my groin. "First things first."

Her fiery glare promised a battle, and battle we would after I said my peace.

"I've kept my mouth shut about the other night. Figured if you wanted to talk about why you spent all day drowning your sorrows, you would."

The spark in her eyes fizzled. "That's nobody's business but mine." She studied my face, waited for a reaction, no doubt ready to run if I gave her grief. "My private pain to process."

So help me, my chest cracked open, all fight draining.

"All right, gorgeous, I won't bring that night up again." I brought our mouths together until she softened against me. "But we do need to talk about something else."

"Joe," she purred, grinding down on my groin. "I didn't come here to talk."

I managed to mutter through the torment, "There was a man at your house the other morning."

She listened without a lick of emotion on her face while I described the vehicle. But when I said, "I've seen that same car three times since, driving by real slow. Sometimes stopping, then moving on."

"You think someone's following me?"

I nodded.

"One of my customers?"

"Wouldn't rule any of them out." Then, to test the waters, I threw in, "Any old boyfriends been harassing you? Anyone back in the picture?"

"No. I don't know anyone who owns a Z or recall any white Nissans driving through the stand recently."

What is your fucking connection to Johan Harper? I wanted to ask but bit my tongue, because if Marley and Harper were in business, she'd clam up and shut me out. A partnership with that man was something you kept on the down-low.

"Do you have a security system?"

"At work? Yes, of course."

Good answer, but not what I was looking for. I cupped her face with both hands. "At home?"

"No. But I've been looking into home systems."

Since the attempted break-in, I left unsaid. "Would you let me install one for you?"

With my hand, I tried to nod her head up and down in the yes gesture, but she shook back and forth. "No!"

God, she was cute, and I wanted her lips on mine, but instead I asked, "Why the hell not?"

"Because I can install one myself."

"But you haven't," I argued. "And with the line of work you're in—"

"Don't, Joe," she interrupted, jerking free of my grip, then shoving a pointed finger in my chest. "Don't go there." Her cheeks pinked, her lips parted. Those wild eyes shot deadly warnings my way.

But when she rose on her knees, moving to get up, I hooked her waist and secured her in my lap. The more she wiggled, the more she fought, the stronger my determination to make her melt.

Some other fucker might hold her heart in his fist, but the rest of her flesh and blood? Mine. All fucking mine.

"I've told you before." Marley slapped her palms on my chest to push me away, determined to win a war she'd already lost. "I can take care of my own shit."

So much for talking. My libido took the lead.

I slid a hand up her back to her nape, then fisted her hair. "It's cute you think you're strong enough to fight me off."

"Let me up, Joe."

"Now, now." I laughed before nibbling her neck, knowing she'd surrender. "You don't really want that, do you?" I growled into her ear, thrusting my hips just enough she'd feel the hard heat. "You love my hands on you."

She squeezed my hips tighter with her knees, and her breasts heaved, smashed between us, those tight buds hardening. Pupils dilated, she glared, her soft breaths growing labored, heady with need.

Hell, yeah.

"You wanna fight me off, gorgeous? Give me your best." My cock throbbed between us. "I'm a man raised by strong fucking women. Women I would die for. Women I'd kill for." I leaned closer, brushing her hair away with my nose and whispering in her ear, "And I'll do the same for you."

I slid a hand inside her waistband to knead that perfect ass, then slipped a finger between her cheeks, then lower, finding her slick and warm.

Her breath hitched, and she opened her mouth to argue, but I continued. "Fight me, baby. But know this. I play dirty. And I'll win." I nipped her bottom lip.

She whimpered.

I chuckled. "We both know you're into me, and it's not just my cock you enjoy, is it gorgeous?"

Her frame hardened like a seasoned warrior, but I wasn't fooled. Marley was delicate as a fucking princess. God, I loved her weight in my lap, the fit of our groins, her feminine heat nestled in that space between my arms that'd been empty and cold for too damn long.

I didn't have to claim her mouth; the little firecracker offered her lips freely, moaning her surrender. If that woman wanted to kiss me into oblivion and tease me to death, I'd die a happy man.

And die I did. Once on the La-Z-Boy. Twice in my bed.

When I woke alone the following morning and rushed to the window to watch Marley head out for work, the ache in my chest was present, but damn if my cheeks didn't hurt from smiling.

CHAPTER
Eighteen

MARLEY

My smile lingered all morning, my cheeks aching from overuse. My nerves, though, remained in a constant state of agitation as if allergic to the giddy emotions. Despite numerous attempts, I could not wipe last night's dinner and sexcapades from my memory. Hell, I couldn't even tuck them behind a dusty shelf. For the past week, Joe had treated me like a queen while he fed me, then adored me like his favorite fantasy for the rest of the night.

A twinge or ache reminded me of our erotic workouts every time I moved. A girl could get used to such treatment, and what an unsettling thought.

Lilly stood at the closet, ruffling the tulle of her pink mini tutu, her tan ass cheeks on full display. "So you boink. He rolls out of bed and heads home?"

I wore a mesh minidress with a lacy thong to cover my cooch and sequined pasties to cover my nips. "I roll out of his bed and head home. Big difference."

She stared at me through the mirror. "He hasn't been in your place yet?"

"No," I admitted, avoiding her glare and focusing on our IG posts for the day. We'd hit ten thousand followers two days ago, and I wanted to keep building momentum. I hadn't told the girls that I'd hired a professional photographer to come in once a month and get shots so that they could focus on work and not on taking their own pics. Not that the selfies they posted were lacking—they were gorgeous, really—but professional photos would up our game and keep those curious customers driving through our stands.

"Why not in your bed?" Lilly asked, applying tape to her lacy pink bralette to keep her breasts from spilling out.

She would never understand, but I explained anyway. "Because then Joe would know about Dylan, and then we would have to talk. Talking leads to feelings, and feelings lead to relationships."

"Well." She pointed a perfectly manicured finger my way. "There, you're wrong. Only mutual feelings lead to relationships." She fanned a fake eyelash, attempting a wink. "Maybe he doesn't like you all that much."

Joe liked me.

I liked Joe so much that I didn't want him to be the next man to crush me.

Lilly tapped her acrylics on the counter, lips curled in contemplation before suggesting, "You could put the pictures of Dylan away."

"No. Absolutely not." I shook my head in defiance. Dylan was my life, and he'd hurt me more than any man ever had, but he was and always would be my reason for getting up every morning.

Sadness consumed me, the smile fading, the ache penetrating my bones. If I granted that pain more than a breath, I'd be useless for weeks. Desperate for a subject change, I teased, "Besides, Joe has a nicer bed than mine. He also has a great couch. Perfect height for bending me over."

Lilly laughed, fluffing her hair. "Oooh, do tell."

"His kitchen table is pretty damn sturdy." I closed my laptop and turned to face my favorite employee.

"Gross." Her button nose scrunched.

"Don't get me started on the garage. Seriously, who knew how versatile a workbench could be?"

Lilly smacked my ass and gestured toward the security screen. "Enough of the dirty details. Here comes your best friend."

I threw my sweatshirt over my head, slid open the window, and waited for the smug face to appear as the tinted glass lowered. "Hey, Harper."

He wore a navy blue dress shirt and more cologne than should be legal. "Marley."

"How's your morning?" Ugh. The fakery was exhausting.

"Better now that I've seen my favorite girl," he said to my breasts, his throat thick like he'd sucked down too many cigarettes before his visit.

"How sweet." I played nice, but not too nice, offering only a halfhearted smile. "We're not open yet. What do you need?"

"I was thinking about your unfortunate accident." A long pause. Harper's left brow raised just a smidge before he finished with, "You know, the fire."

My arm hairs stood at attention. "Appreciate your concern."

"You know, this is a tough business." He draped a long arm out his door and rubbed at a smudge on his side-view mirror. "Not safe for a good girl like you."

"Whatever gave you the impression that I'm a good girl?" I asked, playing his game, continuing with the ridiculous banter.

"My offer still stands." He tapped on the side of his door, then finally met my eyes, his own gaze dark and full of warning. "We work together, nobody would dare touch you."

Translation: Give me what I want and no more unfortunate fires.

My legs turned to rubber. Fear slithered under my skin, leaving prickly bumps from my neck to knees in its wake. Why had he waited so long to make his play?

"Thank you." I wanted him gone, but I hadn't much fight, so I said, "I'll give your offer some consideration." Then, hands shaking, I closed the window and turned my back on a man nobody turned their backs on.

First, an attempted break-in, then someone casing my house, and now, Harper laying down a threat. Warning bells anyone?

I did need a home security system. Or maybe gnarly, killer attack dogs like Halle Berry had in the *John Wick* movie.

Lilly threw her hands up in frustration. "Why don't you tell him where to go?"

"Because I know his type too well."

Though she'd heard tales of my deadbeat dad and his epic misadventures in fathering, she didn't know the extent of what he'd put me through or his past dealings with Johan Harper.

Thankfully, Lilly was brilliant at reading my moods and knew not to question further. She moved around me and stood at the register. "So, Joe invited Marco for a BBQ this weekend."

I played it cool. "He did, huh?"

"He didn't tell you?" she asked over her shoulder. "I was hoping you could fill me in because, apparently, it's men only."

My gut sank. No good could come of that private event. "Men only? That's strange, isn't it?"

"Right? I mean, they only met once that I know of, and

Marco hasn't spoken a word to Joe since." She turned around, arms crossed. "Joe didn't say anything?"

"Like I said, we boink, I go home." I shrugged, pretending not to care. "Not much time for talking."

"Whatever." She rolled her eyes before asking, "How many orgasms have you had in the last five days?"

"Twenty-six." I threw out the number at random. "Not that I'm counting."

Her eyes widened. "Twenty-six?"

"Something like that." I waved a hand like her line of questioning was bothersome.

"That's, like, five a day." She crossed her arms, head shaking in awe. "I can't even do that with my vibrator."

"Mornings. Nooners. Evenings." Yes, I exaggerated, but I rarely got one over on Lilly, and when I did, I had fun. "We get started early. It's amazing what you can accomplish with no talking or feelings involved."

Lilly stared long and hard, her wheels clearly churning. Then she laughed and smacked me with a towel. "You're so whooped."

"I like sex," I said with a shrug. "Joe's good at sex."

"Liar." She huffed. "You've got it bad."

I couldn't afford to have it bad.

Joe and I had fun, and that's all our trysts would ever be —a good time with no expectations.

"Get to work," I ordered, pointing to the pink neon *Open* sign.

No longer cursed with the perma-grin, but unfortunately still agitated, I continued with my morning routine. My thoughts ran rampant. Aside from being a freaking juggernaut in the sack, Joe was fun, and I looked forward to seeing him every day, even if I only stole a peek through my curtains when I heard the rumble of his motorcycle or the annoying squeak of his garage door.

When he kissed that ugly mutt? Panties melted.

Oh, shit. Lilly was right. Maybe I was whooped. Perhaps I'd made a mistake asking him to be neighbors with benefits. Maybe I wasn't capable of halfhearted affairs.

Or maybe, though I'd never say it out loud, I was less scared or vulnerable when Joe and I were together.

Or perhaps, like Joe, I was just lonely.

One thing I knew for sure—I needed a dog.

Dry lips and a wet tongue made for torturous pleasure, whispering along that spot on my neck that always made me squirm. Joe moaned, hooked my waist, and rolled, placing me on top of his warm body, chest to chest.

My skin buzzed, gearing up for round two, until Joe asked, "Wanna tell me why Harper paid you a visit today?"

My post-coital haze fizzled like lit dynamite plunged into a tub of ice water. "How do you know Harper visited me today?" I sat up straight and rested my butt on Joe's knees, doing my damndest to keep my voice in check. "You spying on me?"

He studied me long and hard, those Nordic blue eyes darkening, a small dent forming between his brows. "My best friend works for the SPD. Harper's on everyone's radar. Local law. Feds." Strong fingers pressed deeper into my waist, not hard enough to bruise, but firm and sure, a silent communication that he would not let me slink, storm, or pout my way out of the conversation. "Tell me. Is he harassing you?"

"Not any more than usual," I blurted. "But again, how is it okay that you know this?"

"Not any more than usual?" He ignored my question. "How long has he been bothering you?"

Joe was genuinely concerned for my safety, evident by the crinkles at the corners of his eyes.

He cared, and sweet caramel macchiato, what a delicious sensation knowing someone worried for me. Joe officially had the power to hurt me.

How careless I'd been to let that happen.

I tried to rise. My beautiful, too patient neighbor held me in place.

The bastard enjoyed our size difference, always holding me close or tossing me around in bed like I was his personal bendy blow-up doll.

When he took charge in the sack, my body ignited. However, when he acted the overprotective brute, my internal furnace overheated, nothing but steam and smoke piping out my ears. "Crossing a line here, Joe."

"Not crossing anything," he stated, absorbing my glare and countering with a scowl. "If my friends wanna keep tabs on my girl and report back, nothing I can do to change their minds."

My girl. Ugh. If I weren't so heated, I might've swooned, but I was Marley, and I had an argument to win. "I can handle my own business." I crossed my arms and huffed. "My encounters with Harper do not concern you or your friends."

Joe glared hellfire, jackknifed to cage me in his massive arms, then pulled me flush against his sweaty chest, back to where we'd started, stretched out on his mattress. "You make me fucking crazy, you know that?"

"Back off." I shoved at his chest. "I have this covered. I don't need babysitters."

"You don't want to tell me about Harper." Joe lifted me off his lap and deposited me to his left. "I can't make you talk, but I won't let the subject go." On his way to the bathroom, he said, "You're good at what you do, but nonetheless, your line of business is not safe."

"Says the criminal," I tossed back, bitch mode kicking in.

"I'm serious," he yelled from across the hallway. "You're not selling your body, but you're in the sex business regardless. That's a dangerous place to be."

The toilet flushed, water ran, then stopped. Joe's naked frame filled the doorway. I held my gaze above his shoulders with great effort because, man, that guy could make a girl stoopid. My wits needed to remain firmly intact.

"You say you love your girls." His voice came too gentle, too calm.

"I do," I mumbled.

Arms crossed, he leaned against the jamb. In my periphery, his giant cock swung and bounced with his movement, a heady temptation, but I would not falter my glare.

"They're not safe," he stated. "Guys like Harper won't stop preying on you."

He wasn't wrong, but because of feelings and all that, I argued, "If a man's gonna prey on a woman, he'll do it whether she's wearing lingerie or a turtleneck. Fucked-up men prey on women." I grabbed the only article of clothing within reaching distance. Pulling Joe's T-shirt over my head, I continued, volume rising, "It doesn't matter if she works as a stripper or on Wall Street, if she's a stay-at-home mom or a single lady out for a drink with her friends."

Joe opened his mouth to speak, but I wasn't finished.

"I have taken measures to keep my girls safe."

Joe's glare dropped, lingered, then lifted again.

My hurt lurched. The compassion in his blue eyes was unbearable. I needed to move, break the connection, keep my head in the game. I hopped from the bed.

My Levi's lay on the hardwood floor, one leg bent over itself, the other twisted like my guts. I tugged them on while continuing, "You stand there and scold like I don't understand the risks. I understand more than you ever could. I've dealt with men like Johan Harper since I was in diapers, and they don't scare me."

One flip-flop lay under the bed. I shoved my toes under the rubber strip. "You know what scares me?" I turned to face him but couldn't make eye contact because I was on a tangent. Later, I'd be embarrassed, but I'd deal with "later" when the time came. As my soul bled all over Joe's pretty feet, I knew I was safe because Joe was a safe haven. He would let me bleed, then, no doubt, take every ridiculous line of self-defense bullshit I spewed, and clean up after I finished. So I was safe to confess, "Men like you. That's what scares me."

I dropped to my knees and searched for my other shoe, rifling through a pile of bedding that'd fallen to the floor earlier. "You saunter into our lives, all pretty, tough, protective, and pretending to give a shit. Make us feel. Make us trust and believe that, maybe, we do actually deserve something or someone good."

My cheeks burned with anger. Not at Joe, but myself, for sabotaging a great evening and probably ruining any chance we had at being more than neighbors.

God, I was a mental case. No wonder Dylan left.

My shoe no longer mattered. Ginger could chew the damn thing to pieces.

I hopped to my feet, met him toe to toe, and gave him the last of my rant. "Men like you scare me because you make me forget I had the balls to start a business." Rising on my toes, I poked his chest with a pointed finger. "With little money and no college education, I turned that business into something successful, all by myself, without a growly, strong, supersmart man to hold my hand along the way."

"I wasn't—" he managed to sputter before I shoved my way through the door and headed down the stairs.

"Marley!" Heavy footsteps pounded behind me.

"Thanks for the fabulous fuck, Joe." I waved over my shoulder. Then, after slamming the door behind me, I wiped the first tear away and whispered, "Fuck you, feelings."

* * *

"You sure?" Equal parts mesmerized and horrified, I stared into a set of dopey brown eyes, waiting for the cosmic connection, hoping for a sign, something to tell me, "He's the one."

"Yeah, I'm sure." The man who had introduced himself as Marshall scratched the stubble on his chin. "Knows his commands. Well mannered. Best sidekick you could ask for."

"No females?"

"Not today. You have a problem with males?"

Marshall was attractive, and I might've liked the guy if his gaze hadn't landed on my chest more often than my face. "Men have a history of leaving me," I told him. "You think this guy is a runner?"

Marshall laughed, but I wasn't being funny.

The mutt's black-and-brown fur wasn't too long or too short and soft to the touch. "Is there a return policy, you know, in case we don't mesh?"

"You ever have a pet before?" The kennel manager

leaned against the painted brick wall and crossed his arms, clearly irritated with my uncertainty.

"Not since I was a kid," I confessed, feeling chastised.

"Listen, if you're not sure, go home and give this guy a ponder. Come back when you're sure." The man shrugged, standing upright. "Or not. He's a good guy. Loyal, too. He'll love you harder than anyone. He'll be gone by the end of the week. Of that, I'm sure."

The dog was big, shoulders wide, head boxy and massive, and I was confident that if he snarled, he'd look intimidating, which was why I'd picked him. Studies showed that burglars were deterred by dogs, big dogs especially, and after Harper's threat, the thwarted break-in, and some guy in a sweet car doing drive-bys, I'd sleep better knowing I had an extra line of defense. Besides, although pleasant, the eighty-mile trek to the dog rescue oasis in the woods was not a trip I wanted to make again. Decision made, I blurted, "I'll take him."

"You won't be sorry." Marshall smiled and clapped his hands together, leading me into his office. "I promise."

"What's his name?"

"Bruce." Marshall chuckled. "Guy who owned him before was a *Die Hard* fan." He gestured for me to sit, then made his way to the other side of his desk. "You don't like that name, you can always give him another one. He'll adapt. You're his mom now."

My stomach sank at the mention of that word. *Mom.* But Bruce gave my hand a lick, my maternal instinct kicked in, and an ache I'd suffered for too long suddenly didn't throb so hard.

Thirty minutes later, paperwork signed, I stood outside the kennel and stared into those adoring big brown eyes and whispered, "Let's do this, Bruce."

His stubby tail seemed to flick twenty beats per second.

As if he knew he'd found his forever home and bestie, the mutt bared his teeth, his paws tapping the cement floor while Marshall hooked the leash onto his thick collar.

We left the building, and the moment the sun hit his face, Bruce took off, doing the Scooby-Doo leg spin, his feet slipping on the pavement.

I braced for what was sure to be a painful fall, but the leash stretched to its limit, and Bruce stopped. The handsome beast looked over his shoulder, panting, and waited for me to catch up.

"Good boy," I cooed, stepping forward.

Bruce settled into the back seat like we'd enjoyed a thousand road trips together. Three times on the drive home, he stuck his head between the front seats and gave me a big lick. Twice, he rested his chin on my shoulder and sighed.

He was mine. I was in love.

And I was confident that as long as I kept him fed, Bruce was one guy who would never abandon me.

⁂

My new roommate followed me from room to room, sniffing everything his nose could reach. The exploration lasted a good twenty minutes before he stood at the back door and whined.

We headed outside. "Okay, Bruce. This is the backyard." I gave his butt a pat, and off he ran, enjoying his new kingdom. For a few minutes, I watched, my heart expanding.

Music came from the other side of the fence, and I glanced at the house next door, my heart shrinking right back to its original size.

I hadn't spoken to Joe in days. And while I missed our rendezvous, I appreciated that, again, he'd given me the space I needed. I only hoped I hadn't chased him away for good.

The volume stayed at a respectable level, and his choice of radio stations wasn't disappointing, so I left my earbuds dangling around my neck.

I headed to the shed to grab my ladder, then stopped dead at the sound of Joe singing—deep and rich, hitting the high notes like they were nothing. His voice traveled to his back porch and then into his backyard. Unwelcome flutters erupted in my belly.

Bruce ran toward the fence, then sat, ears cocked. He shot up and danced in a circle, then sniffed the ground along the fence line, his tail taking his butt for a ride.

Patches of gray disrupted the warm sunshine in small bouts, but not enough that I worried about rain. Good day to clean the gutters. My ladder hung at the back of the shed, and it took some creative maneuvering to get it down. As much as I hated climbing the metal contraption, I hated paying someone for a simple chore even more.

By the time I found my work gloves and climbed to cleaning level, Bruce had settled in a shady corner of the porch.

I had an excellent view of Joe's backyard from my perch. In particular, the rose garden where Joe stood dead center, a Seattle Mariners cap shielding his eyes.

Shirtless and wielding red pruning shears, he sang to the rose bushes while he trimmed, handling each flower with tender grace like Alice used to do, except Alice was never shirtless and she always sang off-key.

God, I missed that woman.

I missed that man, too.

Though the view was spectacular, Joe posed a dangerous distraction, and I couldn't afford to be laid up because of an unfortunate fall caused by ogling my neighbor. Forcing my attention to the task at hand, I tucked my headphones into my ears and cranked the volume.

By the time I finished, Joe was nowhere to be seen. I put my tools away and returned the ladder to its hooks in the shed. When I stepped back into the sunshine, blinking against the harsh light, I smacked nose to chest into a wall of sweaty, sun-kissed muscle.

"Holy shit!" I slapped his hard pecs and tore my headphones out. "You scared the shit out of me."

That deep chuckle soothed my agitation.

"Hey, neighbor." Joe cupped my face and stole a kiss, quick and innocent, but toe-curling nonetheless. And when he pulled away and groaned, "Damn, I like you dirty and sweaty," every cell in my body sparked to life.

My teeth ached from his sweetness. My hard, weathered soul softened like biscotti dipped into a hot cup of coffee.

Joe's eyes darkened, reflecting my desire.

Heaven help me.

I moved to escape his heated gaze, but my back hit the side of the shed.

With a grin full of evil intent, Joe braced one hand over my head and captured my chin with the other. Lips dangerously close, he asked, "Are we still fighting?"

"We weren't fighting," I whispered, debating whether to bite his bottom lip or shove my tongue down his throat.

Joe's face cracked into a wide grin, happy wrinkles forming at the corners of his eyes. "Are you still mad?"

"It would be safe for you to assume yes." I swallowed. Moistened my lips. "Always yes."

Bruce barked from the other side of the garage. Joe

rubbed his thumb over my cheek, his breaths getting heavy, the rhythm matching my own. "You got a dog."

"Yes." I nodded, reeling from his tender hold on my face. "A guard dog who obviously failed at his job."

"He wouldn't let me in the gate. I had to bring Ginger over to distract him."

"Oh, my God. No!" I pushed Joe out of the way. "He'll tear her to shreds."

"Don't worry." He chuckled. "They're playing."

"Joe. Ginger is a tasty treat. Bruce is a beast, and I haven't fed him yet today."

"Marley." He gripped my arms just above the elbow, his gesture meant to soothe but flooding my psyche with unwanted memories. "Relax. They're fine."

Relax. They're fine.

Suddenly, I couldn't breathe. I was six again, watching the men in blue drag my daddy away while he cried and yelled, "I'm sorry, baby girl. I'm sorry," while an officer held me back, kept me from running after my dad, his large hands squeezing my arms hard enough to leave bruises.

Over and over, that cop tried to reassure me, chanting, "Relax. He'll be fine. He'll be fine."

"Let go of me!" I jerked free of Joe's grip and rubbed the sensation away. He hadn't hurt me, but they lingered anyway—the ghost pains.

Angry tears escaped.

"Marley." Calm and cool, Joe asked, "What just happened?"

My father happened. His recent resurfacing had my gray matter all mashed up. "I gotta go."

"Hey, listen." Joe allowed a few more inches to separate us, scratching the top of his head, clearly confused and, oh, God, was that worry or realization? Maybe the puzzle pieces had clicked into place. He finally understood that my life was a pile of shit, and whatever fun we had in the sack was not worth all my crazy.

"Just go!" I shooed him away, seconds from an epic tear duct malfunction. "Take your dog. Go home."

"Marley," he pleaded, voice laced with emotion.

"Bruce!" I yelled.

Bruce ignored me, distracted by the little creature running circles around his massive paws.

"Bruce!" I called again, voice breaking on a sob. Nobody, especially my sex partner, needed to see my breakdown.

"Marley. Hey. Shit." Joe came at me, arms lifting for an embrace I didn't think I could handle.

I shoved at his chest, attempting to put distance between us.

Joe snapped a massive hand around my wrist and hauled me against him.

No hesitation. No awkward pauses. That man hugged me with steel-spined resolve like he wanted to absorb every sob, sniff, and tear, or shield me from every ugly experience. I'd gone from teasing to tormented in the blink of an eye, and when others would've run, he stayed.

Embarrassed because, again, I'd gone mental in front of the guy, I wanted to slink away, lock myself in the house for the rest of the day. Instead, I melted into his solid embrace, and I fell apart.

I sobbed for the little girl who had so desperately needed her daddy. I hated my father, yet I missed him terribly. I cried for the bitter woman I'd become. I mourned the boy who'd taught me the true meaning of love, only to slice me to the core, inflict unfathomable pain, and leave me ruined.

When I sucked in my last shaky breath and pushed

away from my flesh and blood rock, Joe pulled a bandana out of his back pocket and helped me wipe my nose.

No probing. No halfhearted condolences. Joe waited until I was steady, then scooped Ginger into his arms and scratched Bruce behind his ear.

"I'm sorry," I murmured. "It's just... when you grabbed me like that..." I rubbed my arms again. "It brought back a bad memory."

"*I'm* sorry," he whispered, stepping closer but not touching.

"I'm not a freak. I promise." I sniffed, studied the ground, then mumbled, "We met at a bad time in my life, that's all."

"Or the perfect time." Joe tapped a knuckle under my chin, urging me to look up.

For a moment, I believed him.

"You ever trust me enough to talk about it, I'm here."

CHAPTER
Nineteen

"We've got a lot to talk about, but first"—I flipped open the cooler—"beer."

Con was the first to dive in, followed by Singleton. Frank had an afternoon shift, so he passed on the libations but stood at the grill, tongs in hand, wearing Alice's *Kiss The Cook* apron.

"All right, Kaine." Marco snagged a Manny's, popped the lid, and settled back in his chair. "What's up?"

The guy was intelligent and protective of Lilly, and that was precisely why I'd invited him. Singleton, I suspected, had a thing for Marley, and he was an accountant, which would come in handy.

We hadn't gathered for afternoon tea and gossip, so I laid my agenda on the table. "Marley's in some shit. I know how to help, but I can't do it alone."

Marco chugged his beer, then shot Singleton a quick glance before he hit me with a stony glare. Jaw tight, he asked, "In some shit, how?"

Yeah, we were cut from the same cloth. "You aware Johan Harper pays our ladies a visit once a week?"

I could swear Marco's jaw cracked. "Lilly's mentioned he comes through."

"Who's Harper?" Singleton asked.

"Biggest piece of shit this side of the Cascades," Frank

growled over his shoulder while he flipped brats. "Slipperier than a greased weasel."

"Wait. Wait. Wait." Singleton waved his free hand in the air. "Johan Harper, that mob boss wannabe that shows up on the ten o'clock news every coupla months?"

"That's the one." I nodded. "He's watching her stands. I suspect he's got someone on her home, too."

Con cleared his throat. "So, she's got this Harper prick breathing down her neck. Have you asked her about it?"

"Tells me it's handled," I said. "Whatever the fuck that means."

Marco tossed his empty bottle into the recycle bag and directed his question toward Frank. "What's your take, cop?"

"Harper's hands are in everyone's pots. Figure he wants a piece of her pie." Frank wiped the sweat from his brow with his forearm. "He's in business with her competition."

"Dirty Dreamz," I threw in. "They've been busted multiple times for illegal exposure and prostitution."

"Suspected of money laundering," Frank added.

Marco cleared his throat. "Lilly told me you did time. You sure it's Harper we should be worried about?"

Frank dropped the lid on the grill and pointed his tongs our way, looking taller than a pine tree and meaner than a grizzly. "My brother here took a life to save a life. Nothing more to be said on that subject. You got a problem with him, leave. We'll deal with this shit on our own. But hear me loud and clear. I'd rather have this guy watching my back than any other fucker on the planet."

Marco stared right through me, working something out in his head, I assumed.

Singleton laughed, leaned back in his chair, hands clasped behind his head, and sized me up. "Who'd you kill?"

I needed these guys on my side. How much of my soul could I expose without scaring them off? "The man who beat my aunt for the entirety of their marriage."

And because my brothers always had my back, Con spoke up, "Any of us would've done the same and, again, no more to be said on that subject."

Singleton and Marco exchanged an unspoken communication, then Marco turned, his lip curled at the corner. "What've you got in mind?"

Bridget busted through the back door. "All right, boys, I'm here. Let's get down to business." Donned in full work attire, hair pinned up, face art flawless, and a shiny black leather briefcase hanging from her shoulder, she maneuvered the steps of the back deck with grace and purpose. "We doing this out here?" she asked.

"Bridget fucking Cross." Singleton shot from his chair and captured her in a one-sided embrace, kissing her cheek and holding her too close for comfort.

"Hey, Isaac." Bridget tried to dodge his lips with no success.

Interesting.

Con barked, "Hands off my sister, man."

Singleton let go and stepped back, his gaze glued to Bridge while she found her balance. She straightened her red blouse, shot Singleton a sideways glance, and turned to ask me, "We doing this out here?"

"Yeah." I opened an empty chair and set it to my left, putting her between Con and myself. "Unless you need the table."

"Outside is perfect. I need some vitamin D." She toed off her heels and sat, raising her pretty face to the sky.

Isaac Singleton could not take his eyes off Bridge, and I made a mental note to Google the hell outta that fucker later, although I'm sure Frank was already running a background check from his cell.

I cleared my throat, drawing Singleton's attention my way. "She's off limits, bud."

The fucker chuckled. That guy thought everything was funny.

"First off," Bridge said, ignoring the horndog and placing a hand on my thigh like a mother about to break bad news, "let me start by saying I'm not sure this is a great investment. Risky if you ask me, but—"

"It's a great idea, Bridge, and you know it," I interrupted, defenses up. "Your issue is that my proposal is small potatoes compared to your everyday dealings."

Bridget Cross was rumored to have the most lethal glare west of the Cascades, but I'd developed an immunity to her female wiles years ago, and her death lasers fizzled at my feet.

The woman knew I was right and didn't argue. Instead, she pulled folders out of her briefcase and handed one to each of us. "I assume Joe has filled everyone in?"

"Not yet," Frank grunted, dropping a Spanish chorizo into a cut up rustic baguette.

Again Bridge glared at me. "Joe. Really? I've got less than an hour to get this shit signed."

"We were getting to that before you busted through the door. How'd you get in anyway? I never gave you a key."

"I have my ways." She winked. "Now, let's get to business."

Step by step, I laid out my business plan, took a shit-ton of ribbing as I'd expected, but after a heated debate over pros and cons, my future took shape. I had something to look forward to, something tangible to call mine. I'd only had to auction off four pieces of Alice's old jewelry to make enough money to finance the endeavor on my own but, gotta admit, felt good to have this group of men on board.

Bridget stood and collected signed documents from each of us, grabbing mine last. "I can't believe we're doing this." She rose on her toes to kiss my cheek.

I wrapped her in a tight hug. "I owe you."

"Oh, yes, you do." She said her goodbyes and headed toward the house.

Singleton made to follow, but was thwarted when Con wrapped an arm around his neck and steered him in the opposite direction.

Marco clapped my shoulder. He'd liked my idea so much he'd been the first to offer a partnership. "Got a name for this ridiculous business?"

"Yeah." Marley's face flashed into my mind. I liked her sweet, but something about her spunk when she was riled stirred my blood. And that woman was about to get her feathers ruffled again. "Got the perfect name."

. . . .

Fifty-seven minutes. I lasted one measly hour after Marley pulled into her driveway before I turned off the baseball game and headed next door.

Hi. Nice to meet you. I'm Joe, and I'm a pussy-whipped motherfucker.

I knocked. Waited. Knocked again. A litany of profanities came from around the corner. I followed the colorful language through the gate and found Marley storming my way, shoving her hands into a pair of work gloves.

"What's that grin for?" she asked, moving past me, her lack of greeting rude but not entirely out of character.

Sawdust stuck to her baggy jeans. A wide tool belt cinched her dirty, white T-shirt at the waist.

"Ah, had a good day, that's all." She dodged my kiss and bent to retrieve a plywood board from where it leaned against the side of her house.

"Let me get that." I moved to help, but she twisted away and headed in the opposite direction.

"I got it" came her clipped reply.

The woman was in a mood, but I was pumped for battle. *Bring it, baby.*

I followed, uninvited, to the back, drew a deep breath when I spied the shattered window, then took time for another long inhale and exhale before asking, "What the hell happened here?"

My question fell on deaf ears. Marley plucked two screws from her belt, stuck them between her teeth, lifted the board like it weighed nothing, then ascended the step ladder.

"Here." I moved to her side, ready to bear the weight of the cutout. "Let me help."

With a huff, she bumped me out of the way, mumbling through the screws, "I can do it myself."

Her fight was lackluster at best, which meant the shit on her mind weighed heavy.

"I know you can do it," I grumbled, then shoved myself between her and the board. "But I'm right here. Let me help."

"Fine."

Temper in check, but barely, I asked through gritted teeth, "What happened?"

"Bird," she grumbled, tugging a drill from her belt.

"That was no bird."

Marley huffed, "A flock of birds."

I called her bluff. "Bullshit."

My blood boiled, and my heart threatened to burst through my rib cage. She could've been hurt, or worse.

"What did they steal?"

"Don't worry about it, Joe."

"Woman!" Done with the back-and-forth, I dropped the wood at my feet and turned to face my frustrating lady. "You do not get to tell me what I can and cannot worry about. Did someone break into your house or not?"

"They tried," she said to the sky, blinking rapidly, then shaking off her emotion. "Bruce must've scared them off."

"Thank fuck for that beautiful beast." That dog was getting a fucking T-bone steak, fresh from the butcher.

"Did you call the police?"

"No," she muttered, voice trembling. "What good would it do?"

That was an argument for another day. "Why didn't you call me?"

"Joe." Finally, her eyes met mine. "I've taken care of myself for a very long time."

"I get that." I reached for her cheek and wiped at the moisture under her eye. "And I know you're capable. But you have a sexy fuck buddy right next door, who, if you haven't noticed, finds every excuse he can to spend time with you." Willpower drained, I pulled her close and kissed her nose, then her ear before whispering, "Call me when you need help. Use me, for Christ's sake."

"Can you stop?" Her voice cracked, but she didn't move away and instead leaned into my touch.

That slight concession, accepting my comfort, seemed a monumental shift in our dynamic.

"Yeah. Sure. I'm done." I'd never be finished with Marley.

She looked smaller despite the baggy clothes. As she stepped down from the stool and avoided my gaze to hide tears I'd already seen, it hit me—Marley and Alice were too much alike. Bullheaded. Proud.

My neighbor would never ask for help.

Well, her pride was about to take a hit.

Marley attempted to move the ladder, but I hooked her waist and spun her away from the house. "Go inside and clean up the glass. I'll finish this."

"I'm okay." Her lip quivered, tears spilling. "Really, I've got this."

Like I said—bullheaded. Gripping her chin, I stole a salty kiss and distracted her with my tongue while I unclasped her utility belt. With a hard slap to her ass, I ordered, "Go inside," then turned my back, nixing any further argument.

Soft footfalls retreated, followed by a door slam. Heh, I'd won that round. What a sweet victory, too.

I finished securing the plywood, put the tools away, considered knocking on her door but instead, headed home and dialed Con.

"Hey." His voice was gruff, making me wonder if he was alone or halfway to wooing a woman into his bed.

Didn't matter. Con wouldn't have answered were he on a date. "Remember last month when that cashier at Home Depot slipped me her number, but I gave it to you?"

"And I got the best blow job of my life?"

Ginger leapt onto the couch, pushed under my arm, and settled against my side. "Yeah."

"What? You see her again? She ask about me?"

"Time to return the favor." I stared at an old stain on the ceiling. More shit to add to my to-do list.

"You need a date? Did Marley finally kick you to the curb? 'Cause I know a few ladies who're actually into criminals."

Though his jab stung, I didn't take the bait. "No. I need someone to replace a window. Today."

"I've got a guy on speed dial." He huffed a laugh. "I'll have him give you a call."

"You're the best, man." Seriously, I couldn't ask for better friends, and their career choices came in handy on countless occasions. Frank being a cop, and Con, a construction king.

"Like I said, best blow job of my life."

"Yeah, yeah." Con would've done me a solid regardless, but I enjoyed reminding the cocky bastard that the hot chick in aisle nine had hit on me first.

Forty-five minutes later, Ruston Howerton of Rusty's Window Repair met me outside of Marley's house. She watched from her porch while he backed his red Tundra into her driveway.

I figured she'd be unhappy. Expected a fight when she glared hellfire in my direction. It killed me when her red, swollen eyes started to leak again.

When I smiled a reassurance, she turned on her heel and retreated without a word.

Round two: Joe.

And though I missed the banter, I'd take that victory, too.

. ˙ . ˙ . ˚ . ˙ . ˙ .

Ginger pranced at the door before the first soft rap. I hadn't expected a visit after the day's earlier events. Heavy knocks beat my rib cage, and I forced my joy down a notch, clearing my throat before opening the door. "Hey, gorgeous."

Marley's face was a mess. No makeup. Puffy eyes. Red

nose. Chapped lips. But she smiled, and that smile knocked me back a step. Or maybe the garlic aroma wafting from the foil-covered pan was to blame.

Bruce stood at her hip, sniffing the air, clearly hoping for a chomp at the goodies. Ginger caught the aroma as well. The little queen danced on her hind legs, nose in the air, trying to get at the food.

"I made you dinner." Marley stared at my chest, then met my gaze with a vulnerability that pierced my soul.

She cooked for me. My ticker kicked into high gear, beating something fierce. I could've fallen to my knees and wept at her feet.

Instead, I moved aside. Marley made her way to the kitchen, the mutts hot on her heels. I hung back a few paces, taking note of her attire, gray sweats that cinched at the waist and ballooned at her Nike-clad feet. A black T-shirt that hugged her tits and didn't quite reach her hips.

Every night, I waited, an addict jonesing for his fix, desperate for her company. This house call was different. This visit was Marley shedding a layer and letting me closer, and though my cock was eager to sink into that hot body, my heart floated on a whole different plane. Moon high.

As if the kitchen were hers, she grabbed plates, collected silverware, napkins, two beers from the fridge, and set them on the table before seating herself.

I watched in awe, in silent worship, in gratitude deeper than marrow, while she served me a brick-sized serving of cannelloni stuffed with meat and oozing cheese.

She dug in. I followed suit, and the flavor exploded on my tongue, inciting a moan. Praise the good Lord above, the woman could cook. I'd hit the girlfriend lottery.

"I'll probably burn in hell for saying so, but this is better than my mom's."

"Every boy thinks his mom's cooking is the best," she said to her plate, a forkful of noodle and sauce suspended halfway to her mouth. She blinked, glanced at me, faked a smile, then continued to eat.

"Your mom teach you to cook like this?" I asked around a mouthful of food, manners be damned.

Marley nodded, chewing, and cut into her pasta.

"Tell me about her."

Her shoulders relaxed. Leaning back into her seat, she said, "My mom is great. Lives in Whisper Springs. I get over there every couple of months for a visit."

"She married?"

"Yeah." She reached for her beer. "She and her husband, Grant, own a bed and breakfast on Lake Willow. Beautiful piece of property. She's so happy, and Grant's the best. I'm heading over there in a couple weeks to spend a few days."

"Siblings?" I asked, resting my fork on the plate, one hundred percent tuned into the convo.

Marley gulped two deep draws of beer, then dabbed her lips with her napkin. "I have an older brother, Wade. He has a couple of restaurants in eastern Washington and Idaho."

"You close with him?" My mouth watered, craving more food, but my head and chest were ravenous for more of her personal offerings.

"No." Sadness stole her smile. "We call each other at Christmastime."

There was a story there, a tale I wanted to hear, but I settled with, "I'm sorry."

"Why are you sorry?" She filled her fork with a large bite.

Simple. "If I had a little sister, I'd check in weekly, at least."

"We're adults," she said, shrugging. "Wade is busy with his business. Life is just like that sometimes."

"I suppose," I grunted, irritated that another man had failed her.

There was more to be said on the subject, but another time perhaps. As much as I loved Marley's fight, I was grateful for the open, honest, and friendly conversation.

While I scooped my second helping, Marley twisted her napkin, and after a long bit of silence, she whispered, "Thank you. For today."

My mouth was full, but I managed, "You're welcome."

"I don't like needing people." Spine rod straight, she shifted in her chair.

"I picked up on that."

A flimsy napkin bore the brunt of her nervous energy, and she dropped the twisted pulp on the table, drew a deep breath, and admitted, "It's not easy for me. I like to be in control."

"So nobody can disappoint you," I stated. I could relate.

"I guess," she mumbled, staring at her plate.

Pushing my food aside, I leaned forward, drawing her gaze. "I understand your dad did a number. Believe me, I get that. Who else hurt you, Marley?"

Brows raised, she released a slow breath. "Just every man who's been in my life."

"You seem friendly with Marco and Singleton."

"They don't count."

So, she had selective walls constructed. "They're men, and they're in your life. Have they hurt you?"

Marley smirked. "Not yet."

"Hmm."

"Hmm, what?"

"You're waiting for the other shoe to drop. You're still waiting for me to hurt you."

"I don't know," she said to my chest, then shook her head and met my eyes. "Yes, I suppose I am."

"News flash." Elbows to the table, I crossed my arms. "People hurt each other. Sometimes it's intentional. Most of the time, it's not."

"You're right."

"I will never hurt you on purpose."

"I know."

"Do you?"

"I'm trying, Joe."

Marley was in a sharing mood and on a roll, so I pushed, but not before stretching my arms across the table and offering my palms. "Why have you never invited me inside your house?"

Head tilted, she considered her reply before sliding her delicate hands into mine. "Because that's the one space in this world that's mine and mine alone. The only place I feel safe."

"That's a great answer. But it's bullshit." I released her fingers and sat back, throwing my hands in the air. "You don't wanna talk about whatever you've got to hide, that's fine, but don't lie to me, gorgeous. I've got thick skin. If you're hung up over some guy who broke your heart, we'll work around it."

The flame was back, brightening the gold in her hazel beauties. "There's nothing to work around."

"No?" My stomach soured, but hell, relenting was not an option. "You cried for hours in my backyard over some man, drunk outta your gourd."

She opened her mouth to speak. Studied me. Then dropped her head and poked at a piece of noodle. "You wouldn't understand."

Frustrating woman. "Try me."

"He was my world. One day he was there, and the next, he was gone."

"He died?" The words lost steam through the lump in my throat. How the hell could I compete with a dead man?

"No," she whispered, face going ashen.

Okay, the guy Marley clearly loved was still alive, and by the look on her face, she had more to confess. At that point, though, only one thing I needed to know. "If he came knocking on your door, you'd take him back."

"With open arms." She fucking smiled through the sadness haunting her eyes.

Christ, that hurt. "And where would that leave me?"

"Joe," she whispered.

"I really am wasting my time, aren't I?"

Wiping the moisture from her eyes, she rasped, "What do you want from me?"

"Just you."

"I don't believe you."

"Why?" God, my chest ached. I slammed my hands on the table and pushed to my feet. "Why's that so hard to believe?"

"Men, Joe!" Marley stood, too, grabbed her plate and mine, then looked up, staring me down. "Men tell you, 'I want you. I love you. I need you.' They tell you what you want to hear, they squeeze you dry, and then..." She headed for the sink. "And then they leave."

Hands clasped behind my head, I stared at her back, frustrated, but not enough to give up. "Name them."

"Who?" she asked over her shoulder.

"The shitheads who did that to you."

She huffed. "Name them?"

"You heard me. Say their names," I challenged. "Out loud. I want to hear their names."

"No." She turned on the faucet, ran a plate under the water. "This is ridiculous."

"You give them too much power."

The plate dropped into the sink. Slow and steady, Marley turned off the faucet, dried her hands, then turned and leaned her hip against the counter.

"You're right." With a nod, she came closer, gripped my waist, rested her forehead on my chest. Then she broke my fucking heart when she raised glassy eyes to mine and, spirit drained, she said in a quiet but sure voice, "I gave them too much power. I gave them everything. Because that's what we do. That's what moms and daughters do."

Marley walked away, and I let her go, processing her statement. I watched her leave, Bruce trotting behind, and I swear to Christ, the mutt shot me a glare over his shoulder.

°°°°°°°°°°°

I took five minutes to digest Marley's parting words: *That's what moms and daughters do.*

Ginger followed me to the door as if she knew exactly where I was headed. She grunted when I scooped her off the ground but gave my chin a lick in a show of support. That, or I had grease on my face. Either way, I appreciated the gesture.

Marley answered her door on the fourth knock.

"You said 'moms and daughters.'"

Shoulders rising and falling on a deep inhale and exhale, she studied me, then stepped aside, pushed the door open wide and gestured for me to enter. I didn't hesitate. I was in. Her last wall breached.

The home was small and cozy. The entryway took me

234

into an open space with a living room to the right and a dining room to the left. A long countertop separated the eating area and outdated kitchen. Straight ahead, a hallway led to the rest of the house.

There was no rhyme or reason to the color scheme. The furniture didn't match, as if she'd collected different pieces over the years and made them fit. One wall was painted beige, another a soft green, and the hallway was some shade of reddish brown.

What caught my eye, what made my guts knot, were the pictures hanging on her walls. Sticking with the hodge-podge theme, none of the frames matched, but the subject was the same: a boy as a baby, a toddler, an awkward kid, and a punk-ass teen.

"Who is he?"

Marley uncrossed her arms and dragged a finger down one of the photos. He wore baseball gear and a familiar smile. "This is my son, Dylan."

My vision blurred, and the air left my lungs. Dizzy, I stumbled back a step, and after I could see straight and breathe right, I replied, "Your son?"

Of all the things I'd expected her to say, "son" was not one of them.

"You have a kid?" Ginger wiggled in my arms. I set her down, and she sniffed around, ignoring Bruce's attempts at getting her attention.

Marley nodded, gnawing her bottom lip.

"Where is he?"

"I haven't seen him since his eighteenth birthday."

"Military?"

"No."

"Wait." I scratched at the tingle on my forehead. "You have an adult son?" I'd never considered her age. "You're too young."

"I got knocked up when I was fifteen. And before you judge, I know"—Marley threw up her hands—"Daddy issues. Looking for love in all the wrong places. In my case, that's true."

"I'm not judging. Took me by surprise, that's all." I stepped close, but she backed away. "Hey." I needed her to know we had another thing in common. "My mom was sixteen when she had me."

Her worried expression softened.

"Why did you wait this long to tell me?"

"It's hard to discuss. I mean, if my only child wants nothing to do with me, why would any man? There has to be something seriously wrong with me, right?"

There was no right or wrong answer. None that would ease the pain. "Why haven't you seen him?"

Marley started to speak but stopped, her lip quivering. Seconds passed while she gained her composure. "On his eighteenth birthday, he said goodbye and left for school. Never came home. I was terrified. I called his phone, called the police, all of his friends. That night, I found a note on his bed, said he'd moved out and he'd contact me when he was ready to talk."

"That's fucked up. You tried to find—"

Marley held up a hand, stopping my question. "I don't want to talk about Dylan. My father abandoned me. Dylan's dad and parents wanted nothing to do with us. Every guy I dated left the second things got real, like temper tantrums, dirty diapers, or anything to do with parenting. Not one of those men hurt me the way my son did. Dylan hurt me so deep I can't find words to describe the pain."

Marley drew a breath, leaned back against the wall. "So, yes, I'm bitter. Yes, I'm hesitant to open myself up to rejection again. I'm not hung up over one guy. I've been battered and bruised by every important man in my life since I was a child."

Damn. There weren't words. No words. I thought of my mom. The sacrifices she'd made. The love she'd given. Had I been appreciative enough? Had I thanked her enough? Sure, we'd fought, and I'd rebelled. But never had I considered turning my back on that beautiful woman.

What could I say? Not a goddamn thing. Instead, I wrapped my arms around Marley and squeezed. I held her until her taut muscles relaxed and her arms looped around my waist. I hugged her until she snuggled closer, her breaths slowed, and she whispered, "I'm not in the mood for sex tonight."

Sure, Little Joe was disappointed, but truth be told, she'd already given what I came for—answers. A piece of herself that hurt her to share.

Arms still around her, I walked her to the couch and eased her into the cushions. Bracing her head, I leaned down to drop a kiss on the worry wrinkles between her brows. "I'll be right back." I kissed her nose, then grabbed her remote off the coffee table and laid it in her lap. "Find a good movie. I need to go put the cannelloni away. You want beer or wine?"

Blinking up at me, she said, "I'd love a cup of herbal tea. Do you still have Alice's stash?"

Fuck me. I couldn't hide my grin. "Coming up."

I jogged to my house and took care of the dishes. Then I returned with a box of Celestial Seasonings and Alice's favorite teacup because I had a feeling my aunt and a warm cup of chamomile had nursed Marley through many a grieving night.

Marley didn't say a damn thing, just scooted over and made room for me on the sofa. An open bottle of Guinness waited for me on the coffee table.

Marley fell asleep an hour later with her head on my lap. At midnight, I followed her to her bed. At six AM, I woke with Ginger snuggled against my left hip and Bruce's hot breath on my right cheek. Marley was MIA, but still, I'd never been more content.

CHAPTER
Twenty

Jazz, my newest employee, leaned over the ice machine, her sheer white teddy riding high to reveal the glitter-dusted globes of her ass. "What do you suppose they're doing over there?"

I glanced past the Ford Focus at the window and across the street to the once empty lot. Four men had worked tirelessly since sunrise. The fruits of their labor? A two-story finished frame.

"Looks like they're building a coffee stand," I said over my shoulder.

The man in the Ford stroked his swollen, purple cock, staring at my tits, eyes glazed, but paying no mind to our conversation. Once again, I offered him his coffee with cream. This time, he blinked away the lust haze and accepted his drink.

I forced a smile, mustered sugar through the sour tang in my mouth, and said, "Have a great day," before sliding my window shut. The masturbators got off faster if we watched them finish, and some paid well if we did. I never watched. No tip was worth that freak show.

"Hmm. A little competition. Sounds exciting." Jazz's deep rasp matched her appearance—tall, dark, and gorgeous. Face art was her forte, and every shift she arrived in a new disguise. Were I to bump into her in public, sans her barista costume, I wouldn't recognize the girl.

"That lot has been vacant since I've been here. Glad to see someone moving in." Feet aching, I headed to the closet and kicked off my peep-toe platforms.

A familiar rumble sent a shiver over my skin, drawing my attention to the security feed. And oh, jeez, my sappy, syrupy heart beat double-time.

Joe rolled into line behind a black Lexus. He wore his helmet, dark glasses, and jeans that hugged his solid thighs.

I shoved my feet back into my heels, checked myself in the mirror, and poured drinks while Jazz took care of customers. When it came Joe's turn at the window, I shooed her away and said, "This one's mine."

The man stole my air, and I drew a deep breath before greeting him. "You're not here to harass me, are you?"

"Tried to call you," he said, removing his Oakleys, flashing a gorgeous grin. His ridiculous muscles bulged and flexed, making it impossible to think straight.

"Sorry. Been busy." True. I hadn't time to check my cell all day. Sunny days brought the boys out to play. "What's up?"

"Bruce dug under the fence." His whole body shook with laughter, those eye wrinkles making an appearance. "Found him stuck halfway through."

"Oh, my God." I laughed. "Is my baby okay?"

"Dog's fine. Had to tear a few boards out to free him."

"I'm so sorry." Not sorry. Not one little bit upset that Joe paid me a visit.

"No need to apologize. Patched up the fence. Ginger and Bruce are safe in my backyard, happy as clams."

"Thanks, Joe."

He nodded toward the crew across the street, a playful twinkle in his eye. "Looks like you've got some competition moving in."

"Yeah. Seems so."

Those eyes brightened from brilliant to blinding. "Could be fun."

"How's that?"

"You got competition." He waggled his brows. "You're gonna have to get creative."

"Only if it's a topless stand," I retorted, rolling my eyes.

At the word topless, Joe's gaze drifted to the mesh crop top that reached only to the bottom of my breasts. Kudos to the guy. He'd held on longer than most.

"It's torture keeping my eyes above your chin right now," he admitted, his voice unbearably dark and hungry.

"Does it hurt?"

"Li'l bit." He chuckled, his shoulders bouncing, his blue eyes finding mine. "A kiss would make everything better."

"No, Joe." I shook my head, pointing a finger his way. "We're just fuck buddies. No PDA."

Joe tore his gaze from me and stared straight ahead for an uncomfortable spell before huffing and raising a brow. "You wanna kiss me, too. I can tell."

A kiss from Joe was everything. The problem was, one lip-lock was never enough. "I'm working. Knock it off."

He stared at my mouth, his tongue sweeping across his lower lip. My nipples hardened, threatening to break the seal of tape holding my cherry-shaped pasties in place.

I was screwed. Head over heels in lust. If he'd said please, I would've jumped through the window and onto his lap. Joe was that potent. And I, shamefully, was that weak to his charms. "I'll pay you back for the fence repairs."

"Not necessary." He allowed himself a gander up and down my body, neck to toes, a mischievous grin lighting his face. "I gotta get to work."

"Work?" I leaned against the window frame, arms crossed, and teased, "You work?"

"Didn't I tell you, Masters?" He shoved his glasses back onto his face and looked straight ahead. "Got a job."

"Ooh. Mysterious." Shame weighted my shoulders. The last few nights we'd spent together, there'd been little talking, and he'd clearly been exhausted, bags under his eyes, no appetite, though that hadn't stopped his performance in the sack. "Gonna tell me about this new job of yours?"

The left corner of his lip lifted, cocky and playful. "Later, neighbor."

Before I could respond, he revved the engine and rolled away.

His retreat left me wanting and jealous of every woman who'd ever sat on the back of that bike. With a sigh, I turned and bumped into Jazz, who'd been ogling over my shoulder.

"Girl"—she fanned herself with a punch card—"please tell me you're tappin' that."

"We're just fu—" Jeez, I would not indulge. "We're friends."

"Not buying it." She shook her head, pointing a sparkly silver claw-shaped nail my way. That man is into you."

Again, I headed to the closet and stepped out of my shoes. "Every man who visits Pink Sweets is into me, long as I'm mostly naked."

Jazz rolled her eyes, not fooled. "Whatever. He's hot. And I've never heard you talk like that to anyone."

"Like what?" I faked offense, slapping a palm to my chest.

"All gooey and sweet." She batted her lashes, then turned to help the next patron.

"Gooey and sweet is not in my DNA," I protested, then turned to change out of my cheeky shorts.

Boom! Our neon *Open* sign exploded, sparks flying. I screamed. Jazz stumbled backward, her ankle twisting, dropping her to the floor, thank God, because there was another loud bang, and a bottle of syrup exploded right behind where she'd stood.

Covering my head, I dove to the floor, grabbed Jazz's wrist, and tugged until she scrambled on hands and knees to shelter with me behind the closet door.

Tires squealed outside. Horns honked.

Jazz and I clung to each other, shaking and cursing, and we didn't move from our cubby until sirens and flashing lights blared outside.

⁂

Tucked in Joe's arm, head on his shoulder, and floating in that fuzzy state of post-coital bliss, I traced the lines of artwork on his chest. "When are you going to tell me about your new job?"

The muscles in his arm tightened. "I'll tell you about my new job when you talk to me about the shooting."

"You know what I know. Those bullets were likely meant for the customer at our window." The man had sped off after the first shot, but our cameras had captured his license plate, and he was a known member of a violent south end gang. Unfortunately, the shooter was not caught on film nor by any witnesses.

Joe grunted, rolled on top of me, then hooked my knees with his arms and drove his spectacular cock deep, folding me in half.

Staring down at me, he said, "That's not what I meant," before rolling his hips and drawing an erotic whimper from my lips. "I don't want the facts," he growled. "I want to know how you're doing."

"Right now," I managed to rasp, "I'm grateful for the

past two years of yoga." I gripped his forearms and squeezed, my body so consumed and contorted by Joe, I was utterly helpless and at his mercy.

I loved the way his muscles rippled under my fingertips, loved that glassy, heady way he stared into me, jaw tight, neck muscles straining, on the razor's edge of control.

"Dammit, woman." He half laughed, half yelled, driving deeper and curling over me, his knees at my ribs, his face in mine. "You had to be terrified. You haven't cried or thrown a fit. Don't hold that shit in, gorgeous."

Seriously. Was Joe Kaine for real?

"I'm good. I promise." Ever since the gossip train had informed him of the incident, Joe hadn't left my side. The truth hit me then, and though I hated depending on anyone, I confessed, "I'm okay because you've been with me."

Joe stared, long and hard, his arms trembling. Then he muttered, "Good answer, babe," dropped my legs, kissed me hard, and fucked me deep.

My orgasm was so intense, I cried.

We lay in bed, sweaty and sated, neither of us eager to move.

Into the darkness, I blurted a question that had bothered me for days. "You said Alice inherited millions?"

"Yeah." Joe shifted next to me.

"Why did she buy this house in this neighborhood?"

Joe sighed as he rolled toward me and draped his arm across my belly. "Alice and Bill had property on the lake. Big boat. Expensive cars." His chest rose and fell against my shoulder. "Only thing Bill let Alice invest in was property, even though the money was hers to begin with. This was one of three houses she owned. It was a rental for a while." Another sigh, followed by a long pause. "Long story short, Bill gambled, borrowed from the wrong people, made shady deals. He lost everything."

"Poor Alice," I muttered.

Joe laughed. "Alice was smart, though. While Bill was living it up, she put herself through school. Got a job as a social worker, so she had her own income. She moved into this place, and the rest is history."

"I don't understand. How can someone lose five million dollars?"

"Good fucking question," he grunted. "But I'm not surprised. You weren't entirely wrong about me when we first met. I come from a long line of criminals."

My heart sank. I'd made hurtful assumptions based on one fact. Did I trust myself to hear the whole story?

Joe left me no choice by continuing. "My great grandfather ran underground gambling and bars. Made his own moonshine. My grandfather took over when his father passed. Brought drugs in at that point, and the criminal activity snowballed from there." He laughed, shook his head. "They were shitty criminals. Spent more time in lockup than out. Spent their money faster than they earned it."

I braved the question, "What about your father?"

"My dad?" Joe rolled to his back and lay silent for a long while, the only sound his heavy breaths. "Blackhearted from the get-go. In and out of juvie. Mom was a doe-eyed Catholic girl who fell for a boy from the wrong side of the tracks. Bastard knocked her up, then left town when my mom's dad threatened to have him thrown in jail for statutory rape."

"Oh, jeez. Your mom must've been heartbroken."

"She loved him," he whispered, then continued. "He came back three years later, the day Mom turned eighteen, riding a Harley and wearing a leather cut with a skull and snake on the back."

"MC?"

Joe huffed. "Yeah. He was dead set on taking Mom and me to Montana. She refused, thank God. She wanted better for her only son."

"You didn't miss growing up without him?"

"Sure, I did. Dad came around once or twice a year, threw money at Mom, gave me expensive gifts, said we could have a better life if we lived with him. Then he'd leave, and we wouldn't hear from him for another six months."

I hated the man for hurting Joe. "He's still there?"

"He'll die there." His answer was gruff, and he swallowed hard. "That club is his family."

"Jeez, Joe. I'm sorry."

"Don't be sorry for me, gorgeous." Joe rolled back to his side and drew lines around my nipples with his finger. "Mom was the best. My grandparents helped as much as they could until they passed. I had Frank and Con, and I had Alice. My life was good."

When I asked, "Do you see your father anymore?" Joe moved his hand to rest again on my belly.

"Spent the past six years working for him," he mumbled.

He may as well have punched me. "What?" I flipped to my side, bringing my nose to his neck. "I thought you had just gotten out of prison when you came back."

The jerk had the nerve to laugh. "You assumed."

"And you let me keep on assuming."

Warm fingers dug into my waist and rocked our bodies closer. "Would you have heard me out?"

"I don't know," I answered honestly, then threw a leg over his hip because the man was hard again and I wanted that thick erection between my thighs.

My phone chimed.

"Not now," I groaned.

Joe reached over my head, snatched my cell from the nightstand, and placed it in my hand.

The text was from an unknown number.

It's your dad. We need to talk.

I hit delete. The phone chimed again.

Don't ignore me, baby girl. We need to talk.

"Speaking of shitty dads," I grumbled.

The annoyance was plucked from my fingers and tossed to the end of the bed. Then Joe helped me forget about the sins of our fathers with a few of his own wicked tricks.

⸺ ⸻ ⸺

My internal alarm blared, jolting me awake. "What time is it?" I reached for the phone that wasn't there.

Joe rolled over, checked his cell, mumbled, "Four-thirty," then dropped his head back into his pillow.

"Shit. Shit. Shit!" Panic fueled my frenzy while I searched in the dark for my clothes and hopped around attempting to dress. When decent enough, I jumped on the bed, slapped Joe's fabulous ass, and said, "See ya later."

"Wait, I'll drive you."

"No. I'm fine." I jogged down the stairs, hollered for Bruce, and made it out the door just as Joe stumbled down the steps, trying to wrestle into his sweats.

"Marley, wait."

When I passed my driveway, a cold chill crept up my spine. My skin prickled, and a heavy dread weighted the air. At the door, I glanced left, then right as I wiggled the key in the lock.

A low whistle came from the direction of Mr. Slavic's yard. Bruce barked at the same time I whipped around. A hooded figure stood in the road, and my blood turned frosty.

He stared. I couldn't move. Bruce continued to bark but stayed at my feet, the hairs on his nape raised, his butt rubbing my thigh like he was trying to herd me inside the house.

Good idea.

I forced my legs to move and turned back toward the door, knocking the keychain to the ground in the process. Profanities spewed from my lips, muffled by the roar of my racing heartbeat.

Bruce growled, and I chanced a glance over my shoulder. The man was closer, almost in my front yard. Still, my bodyguard didn't advance but stuck to my side.

The cold metal was heaven to my fingertips as I scooped the keys off the porch and worked the lock, my hands shaking something fierce, my heart threatening to explode.

I shoved the door open with my shoulder and slipped inside, Bruce hot on my heels. After engaging all three locks, I flattened my palms and forehead against the door, eyes closed, measuring my breaths until my pulse slowed.

Bam. Bam. Bam.

Three hard knocks hit the door, and I could swear, lightning struck my spine, jump-starting every nerve in my body. A scream tore through me fast and fierce.

"Marley. Hey. It's me." Joe's voice came muffled through the solid wood. "You left your phone. Thought you might need it."

I ripped the door open and curled myself around his half-naked body, arms around his neck, ankles locked behind his glutes. "You scared the shit outta me."

"Jesus. Sorry."

He carried me through the door, then shut and locked it behind us. I couldn't have let go if I tried. Fear and relief poured out of me in violent trembles. Joe didn't mock or coddle, only held me close, one hand supporting my butt and the other bracing my back, his fingers digging into my skin, grip tight, silently assuring me, *I've got you.*

Nobody had ever had me.

"What's going on?" His voice vibrated with worry.

Embarrassed to meet his gaze, I whispered into his neck, "Did you see the man out there?"

"I didn't see anyone." He tried to set me down, but I wasn't moving, not for a million dollars. With a grunt, he turned to look out the window. "Nobody's there."

"He was there. Middle of the street. Staring at me."

"That's why you screamed when I knocked?" he asked. "Christ, you're trembling."

My criminal, my fuck buddy, my neighbor with scary tattoos and impossible muscles, soothed me with kisses and hushes and soft caresses. I savored every pathetic second and soaked up his strength, affection, and touch like a love-starved child.

God, I *was* acting like a child.

And I didn't care. Somebody had my back. Joe had me, and I'd never felt more cherished.

. ° . ° . ° . °. °. ° . ° . °

Joe parked next to the door, cut the engine, then turned to me. "Thanks for letting me drive you to work."

"You didn't give me a choice." When I'd finally calmed, he'd waited on my couch while I showered and dressed. When I'd told him goodbye and handed him my spare key (because I decided he needed one, just in case), he'd thrown me over his shoulder and carried me to his truck.

"Bothered me seeing you shaken up. I can relax a little, knowing you're here, locked in, safe and snug. You will lock up, right?"

I jingled my keys in his face. "Always do."

"Good." He didn't look convinced.

"I've done this for years and never had a problem," I assured him. "I might've overreacted this morning. You know, considering all that's been going on." *Fires, shootings, attempted break-ins*, I left unsaid.

"Don't discount your fear like that." Joe leaned back, crossed his arms. "Listen to your gut. You were creeped out for a reason."

Truth. Still, I shriveled like a scolded child while my cheeks heated, embarrassed that I'd behaved the way I had.

Joe nodded toward the nearly completed stand across the street. "Find out about your competition yet?"

Bless his heart for knowing when to change the subject.

"Haven't delved too deep. Whoever the owner is has brass balls, that's for sure."

Prius Guy sped by, slammed his brakes, and rolled to the window.

"This guy for real?" Joe growled.

I rolled my eyes. "First customer every morning."

"He looks like a serial killer."

"He's harmless." I waved his comment away. "And the most well mannered of all my customers." I refrained from mentioning he'd never arrived more than ten minutes before opening until the day Joe had beat him to the window.

The Prius shut off, and I could swear the man was glaring at us through his side-view mirror.

"I better get in there." I reached for the door handle.

"Hold up." Joe hopped out of the truck, jogged around the hood, and opened my door.

"That wasn't necessary."

"Says who?"

"Um, me?"

"Shut it, neighbor. I open doors for my ladies. My mom would slap me silly if I didn't do otherwise."

My ladies. Like he'd laid claim. Crazy how that statement didn't bother me in the least. "Okay then, for Mama Joe. Not because you're my boyfriend or anything."

Joe's truck was tall, and I was short, so I didn't protest when he gripped my waist and helped me down, nor did I mind when he kissed my forehead the second my feet hit the pavement. I might have swooned when he moaned and squeezed my ass before letting go.

He followed me to the door, though it was mere steps away, and waited, hands shoved deep into the pockets of his sweats, until I'd entered and fired up the power on all machines.

"I have a few meetings today," he informed me. "Should be back around noon."

If I had it my way, I'd tuck him in the closet for whenever I needed a quick Joe fix. "I can get a ride home."

"You're leaving for your mom's tomorrow." His gaze dropped to the floor, and he rubbed the back of his neck. "Getting my fill of you today. I'll be here to drive you home. Got an issue with that?"

"No issues whatsoever." My cheeks ached from grinning so wide.

He pulled his bottom lip between his teeth and studied my mouth, nodding. A million questions swirled in those eyes.

"What?" I asked.

Joe sighed. He looked over my shoulder before he hit me with a compassionate gaze. "Why do this if you're the boss? Not judging. Genuinely curious. Why aren't you more behind the scenes?"

"If I expect my girls to serve coffee half-naked, I should be willing to do the same. Wouldn't you appreciate and respect your boss so much more if they were down in the trenches with you?"

"I suppose."

Another car pulled in, the headlights blinding. A quick glance at the clock reminded me it was time to dress. "I gotta go."

He leaned forward as if to kiss me goodbye, but I stepped away.

"Not here. I'm on the job."

"And the horny fuckers who drive through will tip better if they think they stand a chance with you."

"Bingo." I reached up, gave his cheek a pat, and said, "Bye, Joe," then closed the door and locked myself in.

Faster than a Broadway dancer, I stripped out of my sweats and slapped on my outfit, a simple black bikini. I made myself an espresso, flipped the lights to the *On* position, then fixed my lipstick, feeling only slightly guilty for making Prius Guy wait.

I slid open the window and gave him a perky, "Good morning."

He wore his usual attire, dress shirt and tie. Hair was the same, combed back off his face. But those eyes? Dark. Vacant. And staring straight at me. Never once in all the years of patronage had he made direct eye contact.

"Morning," he said, tone brusque.

"Usual?" I forced sweetness into my voice, feeling anything but.

Lips pursed, he nodded, and the same painful tingles I'd felt a mere hour ago shimmied up my spine and over my scalp.

I made his soymilk latte, ignoring the prickles on my

bare skin, and for the first time since opening Pink Sweets, I considered retiring my pasties.

Maybe the time had come for me to step behind the scenes. Age was nobody's friend, especially mine. My figure was harder to maintain, and my youthful glow was more a flicker, as tended to happen when you had to grow up too fast. Or maybe Joe had wormed his way inside my head, made me question my future in the sexy coffee industry.

Either way, the vulnerability was raw and honest and pissing me off.

Before turning to face my customer again, I drew a deep breath and released the air nice and slow, willing my shoulders to relax and my thoughts to calm.

When I turned, he held a fifty-dollar bill toward me. I exchanged the bill for his mug, and he drove away before I could make change. No nod. No "thank you." Just gone.

"Thank God," I mumbled to the ceiling. The knot in my gut finally loosened.

Until I noticed Joe rolling out of the lot. He, too, failed to acknowledge me as he followed the Prius north, a deadly glare aimed at the tiny car.

CHAPTER
Twenty One

Bruce dashed after the ball, surprisingly agile for his size. He loped back and dropped the sloppy mess at my feet, a smile on his face, his stubby tail wagging. I glanced at Joe's house. No sign of life.

We'd only been home from Whisper Springs for a few hours, and though I'd needed that visit with my mother, I'd spent every day of the past week missing my neighbor.

Joe had texted obsessively. Checking in. Sending stupid memes. Dick pics every night. Never thought I'd be a girl who liked getting dick pics, but Joe made everything fun, and his cock was a work of art.

My phone buzzed, setting my heart to flight, and I tugged the cell out of my back pocket.

Lilly. Not Joe. My ticker crashed back to earth with a splat.

"Hey, girl. Everything okay?"

"I know it's your last day of vacation, but you need to get your ass over here."

Horrible scenarios flashed through my mind. Most of them involved Prius Guy, a machete, and bloodied baristas. Not sure why, but that guy had weaseled his way under my skin. "What happened?"

"Our new neighbors moved in."

A wave of relief washed over me. Nobody was hurt, thank God. "That bad?"

"Worse," she huffed. "So much worse."

"Goddamnit!" I shouted, kicking Bruce's ball in frustration. "Just tell me."

"Did you just use the Lord's name in vain?"

So not the time for humor. "You are so fired."

"Just get your butt over here, and bring your boxing gloves." Lilly ended the call.

I hustled Bruce into my Subi and reached Pink Sweets sixteen minutes later.

I parked next to Lilly's Charger and stared across the street, disbelieving.

Thank goodness I was alone because the litany of profanities I spewed would've caused others' ears to bleed.

The building itself was beautiful. Blacks, grays, and industrial steel. Every element looked repurposed, even the bricks that trimmed the bottom floor. Put my little shack to shame, for sure.

One shirtless man worked the window. Muscles. Tan. Chiseled jaw. Faded jeans that hung dangerously low on his waist.

Another stood outside leaning against a Harley. Tan. Muscles. Beard. He smiled. Chatted with the ladies as they passed. He, too, was shirtless. Black riding pants hugged his physique like a glove.

The line stretched around the building, five cars deep, two of which were minivans carrying three or more women each.

The coup de grâce? The name. Bold, bright, in-your-face letters.

Average Joe.

Average fucking Joe.

Fuck.

Speak of the devil. Joe stepped around the corner of the building, wearing a smile I could've spied a mile away. He looked my direction, then to the guy on the motorcycle. His head whipped my way again and then, jaywalking laws be damned, he jogged across two lanes of traffic.

I cracked the windows for Bruce and stepped onto the pavement, shielding my eyes from the sun as I tried to make sense of the scene.

"Welcome home, gorgeous," he drawled, assessing me with a hungry gaze.

I was irate, but no one would know by the way "Joe" left my lips, breathy and desperate because, sweet vanilla latte, the man was a sight for horny eyes. Those thick lips landed on mine, those talented hands slid to my ass, and with a grunt, I was lifted into strong arms and pinned against my car. Joe kissed me dizzy, and I reciprocated with five days' worth of pent-up frustration.

When we broke for air, he cupped my face and, forehead to mine, whispered, "Fuck, I missed you."

Bruce scratched and whined at the window my back was pressed against. Joe laughed, set me on my feet, then opened my car door and greeted my dog with coos and cuddles and panty-melting tenderness.

I turned again to face the scene across the street, and the line had increased by two vehicles.

Bruce whined when Joe secured him back inside the car.

"Quite a spectacle, huh?" He hung an arm over my shoulder, tucking me against his hard body. "Fucking genius, don't ya think?"

Average Joe. I'd told Joe he was average all those weeks ago.

Unholy heat blasted through me.

He wouldn't. Couldn't.

But, damn, that shit-eating grin on his face told me he had.

"You did this." I spun out of his hold.

"Me and the guys." Joe crossed his arms, settled back on his heels, chin high, proud.

"What guys, and why?" I mimicked his pose, chin raised, pissed.

"Guys that care about you and your girls." That sharp gaze sliced from Average Joe to me, then with a wink, he declared. "And because you said I couldn't do it."

I'd said he couldn't do it a million years ago before I'd known better. Before I'd known *him*.

The bastard had the nerve to boop my nose with his forefinger. "Hope you're ready to bring your A game 'cause it's on, neighbor."

Joe pulled off his T-shirt in that sexy way only men can do and jogged across the street to join the other shirtless boys.

Lilly appeared at the back door of Pink Sweets. "I swear, boss, I had no idea Marco was in on this. I just found out and, believe me, that man will be sleeping on the patio for the foreseeable future."

"Marco? What do you mean?" I rubbed my aching temples. "I'm so confused right now."

"Marco. Joe." Her volume rose. "A couple of Joe's buddies. They partnered on this bullshit." She waved her hand in the direction of Average Joe. "I swear to the good Lord above, if that asshole thinks he can spy on me..." Lilly's rant trailed off, her face turned a shade of red I'd never seen, and she curled her lips between her teeth, shaking her head and fighting tears.

Spy? Marco was protective, but he'd never crossed a line.

A million questions bubbled in my head, but two cars pulled into our lot, and Lilly headed inside.

Bruce whined. I ignored the rising irritation and shot

one more glare in Joe's direction before slinking back into my car and heading home.

CHAPTER
Twenty Two

"You've been quiet today." Frank slammed the locker door shut. "Neighbor lady still mad?"

"Haven't heard from her." Three days had passed. Ginger and I missed the hell outta Bruce and Marley. I'd almost crawled to her door last night and begged her to come to bed with me, even just to sleep, but I'd made a dirty play by keeping Average Joe a secret, and the ball was in her court.

Frank shoved his trainers inside his duffle and checked his face in the mirror before following me out of the locker room. "Those guys you hired are great, by the way. Cyn drove through, gave them hell, and they handled her like a princess."

"Yeah?" I shoved through the exit and headed toward my bike. "They better be great. We're paying them too much to fuck up."

"Gotta admit"—he laughed, matching me stride for stride across the parking lot—"wasn't sure this idea was gonna play in our favor, but shit, the guys stayed almost an hour over closing time last night. There was an endless parade of horny housewives driving through." He tossed his bag into his truck bed. "I'm just worried the novelty will wear off, and in a few months, you'll have to shut down."

That'd been a concern, but I tried to assure him that we

hadn't made a mistake. "Sex sells, brother." I clapped his shoulder. "And we're in Seattle. Coffee is everything."

"Do you even like making coffee? I mean, it's a far cry from being a cop."

True. Though a million times better than sorting people's trash.

"I like being my own boss." Bonus? The view across the street was every man's fantasy. Plus, the shop was mine. I waited for two women to pass before saying, "And the business is legit."

Frank held my gaze and nodded in understanding. The Kaine genes were defective, and he'd watched me struggle to stay on the straight and narrow for too many years.

Our silent communication teetered on uncomfortable before Frank broke the tension and said, "And let's not forget the most important thing."

"What's that?"

"You're doing it to impress the woman you love."

Love? Hmm... Hadn't considered my stake in staying close to Marley, pushing her buttons, proving her wrong about what I was capable of accomplishing. But, hey, the shoe seemed to fit. I ached when she wasn't with me. And regardless of whether we fucked or fought, my soul calmed when she was in eyesight. I hadn't taken time to consider what that meant but, yeah, Frank was right, so I didn't argue.

Instead, I asked, "Any luck with that license plate?"

Frank shook his head. "The guy has a clean record. Not even a parking ticket."

"Nothing, huh?" Not good enough. "Sure you can't give me a name?"

Frank gnawed his lip, looked over my shoulder, fighting an inner battle. "You know damn well I can't tell you that his name is Logan Shaw."

God bless Frank Garcia. I played along, shrugging. "Can't blame a guy for trying. I have a bad feeling about that man."

"You know I've always got your back. I'll look deeper into this guy if it eases your mind." Frank rounded his truck and shouted over the hood, "Just stay away from him in the meantime."

I waved in agreement.

Staying away wouldn't be a problem as long as that creep did nothing more than buy coffee from my girl. Seriously, how dangerous could the guy be? He drove a Prius, for fuck's sake.

. . . .

"No friends today?" Ly asked, gesturing toward the chair.

"Not today. I'm sorry." Con was out of town, and Frank had court, so I'd found myself alone for our standing appointment at Emerald Glow.

I stepped out of my shoes and into the churning water before getting comfortable in the chair. Twelve-hour shifts for the past seven days had done a number, and my feet were in dire need of Ly's skills.

"How's business?" I asked, playing with the settings on the chair's remote.

"Good. Always good."

Trudy emerged from the back room, shot me a wink, and said, "Hi, Joe."

A grin cracked my face. The tiny woman held two white paper cups with the Average Joe logo stamped on the front. She set one at her mom's nail station, then sat at her station and held the opening of the lid below her nose, drawing a deep inhale.

"Good?" I asked.

"Mmm," she nodded.

Ly said something in Vietnamese to her daughter, and Trudy responded, then came over to fill the tub in the chair next to mine. The three of us exchanged small talk while Trudy got ready for her next appointment and Ly worked her wonders on my tired feet. I hadn't even considered asking about the comings and goings at the coffee stand outside. Eventually, I closed my eyes and let my head fall back.

The bell on the door rattled. I was too exhausted and too damn relaxed to look.

"Hi!" Trudy greeted her customer.

"Hi, Trudy. Hi, Ly," came a perky voice from the front door. "Thanks for fitting me in on short notice today."

My whole body jolted awake. I'd missed that voice something fierce.

Ly responded, "We had two cancellations this morning."

Marley came our way, stopped when our gazes clashed, then worked that killer smile like she was thrilled to be in my presence. "Well... now I know why your feet are so pretty."

She wore black leggings, a Seahawks T-shirt that hung just below her hips, and mismatching flip-flops, one red, one blue with white stripes. That beautiful reddish-brown hair sat knotted on her head, and she wore no makeup on her face. She also, I noticed, wore zero animosity toward me in her expression and body language.

"Neighbor." The greeting came out garbled, and I cleared my throat. Fuck. She was a sight. "Not working today?"

"I'm always working. Just sticking to office stuff today." She made her way to the other chair, bent at the waist to pull the hem of her leggings up to her knees, then settled in.

I couldn't tear my gaze away. Also couldn't help but ask, "You think my feet are pretty?"

Her smile and laughter righted every wrong I'd ever suffered. "Very well groomed for a hardworking man."

"Didn't know you had a thing for feet," I teased, shooting her a wink.

"Hard not to notice. You're always barefoot or in flip-flops when you're home."

"Oh," Ly cut in, "Marley is your neighbor?" Her wide eyes filled with too much joy.

Trudy snorted behind her mask, then shook her head, trying not to laugh.

"Small world," Ly continued, curious gaze bouncing between Marley and me. "Joe talk about you all the time. Every day I see him, he go on and on about his pretty neighbor."

"That so?" Marley looked my way, a damn adorable smirk on her face.

I was in the shit. No getting out.

"Oh, yes," Ly said, then lifted my left foot to scrub my heel. She shot Marley a scowl. "Why you no like Joe? He good man."

"Mama," Trudy pleaded, rolling her eyes.

"Kill me now," I mumbled under my breath, then turned away, pretending to stare out the window, silently willing an asteroid to fall on the tiny strip mall.

It was then that I saw Harper's car pull up to the stand across the way, and the tell-all convo faded to background noise. My no-good uncle sat in the passenger seat. Both men exited the Escalade. Larry pulled a duffel bag out of the back seat, scanned the parking lot, then followed Harper inside Dirty Dreamz.

"Ly, I think you've got it wrong. I like Joe. Very much. But we can't be more than friends. You see, he built a coffee stand across the street from mine, and I have it on good authority that he did it to spy on me and my girls. Kinda creepy, don't you think?"

The drive-up window to Dirty Dreamz slammed shut, and the *Closed* sign lit up. Strange for eight in the morning.

"Did you hear that, Joe?" Marley spoke louder. "Little creepy, right?"

I couldn't tear my eyes away from the scene across the lot, but I'd heard Marley loud and clear. "I opened Average Joe because you said I couldn't. I never back down from a challenge. The spying part is just a perk."

"So you *are* spying!" Marley's shout bounced off the walls.

"Wasn't my original intention," I said to the window, only slightly sorry for the fib.

"Is that the reason for the second story? Is that your creepy little spy room?"

The second story had been Marco's idea. On-site office/game room. And yes, Pink Sweets was in full view from the upstairs window. Like I said, a perk. Marley and her girls wouldn't agree, so I kept my mouth shut.

Ly stopped scrubbing my foot.

Apparently, my silence was confirmation enough.

"Joe!" Marley scolded. "Why the hell would you think it's okay to spy on us?"

"Harper."

"Harper?" she shrilled.

"And that creeper in the Prius," I reminded her.

"What?"

"And the white Z that parks outside your house."

"Joe!"

I continued ticking off my list. "And that guy who scared the shit outta you the other night."

"You're being ridiculous," she mumbled, losing steam.

"And let's not forget that someone tried to break into your house, one of your stands mysteriously burned to the ground, and one of them has bullet holes." Shitty play, drudging up her recent harrowing experiences, but shit, the woman needed to understand where I was coming from.

Larry exited Dirty Dreamz alone and lit a cigarette before leaning against Harper's SUV. The *Closed* sign stayed on.

"That's just life," Marley muttered. "Shit happens."

"Not to my girl."

"I'm nobody's girl."

Her denial pissed me off. I turned to find three sets of eyes aimed my way, but I locked on the one set that mattered. "You're my girl, and I'll do whatever I can to protect you from snakes like Harper, and even from yourself."

Her mouth fell open, her face darkened three shades, and her fury turned ugly. "What are you gonna do, Joe? Kill someone to defend your girl?"

Insult was Marley's go-to defense mechanism, so I took no offense. But I was done.

I lifted my feet out of the water and snatched the towel from Ly's hand to dry myself. Then I wiggled my damp feet into my OluKais and tossed a wad of cash next to Ly's coffee. I headed toward the door but then stopped and turned back around.

Bullshit she was nobody's girl.

I stalked toward my wide-eyed neighbor. Trudy scooted

out of the way, dropping her clippers on the floor. I bent low, cupped Marley's heated cheeks, and said, "I love you, you fucking crazy bird." Then I kissed her, exchanging my frustration for her rage. Warm palms slammed into my chest, but she didn't push me away. The woman melted.

When I ended the lip-lock, I tilted her face, bringing us nose to nose. "You better be at my house tonight, or I'm kicking your door down. No more sleeping alone. Got me?"

I didn't give her time to answer. I left.

Larry stood outside Dirty Dreamz with his back to me. I climbed into my truck and headed home.

° ° ° ° ° ° ° ° ° ° °

Hours had passed since I'd dropped the love bomb on Marley, and I'd been in no mood to go to the office, so I burned off energy with good old-fashioned physical labor. Weeding had worn me down a bit. Power washing the windows had helped, but not enough. So, I moved to the fence.

I'd just drilled my final screw when Marley barreled my way.

"What did you do?"

Palming a fence post, I said, "I built a gate."

"Why would you do that?" Marley's spark was back, and damn, what fun.

"So you can come and go as you please. We can leave it open, and the dogs can play together. No more digging under the fence." She was pissed, but I couldn't stop. " It's brilliant, right?"

"Why didn't you ask me first?"

I pointed the drill in her direction. "Because you're

266

stubborn, and you would say no, even if you really mean yes."

Throwing her arms wide, she yelled, "You can't just cut a hole in somebody's fence!"

"Says who?"

"The law," she said to the sky.

"The law means nothing to a crooked ex-con," I teased.

Marley dropped her arms, scrubbed both hands over her face, and then held them there, breathing deep.

Angry sex right there in the grass would've been epic and, no doubt, the most efficient way to get over our tiff.

I considered tackling her, but she dropped her arms and whispered, "What was that bullshit at the nail salon?"

"I don't recall any bullshit."

A huff. "You know what I'm talking about."

"Oh." I stepped closer. "The part where I called you a crazy bird? Won't apologize. You are a little off your rocker."

Her shoulders dropped. "The L-word?"

"The L-word." Christ, that woman. "C'mon. You can do better than that."

On an exhale, she said, "You said you love me."

"Because I do," I confirmed, moving close enough she had to tip her head back. "I'm done pretending that we're only neighbors with benefits."

Marley studied my eyes, licked her lips. "But that's what we are."

The woman was drowning in denial. "Yeah, not buying it." I gathered my level and screwdriver and headed toward the shed. The dogs ran ahead of me, then stopped to sniff the air before darting around the rose garden.

Marley followed a few paces behind, her ire heating my back. "That wasn't the deal, Joe."

"I don't recall any deal." I set the drill in its case.

"Fuck buddies until you find someone who can give you a relationship."

"Tell me, neighbor..." I took my time shutting and locking the case before turning around. "Who do think about first thing in the morning? Who is it you can't wait to see when you get home every night? Who did you cry to when you were drunk off your ass and breaking into pieces? Who did you cling to when you were terrified?"

Marley took three slow steps away, eyes wide, glassy.

"I get it. Your shitty father did a number. Every man who should've taken care of you let you down. But what you fail to understand is that I won't abandon you."

"Stop."

Shortening the distance between us, I repeated, "I won't abandon you."

"Joe," she pleaded.

"My heart is yours, you stubborn woman. My yard"—I pointed to the new gate—"my home, my dog. All yours."

"Why are you doing this?"

"You know why."

With a shaky hand, she viciously swiped at the tears wetting her face, another layer of her wall crumbling to dust. Her dogged determination to fight that change would have been awe-inspiring if not so frustrating.

"There's a lock on your side of the gate. You're in full control. It'll only be open if and when you want it open."

Marley looked over her shoulder, then found my eyes again. For a moment, the wrinkles between her forehead smoothed. I'd thrown a lot her way, too much to process. But life was too short for bullshit.

Eyes wet, spirit fierce, she studied me. Then, with a huff, she turned around and headed back to her yard.

She did not, however, close the gate.

At 9:45, she knocked on my door. When I let her in, she

headed straight for my bedroom, stripped naked, and burrowed under the sheets.

I chalked that up as a win.

We didn't fuck, but I held Marley through the night with no resistance.

I woke before she could escape and made my girl breakfast.

CHAPTER
Twenty Three

JOE

Ginger shot from her perch on the bench and sprinted across the lawn, her tiny legs gaining impressive ground. At the back porch, she barked and growled, her aggression mighty, her bark pitiful. Hackles raised, she pawed at the glass door.

Bruce trotted behind, unexcited but curious until he reached the slider.

Someone was in the house.

The only weapons I had on me were a pair of snippers and my fists, so I hoped to God whoever was inside didn't wield a gun.

I forced a false sense of security as I shooed the mutts aside and pulled open the door.

Larry was two steps from escaping through the front.

"How the fuck did you get in?"

He stopped. Turned. Scratched his head. The wheels in that old noggin were grinding with creaks and groans. "Alice gave me a key a while back."

Alice never would've allowed Larry entry.

"That's bullshit. Try again."

He lifted weathered fingers, revealing a house key. "I knocked, and you didn't answer. Let myself in."

So many things wrong with that confession. "What are you doing here?"

"Harper has a job for you."

Liar. I played along. "Not interested."

"Wrong answer." He shoved the key back into his front pocket.

"That a threat?"

His rounded spine straightened. "A warning."

"Let's talk about why you're really here." I pulled a chair from the kitchen table and gestured for Larry to sit. "My rides are in the garage, so you couldn't know I was home, meaning you let yourself in because you thought it'd be safe to search for something. What're you looking for?"

"What's rightfully mine," he had the balls to say.

"Alice's inheritance was never Bill's to fuck with, and you sure as hell have no claim to whatever cash or treasure you think might be hiding around this property."

"My brother died for that money."

And Larry would never forgive me.

"Your brother died because he nearly beat to death a woman I loved."

"You're only alive because you're Andrew's son!" Spit dribbled down his chin, and he wiped it away with a shaky hand.

I hated that he was right. The truth ate at me like cancer. I'd served a short sentence in the correction center upstate, but I'd been released into another type of prison, working for my father. Andrew Kaine had judges and cops in his pocket. His lawyers were the most expensive in the country, and rightfully so. They never lost a case. Getting me out early was child's play.

In return, all I had to do was give my father six years of my time.

And I had no doubt Larry would've commissioned my death, family or not, while I was incarcerated, but Dad was one of a few men Larry feared, and killing Andrew's first-born would've been unforgivable.

"You belong in prison, nephew."

No doubt, Larry knew about the jewelry, but maybe he wasn't searching for money. Maybe Larry had an ulterior motive. He couldn't kill me. However, he sure as hell could find a million and one ways to send me away again. Maybe by setting me up through Johan Harper. Or maybe by planting shit in my home, which fit his MO.

My anger was no longer containable. I charged, grabbed Larry by the collar, and dragged him away from the door. He stumbled but stayed on his feet while I made my way through the living room into the dining room and shoved him into a kitchen chair.

"What did you plant?"

Sirens wailed in the distance. Didn't concern me much. Heard them all the time in our neighborhood.

The old coot had the nerve to laugh. "What's the matter, kid. Worried?"

His laugh grated my nerves. "They say once you're incarcerated, your chances of going back are what? Fifty? Seventy? Eighty percent?"

Well, hell. I was right. He'd broken in to set me up.

Fisting his collar, I raised his face to mine. "Did you plant something in my fucking house?"

The sirens grew louder, closer. My heart rate spiked, my temper boiling over. The dogs continued to bark outside, pawing at the door.

Larry bared his teeth, a wicked chuckle bubbling up his throat. "Gonna kill me, boy? Like you killed Bill. Go ahead. Unleash that wicked Kaine temper." The old man spat, hitting my chin. "Fucking murdering bastard." His eyes were red with hatred.

Of all the Kaines, Larry was the most conniving. Where my father and Bill used brawn, Larry used brains, waiting and watching from the sidelines for the right moment to make his play. He also held a grudge better than anyone. He would never quit. Not until I was dead or back behind bars.

He was a dirty bastard, but he was my uncle, and he was tortured by grief and the need for revenge.

The cold, hard truth washed through me, and I stumbled back a step. Larry was hurting. I'd had no intention of sharing the events of that night, but it'd become painfully clear that neither of us would be free from the hatred until he knew how his brother really died.

And the shit kicker in the whole morbid scenario? Alice no longer needed protecting, did she? Goddamn, my chest hurt.

Larry took advantage of my distraction and came at me swinging. "You murdered my brother!" he wailed, landing a hard blow to my jaw.

I didn't strike back. He was old and tired, and while there was no love lost between us, I'd no intention of hurting or killing the guy.

"Larry," I mumbled through the pain.

His right fist hit my eye, slamming my head back. Motherfucker, that hurt.

The old man was done, his breaths ragged, face drawn and dark. Still, he came at me, his next strike missing by inches.

"Stop. You're gonna kill yourself."

The sirens wailed right outside, loud and blaring. The dogs continued their worry at the back door.

Reining my temper, I grabbed his collar once again, whirled, and backed him against the wall.

Through gritted teeth and a shit-ton of uncertainty, I confessed, "I didn't kill Bill."

Silence hung heavy between us while I gave him time to register my words.

Fisted hands dropped to his sides, his body going limp. "Bullshit."

"I came home that night and found Alice unconscious. And Bill..." I choked down the sticky emotion. "Dead. Alice's face was a bloody mess. Black eyes, split lip, clothes torn. She must've had enough. She finally fought back."

Alice must've lost her mind. Bill had three stab wounds to the neck and one to the chest. The bloody garden shovel had lain between them. The funny thing was, those shallow stab wounds hadn't killed my uncle. He'd probably tripped on the garden hose, shocked that Alice had finally fought back, and hit his head on the cement bench.

"That doesn't make sense. Why the hell would you go to prison in place of that bitch?"

"You know damn well why I had to take the fall. You or Bill's associates couldn't touch me, but that sweet woman would've been fair game. You would've made sure she suffered. She didn't deserve retribution, and she didn't deserve the life Bill gave her. She deserved to be happy. I gave her freedom from the Kaine curse."

"You're lying!"

"Hear me good, old man. I did not kill Bill. Alice did."

*　·　°　·　°　·　°ₒ　·　°　·　°　·　°

Marley

"I did not kill Bill. Alice did."

The barks and growls of the two mutts at my feet drowned out my gasp of horror. I stood, still as a statue, at the back door, watching as Joe pinned an elderly man to the wall.

The scene should've worried me. The purple tint of the old guy's face should've been enough to make me intervene. But I'd heard the whole conversation, and I could not move.

Joe did not kill his uncle.

My neighbor was not a murderer.

Joe had sacrificed his freedom for a woman he adored.

Who did shit like that?

I loved him.

I had to stop him before he did commit murder.

"Joe!" I shoved through the door and barreled into the hulking beast, who didn't budge. "Let him go. He can't breathe!"

Joe released his captive and stepped back, lacing his hands on top of his head, dragging in a slow deep breath.

The man bent at the waist, hands to knees, coughing and sputtering.

The mother in me took over. "You okay?" I rubbed his bony shoulder. "Need some water? A chair?"

Shrugging me off, the man sucked in a slow, deep drag of air, then blew it out as he straightened, a killer glare aimed at Joe. "This changes nothing," he croaked, then on shaky legs, moved closer to Joe. "You chose that crazy hag over your own blood." He spat, hitting Joe's soiled boots. "You're dead to me, boy."

With that, he headed to the front door, favoring his left leg, Joe trailing a step behind.

"Need my key back, Larry."

Larry dug into his pocket, still on the move, and dropped the key on the floor without turning around.

Joe made no move to pick up the trinket. Instead, he watched through the window, shoulders bunched, stance set wide, fingers dangling and twitchy at his sides while his uncle made a slow escape.

Joe huffed. "How much of that did you hear?" he asked over his shoulder.

"Is it true?"

"I didn't kill my uncle." He pushed the door closed with his foot, then twisted the lock and pulled the curtain closed.

"You went to jail for Alice." I made a slow approach because Joe hadn't moved, but his body vibrated, sending waves of tension through the air.

My heart was seconds from bursting. When I grazed his shoulder with shaky fingers, he flinched but didn't turn, so I squeezed between my man and the door, coiled my arms around his waist, lay my cheek on his chest, and waited, measuring his heartbeats, the rise and fall of his chest. I hugged Joe tighter, hoping to convey my gratitude because I wouldn't have had Alice without his sacrifice.

"I had to protect her," he murmured.

"Why didn't you tell me from the beginning?"

"Would you have believed me?"

"Honestly?" I stretched my neck to see into his eyes. "I don't know."

Finally. Finally, those warm, strong arms enveloped me. "You loved her, and I didn't want you to have that image of Alice in your head."

"I don't understand. Alice would've never let you go to prison for her."

"I came home that night to a bloody mess. Found Alice unconscious and Bill..." Eyes liquid, he swallowed then coughed, unsuccessfully hiding his emotions. "I tried to revive my uncle, but he was gone. There was so much blood. I..." He stepped back, looking down at his hands, lost in memories too painful to voice.

Vulnerability fit Joe like an itchy sweater, bothersome

and not his style. I waited, fighting tears while he shed the nuisance.

Avoiding eye contact, he continued. "I told the police I wrestled Frank off Alice and lost my temper. We'd fought, and I'd watched him fall but left him to bleed while I tried to help my aunt.

Shaking my head, I rasped, "But Alice wouldn't have gone to jail. It was clearly self-defense."

"Wasn't jail time I was worried about." Joe raked a hand through his hair before meeting my eyes. "Larry and his buddies would've made Alice's life hell, or worse, killed her. I had no choice."

A full-body shiver tore through me. "Weren't you afraid they'd go after you?"

"I'm untouchable," he sneered, stepping closer.

"Why?"

"My father is the youngest of the three brothers, but he's the most dangerous and the only person Bill and Larry feared."

The space between us disappeared in three strides, and when I gripped his hips and lifted onto my toes, he smiled down at me, and the world became a little less scary.

"Joe," left my lips on an exhale.

"Gorgeous." Head tilted, he considered my lips, licking his own. "I don't wanna talk about this anymore."

I kissed his chest. "But you're not a criminal."

"No." He gathered my hair behind my head and tugged, urging me to arch my neck. "But I come from a long line of them."

Bending low, he grazed my neck with his teeth, sending shockwaves straight to my core. My clit pulsed, warmth swelling between my legs.

"I was so awful to you." I expressed my regret, sliding

my hands down his abs, raking my nails over the bumps and ridges, then one by one, I undid the buttons on his jeans.

Joe was hard, and his erection fell heavy into my hand, hot as fire, smooth as silk.

"You had your reasons." In one swift motion, he removed his T-shirt.

"You saved her life." I pumped his length once, twice, then looked up to find sapphire eyes, hungry and pleading.

Voice gruff, he fisted my hair again. "You would've done the same."

"I'm terrified of prison," I confessed, dropping to my knees, his cock thickening, pulsing in my grip. "I don't think that's a sacrifice I could've made."

I kissed the smooth tip.

Joe shuddered, growled, "I'd do it again," then thrust his hips, silently begging for more. "I'd do the same for you."

"I know," I whispered before taking his length to the back of my throat.

"Ahh, fuck, Marley."

High off his heady scent, I worked his base with my hand and the rest with tongue, lips, and teeth. Joe was sweaty and smelled of earth and hard labor. I didn't care. His moans of encouragement, his grip in my hair, and his thrusts and grunts as he fucked my mouth brought me to the edge of control, reducing me to nothing but throbbing heat and need.

"Ah. Shit. Babe." His cock jerked. "I'm gonna come. Slow down."

I worked harder, taking him deep, choking, and loving every gag and gasp for breath, and when his cock jerked again, I cupped his ass with both hands and took him as deep as he'd go until hot spurts of semen hit my throat. Only then did I relent while he pumped his orgasm into my mouth, cursing, praising, and holding my head with both hands while he purged.

Joe collapsed, his knees hitting the floor, and he curled around me. Exposed and raw, he buried his face in my neck, whispered dirty words, and pleaded for a forever I wanted desperately to give.

MARLEY

"Dinner tonight?" Joe leaned against the doorjamb, arms crossed, one booted foot crossed over the other. His jeans hung low, his T-shirt clung tight to all his bumps and dips, and that grin he wore made me tingle in all the best places. "Testing out my new pizza oven."

"Sounds delish, but I'm closing the stand tonight. Jazz has a stomach bug."

"I don't mind a late meal." He shrugged. "I can wait."

"Thanks, Joe, but when I get home, I need to mow the lawn and whack some weeds. I'll be ready to fall into bed by the time I'm finished."

"God, woman." He reached down and adjusted his cock. "Why does that turn me on, hearing you talk about whacking weeds?"

The sight and sound of him were too much. I couldn't help myself. I sauntered his way and kissed him hard before smacking his chest. "Whack off, perv. I've got work to do."

The groan that rose up his throat was nothing short of pornographic. "I just came in my pants."

"Joe, go." I waved him off and turned to open the window. "I've got customers."

"All right. I'm heading home." With a huff, he grumbled, "Fix your top. These pervs don't get to see your nips. Only me."

He had no idea how much fabric tape I used to ensure

no nippage would occur. "Go." I shot him a glare, though he'd already turned away.

I stole one last glance at his bad-boy ass before locking the door behind him.

Bikini top adjusted, I greeted my next customer.

The afternoon passed in a blur. Ogled. Bad jokes. One steam burn and a paper cut. Two masturbators. Four offers of sexual favors and one marriage proposal. So, a typical day.

And the bonus? I had a marvelous view. Across the way, there was never a shortage of cars waiting in line for their average cuppa joe, and those boys pimping the caffeine? Not one bit shy. No privacy screens in that establishment.

Two guys worked the window. One had dark hair, dimples deeper than the Grand Canyon, and a six-pack that rippled every time he laughed. The second man stood taller and slimmer, with dirty-blond hair and a fresh-off-the-beach vibe.

Average Joe closed on schedule. The lights inside remained on, though the shades were drawn.

Five minutes into balancing the books, a knock startled me. I, too, had closed shop and was locked up safe and tight. I looked at the security feed on my laptop.

"Harper," I mumbled, pulling my sweatshirt over my head even though I'd changed into jeans and a T-shirt before diving into my paperwork.

A visit from Johan was never good. A visit after closing time? My skin prickled, scalp to toes.

I could ignore my caller, but that would only piss him off, and I'd witnessed what happened to people who found themselves on the wrong side of that man's plans.

"I'm fond of my toes," I whispered before yanking open the door.

A sinister smile greeted me. Sweet breve latte, the man had to spend a fortune on teeth whitening.

"Well, if it isn't my favorite girlboss," he chimed, sweet as a snake charmer.

"Harper. What are you doing here? I'm closed." I pointed over my shoulder. "Machines are all shut down."

"Well, darlin', I hoped we could have a chat."

"Not a great time. I'm in the middle of my month-end finances."

His pearly whites disappeared. "I'll only take a few minutes of your time."

The prickles grabbed my nerve endings and beat them silly. "Another night, maybe."

"No." He slapped a beefy hand on the doorframe. "Now's just about perfect."

Before I could push my way outside, he filled the exit space and blocked any chance of escape. Though he didn't enter, his motive was clear. We were going to talk, and I'd never had a choice.

My insides vibrated. My outward appearance? Stone cold aplomb. At least, I hoped so. Standing my ground, I said, "What do you need to talk about?"

"You and me. It's time we work together."

"I do appreciate the offer. Really, I do." I nodded like a maniac, hoping to be more convincing. "But I have no interest in going into business with anyone."

One bushy white brow rose. "You're under the impression that you have a choice." Pushing the door open wider, he hissed, "You work with me, or you'll be left with nothing."

My skin heated, prickles melting, and fuck, I could manage fine without a few toes. I yelled at the man like a lunatic. "Are you threatening me? Is that a threat?"

Harper didn't seem thrown by my outburst. "Have I mentioned what a great kid Dylan is?"

White-hot rage wiped away any fear. "What did you just say?"

"That boy of yours." Harper had one foot in the door. "Great head on his shoulders. Thinks fast on his feet."

"How would you? How do you...?" The room blurred.

"He's done a few jobs for me."

"You're lying."

"You think he could afford that shiny car by delivering pizzas?"

I wouldn't know. I'd never seen Dylan's car. "Get out."

"Thing is..." Harper now stood on the threshold, his smile back. "He developed a bit of a conscience. Wants to pick and choose what jobs I give him. Doesn't understand the way this world works."

"Get out." My voice shook harder than my hands.

"Your father disappeared," he continued. "Now. Way I see it, either you can work off Daddy's debt or Dylan can. Choice is yours."

What insanity was I living in? An Al Capone wannabe, standing in my insignificant coffee stand, threatening me over a debt that I had nothing at all to do with. And really... "How in the hell did Dylan get involved in your criminal shenanigans?"

"Shenanigans." The man laughed a full belly laugh, then closed the door behind him. "God, I like you. What fun we could have together."

"Get out!" I shoved at his chest.

Bad idea.

Harper's demeanor changed in a blink, and those beefy hands curled around my biceps like I was a stress ball. My back hit the closet behind me. For his age and size, the man moved like a ninja.

But it wasn't my first rodeo with a bully, and my knee met his groin.

He doubled over, and his forehead hit my chin, making my eyes water, but he released my arms, and I dove for the bat.

"Marley!" A deep voice called out with three large raps at the door. "Joe said you might have an extra roll of receipt tape we can borrow."

Thank you, Jesus.

Red-faced and quaking, Harper pointed a finger in my direction. "Say a word, and your boy is compost."

Never threaten a mama bear. Bat raised, I whisper-yelled, "Come near my boy or me, I'll kill you." Yes, I had dug my own grave, but the crazy had unleashed, and there was no reining it in. "Think I'm scared of you? Try me."

"Marley!" The door opened, hitting Harper in the ass, and one of Joe's employees, the blond, poked his head in. "Sorry to barge in." He shoved past the fat man like he wasn't sorry at all and positioned himself between Harper and me, eyeing the bat, brows drawn. "Everything okay?"

My heart battered my rib cage, and my hands shook so hard the bat slipped from my fingers, landing with a dull thud.

"Everything is peachy," I managed to sputter.

The space was too small for two large men and me. Their mingled colognes made me nauseous, or maybe that was the fear kicking in, but I needed them out. I needed room to breathe or privacy to have a meltdown, so I ripped open my supply closet door and grabbed a roll of register paper.

When I turned to hand the tape to Blondie, Harper was outside, and the surfer dude stood a foot away, arms crossed. There he stayed while Harper hoisted himself into his SUV, started the engine, then rolled away nice and slow, his glare scornful. Only after Harper drove by Pink Sweets and merged into traffic did Blondie shoot me a wink, jog across the street, and disappear inside Average Joe.

Strange.

My body trembled. Time to call it a night. Paperwork could wait.

When I finally tucked into my car, Blondie waved at me from across the street while he was locking up, although he kept looking in my direction. I should've thanked him or asked why he left without the register tape, but I'd had my fill for the day, so instead, I headed home.

I rolled into my driveway with the window down and Lizzo straining my bass.

My lawn was trimmed, neat rows cut on a diagonal pattern.

My sprinkler was running. The front flower beds were clear of weeds.

I found a note on my front door.

Your weeds are whacked. Bruce is keeping Ginger busy while I make you dinner. Come over when you're ready. Beers are on ice.

God, that man. I don't remember entering my house or changing my clothes, but I found myself at Joe's door. When he greeted me, my muscles sagged, and I fell against my beautiful neighbor, stomach rumbling, my heart drip, drip, dripping, and I pooled into a sobbing puddle in his arms.

. ° . ° . °. ° . ° . °

285

Joe raised my arms over my head, then peeled off my tunic, his grip warm and firm, his intent illicit judging by the twinkle in his eye.

"What are you doing?" My hands dropped to my sides, all energy drained.

"Taking you to my shower."

"Brilliant plan." I rewarded him with the best smile I could muster.

Over dinner, I'd recalled my day and confessed my worries about Dylan. Joe had listened, and though he'd tensed and cursed under his breath more than once, he'd kept his cool. The man handled me like a wounded child. I didn't protest, because any fool could see his fussing was an outlet for his simmering rage.

Joe reached around my back and unhooked my bra, dropping a kiss on my nose, making me shiver. One by one, he slid the straps off my shoulders and peeled the silky garment away from my breasts, exposing my taut nipples. A low groan vibrated his throat.

The scent of garlic and smoke clung to his skin, and though my belly was full, my stomach rumbled.

The beastly man then lowered to his knees, his lips leaving a trail of goose bumps from my chest to my navel. As he rolled my leggings down my hips, he chuckled. "No panties." Another kiss. "Mmm," he mumbled against my hip while helping me step out of my Lululemons.

With those large, warm hands, he explored my calves, my thighs, my hips, my belly, dotting kisses and inhaling my scent. The man was killing me softly with his ministrations.

"If you keep this up, we won't make it to the shower."

Bright blue eyes lifted to mine, and he smiled with his lips to my hip. "I love touching you," he rasped, then rose, hooked his middle finger with mine, and led me to the bathroom.

I stepped into the steam and raised my face to accept the hot, cleansing jets. Soon, rock-solid pecks hit my back, and strong fingers kneaded my scalp.

"Oh, God. That feels so good."

His erection swelled between us. I turned in his arms, the need to touch him overwhelming. I ached to ground myself in his beauty, his scent, his strength.

When our eyes locked, his adoration made my heart swell, and I fought the threatening tears. Joe didn't miss a beat, and before I lost my composure, he gripped my neck and kissed me with a tenderness I'd never survive, assuring me I was wanted and cared for. God, when was the last time...

I sobbed into his kiss, breaking the spell.

Forehead to mine, thumbs caressing my cheeks, Joe whispered, "Talk to me."

"You're taking care of me."

"Of course I am."

"Been a long time since anyone's taken care of me."

He huffed, holding me steady. "Because you didn't let them, I'm sure." Then his shoulders dropped, and his face softened even more. My heart broke when he said, "And you're a mom. Mom's get neglected too often."

He wasn't wrong. Single mothers had no choice but to be everything and everyone to their children. Hell, from what I'd witnessed, most married mothers bore the same weight. Rarely were mothers "taken care of."

That's probably why I'd yet to step back and let my managers handle the shops. Momming was not easy to turn off, and I treated my employees like they were my children.

"You're a beautiful man, Joe Kaine."

My bad boy lowered to his knees, guided my left leg over his shoulder, and "took care" of me.

I came on his face, my fingers in his scalp, my voice

hoarse, body sated, and when I fell limp against the shower wall, he washed my hair, then my body, whispering dirty words and working me into a lather.

He dried me off, combed my hair, and led me to bed, where he loved my body with lips and tongue and finally that magnificent cock. We fell asleep, limbs tangled. I woke to the smell of coffee, Ginger curled in a ball against my left side, and Bruce on his back with all four legs in the air.

What a turn my life had taken.

I found Joe in the kitchen, running pants hung low on his waist, and he wore no shirt. His bare feet looked prettier than ever, and bedhead only made him more appealing. But that smile aimed my direction? Woke places in me that had too long lain dormant. The only other grin that affected me soul deep was Dylan's.

Joe wrapped me in a warm embrace and kissed my head. "Morning."

Heaven help me, he smelled like a rainy afternoon and the promise of snuggles.

"Morning," I mumbled against his chest, clinging tight. "Thank you for last night, but I need to get home, find Dylan. Make sure he's okay."

"Frank's already on it."

"What?"

"I spoke with him after you fell asleep."

"No. No cops, Joe." I moved backward, bumping into the table. "Maybe Dylan hasn't done anything illegal yet. I need to talk to him first."

I was a mess.

But Joe was cool as an iced Americano. "Do you know where to start looking?"

"No," I lied. If Dylan were involved with Harper, my father was involved, and that was a mountain I needed to scale solo.

"Frank has the means to find him. That's all he's doing," he assured me.

"I get that Frank is your friend," I argued, "but he's a cop first, and if my son is involved in criminal activity, he'll do what cops do."

"Calm down." Joe laughed. "Frank knows the score."

"I don't want Frank to know the score," I squealed. "I don't want him involved. I don't want anyone involved. It's my messy life, and I choose who to share my shit with. You had no right to get him involved!"

Like we were having a normal conversation, Joe turned to the coffee pot. "I have the means to help. Let me help."

"I would have called the cops last night if I'd wanted them involved," I said to his back. "I don't."

"I get that." Joe turned to face me, butt against the counter, fingers gripping the edge. "But we have a chance to help your kid, and Frank's our best bet."

We. My heart sputtered. My fight drained. *We.* A powerful punch to the gut. I loved that man. I did. In his mind, we were a couple. In his mind, I was his to protect. Joe and Marley, and man, oh man, I loved the word *we*.

But I needed to file those feelings away for later.

Rising high on my toes, I kissed the stubble on his jaw. "I sure do like being your fuck buddy, Joe Kaine, and tonight, it's my turn to make you dinner. But right now, I have to go. I have to find my son before he gets arrested or before Harper follows through on his threat."

"I'm coming with you."

"No," I said on my way to the door. "Absolutely not."

"Um. You don't get a choice in the matter."

Exit plan aborted, I turned around. "Excuse me?"

"Harper is a grade-A piece of shit. You're not dealing with him alone."

"That's sweet. Really. But I'm not an idiot." I studied

the rooster clock over his shoulder. Eye contact would be detrimental to my resolve. "I'm not going anywhere near Johan Harper. I'm going to call around to the parents of Dylan's friends. I'm going to bribe people if necessary for phone numbers. I'm going to harass anyone who might still be in contact with my boy until someone gives me a damn address."

Joe hadn't moved except for his mouth, which hitched on one side. "That's cute, really. But I'm not an idiot, either. You're planning to find your father, and you're going to ream his ass for getting your son involved with Harper before you beat Dylan's whereabouts out of him."

What could I say? Joe got me.

"Problem with that plan is," he continued, too damn smug for my liking, "you said Harper is looking for your father, too. So, chances are good you might bump into him or one of his goons."

"Fine." Some battles weren't worth the effort, and I really liked the idea of Joe by my side. "You can be my muscle. Meet me at my house in half an hour. I need to go call Lilly, see if she can cover my shift today."

"I did that before you came downstairs."

I wasn't surprised. "What are you, my personal assistant now?"

His smirk bloomed into a full-blown toothy smile. "I'm the guy who's in love with your crazy ass."

. ° . ° . ° . ° . ° . °

"Maybe we should check the prisons," I half joked. We'd visited my father's favorite bars, his last known address, his parole officer, two of his on-again, off-again girlfriends, and

290

four of his frequented "massage" parlors—places I never cared to visit again. We came up with zero, zilch, nada.

Anyone willing to admit they knew Warren hadn't seen him in weeks.

Over the years, he'd called me from several different numbers. I tried them all repeatedly on our jaunt around town. One went straight to a full voicemail box. Two others were no longer in service, and one rang and rang.

"What do you know about your dad's involvement with Harper?" Joe asked, one hand on my thigh, the other on the steering wheel.

"I don't know the details of their relationship. They've known each other since I was a kid. Harper used to come by the house every time my dad decided to grace us with his presence." I shivered. "Harper always brought candy bars. He and Dad would wave them in my face but only give me one if I smiled for them, or fetched a beer, or something ridiculous. Of course, I was a kid and I wanted the damn candy, so I did whatever they asked."

"You wanted your father's attention," Joe said, not a lick of judgment in his tone.

"You're not wrong. I would've done anything without the candy." I slumped in the seat. "I pimped myself out for my dad's love. How messed up is that?"

"Not your fault."

Deep down, I knew I wasn't to blame, but the pain surfaced regardless. "I can't believe this is my life."

"We're gonna get through this. And Dylan's gonna be fine."

I wanted to crawl into Joe's lap and hide inside one of his hugs. Instead, I straightened my spine, rubbed a smudge from his truck window, and replied, "You can't know that."

"I've got an idea."

He didn't wait for a response. A quick glance at his side

mirror, and he darted across two lanes of traffic, then headed for Interstate 5. Thirty minutes later, we parked in front of a brick apartment building, nearly identical to the buildings flanking each side.

Joe grabbed my hand when my feet hit the sidewalk and guided me inside.

"Who lives here?" I asked, trying to ignore the musty stench of the tight hallway.

"My uncle," Joe grunted, his pace quick, shoulders tense.

We stopped in front of apartment 69, and Joe chuckled while pounding three large raps at the door.

"What?" I whispered.

"Nothing." He shook his head and went back to brooding.

A rustling came from the other side of the door. Then silence.

Joe shifted his stance. Huffed. Pounded again. "Open the door, Larry. We can hear you."

He stared into the peephole but gave my fingers a playful tug.

"I've got nothing to say to you, boy," came a muffled voice. "Get out of my building."

"Not leaving. Open up."

Another long pause. Joe's grip on my hand tightened, and I craned my neck to get a read on his face. His jaw was set tight, but he noticed me staring and shot me a wink. "You might hear some ugly shit come outta my mouth in there. Just know that it's necessary when dealing with—"

"I understand," I interrupted. I understood too well. Joe's uncle, Harper, and my father were cut from the same cloth.

Out of fear or frustration, Larry opened the door and gestured for us to come inside, checking the hallway before shutting us in. His gray hair was slicked back and still wet, his beard freshly shaved, and his Tommy Bahama button-up and khakis were neatly pressed. The cologne he wore made my nose tickle, but I refrained from scrunching up my face.

His living space was small but tidy. His decorating obviously inspired by Total Wine & More. Varying bottles of alcohol decorated shelves and side tables, some in clusters, some single bottles on display.

"Who's this?" Larry avoided my gaze but gave my body a quick sweep before glaring at Joe.

"This is Marley," Joe said. "We're looking for her son, Dylan."

Larry waved a weathered hand. "I don't know any kid by that name."

"He works for Harper"—Joe's voice deepened—"so I believe you know the kid."

My heart dropped to my gut. Larry and Harper were connected? Had Joe known this all along?

"If that's the case, then I'm not saying a word." Larry pointed to the door. "Get outta my house."

"Larry." Joe released my hand, stepped closer to his uncle, and seemed to swell, his body tensing, the air between them shifting, warming. "I know you're loyal to that fat, greasy fucker, but Marley here is worried about her boy, and I don't like that she's worried. You have any information about Dylan Masters, it's in your best interest to share."

"Masters?" Dark eyes flashed, briefly meeting mine. "You're a goddamn Masters?" He shook his head, stumbling back, his butt falling into the couch cushions. "As in Warren, the woman-stealing, backstabbing Masters?" The old man rubbed his temples with trembling hands, not looking to me but Joe for an answer.

"Yes," I belted out, shoving Joe to the side and bending

low to make sure the old fart met my glare. "You don't like my father? Good. Neither do I. Now, where in the hell can I find my son?"

The geriatric pig took a lazy gander at my chest, then said to my lips, "Last time I saw your kid, he was getting a blow job from his favorite gal over at Dirty Dreamz." His tongue darted out to wet his lips, and he failed to give me the respect of eye contact.

Either Larry was trying to get a rise out of me, or he indeed was an old-school, womanizing swine.

Mama bear was ready to wrestle, and my claws were lethal. The only way to mess with trash like Larry was to fight dirty. I snatched the first bottle within reaching distance and smashed the end on the coffee table. A chunk of veneer and fiberboard fell to the floor, but the bottle of Maker's Mark stayed intact.

Okay. That didn't go as planned.

Larry shot a confused look over my shoulder to Joe.

Joe would not hurt his uncle, that much I knew. He'd threaten, he'd bully and scare, but he wouldn't cause physical harm. Larry knew as well.

I was the wild card. I had to make that man talk.

I rushed the geezer and slammed the bottle into his groin, then jumped out of the way before he could strike.

A childlike scream tore from his throat, his face twisting in agony.

I smiled because mama bear was just getting started.

CHAPTER
Twenty-Five

Mom was famous for her temper. Hell, my own had landed me in hot water on countless occasions. But never— and I'd spent years living with criminals and a violent MC —had I witnessed anyone blow their top with such reckless abandon.

My looney bird had lost her shit.

I well and truly felt for Larry. The plethora of profanities and testicle-shriveling threats that erupted from the wild-eyed, red-faced, crazy woman while she held my uncle's balls in a bionic fist had my heart racing and my stomach revolting.

Larry should've passed out after the first few minutes. I'd never seen my uncle cry, but lo and behold, he trembled, tears pouring down his wrinkled cheeks, his lips moving but not a discernible word coming out.

Marley was wild. A rabid field mouse about to get stomped by a moose.

"That's enough." I yanked her off my uncle and carried her kicking and screaming to the other side of the room.

The second her feet hit the carpet, she was on him again, this time drawing a wretched sob from the man.

"Where is my son?" Her scream vibrated the walls, and her fist met Larry's nose. "Where is he?"

I blocked her second strike, wrestled her away, then restrained her in my arms. "Enough!"

"He knows." Marley fought my grip. "He knows where I can find Dylan."

Nose to nose, I told her, "He can't tell us anything if you kill him."

Her body softened, going limp. Still, I held firm and whispered, "I need you to go to the car."

"No."

"I'll make him talk." I doubted he knew anything since he didn't utter a word through the torture.

"I'm not leaving."

God, she was gorgeous. I wanted to kiss that fire right out of her, but instead, I leaned close and warned, "Then stay right here. You move a muscle, we're out, and Frank's gonna handle this."

Larry coughed and sputtered, "Crazy, stupid bitch," through clenched teeth, his body curled in a ball on the couch.

Marley shoved free of my hold and leaned against the front door, lips sucked between her teeth, arms crossed.

I squatted next to Larry. "Give me something, old man. That was painful to watch, and I'd hate to let her loose on you again."

His body shook. "I don't keep tabs on every dumbass kid Johan recruits."

"Give me something," I demanded through clenched teeth.

"Kiss my ass," he snarled.

Another tactic, then. "You know, my pops was right about you."

Larry tensed.

I continued. "Said you and Bill were a world-class pair of idiots. Not because you were stupid, but because you spent your life doing shit jobs for Harper when you could've been running your own crew."

Larry huffed.

"Which leads me to believe that Harper's got something on you." I rose from my spot on the floor, snagged a tumbler from the liquor cabinet, then held the empty glass toward Marley.

She rolled her eyes, popped the top off the whiskey she still held and poured a shot.

Larry pushed himself into the sitting position on shaky arms, a wary glare aimed at Marley.

I tried for friendly, approaching him again. "What does he have on you?"

Larry took the offered drink and threw it back, then dropped his gaze to the floor, his shoulders curling.

Too many seconds of silence passed.

"Tell me something. Anything." I swallowed the bile rising in my throat, dreading what came next. "Don't make me call my old man. I don't want him in town any more than you do." I hitched a thumb over my shoulder toward Marley. "But I'll welcome him with open arms if it means finding that lady's son."

I hoped to God Larry didn't call my bluff. Neither of us would benefit from having my father in town. And I sure as hell didn't want to owe Andrew Kaine another favor.

"I don't know where the kid is staying." My uncle turned green. "I know he's got a drop-off scheduled tomorrow night."

"Where?" Marley asked from her spot at the door.

Larry's lips curled in disgust. With a mumbled curse, he said, "That vacuum repair shop in Georgetown, a block up from the strip club."

"Time?"

"After dark's all I know."

Good enough.

Marley came to my side, the bottle of whiskey held close

to her chest. On a long sigh, she filled Larry's empty glass. "I'm sorry about your balls."

Larry flinched, hands shaking, never meeting Marley's eyes.

"But I'm keeping the bottle," she declared, then turned on her heels and stormed out the door.

I followed, a little dazed and confused, but a helluva lot turned on.

. ° . ° . °. ° . ° . °

Marley downed two swallows of Maker's Mark with trembling hands before capping the bottle and nesting it between her thighs.

I headed for the interstate.

The silence was thick and uncomfortable, but necessary. We both had a lot to process. Though successful, our meeting with Larry hadn't gone as I'd expected. I'd figured I'd have to rough up my uncle a bit, make some threats, and pull out the "dad" card as a last resort. Should've led with Daddy Dearest and saved us time and trouble.

Though entertaining, Marley's violent outburst exposed the depth of her fear. The woman was terrified for her son.

"Wanna talk about what happened back there?"

"What do you mean?" She picked at her thumbnail.

"Would you have stopped if I hadn't dragged you away from Larry?"

"I knew what I was doing." She slapped her hands to her thighs and squeezed.

"Did you?"

"He's your uncle." She fought a grin. "I had to be the bad guy."

"The bad guy." Sweet Jesus, that woman. I laughed a deep, eyes-watering, belly laugh.

"Why is that funny?"

"We weren't playing good cop/bad cop."

"I wasn't. I just..." Marley turned her face away, clearly trying not to chuckle. "I'm used to taking care of what needs to be done. He needed to talk. I knew you wouldn't hurt him—"

"Too badly," I interrupted. "I wouldn't have hurt Larry too badly." He was nearing seventy, but the guy was a scrapper.

"Okay. Whatever. You wouldn't have gone for the balls, though, and that's what needed to be done."

A full-body shiver rippled through me. "Remind me never to make you angry."

Marley shifted to face me. "If the bottle had broken like I'd intended, I could've just threatened his jugular." She drew her index finger across her neck.

"How many bar fights you been in, neighbor?"

"Would you believe zero?" She opened the whiskey and downed another shot. "Why didn't you tell me you had a connection to Harper, too?"

"No connection, really," I answered honestly. "Only know about Johan Harper because I used to keep tabs on my uncles. But I tried my hardest to steer clear of them growing up."

"So you don't know him personally?"

"Never met the guy."

"But Larry works for him."

I nodded.

"Small world, huh?" Marley leaned back in her seat, hands folded in her lap, her wheels grinding hard enough to wake the dead.

"Listen, these are not good guys we're dealing with.

Larry's an old-school chauvinistic dipshit, and he has no problem laying hands on women. If I hadn't been standing in that room with you, you'd be in the hospital right now, or worse."

"I know."

"Do you? Because from where I stood, you thought you had things under control, but you were too out of control to read the room."

"I know what kind of men they are, Joe. Give me some credit." She shook her head, lifted the bottle to her lips, then changed her mind. "I watched Harper's goons drag my father out of the house. He showed up three days later, beat to bloody hell and missing toes. Toes, Joe!" Clearly agitated, she fiddled with the bottle cap, huffed, then shoved the liquor into her handbag. "And my dipshit dad went to jail for that man more than once. I don't know why. Maybe he had something on my father, too. Maybe that's how Harper keeps his guys under control." A long pause. "Shit." Marley cocked her head. "That's how he's trying to get me to fall in line. He's using Dylan. But what's he using to keep Dylan under his thumb?"

"You," I said, the answer simple.

"Do you think?"

"Or your father. How close is your son to his grandfather?"

"I had no control over my father's comings and goings when I was a kid. The day I turned eighteen, I got an apartment. Wouldn't let Warren anywhere near us. But once Dylan was old enough, who knows what he did or who he saw?" She slapped a hand to her forehead. "Oh, God. Oh, God. I should've moved far away. I should've gotten a desk job as an accountant or something. Changed our names so Warren could never find us." She groaned, sinking into her seat. "I should've married that computer geek that used to text me poetry and hack my laptop so that every time I turned it on, a new bloom of flowers appeared."

"Okay, babe. Taking it a little far here." I gripped her shoulder and squeezed. "Listen. From what I can tell, you did nothing other than love your son and try to protect him."

Eyes glassy, she nodded.

"Just like my mom did for me. She protected me from my father's dangerous lifestyle. But I'm a guy. I did enough stupid things without my father's influence and gave her every one of those gray hairs on her head."

Marley nodded.

I continued. "Mom tried to keep me in line, but I drove her insane because, again, I'm a guy. We're selfish. We make stupid choices—for our dicks and egos. Mom and I fought all the time from the day I hit puberty. But I never stopped loving her. And I love her all the more now that I can look back and see all the shit I put her through."

I rubbed a runaway tear from Marley's cheek. "Dylan will come around. The kid just needs time to be a guy and learn who he is without his mom."

"What if he doesn't?"

"He will," I assured her.

If not, I'd find that little fucker, show him what road his current choices were going to drag him down, then make sure he made his mother feel appreciated.

. • . • . ° . °. ° . • . • .

Rain pinged the roof, the staccato slowing, then speeding up again with each gust of wind rocking the cruiser.

Frank leaned on his elbow, chin perched in his hand. "Where the hell is the runt?"

301

The clock read 1:17 AM. "Larry said after dark. That's all he knew."

The run-down "vacuum repair" building sat on a busy corner of a shady south Seattle neighborhood, where old homes, some still lived in but most converted to offices, were tucked between new industrial buildings. Homeless camps littered most of the alleys and spilled onto the sidewalks.

The place looked vacant, no lights on, no cars in the parking lot, but we knew at least one person was inside, because he'd come out to chase away a crackhead that had tried to break in two hours earlier.

"We grabbing him before or after?" I asked, fidgeting with the red-and-white bag in my hands, my skin itchy and tight.

"Let him make the drop. If we nab him with whatever shit he's delivering, then I'll have to take him in for real. Besides"—Frank sniffed—"it'll buy the kid more time."

"I owe you, brother." I plucked a handful of sunflower seeds out of the bag, then offered the snack to Frank.

He snatched the bag from my hand and set it in his lap. "Not a problem." He smiled, rolled his head in my direction. "You love her."

"Fuck yeah." I sucked the salt off a seed, then cracked the shell between my teeth.

"Cyn wants to meet her."

I lowered my window and spit, blinking against the rain hitting my face. "We'll have a dinner date."

A white Z, the same white Z that had driven by Marley's house too many times, parked on the street in front of the shop.

"Fuck me," I grumbled, my guts knotting. "That's the car that's been casing her house."

A tall kid untucked from the front seat of the NISMO, same guy who'd stood in Marley's driveway all those months ago. He wore dark clothing and a backpack slung over his shoulder. He assessed his surroundings before jogging to the entrance. He knocked twice. Seconds later, the door opened, and the kid disappeared inside.

"Take the long way, yeah?"

Frank chuckled. "You got it."

I unfolded from the car, spit more shells, then crossed the street, where I waited in the shadow of a magnolia tree.

Four minutes passed before the kid reappeared empty-handed. As soon as he grabbed his door handle, I slammed him against the car.

He grunted and tried to fight me off, but the kid hadn't fully matured, and where he was lean, I was mean, and it took all of two moves before I had him folded over the cold, wet Z with his hands secured behind his back.

"Okay, kid. Here's what's gonna happen. You and I are gonna get in the car, then you're gonna follow my buddy, Officer Garcia." I flipped his face so he could see Frank's car behind his.

The lights on the cruiser flashed once.

"You got any weapons on you or in the car?"

Dylan tried again to shake me off. "Fuck you."

I grabbed the back of his head and gave him a hard smack against the hood, not to damage his pretty mug but to let him know I wasn't fucking around. "Any weapons?"

He mumbled, "No."

"Good." I removed my body weight and let him straighten. "Get in."

He obeyed.

I slipped into the passenger side, then pulled the Kershaw out of my boot to rest on my thigh. I'd no intention of using the fixed blade, but I'd every intention of scaring any fight outta the kid.

Frank pulled his cruiser around and started a slow roll toward home.

"Drive," I commanded, raking wet hair off my face with my fingers.

When the engine purred, the radio blasted, vibrating the interior. I punched the power button on the stereo.

"Are you a cop?" Dylan asked.

"No. I'm a friend." I yanked the hood off his head to get a look at his face.

Good-looking boy. Dark hair—messy but not stank. Large, bright eyes, straight nose, skin a shade or two darker than his mother's.

He jerked away but kept his eyes on the road. "A friend of who?"

"Your mother."

"Fuck." He seemed to shrink.

Good.

"She's worried sick," I growled, tapping the knife on my leg.

"What does she know?" He'd lost his cocky facade.

"Harper's threatening her. Using you to get her to bend."

He pounded the steering wheel with his palm. "God! I hate that guy!"

Seemed my job would be easier than planned, thank fuck.

"I'm here to get you out. That's what you want, right?"

Worried eyes shot my way, then fixed back on the street. "How do you know this?"

We hit the highway, and the kid worked the clutch and shift like a pro. Damn, I wouldn't mind giving the sweet ride a spin myself.

"Doesn't matter how I know. I can help."

"How?" His voice cracked, maybe in relief, or perhaps fear. "How you gonna get me out?"

My shoulders relaxed. Smart kid. He'd play along.

"I'll get you out of town. Have a buddy in Whisper Springs. Already spoke to him. He's got a job for you."

"My grams is in Whisper Springs," he muttered, nearly cracking a smile.

"Spoke with your grandmother, too. She said you've got a place to stay if you decide to let us help."

"Mom?"

If Marley didn't kick me to the curb, I'd be shocked. "She doesn't know I made arrangements. Didn't wanna get her hopes up if things went south."

Dylan stared ahead, silent, the *whoosh, whoosh* of the wipers a welcome break from the convo.

I waited until we were close to the drop-off location before telling the kid, "You'll have to leave the car behind."

Dylan nodded, but his hands tightened on the wheel. "I just want out."

CHAPTER
Twenty Six

I'd chewed my fingernails to the quick, my left thumb-nail to the point of bleeding. I'd stubbed my toe twice while pacing in the dark, and under my skin, fluttery, out of control vibrations wreaked havoc.

Six hours had passed since I'd watched Joe and Frank drive away. Six miserable, gut-churning hours since I'd waved from my front porch, then ran to the bathroom to barf.

Undefinable emotions battered my insides, the pain as raw and destructive as the day Dylan left. What if Joe found him? Would he come home? Would he be angry? Had I ruined any chance of hugging my son again by sending Joe? God, I needed to hug my son.

Grief is supposed to ease with time. Bullshit. Grief gets buried under all the junk life throws your way, but the agony is always there, simmering, thickening, growing more pungent.

Guilt was the one emotion that rivaled my heartbreak. I felt guilty for mourning a child who was alive and well, only dead to me by his own choosing. Guilt for going on with my life when my baby was alone in the world, possibly hurting and scared, and I couldn't protect him.

Fear was a slithering entity, hitching a ride on my journey of self-reproach. I feared never seeing my child again, never laughing with him or watching him mature through life's ups and downs. I was terrified I'd never get to watch him fall in love, or God forbid, never meet my grandchildren. Shamefully, I feared judgment. What kind of horrible mother must I have been that my only child left with no word? Did he hate me? Did I love him too hard? Not hard enough?

Why was I so unlovable?

God! I had to stop.

I parked my ass on the sofa, making Ginger bounce from a tucked ball to her back, her legs sticking straight in the air and her tail wagging.

Bruce grunted at me from his bed in the corner.

I slid to the floor, crawled his way, and kissed the big, beautiful mutt. "Thanks for sticking around, boy. Please promise you'll never leave me."

Joe found me that way, a misty-eyed mess on the floor, holding tight to the one warm thing I had to cling to at the moment.

"Baby," he whispered.

I hadn't heard him come in. Maybe he'd been afraid to wake me. Silly man had no clue the torture I'd put myself through.

I exchanged one warm embrace for another, throwing myself into Joe's strong, steady arms, tucking my face into his neck, where sanity thrived.

"Babe." He slapped my ass, prying my arms from around his neck. "We're not alone."

Time froze. My fingers curled into Joe's shoulders, and I dared a peek around his bulk. My ticker dropped to my gut and bounced back up into my throat.

Dylan stood in the doorway, hands in his pockets, shoulders slumped forward, head down, but those golden eyes lifted to mine. Strong and healthy. So fucking beautiful.

"Hi, Mom."

A strange euphoria washed over me, and I could swear I caught a glimpse of Heaven. My baby. My baby. Oh, my God, my baby! My voice wouldn't work, but my eyes leaked something fierce.

Joe lowered me to my feet. On a sob, I threw myself at the poor boy, making him stumble backwards, but his lanky arms wrapped around my back, and he squeezed like he'd missed me every bit as much as I'd missed him. How could I ever let go? How could I ever let him out of my sight again? I breathed him in. He smelled like the same sweaty boy, and dear God, how I'd missed that dirty funk only boys could pull off.

Minutes later, Joe slipped past us, dogs in tow, and before he shut the door behind him, he clapped Dylan on the shoulder and said, "See you later, kid."

I was so fucking in love with Joe Kaine.

Minutes passed before I mustered the courage to let Dylan go. I released my death grip and stepped away, giving him room to breathe.

"We have so much to talk about," I croaked, taking in every inch of him.

Dylan nodded. Dark circles framed his eyes. We needed to talk, but he needed sleep. I never wanted to close my eyes again for fear of losing another second with my son.

"There are fresh sheets on your bed. Why don't we talk after some shut-eye?"

Dylan nodded, kicked at the floor, then hit me with a gaze that held deep regret. "I'm sorry for hurting you," came out a mumble but had no less impact than if he'd shouted.

"I know." I hooked his arm and led him down the narrow hallway and to his room.

Dylan stepped inside. Other than cleaning, I'd left everything as it was. He studied the small space, scrubbed a hand through his dark hair, kicked off his Nikes, and said over his shoulder, "You got a dog."

"He's a great dog." I blew a kiss and closed the door, allowing him privacy despite wanting to jump into his bed and hold him forever.

Then I snagged a pillow and blanket from my room and curled up on the couch, right next to the front door, just in case.

. ° . ° ° ° ° ° . °

You'd think I was the luckiest woman alive, sitting across the table from two of the most beautiful men ever created. But for the moment, I wanted to kill them both because they had just pierced my chest with a lethal dart.

"You're taking him where? And when did you decide this?" I'd had zero minutes of shut-eye. Safe to say, my mood was volatile.

"Mom." Dylan's overgrown hair fell in his eyes, and he shook his head as if that would help. "It's a good idea."

"I know." I refrained from touching his face and brushing his locks aside. "But shouldn't I have been involved in this decision?"

Joe and Dylan both blurted, "No" in unison.

Then Joe added, "You're too emotionally involved."

"I'm his mother." I aimed my anger and frustration at Joe.

"Exactly." He reflected my glare with his own.

"And when did you have time to arrange all this behind my back?"

"Mom." Dylan reached across the table and took my hand, his twice as big as mine. "Don't be mad. Getting out of town is the best thing for me. I fucked up." His breath hitched. "Got caught up in Grandpa's shit. You warned me, and I didn't listen. I tried to come home, tried to tell you, so many times."

"You can tell me anything, Dylan. Anything."

"I didn't want to see that look on your face, that look you got every time Gramps showed up or called."

Tears threatened, but I fought them back, my face scrunching. "I just got you home."

"I promise to call every day."

I could fight, but even bullheaded me knew Dylan and Joe were right. My son would only be safe outside of Harper's reach. "When are we leaving?"

Joe piped in, "We need to take off soon."

"Today?"

"It's better to have him clear of Seattle before Harper realizes he's gone."

"Oh." The cracks in my chest were audible, my heart splitting, tiny fissures forming. "Okay. I'll call Lilly. I'm sure she'll cover my shifts."

Dylan shot Joe a nervous glance.

Joe nodded.

The little green monster slithered in my belly. Those two shared silent communication after knowing each other all of five minutes. I didn't love Joe so much at the moment because I knew what that exchange meant. "You don't want me to go."

"Harper's got eyes on you. If he hears you left town, he'll put two and two together." Joe scratched his forehead with his thumb and, clearly, he was as uncomfortable with the situation as I. "You need to carry on as usual."

"If he's got eyes on me, surely they saw you march Dylan into my house last night." I was grasping for straws.

"We were careful. Ditched his car first thing. Made sure

we weren't followed. My truck was at the station. Dylan was outta sight the whole ride home. Parked in the garage, brought him through the backyard. Nobody saw a thing." He shot me a wink. "See, that gate came in handy for something."

"God, this sucks!"

"I'll give you two some time." Joe pushed from the table and stood. His gaze sliced to Dylan. "Head on over to my place when you're ready."

Joe sauntered to the back door, his jeans hugging his ass and thighs, those thick-soled boots adding an edge to his already daunting form. He stopped, turned, hit me with warm, inviting eyes, and waited.

Did he want me to thank him? Was he expecting a grand send-off? A kiss goodbye?

I had nothing to give. Dylan was home. Mere hours were not enough to make up for our lost time. Every emotion, every smile, laugh, tear, spoken word, every single ounce of energy were for my son.

Joe dropped his head, nodding, and left.

"What do you need for your trip?" I fought a lip quiver to no avail.

"Joe and Frank helped me grab all I needed from my apartment last night."

"I see." I stood, fidgety and struggling to stay composed.

"Mom."

"If I'd known you were leaving today, I wouldn't have let you sleep last night. I would've made you stay awake and talk to me about everything, or anything." Arms crossed, I brought a finger to my mouth and gnawed a nail. "You can't possibly imagine how much I've missed you, how empty my chest has been."

"I know," was all he said as he pulled me into his arms

and hugged me like he really had missed me, too. "I'm so sorry."

My boy was taller, wider, and more muscular than when I'd last seen him. His hair was still a thick mess, his voice more mature, his eyes wiser, and as he rocked me, whispering, "I'm sorry," over and over, I realized his heart had grown, too.

My boy wasn't a kid anymore. He'd spread his wings. Flown the coop. He'd made bad choices but owned up to them. Dylan would stumble and fall a million and one times in his life, but he was a good kid, well on his way to becoming a good man.

Hard as it was to admit, that journey was for him to navigate. I'd been blessed to be a part of his life for eighteen years. My job was done. I only hoped he'd remember to share his failures and celebrations with me along the way.

We said our goodbyes. I watched my only child cross the backyard, confident he'd flourish while terrified I'd crumble to dust. When he disappeared into Joe's yard, I allowed myself one long, hot shower to cry, and then I dressed, painted my face, styled my hair, and drove to work.

⁂

The words and numbers on my calendar faded in and out of focus, my perpetual blinking making little difference.

Lilly closed the window, stuffed her tip in the jar, and turned to wipe down nozzles. "You've been at that schedule forever. Need help?"

Blink. Blink. I would not cry. I'd finished the schedule at home and only needed to post the changes on our employee portal. For some reason, I struggled to hit the submit button on my laptop. "I'm giving my shifts to the other girls."

"Well, I'm sure you won't hear any complaints from them. But why?"

Fear. Exhaustion. "I'm not getting any younger."

"You're young at heart," she sang, snapping my ass with a damp towel.

I tapped the *Submit* button and snapped my MacBook shut. "You practically run this stand already. I'd like you to manage both, as far as scheduling, hiring, and whatnot."

"Marley, are you serious?" she shrieked, hopping on her toes and clapping, her breasts bouncing in her leather-studded bustier.

"I'll still be here behind the scenes, but I'd like to go back to school. Get my business degree. Maybe expand into some clothing-required coffee stands."

"Well, more power to ya! So, does this promotion come with a hefty raise?"

"You know it does."

"Then I wholeheartedly accept." Lilly nodded toward the security camera. "Well, look here. Prius Guy is off schedule."

"Strange." I was not in the mood to be friendly. "You wanna take him? He tips great."

"Nah." She winked. "He comes for you, boss."

Prius Guy rolled up to the window, face grim and facing forward. Nothing new. His attire, however, made me do a double-take. Seahawk's cap. Tight black T-shirt. Black watch with a thick black band and face. He wore a five o'clock shadow that aged him by years, hiding his baby face.

"Hi," I said, mustering my sweet work voice.

Those dark, steely eyes turned my way. His leer landed on my chest, then took a slow trip up to my neck and face.

Dear God. The man had never looked me dead on. And

though he was clean-cut and handsome, something messy and ugly lingered in that glare.

"Well, this is a nice surprise."

He didn't blink. "What is?"

Tingles zipped up my spine and over my scalp. His voice carried an edge that I couldn't decipher.

"Not used to seeing you in the afternoon. In casual attire. Looks good on you," I threw in because he gave a hostile vibe, and I was trying to make nice.

The man clenched his jaw, staring straight through me. "Not used to seeing you in the afternoon."

Yeah, I needed to wrap this transaction up, and fast. "The usual?"

"Why wouldn't I order my usual?"

My skin prickled. "Right, sure." He'd thrown me off my game, and I was always on my game.

I turned to grab the soy milk from the fridge, the shake in my hands unnerving.

Lilly stood out of sight, her eyes going wide, silently asking, "What the fuck?"

"I know, right?" I whispered back, then finished making his drink.

When I turned again to face the man, he wore a grin that reminded me too much of Charles Manson. Or maybe that was my overtired imagination. Regardless, I forced a smile and said, "This one's on the house. Have a great day," before slamming shut the window.

"That was weird, right?" I asked Lilly, palms to my hot cheeks.

"That was creepy as heck."

We shared a simultaneous shiver, the spine-chill factor dialed too damn high for my liking.

Without a second thought, I declared, "No more working alone for a shift. From now on, we're doubled up, always." Normally, I'd dismiss the weird vibes as being over-tired and overstressed, but there was no ignoring the warning bells ding-donging in my head.

Lilly turned to face me, arms crossed, hip rested against the counter. "That will not make the girls happy. Tips are everything in this line of work."

She was right. On a good day, my baristas could earn a grand, give or take, and on a bad day, they rarely collected less than two hundred.

It wouldn't be fair to cut their daily income by half. I'd lose my employees to our competitors.

But how could I ensure their safety? Between Harper's threats and now Prius Guy's one-eighty, my guts were knotted and my head was a mess. Something had to change.

The rest of the day passed without incident, thank the good Lord. My heart couldn't take another hit. My mind was on Dylan, and while I trusted he was in good hands, the ache in my chest would forever linger, as was the curse of all parents, I suspected.

And Joe? He'd earned bonus points by freeing my son from Harper's clutches, but he'd crossed a line planning Dylan's move to another state without talking to me about it first. I was torn between adoration and indignation.

Staying busy helped stifle my erratic mood. So, during lulls, I deep cleaned, reworked the schedules, and planned a company meeting.

When it came time to visit the Georgetown stand, I retrieved my pepper spray and set it on the counter. "I'll try to be back before closing. If I'm late, I want this in your hand to and from your car. Got me?"

Lilly looked at the little can, then me, her grin spreading. "Seriously?"

"Yes. I'm going to stock both stands. Pepper spray. Maybe stun guns, too."

Lilly dropped her arms to her sides, her face going stone-cold serious. "Boss. I carry a gun. Most of the girls carry guns."

My heart dropped to my gut and bounced around. "What?"

"We didn't say anything because we know how you feel about them."

"You're licensed?"

"Of course. Marcus and I hit the gun range at least once a week."

"Lilly! How did I not know about this?"

She pointed a finger in my direction. "Because of that look on your face right now."

Apparently, I had a "look." Dylan had said the same thing to me less than twenty-four hours ago. "I don't have a look," I retorted.

"You do. It's a mix of condescending and disappointed with a splash of brokenhearted." Lilly laughed, shaking her head. "It's a mom look."

I threw my arms up in frustration. "I'm a mom!"

"You're a great mom and a great boss. All the girls adore and respect you, and nobody wants to disappoint you." She shrugged. "So we didn't tell you about the guns."

"Huh," seemed the appropriate response.

I had always been vocal about my distaste for firearms. Only because when I was in third grade, my classmate was shot by his cousin when they found a loaded weapon in his parents' closet. His was the first funeral I'd ever attended. Left a mark. My dad carried guns in his cars, sometimes his coats, and when I'd see them, I'd hide in my room. He'd tease me relentlessly.

"Have I failed my crew?" I fell back onto my stool. "Does nobody feel safe?"

"The world has failed us, Marley, not you. I don't feel any safer in my home, the gym, the store, or even church."

Again, I said, "Huh," then stuffed the pepper spray back into my handbag and headed out, feeling absurdly under protected.

。˚˳°。˚˳°。˚˳°。

"That went well, yeah?" I hooked my arm around Lilly and walked her to her Charger. "The girls seemed supportive."

"That was a much-needed team meeting. You're doing the right thing, stepping back." She gave me a long, tight hug. "Don't get me wrong, you're great at the window, but you're the boss, and you need to focus on the business side."

We'd had our impromptu gathering at the Dusty Dive Bar and Grill. Great burgers, the best draft beers, and an old-school jukebox. They also had a backroom table large enough to seat eight employees.

"Have I told you lately that I love you?" I sang, squeezing her waist.

A stinging whack hit my backside. "Now, go home and take some quality you time. Get some lovin' from that man of yours."

Joe was getting something all right. But, good or bad, I'd yet to determine. Neither he nor Dylan had contacted me in two days, and I hadn't called them for fear Johan Harper was keeping tabs.

I'd kept all the Dylan business to myself, for obvious reasons, not that I didn't trust Lilly or any of my girls, but because I knew what Harper was capable of, and if he wanted information, he'd find a way.

The black sky promised a soggy night. The clock in my

Subi read 10:12 PM. Our meeting had ended hours ago, but we'd hung around, chatting, drinking, dancing. Rarely were all of us in the same place at the same time. Turned out, my girls were freaking awesome and fun. My stomach ached from laughing so hard at their creepy, and crudely hysterical, customer horror stories.

I'd cleared two blocks when blinding headlights hit my rearview. I slipped into the right lane to let the car pass.

The vehicle pulled right behind me.

My first thought was *asshole*. My second was *shit*.

At the next light, I took a last-minute turn. The car followed, and I continued with the right turns until I'd completed a full circle. Those headlights still shone in my eyes, never backing off.

After checking all of my sight points, I pulled my wheel and performed a painfully slow, illegal U-turn, catching sight of the vehicle. A fucking blue Prius.

The car followed, executing a turn more precise than mine.

While I wanted to get out of the car and smash some headlights, I instead headed toward the closest police station.

When I turned into the parking lot, my stalker blew past. At that point, I figured I was safe, but my adrenaline pumped, and I needed air and motion, and though I didn't want the police involved, something had to be done.

I marched inside and demanded to speak to Officer Frank Garcia.

"He doesn't work at this station, ma'am," the woman said, her skin dark, her makeup flawless, her black hair pulled into an impressive knot in the back of her head. Bless her heart for not laughing at my idiot assumption that Frank worked at the first police station I walked into.

"I don't have his number. Is it possible for you to contact him for me?" I leaned forward, palming her desk.

Her gaze dropped to my trembling hands, then bounced back to my face. "I'll see what I can do." She nodded toward the wall behind me. "Have a seat."

"Thank you."

Frank stormed through the door thirty minutes later and found me blindly skimming a community events packet.

"Marley." He approached, sans uniform, and sat next to me on the small, and might I add, uncomfortable bench.

His brown eyes held wisdom and fiercely protective resolve.

"I was being followed," I blurted. "I didn't know what to do. I didn't want to drive home. I couldn't call Joe."

Frank was tall and built, so when he leaned forward, elbows to knees, I was shielded from any onlookers. "You did the right thing. Do you know who was following you?"

"There's this guy at work. He's a regular, never given me trouble—"

"Logan Shaw," he mumbled. "The guy that drives the Prius?"

My voice trembled. "How do you know about Prius Guy?"

"Joe asked me to run his plates."

"That motherfuck—"

"That doesn't matter right now," Frank cut me off. "Tell me everything."

I relayed all the details. Frank hmmed. Nodded. Didn't say a word until I finished.

"And that's it. I drove straight here. Didn't want to talk to anyone else. I don't like cops much, no offense, so I asked for you."

"You can always ask for me. Got it?" He laid an open palm on my thigh. "Give me your phone."

I complied, unlocking the screen before handing my cell over.

Frank pulled up my contacts and entered more than one number. "There. You've got my personal number and direct work line. I also added Con's cell and work numbers. You have any issues, ever, you call us."

"Con's not a cop."

"But Con will be there for you at the drop of a hat."

Instead of asking why, or are you for real? I said, " Thank you."

"Let me do a sweep of the area, make sure he's not stupid enough to stick around and wait for you to leave." He pushed from his sitting position, then dropped back down. "Unless you want to stay with Cyn and me tonight."

"Oh, no. But thank you."

"You sure?" He stood and shot me a killer wink, his grin exposing dimples I'd never noticed. "She makes a mean omelet."

"I appreciate the offer, but I'd really like to sleep in my own bed tonight."

"Sit tight." His heavy hand landed on my shoulder. "I'll text you in a few, let you know it's okay to go, then follow you home."

"Thank you, Frank."

"Anything for Joe's girl."

"I'm not his girl."

He chuckled, then shouted over his shoulder on his way out the door, "That's what Cyn says, even though she's wearing my engagement ring."

Twenty minutes passed before I got the go-ahead, and fifteen minutes later, I was home. Frank did a sweep of my house, dodging licks and nudges from two riled-up mutts, and dropped a kiss on my forehead before leaving.

He'd offered to stay, but I refused despite my rattled nerves. I fell asleep with two dirty dogs flanking my sides and all the lights in the house turned on.

CHAPTER
Twenty Seven

*J*OE

Two AM and every damn light shone in the house.

I made the rounds, hitting every switch to OFF, while a cacophony of barks and growls came from behind the closed bedroom door.

Marley hadn't greeted me. Either she was dead asleep or still angry, and I'd put my money on the latter.

I hadn't planned on staying in Whisper Springs so many days, but Marley's mom, Lori, had insisted I spend the first night.

Their bed and breakfast was a renovated three-story Victorian home, painted in earth tones that blended with the wooded landscape. The house sat on a plot of pristine land, half an acre from a private beach in a secluded bay of Lake Willow.

Lori's husband, Grant, was laid up with a torn meniscus, so I'd offered to help repair a gutter that'd been knocked off its perch during a recent windstorm. That DIY project ate an entire day. Good news? I'd gotten to know Marley's son, and that kid was golden. Good head on his shoulders, big heart like his mom, and grateful as fuck that I'd snagged him from Harper's clutches. His only complaint? Having to leave his NISMO behind. I'd cry about that, too. But, that 370Z was a tool Harper had used to keep the boy under his thumb, and Dylan's life, his safety, was worth more than any shiny car.

After a long couple of days and a lonely drive home, I needed to wrap my arms around Marley and sleep for a week.

When I hushed the dogs, saying, "Chill, guys, it's me," their warning snarls turned into happy whines and door scratches. Before I reached the knob, the door tore open, and a wild-eyed Marley tackled me to the ground.

"You son of a bitch!" She attacked with bruising kisses. "You scared the shit outta me."

The dogs flanked us, dancing, pouncing, greeting me with licks, sniffs, and grunts.

Marley lay stretched across the length of me, her arms coiled around my neck, red-rimmed eyes staring down at me. "You were gone too long."

"Your mom bribed me to stay with her potato pancakes."

That earned me a laugh.

"You men and your bellies." Marley rolled her eyes. "Too easy." Planting her palms on my chest, she pushed to stand, then retreated to her room, leaving the dogs to their attack. "How's Dylan?" she asked from out of sight.

"He's good. Settling in." Ginger hopped to my chest, and I accepted her licks while giving Bruce a good rub with my free hand.

I found Marley in bed, fully clothed, buried under her bedding. Not the reception I'd anticipated. But hell, I was home. Stripped down to my boxers, I crawled into bed and curled around her body.

"Talk to me." I squeezed her middle. "Why were all the lights on?"

After a dramatic inhale, exhale, she whispered, "I was followed on my way home tonight."

My body fevered with violent tremors.

"It was a Prius."

I rolled to my back, worried the rage would spread from my skin to hers, smother the words before she could speak them.

Marley stayed put, her back to me, her voice gone soft. "I drove to the police station and had them call Frank."

Thank fuck.

"Frank followed me home and checked the house. He was great." Marley laughed, then added, "For a cop, he ain't too bad."

"Yeah. Frank's the best." He'd called me before meeting Marley at the police station, then while he followed her home, and again to let me know he was stationed outside her house for the night. But, of course, I kept those details to myself.

Marley sighed, turning to face me, but didn't touch. "I was scared, Joe. But worse? I hated that you weren't here. Hated that I missed you, that I needed you to make me feel safe."

"Because you believe that gives me the power to hurt you."

Marley shifted, laying her head on my chest. "God, I'm such a mess."

"You're my mess." I slid a hand under her flannel pajama pants to grip that ass I hadn't touched in too long. "You have the power to hurt me, too, gorgeous."

My boxers strained against the thickening erection, but Little Joe would get no relief. Marley's body had already gone soft, dead weight. Better that way. She needed tender and slow, but after hearing about her night, I had nothing to give but fury.

Limbs heavy, head fuzzy, I kissed Ginger on the snout, gave Bruce an ear scratch, fumbled into my jeans and tee, and searched for Marley. Living room empty, I headed to the kitchen, where a pot of coffee sat in wait. The clock read 9:48 AM.

Marley made her coffee strong, as java should be, and as I savored my first sip, I glanced out the window. The mug slipped from my fingers and crashed into the empty sink, splashing scalding liquid in every direction. The burn on my neck and arms registered, but I ignored the pain and stormed outside. "What the ever-loving fuck are you doing here?"

My father stood next to his bike, arms crossed over his broad chest, a shit-eating grin parting his overgrown beard. He nodded my direction, then said to Marley, "See. Told you he wouldn't be happy to see me."

Marley stood, feigning casual, with her hands tucked into the back pockets of her baggy jeans. She wore a threadbare Guns N' Roses T-shirt, half-tucked in the front, and a fake smile.

"Dad," I mumbled, eyeing him, then the two men wearing matching cuts and standing guard at the end of the driveway. "Hey, guys."

Arms crossed, they both nodded.

"Son." My father had a deep, demanding voice that I'd always respected.

"What are you doing here?" I asked. Andrew Kaine didn't do casual visits.

"Got a call from my brother."

Larry? Interesting. "And?"

"Said you were outta line, messing with Harper." He smirked. "Told me to get you in check."

"You could've called."

"Wanted to see my boy. That so bad?" He reached into his saddlebag, pulled out a loosely wrapped package, and shoved it at my chest.

I recognized the weight. Choked back bile but held the offering tight.

"Go home, old man. I've got shit handled." I wanted those men far away from Marley.

"I've no doubt you've got things under control. I've got one thing to say, then I'll be on my way."

"Say what you need to say."

"I've got your back. The club has your back. You need anything, say the word."

"I've got it handled."

Dad and I had opposing views about "handling" things, hence the personal delivery.

"You don't wanna owe the club. I respect that." He nodded, scratching his bearded chin. "You've more than paid your dues. You don't wanna patch in, that's your mistake to make, but you're my boy, and that makes you one of us." He nodded at Marley, then me. "What I'm saying is, you need me, you call. Harper thinks he's untouchable. He ain't."

"Appreciate the offer." I stared into the same blue eyes I saw in the mirror every morning. Holding his offering, I thanked God that Mom had resisted his charms all those years ago. Dad was proud, strong, and demanded respect, but he was also a stone-cold killer when necessary. He would have crushed my mother, and he would have molded me into a man who would have broken his mother's heart.

"How's your mom?" The fucker could read minds, too.

"Never been happier."

"Good to hear."

Dad stepped around me, cupped Marley's face, and pulled her in for a kiss on the forehead. "Nice meeting you, Marley."

Marley jerked back, brows pinched.

My father laughed, mounted his bike, and said, "I like her," then backed out of the driveway and left with a bone-rattling rumble.

"Are you kidding me, Joe?" Marley whisper-yelled. "Satan's Slayers?"

"I'm not one of them."

"But you were." She slapped a palm to her forehead, realization settling in. "For years."

"I had no choice at the time."

"Satan's Slayers?" Marley's voice rose an octave. "You know how dangerous they are, and you've brought them to my house?"

"Jesus, Marley. I can't do this right now." Not with the heavy metal in my hand. I headed back inside. I grabbed my shoes, my dog, my keys, and made for my own front door, mind spinning.

"Joe," Marley called. I waved a hand over my shoulder, not sure what to say but acknowledging that I'd heard.

Unsatisfied, she followed with Bruce trotting behind. "Do I need to worry about your dad?"

"No." I unlocked the door and stepped inside.

"Why was he here? How did he know to look for you at my house?"

"Fuck! Calm down for one minute, and I'll explain." I set Ginger on her feet and the package on the side table. Hands to hips, I drew in a deep drag of air. "You should thank that criminal for making an appearance at your place and kissing your head. He did that because he knew Harper's guys were watching. That gesture made you untouchable." I paused, waiting for my words to register.

Marley only blinked, arms trembling at her sides.

"My father just saved your ass. That was all about you." Frustration got the better of me and I shouted. "Get it? He knows you're mine, and that makes you his."

Like a kettle about to blow, Marley's face reddened. "I'm not his. I'm not yours!" Then she blew, arms swinging wide. She knocked the table lamp over, sending the package to the ground.

Out fell my Glock, skidding inches across the hardwood.

Marley shrieked, jumping back. "A gun? Why did he give you a gun?"

Ah, shit. "That's mine. He's only returning the damn thing."

Her voice lowered to a deadly growl. "How are you taking care of things exactly?"

"I'm not shooting anyone, if that's what you think."

"I don't know what to think right now."

My head hurt, and I needed coffee and time to sort my shit. Mostly, I needed Marley to know how things would play out.

"Listen. I've got eyes on you at work. I'm here with you at home. Harper can't touch you, even if he was suicidal enough to try. As for the fuckhead who followed you last night, no more going anywhere alone. Got me?"

Wrong thing to say.

"Got you? Got you? Are you serious right now? Is that an order, sir?" Wild-eyed Marley was back, the same girl who'd gone apeshit on my uncle.

Riled, tired, and vexed by Dad's unannounced and unwelcome visit, I threw back, "That's right. You're not going anywhere alone until I set that Prius-driving shithead straight. I knew he was trouble. Should've taken care of him that first day."

Marley snatched my gun off the floor and dangled it on her finger by the trigger guard. "Taken care of him, huh? What would you have done, Joe? Tell me. Roughed him up a bit? Beat him to a bloody pulp?" She licked her lips, eyeing the Glock, then pointed the damn thing toward the kitchen. "Or maybe you would've shot him. I mean, you spent five years with a dangerous gang."

"Club" came out of my mouth by habit. "They're a club. Now give me the fucking gun."

"What did you do for your club exactly? How did you pay your dues? Why did you need a gun?"

"Stop pointing that thing and hand it over."

Eyes aimed at the weapon, she whispered, "I hate guns. I hate criminals." Gaze fierce, face crumpling, she said, "But most of all, I hate bossy assholes."

Her hands shook. She'd had enough. Dylan. Prius Guy. Harper. My dad. Marley was breaking, and it killed me to watch her fall apart.

"Babe. C'mon, please. You want an apology? Okay, fine." I dropped to my knees. "I'm sorry that I'm an overprotective dickhead. Sorry for falling in love with a woman who has a fan club full of psychopaths. I'm sorry my dirty history upsets you." Slumping, butt to my heels, I purged because apologies weren't enough. "Until you, my life had no purpose, and now my only goal is to wake up every morning to that gorgeous smile, knowing you're happy and safe. And I'm not sorry for being the bossy asshole to give that to you."

Chest rising and falling, her glare softened. "That was a shitty apology."

"Neighbor, listen," I pleaded, hands steepled. "My old man doesn't carry a gun unless—"

"No. You listen," interrupted my spirited girl. "I'm a grown woman who runs a successful business. I raised an amazing human all on my own. I've survived for years without a man telling me what to do, having me watched, or—"

Marley continued her rant, unaware that Ginger had caught a case of the zoomies and barreled our way, Bruce loping behind. Ginger skidded, avoiding a collision, but when Bruce tried to stop, he slid across the floor and knocked Marley off her feet.

A deafening crack pierced the air. A punch to my gut threw me to my back. Marley scrambled, screaming, climbing over me, but I couldn't hear a word out of her mouth.

Rage I'd never known rumbled through me. "You shot me!"

⁕ ⁕ ⁕ ⁕ ⁕ ⁕ ⁕ ⁕ ⁕

"I can't believe she shot you," Connor howled, slapping his knee, his face red from laughter.

"Shut up." I slid my feet into my OluKais, then tested my balance, rising to stand.

The room swam around me, and I gripped Con's shoulder. As always, he had my back, bracing an arm around my midsection and helping me into the wheelchair.

Ominous clouds and misty rain greeted us when we passed through the emergency room doors. Frank's truck idled curbside, the back passenger window dirtied with smudges that only sloppy tongues and wet noses could create.

Bruce's giant mug appeared as we approached, and I

could swear he smiled. Ginger sat in Frank's lap, tail spinning, body shaking. Frank held her tight until I settled in my seat, then released the little ragamuffin to say her hellos.

My eyelids weighed a thousand pounds each. I hurt everywhere, but more than anything, my ego was bruised, maybe beyond repair. Still, I asked, "How is she?"

"Marley wouldn't talk to me," Frank said, chuckling. "Feisty little shit."

"She home?" My question seemed to come from someone else.

"Nah," Frank said. "They're keeping her overnight. Are you gonna press charges?"

Press charges? Yeah. Good idea. Maybe my hot-tempered Calamity Jane would learn to calm her shit while holding a loaded weapon. "Let me think on it a bit," was the last thing I remembered saying before passing out with my head against the window.

CHAPTER
Twenty Eight

MARLEY

Patches of gray mottled the pale blue sky. One dog-shaped puff stood out from the rest, making me smile despite my circumstances. Face raised to the sky, I sucked in a dose of fresh air. Smelled heavenly, tasted like freedom.

It was a bit disheartening to find zero messages on my cell, but what did I expect? I'd shot a man. My lover of all people. I'd yet to hear if he'd been released from the hospital or the extent of his injury. And I just needed to know he was okay.

My lawyer explained I wasn't out of the woods, but I considered myself damn lucky to be standing on a sidewalk and not behind bars.

Though, a six-by-six cell might be safer. Joe probably wanted me dead.

My Uber driver, Hanish, arrived, and I wondered, while lying to him about my career, if he sensed danger in the presence of a gun-wielding boyfriend slayer. I giggled, probably because I was crazy, but most likely because I was exhausted. Hanish glanced at me through the rearview, then turned up the volume on his stereo. Yeah, men, too, had a sixth sense about danger.

Hanish dropped me at home. Immediately, I headed for Joe's door. Ginger and Bruce barked from the backyard, but nobody answered.

I headed to my own house, called the dogs inside,

absorbed their exuberant greetings, then, overdue for a shower, I stripped in the hallway and stepped into the bathroom and under the hot spray, where I stayed until my skin was red and the stench of my mistakes swirled down the drain and into the abyss.

Towel secured around my hair, I headed, naked, for the bedroom, mind set on driving to the hospital and demanding answers.

Joe stood in the hallway, shoulder against the wall, one foot crossed over the other, eyes red-rimmed and swollen.

"Fucking shit!" I screamed, startled, a whoosh of air leaving my lungs. "You're okay. Thank God!"

Joe held my gaze, silent, stiff. He was a battle-worn soul who stunk of body odor and antiseptic. "I'm far from okay," he rasped, standing straight, towering over me, every muscle in his jaw and neck tight.

Fear coursed through me, buckling my knees.

Joe's gaze dragged along the length of my naked, trembling body. He shook his head, releasing a breath, then turned and headed toward my room.

"I'm sorry" seemed insignificant, but I said the words regardless, following behind.

Joe reached the bed, cleared his throat, then broke my heart. "You could've killed me." His shoulders rose, then fell on a long sigh. "These pain meds are doing a number. I need sleep." He kicked off his shoes, stumbled, caught himself on my dresser, then mumbled, "I don't wanna be alone."

How could he possibly want me in the same room? "Joe—"

"Please." He scrubbed a palm over his face. "Get in bed."

I obeyed. I owed him that much.

He slid between the sheets, mindful of his wound. I

eased next to him, leaving ample and painful distance. I ached to touch, soothe, connect, anything, but was I allowed after what I'd done? I watched and waited until his body melted into the mattress and a faint snore filled the silence. Only then did I dare reach out, stroke the stubble on his face, trace his pulse.

Thank God he was alive. Thank God I hadn't destroyed one of the good ones.

My heart ached for Joe and beat too hard, too fast, my mind spinning, showing no sign of shutting down.

I'd nearly killed a man, yet he lay in my bed, resting peacefully. He'd come to me for comfort after my foolish behavior.

If I'd kept my temper in check, I would never have picked up that gun.

If I had followed my own rules and never dropped my pants for Joe, he'd be happy and healthy with a good woman who carried no baggage. Then again, I wouldn't have discovered how wonderful a bad boy could be.

Joe Kaine was an angel dropped from the sky into my crazy life, and time and time again, he'd proven that he was playing for keeps. But, not even the best of men should be expected to forgive being shot by the woman they love.

The dogs barked, snarled, and clawed at the front door. Brain half in dreamland, I wrestled from the bedding and stumbled through the dark living room.

The mutts circled my legs, whining, then continued their defensive routine. A peek through the window revealed nothing or no one outside in the immediate vicinity.

"What are you brats making a fuss about? Was there a critter outside?" I cooed, patting their heads to calm them, though my skin prickled with a warning.

After double-checking all the locks, I shooed my protectors back to bed, snuggled into my pillow, then breathed deep, inhaling Joe's scent.

My alarm blared at five AM. Joe mumbled, then fell silent, his lashes fanned over his cheeks, adding boyish charm to his chiseled features. Ginger groaned. Bruce leaped to the floor and scrambled for the back door, ready to take on the day. I waited patiently for the pitter-patter of four tiny paws to catch up before letting them outside.

I had just poured steaming coffee into my mug when Joe shuffled around the corner, hair a mess, lips pouty, eyes sleepy and so damn dreamy my nipples pebbled.

"Got one of those for me?" he asked, voice thick with morning rumble.

I handed him my cup, mumbled, "Good morning," and poured another.

Joe leaned against the counter, too far away for my liking. He didn't look happy to see me, nor did he look sex starved as I'd become accustomed to. He looked like a man ready to end things, and for that, I was devastated.

My gut churned. Steeling my spine, bracing for the inevitable impact, I started, "Joe, I, uh—"

"You shot me."

Once the first tear fell, there was no stopping the flood. "I—I don't... I can't tell you how sorry I am. There are no words to convey how horrid I feel, how disgusted with my behavior." I sniffed, swiped the moisture from my face. "I hate guns. I absolutely hate them, and I flailed that thing around like a lunatic. I could've killed you or one of the dogs."

Joe sipped his coffee, arms crossed, showing no emotion but holding my gaze.

"It's not like me to be so careless or out of control. But lately, I have no control over anything, especially my temper, and... I need help. I know that."

While I purged, Joe watched, stiff and still.

My body shook, overloaded with emotion. "I'm going to see a counselor or a therapist and work through all the craziness in my head. And my lawyer said I could serve time." I pressed my hands together and begged, "If I do, please, please, will you take care of Bruce? You're the only one I'd trust him with, and I understand that you hate me, but Bruce and Ginger, they're good together. They need each other, and I don't think we should punish them just because we're not going to see each other anymore."

Still, nothing from the man. No smirk or sneer, not even an eye roll.

"So, if you want him full-time, that's okay, too. He likes your house better anyway. It's bigger. And you've got your shit together unlike crazy ol' me." I had to stop rambling. I drew a deep breath and said, "I'm just so, so sorry."

Joe set his mug on the counter, ripped a paper towel off the roll, then dabbed my tears. "I forgive you."

"What?"

"You heard me."

"You forgive me. That's it?" I had to be dreaming. "No yelling, screaming, making me suffer?"

"You didn't aim the gun at me. You didn't shoot me on purpose."

"No." Another sob escaped. "Of course not."

"I'm pissed, Marley, and I'm a grouchy fucker when I'm in pain. And that whole situation was shitty." He dropped the napkin in the sink. "Had every intention of making you suffer. But then..." He stared over my head for a beat, as if searching for the right words. "Listen. The thing is, life is short, and I refuse to waste time being angry over an accident. That's all it was, an accident."

"Joe," left my lips on a sigh.

"I love you, and I forgive you." He pressed a finger over my mouth. "You don't have to say it back. I see it in your eyes every time you look at me. Read it in your smile. Feel it when you touch me." He cupped my face, tilted my head. "I get that you're not ready to admit defeat. But we're good. I forgive you for giving me a new scar just like you'll forgive me for being an overprotective, bossy asshole. We'll always forgive each other because that's what you do when you love somebody."

"You make it sound so easy."

"It is." He smiled his *I've got you* smile, then winked.

I eased my arms around his middle and rested my cheek against his chest. My heartbeat steadied for the first time in days. Emotion clogged my throat, so I hugged all the gratitude I couldn't speak into my incredible man.

. . . .

Lilly's eyes filled with tears, and she clutched her chest. "So, Joe's going to be fine, and you two are good?"

"Yes." I nodded, biting my lip because I'd cried enough and wasn't about to start again. To say I was overwhelmingly grateful would be the understatement of the century. "How are things with Marco?"

"I'm still pissed," she huffed and leaned against the counter, gripping the edges. "I mean, really, he crossed a line. They all did. But, he's groveled enough and his intentions, though extreme, were pure. I suppose it's time to let him off the hook."

"And if Joe can forgive me shooting him," I added, "I sure as hell can forgive him starting a business across the street just to prove me wrong."

Lilly wrapped me in her arms.

I melted into her, so thankful for the people in my life. "I appreciate you taking care of things the past couple of days."

"It's been smooth sailing." She rocked us back and forth.

"No Harper?"

"No Harper."

"Prius Guy?"

"Oh, Prius Guy hasn't strayed from his morning schedule, but when it's not you, he says, 'never mind' and drives away."

A full-body shiver tore through me.

Lilly grabbed my shoulders, held me at arm's length. "He's not happy with your retirement from the window. This morning, he looked terrible. Stubble. Messy hair. Dark bags under his eyes. When I greeted him, he looked at me like I was roadkill, yelled, 'fuck,' then punched his dash and drove off."

"Lil, I'm sorry you have to deal with that."

"It is what it is." She shrugged and turned to look out the window. "The Average Joe's are here before I open, stay until after we lock up in the evenings. They're watching us. And though it's bullshit that our men concocted a whole business for the sole purpose of keeping tabs, I must admit, I feel safer."

"Me, too. And if you tell anyone I said that, I'll fire your fabulous ass," I teased.

A customer approached. Lilly headed to the window, and I continued restocking the supply closet.

When I was finished, I said, "I'm heading to Georgetown to check on Jazz. You need anything?"

"A night out with my girl?"

"Soon," I promised.

We said our goodbyes. I waited until Lilly locked up behind me, then I headed for my other stand. I had only just pulled my parking break when an Escalade rolled to a stop next to me.

I envisioned a gang of beefy men dressed in black jumping out of the SUV, then stuffing me, kicking and screaming, into the back seat. Heart rate spiking, I dried my sweaty palms on my jeans.

But when Johan Harper stepped around the front of his vehicle and then opened my car door, I only grew angry. He moved aside, allowing me room to stand and gain equal ground.

"You are no longer welcome at any of my establishments." I stood toe to toe with the man, daring him to challenge me.

"Good morning to you too, Marley."

Much to my dismay, he stepped back, shoved his hands into his gray slacks, and leaned against his Caddy.

"What do you want?"

Harper studied my attire, scratched his chin. "Haven't seen your boy."

"Welcome to the club." I held his gaze and balled my fists, struggling but succeeding in keeping my shit together.

"Heard you're tight with Satan's Slayers."

"None of your business."

Harper dropped his gaze to the ground. Nodded. Shifted on his feet.

Hmm. Joe had been right. Harper had heard Mr. Kaine was in town, and the old man was riled.

"Wrong crowd, doll. Are they the reason you've been putting me off? They running shit through your stands?"

"What the hell are you talking about?"

"Don't play stupid. You're your father's daughter."

Despite that insult coming from a lifelong criminal, I was offended. "I'm nothing like that man." Except for the erratic temper and running whenever life got uncomfortable. I stabbed a pointed finger into his chest. "I'm one hundred percent legit, and I'll close shop before partnering with the likes of you or some sleazy, no-good biker gang."

"Club," he mumbled, correcting me.

What was with these men? Club. Gang.

Whatever.

I continued, waving him away. "Get back in your fancy car, and go intimidate someone who gives a shit."

Harper's white hair blew loose in the breeze, and he made no move to pat it back into place. He stared at me long and hard, no emotion on his face, then nodded. "My weekly visits are over, but hear this, little lady. I'm watching. I don't take kindly to outsiders sniffing around my territory. If I hear you've got something going on with the Slayers, you won't like the backlash."

Threats, threats, threats. What a piece of work. I was done. Cheeks aflame, I promised, "You hear this, little man. Go anywhere near my son, so much as speak to him, you'll beg for death by the time I'm finished with you."

Harper stood straight, laughing. "Deal." He headed back around his vehicle, still chuckling, then shouted over the hood, "I like you, kid. It's a damn shame we can't work together."

I responded with a middle finger. Classy, I know.

He rapped his knuckles on the hood twice, then made

an undramatic exit, rolling into morning traffic and hopefully out of my life for good.

. . . .

"I told you not to go anywhere alone," Joe growled at me from his spot on the sofa.

He was livid. Understandably so. I'd waited until after dinner to bring up my conversation with Harper. Perhaps I should've given him another day or two.

"Joe, listen." I skirted the coffee table and straddled his thighs, resting my butt on his knees. I raked my fingers through the scruff on his face and reminded him, "I have a business to run, and you've been busy healing from a bullet wound."

"No. You listen." He curled his strong fingers into my hips, tugged me to his groin, and hit me with those worried blue eyes. "You just need to stay safe, please. It would kill me if anything happened to you."

Oh, my heart.

"Joe—" I started on a sigh.

"What if Harper had wanted to hurt you?" he interrupted. "You were defenseless."

I wanted to remind him that Harper wouldn't risk a public display but chose wiser words, hoping they'd soothe the riled beast. "I trusted what you told me—I was untouchable because of your father."

His hard features softened, and those bunched shoulders dropped. And when he didn't respond, I whispered, "Harper said he would leave me alone, and I believed him. You were right about your dad."

Lips drawn tight, Joe nodded, cupped my cheeks, and

dropped a kiss on my nose, then on my forehead, lingering there. Eyes closed, I breathed him in. His breath wreaked of garlic, and I suspected he'd snuck a third helping of linguini and pesto while I was outside with the dogs.

"You're an amazing man, Joe Kaine."

In one fluid motion, Joe flipped, tossing me on the cushions and crashing over me, a man on a mission. "You're so fucking into me it's embarrassing." Hair fell over his face as he stared down at me, fighting a grin.

"You're so pussy-whipped it's pathetic," I teased back.

Joe yawned, dropping his head into my neck.

"Let's get to bed. It's been a long day."

Beautiful and weary, he nodded, then pushed off the couch. He grabbed my hands, helped me up, then tugged me toward the stairs. I followed without a fuss. I'd follow him anywhere. When we reached the bedroom, he steered me inside, where he stripped my dress, slow and lazy, then removed my bra and panties. Joe kissed me dizzy against the wall while I fumbled to remove his shirt. His running pants and boxers proved easier to remove.

My guy was exhausted. I sucked him off where we stood and refused when he tried to return the favor. He needed a good night's sleep more than I needed an orgasm.

We fell into bed, and Joe held me close. I only drifted off when his arms loosened and soft snores filled the silence.

Morning came too soon. Dogs barked outside. Joe's side of the bed was empty and rumpled. I snagged a T-shirt out of his drawer and trotted down the stairs, yawning, searching for signs of life. The back door was open, screen, too, and as I drew nearer, Ginger caught my attention, working her little paws in a fresh, deep hole near a rose bush.

"No, Ginger," I scolded, scooping her up and nuzzling

her into my neck. "Not Alice's rose bushes. Naughty girl," I said, kissing her nose.

Bruce barked from my side of the fence, and I headed for the open gate, the dewy grass cold and muddy. Men's voices reached my ears, one familiar, both of them tense.

The strange voice shouted, "You took her from me. She's mine and you stole her right out from under me."

Joe replied, "Relax, man. Let's sit down and talk about this."

When the men came into view, my heart sputtered. Joe stood barefoot and shirtless next to my firepit, basketball shorts hanging low on his waist, his hands in the air, level with this shoulders. Logan Shaw, aka Prius Guy, stood with his back to me, arms raised, gun pointed at Joe.

Bruce bounced back and forth between them, vying for attention.

The world silenced to nothing but a deep buzz. My chest pounded, limbs trembled. Ginger grunted, trying to wiggle free, then yelped when I squeezed her too tight. Through the foreboding dread, I managed to duck behind the fence.

Too late.

"You said she wasn't home."

"Run, baby," Joe yelled, voice low, commanding. Terrifying.

I ran. Straight toward the house, setting Ginger free somewhere between the rose garden and the back porch. I'd reached the kitchen when the crack of a gunshot knocked me to my knees.

Joe. Oh, God. Joe.

My foot caught in the hem of the tee when I tried to stand, and I stumbled into the cupboard, catching the edge before smacking my head on the sharp corner.

I reached for the phone, two fingers making contact

when an arm hooked my waist. A low growl. The room spun, and my back slammed against the fridge, knocking the air from my lungs but spurring my fight.

I pushed and shoved, scratched and kicked, grunting and screaming until I was free of his grip.

Logan might've been speaking or shouting or trying to calm me, but I couldn't make out a single word over the heavy thrumming in my ears.

"Shut up!" registered a blink before his fist met my temple.

The room went dark, then shimmied back into focus.

I swung in reflex, hitting his nose, and Logan's head flew back. He cupped his face with both hands, releasing me, and screamed, "Ow! Fuck!"

Again, I ran, though my surroundings were fuzzy and my head hurt like a son of a bitch.

"Joe!" I screamed while heading toward the shed. I don't know why. To hide? To find a weapon?

Rocks tore my feet, but I pushed forward. I spotted Alice's hedge sheers propped against the bench at the same time gravel crunched behind me.

I dove for the handle, and with a mighty roar, swung around before looking and hit Joe in the shoulder.

"Fuuuuck!" He stumbled to the side, gripping his arm, then tripped over his feet and landed on his ass.

That's when I spotted Logan, barreling my way, gun aimed, eyes black as insanity, yelling, "You left me! You left me!"

They say your life flashes before your eyes before you die. My only thought was *no, not yet*. Breathless and nauseous, I gripped the handle of the sheers, bracing for a fight because I wasn't ready to go. I hadn't loved Joe long enough, and I would kill Logan before letting him take me away from my boys.

Joe powered to his feet and rushed toward the crazy man. Before he made contact, the toe of Logan's shoe caught in the hole Ginger had dug, and he went down, his eyes going wide, the gun flying through the air. His head hit the corner of the cement bench with a sickening thud, and he fell limp.

CHAPTER
Twenty Nine

*J*OE

Logan Shaw's blood had washed away long ago, but I continued to cleanse the ground with the cold spray. Not even the cool water could soothe the rage that bubbled and burned under my skin. Alice's sacred garden had once again been desecrated. I'd failed to protect Marley from the cuts and bruises marring her skin. She could have been killed in the same spot I'd found Alice beaten half to death all those years ago. Fury like I'd never known vibrated my core, and suddenly, I hated every fucking petal and thorn on every fucking stem of every god forsaken bush.

More so, I hated that cold gray bench.

I'd made a terrible error in judgment, vowing to keep Alice's rose garden alive. She'd tended to her garden with fervor, but had they ever made her truly happy, the thorny reminders of Bill's betrayals?

Time to start my own damn garden. Fuck that. A good excavation was in order. Maybe I'd build an outdoor kitchen. Yeah. Good plan. I shut off the water, coiled the hose, and headed to the shed. The one tool I needed was nowhere to be found.

"Hey," came Marley's sweet voice. "You okay?"

I couldn't meet her gaze, the bruise near her left eye a reminder of how I'd failed my girl. "Fine. Just cleaning up this mess. You don't happen to have a sledgehammer, do ya?"

"Of course I do, but why?"

"Demolition day." I gestured to the bench, then the roses.

"But Alice—"

"Alice built this garden as a fuck-you to her abusive, unfaithful husband. He died in this spot. Alice almost died in this spot. Now Logan. And you..." I couldn't finish that train of thought. I swallowed past the lump of emotion in my throat. "No good comes from these bushes. I don't think she would've wanted me busting my ass to keep them alive. They have to go. I can't look at them another day."

Marley blinked up at me. "I'll get the sledgehammer."

She hurried off. I found the shovels and gloves. Marley returned with two orange-handled Fiskars, her own goggles, and protective gear. "We're doing this together."

Good Lord, my girlfriend was badass. "Why?"

She ignored my question, asking, "Who gets first swing?"

"All yours, baby."

My gorgeous girl stepped next to the bench, braced her feet, and wrapped both hands around the handle. "Joe?"

"Yeah?"

"I want to help because I love you."

Air and rage left my body in one ferocious exhale, replaced by the freshest, freest inhale I'd ever experienced.

"Good goddamn answer, neighbor," I told her. "Now, show me what you've got."

She swung, chipping a corner off the bench, then yelled, "Ah, that feels good!"

She needed to purge, too.

She took three more turns before I dropped a kiss on her nose and then above her bruise before I said, "Love you too, gorgeous."

I aimed for the center of the seat. The cement cracked

but didn't fall. I struck again, hitting dead center, splitting the slab down the middle. The two halves folded, falling to the ground, and exposed the hollow centers of each columned leg. Inside each leg sat capped pieces of PVC pipe.

Marley hummed, stepping closer. "That's strange."

I set my sledgehammer aside, bent at the waist, hands to knees, and stared, disbelieving.

Alice's letter came to mind. She couldn't have, could she? But what else could that be? I laughed, belly deep, tears falling.

Alice. That shit.

Marley watched, brows knit, her own body shaking with humor. She had no clue. In hysterics, I fell to my ass, hands to my face.

A good five minutes passed before I pulled my shit together and removed the pipes from the bench. "C'mere, babe." I headed to the garage, where the miter saw was currently stored. Took a minute to set her up, adjust the angle, and clamp the pipe, but when I cut the end off that damn tube and pulled out a rolled-up stack of cash, I wept. Honest to God, tears of gratitude and bittersweet joy erupted from my core.

Marley watched, still clueless, and if I wasn't mistaken, worried for my mental health. "What's going on?"

"Alice. That crazy nut." I shook my head, then slapped the money into Marley's palm. "I should've known."

Dig deep, she'd written. Dig deep.

Alice's "fuck you" to Bill was also her "you got this, girl" to herself.

Marley followed me back outside, where I grabbed the shovels, handed one to her, and instructed, "Get your sweet ass over here, babe." I picked the closest rose bush and dug, directly at the roots, telling my love, "This is you and me getting out of the sexy coffee business. This is you and me having the honeymoon to end all honeymoons. This is you and me doing whatever the hell we want for the rest of our lives. What's your favorite charity? We'll start there."

"Honeymoon?" Marley forced her shovel deeper with her foot.

"Don't pretend you don't know that's where we're headed." Scoop. Toss. "And Alice left us one helluva wedding gift."

My gorgeous neighbor slapped a hand to her mouth, eyes wide. "Oh, Joe." She shook her head. "Bill didn't whittle away her money, did he?"

Words failed, so I laughed. What else could I do?

"Alice, you crazy, beautiful woman," she yelled to the heavens. Her eyes glistened, but she wore an unbearably beautiful smile while she helped me dig deep.

Hours passed. By the time we'd removed all of Alice's revenge roses, we'd unearthed twenty-three tubes of PVC pipe, each filled with rolled and carefully preserved hundred-dollar bills. I had a hunch there was more hidden in odd places throughout the house and property. We'd get to them eventually.

My heart was content. Money or not, Marley loved me, and a man like me couldn't ask for anything better.

Ly brushed the clear polish over Marley's Tinsel Town Red. "When you two marry?"

Trudy huffed, "Mama," then shook her head and rolled her eyes.

I laughed, hit Marley with a wink, and said, "Soon as she agrees to be my bride."

Marley had mentioned she didn't like big weddings. I wanted to watch my girl walk toward me in a gorgeous gown in a church full of our loved ones, then steal her away to a clothing-optional, secluded beach somewhere tropical.

"You haven't even proposed," Marley chastised.

"You love me?" I asked, turning in my chair to face her full on.

"More than anything." Her blush did unbearably good things to my insides.

"You ever gonna love another man?"

No delay. "Never."

"Then what's the problem?" I sat back, folded my arms, closed my eyes. "We're a done deal."

"I might not want a big wedding or a wedding at all," she teased. "But I deserve a little effort. You need to work harder than just telling me we're getting married."

God, I'd never tire of riling her up.

Ly patted Marley's leg. "Okay. You sit here few minutes." She scooted her chair back to clean up.

Marley and I were Ly and Trudy's only customers, so I stayed in the chair to enjoy the massage rollers even though my pedicure was finished.

"And besides," Marley said, "I'm too busy trying to run you out of business. Your hot Joes are distracting my girls."

Trudy chose that time to slurp on the straw of her iced drink fresh from Average Joe.

"Let's spice things up a bit."

Marley cracked a grin, wiggling her brows. "What do you have in mind?"

"A contest. See who can sell the most drinks in a day."

"Winner gets?"

"You win, we elope. I win, we go all out."

The little shit pretended to ponder my proposal, tapping a finger to her temple. "Deal. But let's make it a charitable event. What d'ya say?"

"Looking mighty smug, future Mrs. Kaine."

"I'll win," she said, chin held high.

"I might have a few tricks up my sleeve."

"I'll always win." Such confidence.

"Yeah? Why's that?"

Marley laid her head back, closed her eyes. "Sex sells, and men are pervier than women."

"I'll have to disagree with you there," I argued.

"Whatever." She waved her hand, brushing me off. "Set the date. It's on." Then she smacked her armrest. "And the charity has to be for battered women."

My throat thickened with emotion. Abused women. For Alice. I swallowed that lump and stayed my course. "You realize you just agreed to marry me, right?"

"I did no such thing," she mumbled, fighting a smile.

"I heard it. Ladies? You heard her, right?" I asked the room.

Ly and Trudy nodded in agreement.

"I did not!" Marley sat straight, shooting me a glare.

"You said 'deal' to my challenge."

Christ, I was getting a boner. We needed to get home fast.

"Get on your goddamn knee and ask me then," Marley challenged.

"Like every other average Joe out there? Seems boring."

"Yes," she insisted. "Just like that. A classic, everyday, ordinary proposal."

I stared into twinkling eyes, half tempted to throw her over my shoulder and steal her away to the nearest courthouse. But that wasn't us.

I stood, laid cash on the counter, and sauntered to the

door. Before making my exit, I threw over my shoulder, "Nah, you need extraordinary," then headed to the truck to hide my hard-on.

. ° . ° . °. ° . ° . °

When you know, you know. The morning I met Marley, she'd only heard tales of me as the bad-boy ex-con. Still, she'd comforted me when I'd cried like a baby on Alice's kitchen floor. That was the day I'd known, without a doubt, despite never before having met the woman, that she was the one.

Love at first sight. If someone had told me a year ago that I'd fall victim to that ridiculous sentiment, I'd have laughed in their face or knocked them into next week.

Funny how life proved you wrong.

Take, for example, I'd believed I had our contest in the bag. Con, Frank, and I had pulled out the big guns for our charity contest/event.

We'd recruited cops and firemen for the day, all of whom were more than willing to flex their hard-earned muscles to support a local charity. Two pet shelters had even hopped on board.

I mean, hot men with puppies and kittens? We couldn't go wrong, right?

Our earnings were pretty damn close, but Marley proved to be the true champ. She'd dressed her girls in Seahawks colors, and every person who bought coffee was entered into a drawing to win season tickets or a premium suite for one of next year's games.

Brilliant, right? It should've been my idea.

The girls worked mostly naked that day. Pasties and

thongs, their skin lightly dusted with blue, silver, and bright green glitter.

We'd advertised in the paper, as well as social media, but our following was nothing compared to Pink Sweets, and her blast had gone viral. Two news stations had stopped by to cover the story.

So, a good day for everyone around. So successful, in fact, we agreed to make it a yearly event.

Marley was right. Sex sells. If we decided to stay in the "sexy" coffee business, we could turn what was considered an immoral endeavor by most into something positive for the community.

We could shake the shadows of our father's dirty dealings. We could break the cycle. Alice's suffering would not be for nothing.

Marley and I would never have to work again with Alice's money, and we could own a killer house with a million-dollar view in a neighborhood too posh to worry about break-ins, where we could walk the dogs on pristine streets without looking over our shoulders. But that life was not for me, and I hoped, believed, that Marley felt the same.

Undoubtedly, our neighborhood in south Seattle was below average, but the homes, people, and streets were ours. We'd met, fought, fallen in love, were raised, raised a child, and had Alice on our unimpressive street.

I needed nothing more, except maybe to share my good fortune with those I loved and with others that needed a helping hand.

Yeah. Fuck you, Kaine curse. I was free. An average fucking Joe.

I got my woman, my dogs, and the best buddies a man could ask for.

"What's that smile on your face?" my girl asked, staring up at me with adoration I'd forever cherish.

"Just thinking about how lucky I am is all."

Marley leaned her head on my shoulder, lacing our fingers. "I was thinking, since you insisted on getting married, I could rent out my house. I don't think I should sell. Too many memories. Besides, I'd like to pass it on to Dylan someday."

"That's a great idea." I pressed my lips to her hair.

"So, where is this guy?"

We stood in front of my gym. Cadence Fight Club. The window stretched the entire length of the building, and their logo was a simple gold circle with CFC in the middle.

"He'll be here soon."

Shielding her eyes from the sun, she looked up. "Looks like an apartment building up above."

A man emerged from the alleyway, wearing workout gear, looking like he stepped off a Men's Health magazine cover.

"Cole, my man." I stepped forward, embracing my friend and owner of the gym, then stepped back and made introductions. "This is the future Mrs. Kaine."

"Pleasure." Cole offered Marley his hand.

"Nice to meet you," she said, giving him a firm shake.

Cole led us inside the building to a private elevator, then up to the fourth floor.

"Can't tell you how much your donation means to us." He stepped into the hallway, which opened into a large reception area.

Cole Adams didn't need our money. His family owned most of Seattle.

"What is this place?" Marley asked, spinning a slow circle, taking in the space.

Aside from the large desk, the entryway was unassuming, yet homey and comfortable. You wouldn't know if the offices behind the walls were for accountants, lawyers, doctors, or a tech company.

I knew.

"It's a safe haven," Cole said, turning to face Marley. "For women like Alice. We offer the best security. Anonymity. Our women get free help—medical, legal, counseling. We provide homes, schooling, and childcare."

Awed, Marley grabbed my waist, lifting that gorgeous face to mine. "This is our charity?"

"If you say yes."

"Yes, of course. Why haven't I heard of this place?"

"Discretion," Cole answered. "The system often fails these women. We don't."

Marley brushed a finger over the hand-carved desk. "This is a massive undertaking. You fund this purely with donations?"

"No." Cole leaned against the wall, ankles crossed. "Private funding mostly. Though every bit helps, and nothing goes unused. I do have a proposal for you."

"For me?" Marley stepped back, bumping into my chest.

Couldn't help myself. I curled my arms around her shoulders.

"Yes." Cole tilted his head, glanced at me, then back to my girl. "Joe told me you're opening more coffee stands soon."

"Yes."

"We'd like you to consider employing some of our women. Help them find their footing and transition back into the world outside these walls."

Marley curled her hands around my forearms. "Yes. Yes. Of course. I'll do it."

Cole's brows raised two inches. "Just like that?"

"Just like that." She nodded.

Marley couldn't have said no. She had a mothering spirit, and she bloomed when any opportunity to nurture or guide another human being presented itself.

I pulled her tighter to my chest and kissed her head. "Good answer, neighbor. Good goddamn answer."

Marley laughed, shimmied out of my embrace, then threw her arms around Cole. "Best day ever," she squealed, like the child she never got to be.

CHAPTER
Thirty

MARLEY

Best day ever?

Hands down, it was the day I woke up next to Joe in my mom's bed and breakfast, knowing that Dylan was downstairs.

I slapped Joe's bare ass, then hurried through a shower, shimmied into my jeans and tank, wiggled my toes into my flip-flops, and jogged down two flights of freshly polished hardwood.

The old Victorian was beautiful, clean, and homey and smelled like bread fresh from the oven. My nose led me toward the kitchen.

Dylan sat on a barstool, head down, shirtless, dark hair hanging in messy waves over his forehead. His muscles were more defined. Dark curls dusted his chest and lower abdomen. I'd said it before, but my son was no longer a boy. He was a man. A bittersweet sight for a mother's sore eyes.

"Hey, Mom." He pushed off the counter and stood straight, coming at me with arms wide open.

"Morning," I mumbled against his left pec. He was strong, too. And much taller than I'd ever imagined. "Where's your grandma?"

"She had to take Grant to his doctor's appointment." He snagged a black T-shirt off a stool and tugged it over his head. "C'mon, I'm taking you to breakfast."

"You are?" My heart burst, overfilled with every happy feeling imaginable. "What about Joe?"

"He wants to sleep in." Dylan tucked his phone into his back pocket, his wallet in his front pocket, and grabbed a set of keys off the counter. "I asked him last night."

"Oh. Okay. Let's go."

Dylan drove me through downtown Whisper Springs, then toward the old highway. We exited onto a dirt road that led to a fifties-looking diner on a huge lot that overlooked Lake Willow. The old three-tier sign sat high above the pines and read Truck Stop Diner.

I blew a low whistle. "What a view."

"Cleo works here." His shy smile nearly killed me. "I want you to meet her."

My heart galloped. "You have a girlfriend?"

"She's a work in progress. So play it cool, yeah?"

"Promise."

"You're not gonna cry, are you?"

I shook my head no, biting my tongue.

A cowbell rattled when Dylan pushed the door open for me. From behind the counter and through a service window, a gruff voice hollered, "Hey, it's Dylan! Morning, runt!"

"Charlie!" Dylan greeted, chuckling.

"Who's the lovely lady?" Charlie yelled through the window, uncaring that the dining room was packed and everyone could hear.

"She's taken. Back off, old man."

At that, the double doors in the back burst open. A gorgeous girl emerged, her hair a shade darker than blonde, but not quite brown, petite with wicked curves, bee-stung lips painted a darker shade of nude. Her eyes were dark as sin but somehow sparkled and narrowed at my son.

She delivered her plates of food to a table in the corner, then came our way, a blush creeping over her cheeks.

She pulled two menus from behind the counter and, ignoring Dylan's sweet, "Hey, Monster," led us to a table near the window.

Her dark eyes fell on me, and I resisted the urge to laugh. "Coffee?" she asked, avoiding Dylan's starry-eyed gaze but struggling to hold mine.

"Yes, please," I said.

Dylan cleared his throat, sat straighter in his chair, and said, "You can relax, Monster. She's my mom."

Monster's shoulders dropped two inches at least. She released a loud exhale, then smiled and offered her hand. "I've heard so much about you. Nice to meet you. I'm Cleo." She smirked, nodded toward my son. "But Dylan calls me Monster because he's a dick. No offense."

And before I could react, she was gone, tending to other patrons.

I raised a brow at my son. He laughed, but in that small gesture, I recognized the shimmer in his eyes. He shook his head as if he himself couldn't believe he was in love with that fiery woman. Somehow, I knew those two were in for an epic love story.

Breakfast was the best I'd had in years. A veggie omelet with hash browns because Dylan insisted I had to try the hash browns.

Catching up with Dylan, face to face, filled my soul in unexplainable ways. Neither of us had heard from my father, and what a relief. Though, I was sure he'd turn up again when he needed something from me or his grandson. That man would never change.

Dylan whispered in Cleo's ear on our way out, and she smiled, then nodded.

I suspected they were planning a get-together later in

the day but kept my mouth shut. Joe and I had planned on asking Dylan to move home now that Harper was no longer a threat, but my independent son had already enrolled in the local college, and after witnessing the blooming love affair, I changed my mind.

When we parked around the back of my mother's home, Joe opened my door, helped me out by hooking our elbows, and dragged me down the lawn and to the end of the dock.

As I'd grown to love, he towered over me, so close we could've been one.

"Hi," he rasped before kissing me deep and tender.

The wind blew my hair, birds cawed overhead. Lake Willow was already alive with water skiers and outdoor enthusiasts.

When Joe broke the spell, leaving me gasping and clinging to his shirt, he whispered, "Hi," again and, dear sweet raspberry cappuccino, the love in his gaze made me sigh out loud.

"What was that for?"

Joe smiled so wide and beautiful, my chest hurt and my legs turned to wet noodles. Then the scary ex-con mountain of a man dropped to one knee and shoved his hand into the front pocket of his jeans.

"My beautiful, crazy, cuckoo bird neighbor," he said, his dimples deep. "You're my life, my sunshine, my cool air on a hot day. My favorite badass. I want to fill your holes every day for the rest of our lives." Eyes wet, hands trembling, he raised the box and opened the lid, revealing what I knew to be a ring but couldn't see through the moisture in my eyes.

"Please say you'll marry me, baby, because I'll die right here if you deny me another day."

I was a hot air balloon about to ascend, a baby tasting her first bite of cake, floating and flailing and bursting with joy I didn't know how to express. "Yes, yes, yes," I blabbered, unable to hold still, wiping my face with the heel of my palm.

Joe slid the ring on my finger, but I couldn't look. I couldn't do anything but jump into his arms and wrap myself around my mountain, my safe place, my home, and squeeze and kiss him with all my might.

Applause filled the air. Supporting my ass, Joe turned so I could see the source over his shoulder. Mom and Dylan stood with cameras aimed our way, and Grant held a box of tissues at the ready.

Joe slapped my butt twice, then pulled back to look me in the eye. "Alrighty then. Go with your mother." He kissed me again. "I'll see you in a few hours."

My feet hit the wood like lead weights, but my arms remained locked around his neck, forcing him to bend forward. "What? You propose, then send me away? Seriously? Can't I revel in this moment for—"

Joe silenced my rant with a kiss that left me boneless. "Just go." He laughed, peeling my arms away.

° ° ° ° °₀° ° ° ° °

Joe

While Marley and her mother were upstairs doing whatever ladies do to prepare for their big day, Dylan greeted our guests, sending the women to the third floor and the men to the second.

Pulling off a surprise wedding had been a challenge, but (thank you, Jesus, for Marley's amazing mom) Lori had taken the reins and made my job easy.

Four hours after I'd proposed, Marley walked down the makeshift aisle arm and arm with her son, in the backyard of her mother's home, with Lake Willow as our background.

There was a moment when she glided my way, wearing an angelic, body-hugging white dress, that I feared we'd have to call off the ceremony because my throat closed tight, the scenery blurred, and I swayed in my shiny loafers.

Frank gripped my arm, whispered, "Breathe, Joe. Just fucking breathe."

Con slapped my back, forcing my lungs to work again.

My bride-to-be came closer, and Con whispered, "Holy shit. Will you look at her? Joe, you lucky bastard."

Lucky was an understatement.

Seemed like years before Marley reached us. Lilly and Lori stood by her side.

Con and Frank stood by mine.

My mother and Alejandro joined Grant, Cynthia, Dylan and his "not girlfriend," along with Marco, Ginger, and Bruce under the shade of a willow tree.

At one point, I looked up and could swear I saw Alice's face in the clouds.

I married my girl.

Marley got her small wedding. I got my white-dress moment.

We partied until sunrise the following day, then all spent a lazy weekend together in Whisper Springs.

Marley and I honeymooned for two weeks in Spain and then two in Italy, vowing to visit my mom at least once a year.

When we returned home, Marley started classes at WSU, and what a fucking sexy student she made.

We settled into our new normal as Mr. and Mrs. Kaine, with our furry babies, Ginger and Bruce, and made a new home and a new future, together, in our average little corner of heaven.

Thank you for reading Average Joe. If you enjoyed Joe and Marley, you'll love getting to know Natalie and Cole in **L.O.V.E.**, a friends to lovers romance.

You can visit Whisper Springs, where Joe and Marley married, in the Truck Stop series, starting with **Truck Stop Tango**, a second chance romance.

Gloria Downing and Tyler Rodrigues. Thank you again for taking the time to read Average Joe in its early stages and for your honest input. Big hugs to you both!

Corinne DeMaagd. Oh, my Lord, you are THE BEST. Thank you for your patience with me on this book. I'll do better with the next one, I promise.

Sarah Hansen, thank you for another gorgeous cover. I look forward to working with you on the rest of the series.

To the book bloggers, tiktokers, Instagrammers, and all you social media rockstars, thank you for all you do for the book industry and for authors in general.

And to you, my dear, cherished reader. Thank you for spending time with Joe and Marley. It still blows me away that someone other than my mom spent their hard-earned money to read my stories.